Destroying Angel

Also by S. G. MacLean

Destroying Angel

S. G. MacLean

Quercus

First published in Great Britain in 2018 by

Quercus Editions Ltd
Carmelite House
50 Victoria Embankment
London EC4Y 0DZ

An Hachette UK company

Map created by Liane Payne based on an original map
from *Civitates Orbis Terrarum*, 1612

A CIP catalogue record for this book is available
from the British Library

HB ISBN 978 1 78648 416 1
TPB ISBN 978 1 78648 417 8

10 9 8 7 6 5 4 3 2 1

Typeset by CC Book Production

Printed and bound in Great Britain by Clays Ltd, Elcograf S.p.A.

To Catriona

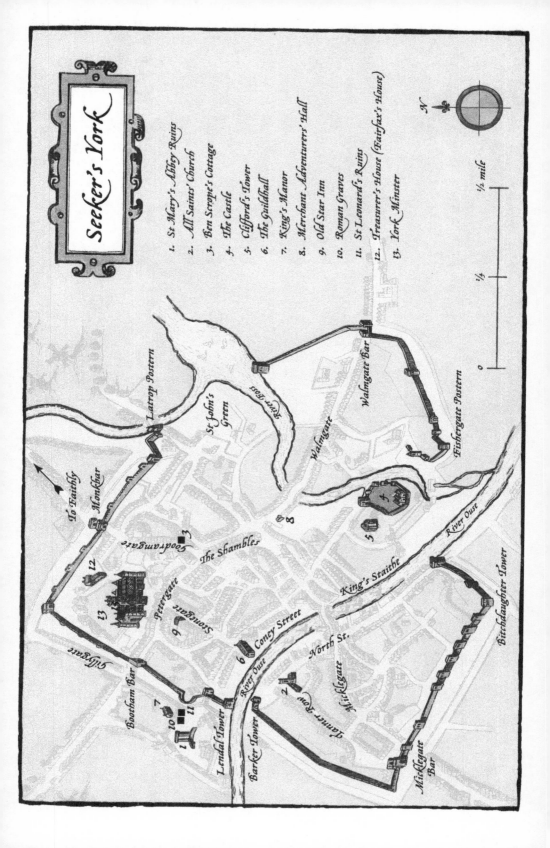

Seeker's York

1. St Mary's Abbey Ruins
2. All Saints' Church
3. Ben Scrope's Cottage
4. The Castle
5. Clifford's Tower
6. The Guildhall
7. King's Manor
8. Merchant Adventurers' Hall
9. Old Star Inn
10. Roman Graves
11. St Leonard's Ruins
12. Treasurer's House (Fairfax's House)
13. York Minster

½ mile

¼

0

N

To Faithly

Bootham Bar

Gillygate

Monkbar

Goodramgate

The Shambles

Petergate

Stonegate

Coney Street

Lendal Tower

Barker Tower

River Ouse

North St.

Tanner Row

Micklegate

Micklegate Bar

Bitchdaughter Tower

King's Staithe

River Ouse

St John's Green

Latrop Postern

River Foss

Walmgate

Walmgate Bar

Fishergate Postern

PROLOGUE

September 1655

Yorkshire, somewhere between York and Halifax

Thomas Faithly laughed; he had heard the joke before, of course: it was filthy, rendered all the more so by the thick guttural tones of the Fleming who told it. The Spaniard to the right of him glanced quickly his way, as if uncertain as to how a countryman and loyal subject might take the slight aimed at Charles Stuart, but Thomas assured him that none had laughed more heartily than the King himself when first he had heard it, and that several around the table on that occasion had eagerly attested to the proficiency of the lady in question.

As well that those who rode alongside their party couldn't decipher the Flemish tongue, thought Thomas. Unless things had very much altered in the four years since he had last touched Yorkshire soil, they were unlikely to appreciate the humour. He'd heard enough to know that they certainly did not appreciate having to act as night escort for the party on its journey from York to Halifax, but Major-General

Lilburne had been adamant, and none of his men would have dared gainsay him.

It was not yet the end of September, but the night was clear and moonlit, and the temperature dropping. However cold it might be for their escort outside, inside their covered wagon, Faithly and his companions were warm enough, and the time was passed in stories and the occasional ballad, sung low so as not to offend their Puritan hosts. The roads so often marched and ridden by one side and the other might have been better kept, but they had not yet had their churning by the coming winter. Faithly had known worse journeys, certainly, and as the fellow opposite him began to intone some ballad of lost love in time to the comfortable rhythm of the wheels rumbling beneath them, he felt his eyelids close and was powerless to prevent himself from drifting off into a deep and comforting sleep.

It could not have been much later, and certainly they were hardly three hours out of York, when Faithly was awakened by a sudden jolt and the sound of rearing horses. The animals' terrified whinnying almost drowned out the shouts of the two mounted guards thundering up from the rear to see what had caused the commotion. When Faithly looked out, just managing to crane his neck far enough to see a little up ahead, all he could make out were the rearing horses, a thrown rider and a huge ball of flame which appeared to be hanging in the sky just above them. There were shouts from the soldiers as they tried to calm the beasts and attend to their downed comrade. It was then that

Thomas's travelling companions began to cross themselves, mindless of the scruples of their escort, and to offer urgent prayers to the Virgin in their own tongues. Thomas might have prayed too, but the thing, swinging, ablaze, from the branches of the huge elm up ahead of them, was beyond help and he, unlike the others, had heard another sound, more hooves, approaching at great speed and from the north. Thomas felt a small glow of triumph and no little relief begin to creep through him. His fears that the one person he could trust might not be capable of carrying this thing off looked to be without substance: his coded letter had got past Cromwell's intelligencers, the instructions had been understood and he was going home. He turned in time to hear a splintering of wood and the rending in two of the thick canvas at the back of the wagon. A shaft of moonlight and the glow from the flames up ahead played on the face that loomed towards them, illuminating the shining eyes of the man on horseback. Prayers in Spanish and Flemish turned to terrified curses and calls for help as the men around Thomas shrank back as far as they could. Thomas, however, shouldered his way past them to lean out through the back flap of the wagon, holding his manacled hands out in front of him, the chain pulled taut, as if in supplication. The face of the man on horseback broke into a strange grin, and he laughed as he swung his two-headed axe up into the darkness above, before bringing its blade crashing down with a sickening crack on the chain.

It was less than a minute later that, breathless, Thomas

managed to clamber up onto the back of the fine beast that must surely have come from his father's old stables, and wrap his still manacled arms, their chain newly broken, around the waist of his liberator. 'Took your time, didn't you?' he said, as the other man dug his spurs into the animal's flank and they galloped off north-eastwards, towards the Ouse and the back ways that would take them at last to the North Riding, and Faithly Moor.

Yorkshire, the North Riding

The bright light of the full moon shone on the clearing, and there they were, white, beautiful against the sparkling frost of the grass: destroying angels. How could something so lovely be so deadly? Satan's bolete, stinkhorn, fly agaric, hoof fungus, false morel: all so foul, so hideous to the eye that no one in their right mind would go near any of those, but the destroying angel? Pure, white, delicate temptations almost, from another world, the world of the Green Man, of Arthur, or further back to the stories and beings that none would speak of now for fear of the witch-finder's flames.

The moonlight was growing dimmer, a pinkish shade starting to creep over the horizon. The arm that stretched out over the wet grass cast little shadow, a gauntleted hand picked one, two, three, half a dozen of the milky-white, flowing caps with their stalks. One alone would have been enough, but caution was always to be preferred to trust, and there might be unforeseen accidents in the coming hours. To return here again, if seen, would raise questions, and anyhow, the thing must be done tonight if ever it were to be done. And if it were not done, then worse, much worse, would surely follow. No basket to draw attention, but a simple muslin packet, soon slipped beneath a cloak, and footprints in the grass that would fade in the warming day to be seen by no one, as they made their way back across Faithly Moor, ahead of the rising sun.

ONE

York Castle

To the south, Seeker could see the mist rising above Knaves-mire. To the north it had already cleared, and the minster stood massive and white against a clear blue sky, dominating the city, the tangle of streets, houses and parish churches bounded by rivers, castle and walls, within which men and women lived their lives and carried on their business in the hope that they might not draw too much attention to themselves. Seeker had become familiar, once more, with those streets these last six months, since Thurloe had sent him north to mop up the dregs of the latest Royalist rag-tag rebellion, and to prepare the way for the rule of the major-generals.

Only the slightest of breezes met at the juncture of the Ouse and the Foss this morning, doing little to disturb the waters of the castle moat, and yet still Seeker thought he could smell the rotted heads of some of those March rebels. They had thought the people of York would open their gates to them: they'd soon learned that the people of York had better sense, and now a good few of them looked out over Knavesmire from spikes at the top of Micklegate Bar, through eyes that the ravens had picked clean months since.

He could hear the clatter of boots running up the spiral stone stairs towards him. When the man finally emerged onto the walk at the top of Clifford's Tower, he was trying not to sound out of breath. 'Major-General Lilburne wants to see you, Captain. Straight away.' Seeker glanced one more time to the south and then turned his thoughts from past troubles to consider what new ones might be waiting for him.

Robert Lilburne was leaning over his desk, hands planted on either side of the letter laid out in front of him. He was still wearing the travelling clothes Seeker had seen him in not half an hour ago, alighting from a barge at King's Staithe.

'How was London, sir?' asked Seeker.

Lilburne didn't look up. 'Stinking hot and full of vice, as ever. And York?'

'Bit colder.'

Lilburne smiled. He was as firm a Puritan as any in the army, but he wasn't without humour. He had a hard soldier's face and the certainty of his cause, but more of a grasp on the possible than his radical and oft-imprisoned Leveller brother, John.

'No trouble, though?'

Seeker shook his head dismissively. 'Nothing worth speaking of.'

'Good,' said Lilburne, 'for I think there may be some

brewing in the North Riding.' He lifted the letter, which Seeker saw had no seal attached, and held it out. 'This was handed to me just before I stepped onto my barge at Whitehall stairs. You'll know the hand.'

The moment Seeker looked at it, he knew why the letter bore no seal, for he did indeed recognise the hand. He looked up. 'Secretary Thurloe.'

Lilburne nodded. 'The same.'

'Am I called back to London, sir?' Seeker had been waiting a long time for such a summons.

'London?' Lilburne almost snorted. 'No, this is nothing to do with London, not yet, anyway. You'd best read it.'

So Seeker did, and with a sinking heart knew he would not be returning south for a while yet.

'Sir Thomas Faithly?'

'Aye. Do you know of him?'

Seeker shook his head. 'Only know that Faithly is up on the moors, a good bit past Pickering. I know nothing of the family.'

'Sir Thomas is the older son of Sir Anthony Faithly. Old North Riding family. He and his father came out for the King in '42, as soon as Charles raised his standard at Nottingham. Father was killed at Marston Moor. Son, Thomas, fled abroad on the same ship as the Earl of Newcastle and a good few of the other leading officers of the King's army in the north. Next heard of in '47, fetching up in Paris, at the Prince of Wales's court at St Germains. Joined the young Charles Stuart in his invasion from Scotland in the summer of '51, and managed to get away again after the battle of Worcester, back to the continent.'

'Charles's court again?' asked Seeker. 'I never came across his name.'

'That's because Thurloe only involves you when there's trouble, and Thomas Faithly hasn't given cause for concern in four years. Dances, drinks, wenches, plays the fool. A perfect playmate for the young King.'

'And now he's disappeared,' said Seeker, looking down again at what Thurloe had written.

'Off the face of the earth,' said Lilburne. 'And not one of Thurloe's informants at Charles's court can discover a thing about where he's gone.'

'Does Thurloe think he's come back here?'

Lilburne indicated the letter once more. 'That's what he wants you to get up there and find out.'

Seeker folded the letter, resigned. 'I'll set out within the hour.'

'Good. And when you do you can take these with you.' He handed Seeker another set of papers, a good deal thicker this time, and bearing the seal of the Council of State. In response to Seeker's unspoken question he said, 'They're the new instructions for the commissioners for securing the peace in the community, to be put in place under the new arrangements.' The new arrangements: the rule of the major-generals. 'There'll be plenty won't like it, but the country's forced this upon itself: the Protectorate must be secured from the Royalist threat and the people from their own vice. Only the godly and the army working together in the localities will achieve that, for nothing else has. Copies are being sent out to every commissioner in the country.'

'Giving the local commissioners greater powers?'

Lilburne nodded. 'They grant them greater powers of oversight and enforcement of the laws of the Protectorate, and give them the power to dismiss those who don't fully cooperate. If they don't do this, they risk dismissal themselves, and replacement by men better affected to the regime. Power has already shifted at the top: this could have it shifting at the middle and bottom as well.'

Seeker nodded. That was the part that wouldn't go down well in some quarters. 'And who's the commissioner at Faithly?'

'Matthew Pullan, wool merchant.' Matthew Pullan. The name was known to Seeker, from his earliest days in intelligencing work in London, before even Thurloe's time. Matthew Pullan had been a soldier and a Leveller who'd been persuaded to turn informant on his own comrades. He was a fellow Yorkshireman, and Seeker suspected this Matthew Pullan would prove to be the same man. What Lilburne said next made it certain.

'Pullan's loyalties are beyond question. He is known to me personally, and I would trust him with my life.' The major-general lowered his voice. 'Matthew Pullan was a friend to my brother, and sought to counsel him against some of his wilder schemes.'

Robert Lilburne rarely spoke to subordinate officers

about his brother. Freeborn John, Honest John who had fought bravely for Parliament, who might have risen as high as his brother in the Commonwealth's cause, but who was in prison more often than he was out of it, and who had, somehow, avoided the executioner's axe for the treason he had spoken and written against Cromwell. Some had it that it was the sheer love of the people for the inveterate Leveller that had saved him; some said it was Cromwell himself that remembered a brother officer's valour too well, but Seeker knew what neither Robert Lilburne nor his troublesome brother could: that it was in exchange for the information traded by Matthew Pullan that John Lilburne had been granted his life.

Lilburne continued. 'Matthew Pullan joined Parliament's militia at the first ordnance in 1642. By '47, he had taken up Levelling principles and was much in my brother's company, and was at Putney as an agitator. There, thank God, General Fairfax brought him back round. Wish that the same might have been done with my brother, but it was not, as you well know. Nevertheless, Matthew Pullan and John remained friends, though Pullan drew back from the wilder schemes and petitions of the Levellers. It was when Fairfax laid down his commission that Pullan finally left the army and returned to Yorkshire, and his home in Faithly.'

'Where he is the authority.'

'Where he is the commissioner,' Lilburne corrected.

'And the justice of the peace?'

Lilburne raised an eyebrow. 'Sir Edward Faithly, the fugitive Sir Thomas's younger brother.'

Seeker took a moment to process this. 'So he didn't go out with his father and older brother for the King. Too young? Or the family hedging its bets?' It was a common enough thing.

Lilburne shook his head. 'Edward Faithly was old enough, and his father would have seen his estate burned to the ground before he'd hold it for Parliament. Edward Faithly, it seems, had a riding accident a week before his father and brother left to join the King. He's hardly fit to get on a horse even now, they tell me.' He paused a moment. 'Unfortunate.'

'Or politic,' said Seeker.

Lilburne looked up from the papers he'd begun to arrange, and grimaced. 'Nothing gets past you, does it, Captain? Well, I've no doubt you'll find out, one way or the other. Make sure you make plain to him our view of Royalist sympathisers, and make sure he knows what'll happen if he gives any sanctuary to his brother.' Lilburne had made his points and returned to his papers. 'Send Parker in to me on your way out. He'll be delivering to the other commissioners in the North Riding, though how he'll get on up on the moors, God alone knows. He trusts everyone he meets, and gets a nosebleed any time he ventures north of Monkgate.'

Whereas Seeker, it was understood, trusted no one, and knew the moors like the back of his hand.

Less than an hour later Seeker and his men were waiting at the drawbridge to cross out of the castle and into the town, on their way north. Seeker held back as a horseman came clattering down towards them. The man slid from his mount in near exhaustion when he came in through the gate. Breathless and dishevelled, he shouted something about an ambush on the road to Halifax, a burning effigy hanging from a tree and a foreigner escaped. Seeker had seen him only the previous day, at the head of a prisoner transport, Dunkirkers being moved on Lilburne's orders from York's overcrowded dungeon to the gaol in Halifax.

'Any of our men harmed?' asked Seeker.

'One with a broken leg and another with burns to his arm. Two horses lost.'

Seeker heard his sergeant behind him mutter something under his breath.

'Take it to the major-general, then,' said Seeker. A fugitive Dunkirker shambling around the West Riding: not his problem. Moving his mount, Acheron, forward onto the drawbridge, he signalled to his men to follow, and they set out through the castle gates for Faithly Moor.

TWO

The Village

Bess Pullan rested her arms on the bottom half of the kitchen door and looked out to the yard. The door to the milking parlour was open and she could hear the girl Orpah singing to their cow, in the belief that her milk came easier that way. Bess permitted herself a smile at the foolishness, but at least the cheese was all made now and stacked for the winter, the butter long-churned and set in the cold store. Soon there would be the last of the milk until the spring. Let the girl sing if she wished.

Smoke was curling from the chimney of Gwendolen's workshop. Shadows of cloud were scudding across the moor: time was getting on. She'd have to call her in soon, the venison pie was still to be filled and the batter not yet made for the fritters. Bess stepped into the yard, shooing the pig out of her way. 'Nothing but your belly with you, is it, Peg?' All her pigs had been called Peg, after a long-dead schoolfellow whom she had never liked. The pig took its telling and ambled, disgruntled, back to the orchard. Bess felt a twinge in her back as she bent to pick more parsley for the pottage; the aches came earlier every year now, and Gwendolen's poultices became less effective with each month that passed.

Another twinge when she stood up. She rested her hand a moment on the drystone wall and looked out at the village. Tansy Whyte was waiting, as usual, by the bridge over the beck, watching for the cart to appear trundling back over the track from the fair at Helmsley, hoping it would bring back her husband Seth, and that he had not stayed too long in the taverns. She'd been waiting there every day for fourteen years. Bess shook her head and cast her eyes towards the churchyard. The Reverend Jenkin was shutting the door to the small schoolroom, his scholars scampering home on the street or up over the moor. As he picked his way past ancient grave slabs to the door of his church, she wondered if he would ever again stand at his desk in that schoolroom, or in the pulpit of that church, after tomorrow. Probably not, if even half of what she'd heard of the trier was true. It didn't matter much to Bess: he'd brought it all on his own head.

They were busy already down at the Black Bull, making ready for tomorrow. Benches that Bess was certain had seen neither soap nor water since her father's time had been scrubbed, floors swept and new rushes put down, fires lit in rooms long disused. All day, farmers and housewives had been coming and going – legs of mutton, sides of bacon, what eggs were still to be had, cheeses – though none of Bess's; they'd have nothing from her larder. The ovens of the Black Bull had scarcely cooled these last two days, Orpah had told her, for the mountains of bread – manchet loaves, cheat bread, oat jannocks – pouring from them, to say nothing of the extra ale laid down and the barrel of wine ordered up from York. Bess knew all about the wine, Matthew himself had arranged its transport – Jack Thatcher at the Bull couldn't find his way to York if he was tied to the back of a packman's horse. 'Fine Puritans, no doubt, this committee,' Bess had commented to the wide-eyed Orpah.

Beyond the Bull, past the bridge where Tansy was now hopping from foot to foot, Bess could see a party of riders coming over the top of the ridge. As they drew closer Bess knew these weren't the ejectors, for the ejectors were local men, and none had horses like these three rode. Nor yet was it the trier, for he was already here, arrived this dinnertime with his wife, Orpah had said. A chill came over her, though the yard was still bathed in a late-afternoon sun: soldiers.

Others had noticed them too, and by the time the party had reached Tansy, several people stood in their doorways, or watched cautiously through windows. In front of the inn, all work was suspended. Bess saw the tallest of the three horsemen bend down towards Tansy and ask her something, and just as surely saw Tansy turn and lift her hand, pointing to Bess's own house. The soldier was about to move on, but Tansy put a hand on his beast's bridle, appeared to ask him something. The man shook his head and Tansy dropped the bridle and resumed her vigil.

Bess went back into the house, through the kitchen to the narrow entranceway, and went out to stand her ground at her front door. The village watched as the horsemen made their way up the street. Maud Sharrock, outside the blacksmith's, gawped like a fish. Close your mouth, Maud, thought Bess, you'll catch something. As they came nearer, the leading horseman pulled away from his companions and drew up in front of her.

'Mistress Pullan?' he enquired.

'Who's asking?'

She thought he bridled a bit at that, though there might just have been a hint of a smile. She couldn't see much for his helmet, although what she could see put her in mind of the Wainstones past Urra Moor.

'Captain Seeker, of the county militia. I have papers to deliver to Commissioner Pullan, from Major-General Lilburne at York.'

Yorkshire, by his speech. That was something. 'You'd best come in then,' said Bess, turning back into the house and leaving the door open for him to follow her.

Accustomed, once again, to army billets and the stone corridors of York Castle, Seeker had grown unused to private dwellings, and he was conscious of his size as he entered the house and followed the woman through to the kitchen at the back. She threw a hand out behind her to indicate a room off to his right. 'I'd take you into the parlour, but I'm busy, so here'll have to do,' she said, throwing some flour onto the board in front of her and beginning to roll out some pastry she'd had sitting there.

'Where's your son, Mistress Pullan?'

'Rode over to Lockton, early. Business,' she said, thumping the mix down again and turning it. 'Won't be back till near suppertime.' She glanced over her shoulder at the papers Seeker had rolled up in his hand. 'You can leave those here, I'll see he gets them.'

'I've to deliver them personally, see he reads them. I'll come back later.'

'As you please,' said Bess, taking the pastry and beginning to line the sides of a deep earthenware dish with it.

Seeker had put the letter back into his satchel and was making to leave when Bess straightened herself and turned wearily to him. 'Wait, lad, you've had a long ride and you're all no doubt thirsty. Will you take a cordial before you go?'

They hadn't stopped since Malton and he suspected both the men had drained their water bottles hours since. 'I wouldn't say no,' he said.

'You sit you down then,' she said, indicating a long, high-backed seat by the wall, 'and I'll fetch you something.' She went to the back door and called out into the yard, 'Gwendolen, bring a jug of that elderflower cordial up from the cold cellar, and then come in and help me -- we'll never be ready at this rate.'

Seeker surveyed the kitchen. The seat, the oak armchair by the hearth, the woman at work at the table across from him, the fine flagstone floor, took him back to something else: it was what he had promised Felicity, what he had believed in, before the war, before everything. He shook himself out of it and looked properly. It was well past the dinner hour and this was no ordinary supper in preparation. 'You've some household to feed, mistress,' he said, inclining his head towards the laden table and the pot of pottage already simmering over the fire.

'Tonight, I have,' answered Bess, leaning back a little and pressing her hands to her weary back. 'Since my husband died it's just been me, Matthew and Gwendolen, my ward. Orpah helps me in the house and tends to the beasts, though she goes home to her own mother come sundown, thank the Lord.'

'What's on tonight?' Seeker knew that subtlety of approach, going around the houses, only wasted time with these people. His father had told him once, 'If you can't say straight what you mean, don't say it.'

'I've to give a supper. Ten folk. As if I haven't enough work.'

'Ten's a lot,' said Seeker carefully, but Bess saw his meaning anyway.

'There's a few of them I wouldn't choose to have sat at my table, I won't lie, but if you're looking for secret gatherings of Royalists you won't find one here. There aren't enough of them in these parts to break the law even should they bump into each other in the street, never mind to set up a cockfight.'

'Not even Sir Edward Faithly?' pushed Seeker.

'Faithly?' Bess snorted. 'Knows which side his bread's buttered, that one. Always has done.'

'Oh?'

She paused and turned to him with an arched eyebrow. 'Oh, you don't get me like that, Captain. You can make your own mind up about Edward Faithly.'

Seeker grunted. So much for Edward Faithly, for now. 'What about the rest of them?'

Bess scrutinised him. 'You don't hang about.'

'Saves everybody's time. I'd get there in the end, regardless.'

Bess sniffed. 'Aye, I imagine you would.' She took a moment. 'I'm making no accusations, mind.'

Seeker nodded. 'So?'

'I know all the folk who'll be round my table tonight save two: Caleb Turner and his wife.'

Caleb Turner. The trier. Lilburne hadn't told him this – maybe he hadn't known. Turner was notorious throughout Yorkshire and right across the Pennines to Carlisle. There was hardly a preacher or teacher from one coast to the other who hadn't come under the scrutiny of his examination, and none but the godliest of the godly, the purest of the pure, by Turner's exacting lights, emerged unscathed. 'What's Caleb Turner doing here?'

'What do you think? He's coming to try our vicar, Septimus Jenkin, that has the church and school up at the end of the village there. Turner and a whole committee of ejectors, and if Jenkin be found wanting, God help him.'

'And will he be found wanting?' asked Seeker.

'Not for me to say.' She nodded towards the satchel Seeker had set at his feet. 'Like as not the verdict's in those letters there.'

Seeker shook his head. 'I'm not here for the trier's court. As I said, my business is with your son.' All the same, he doubted what was in the letters would help the cause of Septimus Jenkin, however worthy and blameless the vicar of Faithly might be.

A shadow fell across the doorway and Seeker saw a young woman – little more than a girl, really – standing there. Pale and thin, but with intensely grey eyes, she wore a simple blue woollen gown over her smock and in her hands was carrying a large delftware jug with a pewter lid. 'Where shall I put it, Aunt Bess?' she said, not seeming to notice Seeker.

'Down on the dresser, and fill three tumblers for the captain there and his men – there's two of them out front.'

Only now did the girl look at him, cautiously from the side, like a half-tamed bird, then she dipped her head to him and did as her guardian had told her. The last rays of light coming through the door glinted off the gold in her hair and sparked the grey in her eyes like sun off granite.

'My ward, Gwendolen,' Bess explained, then, 'Captain has business with our Matthew. Any sign?'

The girl shook her head. 'No, Aunt Bess.' There was plenty of space for her to get past with the tray of filled beakers for his men, but she still seemed to shrink away from

Seeker as she moved from the kitchen to the entrance hall. As she passed him, scents of rose and musk that he had not thought to find in the midst of these desolate moors flitted past him. He sipped tentatively at the cordial and then took a long draught. Bess Pullan was watching him. 'It's good, isn't it? She makes it herself, out in that workshop of hers. What she doesn't find out on the moor or in the woods, Matthew fetches her from York. Never saw a child's head so filled with recipes and compounds and brews.' Then Bess pulled herself up, a frightened look suddenly in her eye. 'Nothing unnatural, just drinks and medicines and perfumes, nothing more.'

Seeker held up a hand. 'Peace, missis. I'm no witch-finder. The girl has a gift, though.'

'Aye,' said Bess, 'but there's them as sees what suits them.' Suddenly her face clouded in irritation. 'And here's one now.'

There was a sound of muttering from the yard, a pig grunting and a woman scolding. A moment later a small, fat woman, red-faced and breathless, stood in the doorway.

'Maud Sharrock, have you no work to do?'

'I've plenty to do, Mistress Pullan, as you might guess, seeing to it that Mr Turner and his wife have all they require.'

'I thought they were putting up at the inn?' said Bess, filling the pastry lining with dried beans and stooping to open the oven door.

Maud bridled. 'Well, aye, but what does Hettie Thatcher know about entertaining folk of quality?'

'About as much as you,' Seeker heard Bess mutter, as she pushed the pie dish across the floor of the oven with her flat shovel.

The other woman had not heard, though, so intent was she now in staring at Seeker, and moving herself little by little towards him. 'I hope you've no trouble, Bess, what with your supper tonight, and Mr Turner and all?'

'None that I know of,' replied Bess, her back still to Maud as she secured the door. 'Captain here has business with Commissioner Pullan, none of your concern.'

'Oh, no, no, of course not,' said Maud, her small eyes brightening and almost skewering Seeker with their interest. 'No doubt Mr Pullan will tell Abel of it tonight.'

'No doubt he won't,' said Bess turning. 'Now if there's nothing else, I have work to be getting on with, Maud Sharrock, and I'll thank you to leave me to it.'

Maud was clearly working up to an outraged riposte when something beyond Seeker's shoulder took her eye. Seeker saw an unpleasant look of satisfaction cross her face.

'Too much work, it would seem, Bess Pullan, to keep an eye on that girl.'

Seeker turned his head slightly, towards where Gwendolen was standing stock-still in the doorway, the tray of now empty beakers in her hands. The girl was staring down at the tray, but Seeker could see that her face was flushed and her hands trembling.

Bess's voice was cold. 'And what, exactly, do you mean by that?'

Maud pretended surprise that she should even have to ask. 'What? Wandering about the moor at all hours, disappearing into the woods at sun-up and sunset, consorting with Tansy Whyte, locked away in that workshop of hers doing what, eh? Doing what, I say?'

Bess straightened her old back and stood as tall as she could. 'Get out of my house.'

Maud, some nervousness showing, nodded towards Seeker. 'It must be asked! It must be answered!'

Before Seeker could muster an intervention, Bess was a foot from where Maud Sharrock stood, brandishing her flat shovel inches from the woman's face. 'I'll answer you tenfold if you don't get out of my kitchen right now!' she said.

Maud didn't need another telling, and was out of the back door and into the yard by the time Seeker had got fully to his feet.

As Maud scuttled away across the yard, Bess sank back against the dresser, letting the shovel fall limp at her side. Behind him Seeker heard the girl's faltering voice. 'I'm sorry, Aunt Bess, I'm sorry. I try and I try. I just don't manage . . .' The rest of her words were lost in deep sobs.

Across the kitchen, the old woman's face suffused with love. She gathered herself and went past Seeker to fold the young girl in her embrace. 'Hush, there, hush. You have nothing to be sorry about. Nothing. Maud Sharrock is a poisonous baggage and no one pays her any heed.'

Seeker shifted uncomfortably in his seat, didn't know

where to put himself, what to say. Whatever was the matter here was not for outsiders to see. Once the sobs behind him subsided a little he cleared his throat and made to fix on his helmet again. 'I'll – ehm – I'll leave you to it then, mistress. If you'd send over to the inn, when your son comes in.'

Bess turned to face him. 'Stay where you are, lad. Matthew'll be here soon enough, and Gwendolen's fine now, aren't you, my love?'

The girl wiped her eyes and managed a smile for her guardian, before dipping her head to Seeker and hurrying past and out to the sanctuary of her workshop again.

'What was that all about?' he asked, once Gwendolen was out of earshot.

'What it sounded like,' said Bess, settling herself at a basket of apples at the table. 'Maud Sharrock spreading poison. Gwendolen's not like the other girls, never has been. Happier out in the woods, gathering plants and herbs, or busy out there in her workshop, than gossiping and gawking like the rest of them do.' She fixed Seeker with a hard look. 'She doesn't understand their ways, and they don't understand hers. Makes her a target. She knows it, and she tries, but it doesn't make any difference.'

'Does it really matter that much?' said Seeker. 'Being different?'

Bess looked at him and picked up her small knife. 'Aye. Sometimes, it does.'

A few apples peeled and nothing further said about Gwendolen, Bess spoke again. 'No point going to the inn.

You'll not get a billet there tonight with the trier's court on tomorrow.'

'We'll commandeer a barn somewhere, and then we'll be gone, once I've been up to Faithly Manor in the morning.'

'Do they know you're coming? Edward Faithly and Lady Emma?' Bess asked.

Seeker laughed, nodding towards where Maud Sharrock had been. 'In a place like this? I'd lay my supper on it.'

Just then, there was the sound of a horse coming into the yard, followed by a man's voice calling to the dairymaid. A moment later Matthew Pullan was filling the back door of his mother's kitchen, assessing what he saw and clearly not liking it. His air of apprehension did not lift when Bess Pullan introduced the captain and told her son he'd come from the major-general in York with papers for him. Matthew Pullan continued to look unflinchingly at Seeker, putting a question without words.

Seeker looked back at the commissioner. Had he come upon Matthew Pullan as a stranger, out in the street, or somewhere on the moors even, Seeker would have known him for his mother's son: dark, almost black hair, grey eyes beneath thick arched brows, a firm straight nose and strong cheekbones. He would have known him anyway, from their days in London as Seeker had gathered Pullan's testimony on the Levellers, but they greeted each other now as strangers, and Pullan was evidently no more disposed than Seeker to tell even his own mother that he and Seeker knew each other of old.

★

A few moments later, in Matthew Pullan's study, with the door firmly closed, Seeker cast his eyes again over the Commissioner of Faithly. There were some flecks of grey in Pullan's close-trimmed beard and his near shoulder-length hair that hadn't been there five years ago, but all in all, he hadn't aged so much. The old wariness was still in his eyes, and he didn't waste any time waiting for Seeker to explain himself. 'Why has Lilburne sent you here? Does he know?'

Seeker shook his head. 'No.'

Pullan was unconvinced. 'You're no courier, Seeker. He could have sent a common soldier to deliver these papers, so why you?' he asked again, waving a dismissive hand towards the new orders from the Council of State.

'Rest easy, Matthew. This has nothing to do with your time in London.' Seeker kept his voice very low. 'The major-general knows nothing of the reports you made on the activities of his brother and his fellow agitators. It was seven years ago and all that is done.'

'For you, perhaps,' said Pullan, 'but it weighs on my conscience.'

'It shouldn't,' said Seeker. 'If you hadn't reported to Fairfax what you heard all those nights at the Mouth in Aldersgate or the Whale in Lothbury, things would have gone far too far: the Levellers might have unseated Crom-well, eventually.'

'Or brought him round,' said Pullan.

'They'd never have brought him round.'

Pullan picked up a clay pipe and began to pack tobacco

in it. 'So I told my tales to Ireton and to Fairfax, and the Levellers' presses were found and smashed and their wives put in prison, and agitators arrested.' His voice was filled with disgust. 'If they knew it had been me . . .'

'They'd have thanked you, if they knew what you traded for.'

Pullan was doubtful. 'Would they?'

'Aye. The ones that got out of prison sooner than they should have done, or others – John Lilburne for a start – that kept their heads on their necks.'

'You're wrong. They wouldn't thank me for it, not Honest John, at least.'

'The past's over, Commissioner, and the Levellers are done. I'm not here for you. I'm here for Sir Thomas Faithly.'

'Thomas Faithly?' Matthew Pullan's face relaxed and it broke into a curious smile that Seeker also remembered. 'You're slipping, Seeker. If you wanted Thomas Faithly, you've come thirteen years too late.'

Seeker told Pullan of Thomas Faithly's disappearance from the court of Charles Stuart, and of Thurloe's suspicion that he might resurface in Yorkshire. The commissioner was doubtful. 'There wasn't much support round these parts for the last Royalist rising, and Thomas Faithly's been gone a long time. Most that thought like him either died with his father, fled with him or learned better manners.'

'Hmmph,' said Seeker. 'Well, if they haven't yet, they'd best learn,' he added, indicating the papers he'd brought with him with the new orders from the Council of State. 'But what about his brother?'

Any humour left Matthew Pullan's face. His tone was dismissive. 'Edward Faithly wouldn't stir himself for anyone but Edward Faithly.'

'So the fall that kept him from having to choose a side thirteen years ago served him well, then?'

Pullan's voice hardened further. 'Very well. He stayed at home whilst his father and brother went to fight. They're gone, and he's still at home. Never roused himself to give any trouble to Parliament or succour to the Stuarts. Edward Faithly's sitting pretty, and I don't imagine he'd be in any hurry to see his older brother back in the North Riding. You can ask him yourself, tonight.'

'Oh?'

'Aye. He's coming to this supper that's been foisted on me. As commissioner, I'm expected to welcome this trier and his wife to Faithly. Sir Edward's justice of the peace so I've to have him too. Whilst Lady Emma—'

'Who's that?' asked Seeker. 'Faithly's wife?'

Pullan looked away. 'Aye, she is.' He shifted a letter knife on his desk. 'She'll make small-talk with the women, you can get your teeth into Edward Faithly and I'll keep the trier happy.'

'If such a thing can be done,' said Seeker. 'Nothing I have heard of Caleb Turner suggests he is a comfortable supper guest.'

Pullan looked up again and some warmth had crept back

into his eyes. 'About as comfortable as yourself, I'll warrant. But never fear, Seeker, there'll be others there to leaven the misery, and we'll always have Abel Sharrock for entertainment.'

'Sharrock?' The fat woman's husband, presumably, and a name Seeker had come across in papers somewhere.

'Aye. Abel Sharrock. Gravedigger. Constable of Faithly, and Puritan to his hard black soul. He's just the sort of man these new orders you bring, of the rule of the major-generals, will put power into the hands of, should men like me prove wanting.'

'Then you'll just have to stay on your game, won't you, Commissioner?' said Seeker.

THREE

The Supper

Abel Sharrock put on his hat with care and considered the impression he would make. Even in the dim candle-light of their small bedchamber, the white of his plain linen collar stood out, pure against the deep black of his doublet. The cloak he had had made had cost a month's wages, but he had told Maud, who was prone to peeve on such things, that before long a sexton's wages would not be their concern. They had but to wait for the committee to do its business; the committee would open such a Pandora's Box in this village that nothing would be the same again.

He'd been back in near an hour from his inventorying of the church and schoolhouse, and Maud was still squawking in his ear about her treatment at the hands of Bess Pullan.

'And that girl, and her secretive ways and strange looks and crying of a night – and you've heard it, same as me, and nothing ever said. And the way Bess Pullan spoke to me in front of the captain!'

'Woman, there are bigger things afoot. Only bide your

31

time: Bess Pullan'll be a sight less haughty before this week is out.'

'All right for you to say, but still I should have been invited. How does it look? What will the trier think?'

Abel turned from the looking glass to face his wife. 'That all wives would do well to model themselves on his own.'

Maud's face was silent fury as Abel lifted his new cloak from the bed and fixed it at the neck, but she said nothing more.

It was almost dusk and all was quiet in the churchyard as he went through the gate and out onto the village street. A tentative bat flew out from the eaves of Tansy Whyte's hovel, then another. Abel took note of it. Up ahead, the coach from the manor was already drawn up outside Matthew Pullan's house. He quickened his pace, concerned that they would speak of him in his absence, or that he would miss something. If Maud had it right that the captain of the militia arrived at Pullan's had been sent from the major-general in York, Abel Sharrock was determined not to miss anything at all.

From habit, he went around the back, through the yard. It was a habit he should train himself from, he thought, although he knew there was more to be heard and learned arriving unannounced and by ways unexpected. There were three strange horses in Pullan's stable, one of which in particular, a big black cavalry horse, Abel didn't like the look of. He gave it a wide berth and hurried on. The door to the girl Gwendolen's workshop was open, but no light showing through it. The heavy perfumed smell emanating from it to mingle with the stench of pigs and poultry caught in Abel's throat and made him cough, bringing that halfwit child Orpah Bigley to the back door. She didn't know how to address him tonight, he saw that and it pleased him. 'Master and his guests are in the parlour.'

'Then show me through, girl,' he snapped. He'd lived in this village his whole life, and he hadn't been in that room once, not once.

They all turned to look as Orpah gabbled, 'It's Abel Sharrock, missis,' and he had almost to push the fool girl out of the way to get in. The room was dimly lit. Bess Pullan wasn't one to waste money on anyone's account, and the candles on the long oak dining table had yet to be lit, what light there was coming from the fire and the candles at either end of the mantelshelf, and a couple along the near wall on a sideboard. He could see nevertheless that the room was large and comfortable – not grand, like the great hall of the manor – but furnished with things of good, serviceable quality, and better by far than anything he and Maud made do with in the two-roomed, cruck-built sexton's cottage by the churchyard. The furniture, well made and sturdy, might have been there from Pullan's grandfather's time, for all Abel knew. There were two sets of benches down each side of the table and carver chairs at either end – he could make out a rose pattern worked across the back of the one closest to him. There were no portraits, but what looked like heavy tapestries hanging from the walls. One near to the fire was of a forest scene – intertwined berries and flowers, nuts and tangles of vine through which the face of a fox or the head of a pheasant or blackbird might be glimpsed, or a rabbit tail disappear. There would be a Green Man in there somewhere too, Abel was sure of it. More superstition to be rooted out. Off to his left, good plate – pewter, not tin or wood – was ranged on the sideboard, where candlelight glimmered in the cut crystal of glasses such as Abel's stubby fingers had never held.

Orpah's announcement of him had been met with silence, broken finally by Matthew Pullan, who detached himself from his place leaning against the mantelshelf to come towards him. 'Constable Sharrock. Welcome.'

Abel took a moment to swallow down the surge of pride that had risen in him like bile. Every day for nearly thirty years Matthew Pullan had given him nothing but 'Abel', or a dismissive 'Sharrock'. Until tonight. But what was Matthew Pullan to him that he should feel pride in being given his proper title by the man?

'Commissioner. I see you are assembled early.'

'Perhaps it is you that's late, Abel.' Abel hadn't noticed Lawrence Ingolby when first he'd come in, but he saw him now in the corner, half-slouching like a long brown weasel in breeches and doublet, watching, that insolent almost-smile as ever on his face. Abel was working for an answer, as he always had to with Ingolby, when the voice of Lady Emma cut through the room. She did not address herself to Abel, didn't even look at him.

'The gravedigger. I see you're determined on entertaining us tonight, Matthew. But where's this famous "trier" that we are all agog to meet? Surely Master Sharrock hasn't had himself made trier now too, as well as constable? He'll be too hard pressed, and then who will dig our graves?'

There was silence in the room. Abel thought he saw a crooked smile play over Edward Faithly's lips. The man should mind his wife better, but then Emma Faithly never had been real quality, little keeping up the roof of her father's hall but his ancient title and some moth-eaten tapestries. If Edward Faithly hadn't married her, the whole crew of them would have been out on the roads, begging their bread. At last Abel found his voice, which nonetheless trembled as he answered her. 'Never trouble yourself over that, Lady Emma. I'll dig your grave for you easy enough.'

'I don't doubt it, Abel,' she said.

Abel gave her a furious look as he swallowed down his short-lived triumph.

'Aye, but where is the trier?' said Matthew Pullan eventually.

'He won't be coming,' said Abel. 'He thinks it more fit that he and his wife should spend tonight in prayer, in preparation for the morning.'

Bess Pullan's lips pursed so tight Abel wondered she didn't suck them in altogether. 'Not coming?' she said at last. 'All this trouble I've been put to, at your committee's insistence, and he's not coming? Since when is he not coming? He was still coming when Maud came nosing about my kitchen this afternoon.'

Abel saw Matthew Pullan shoot his mother a warning glance. 'Your committee was very insistent Mr Turner and his wife should be given respectful welcome. My mother has indeed been to a deal of trouble for tonight, and I daresay Sir Edward and Lady Emma have more to do than come down over the moor at night on the trier's whim. It doesn't speak well of this Mr Turner's manners that he has changed his mind at such a late hour.'

Abel preened himself. 'Mr Turner has more to concern himself with than human vanities or the distinctions of persons, and he's more to consider than the needs of his belly or the inconveniencing of housewives.' Then he turned his gaze upon the man standing behind the settle where the girl Gwendolen Sorsby and Lady Emma sat. 'And it hardly speaks much of manners to expect that he would sup tonight with Septimus Jenkin.'

'The Reverend Jenkin has been found guilty of nothing,' said Matthew Pullan evenly.

'Because he has not yet been tried. Accusations have been made for which he will answer.'

Jenkin fixed Abel with a look of long-nurtured contempt, but said nothing. Abel saw his hand shake. That too would be noted by the committee as a proof, the shake of a man who drank, as Abel had already informed them he did.

'But not tonight,' said Matthew Pullan. 'This is my house, not some trier's court in the taproom of the Black

Bull inn, and none at my table shall be made to answer for themselves.'

Abel scanned those familiar faces and promised himself he would make them answer, every one of them. Bess at last pulled the cord to summon Orpah Bigley back through from the kitchen to light the candles set along the table. And that was when Abel finally saw the man of whom Maud had spoken, 'a giant of a man, near on seven foot tall! Captain of militia, sent from the major-general in York. Dark as a Welshman, but Yorkshire-spoken. A giant of a man!' Abel had told Maud not to be so foolish, because she had babbled all this in front of the trier and his wife, but Caleb Turner had bid him let the woman speak and questioned her in some detail about the man and his appearance. Mistress Turner had gone quite pale at all Maud's nonsense, but then the trier had named him and Maud had said, 'Why yes, that's it exactly! Seeker, Captain Seeker.'

Taking a step forward, Abel removed his hat, which he had hitherto forgotten to do, and made a show of bowing. 'Abel Sharrock, Captain, constable of this place.'

The officer said something in response, Abel was sure of it, but he could not make it out.

For fear the soldier was not fully aware of his significance, Abel expanded on his introduction. 'I have been keeping an eye to matters in Faithly, the business of this village and the wider jurisdiction hereabouts. I have made oversight of morals, private and public, my special interest. You may be assured, Captain, of a welcome amongst the well affected in these parts, and their readiness to assist you in making manifest the rule of the major-generals, even here, in the North Riding.'

Before the captain could reply, Lawrence Ingolby's mocking drawl filled the room. 'Take a breath, Abel, for pity's sake. Now, if you're done, I'm starving.'

In the general hubbub of agreement, Bess ushered everyone to take their seats and Abel managed to curb the outburst boiling up within him. But he would have his time: different days were coming to Faithly, and all at this table would know it.

An hour earlier, as Abel had been running a hand over the fine cloth of his new cloak, spread out on the bed in the sexton's cottage, Seeker had entered the Pullans' dining parlour. None of the rest of the household or the guests had yet arrived. The maidservant, coming in to finish the laying of the table, had almost dropped the tray of preserves she was carrying when she'd seen him standing by the hearth.

He held up a hand. 'Easy there. I'm expected. Your master knows I'm here.'

'Aye, but the mistress?' she gulped.

Seeker grinned. 'Oh, so the mistress is master here also, is she?'

The girl's eyes went wider at him, as if he might be mad. 'No. Commissioner's master and Mistress Bess is mistress, and that's enough. And she'll tan my hide if I don't lay this table right. She's been in a hundred times, chiding me for this not being in the right place and that being wrong, and woe betide me if I shift anything if she's already shifted it!' She went on at some length about her mistress's admonishments.

'Maybe she's worried what the trier will think?' Seeker suggested.

The girl snorted. 'Mistress Bess? She doesn't worry what anyone thinks. Even the Lord Protector, should he fetch up here, would have to take his telling like the rest of us. Now, you'll not touch anything?'

He laughed. 'I give you my word. And if the Lord Protector does turn up, I'll see he behaves himself as well.'

'He'd better not,' she said, 'for there's only eleven places set.' And from then on she averted her eyes from Seeker as much as possible as if by doing so she might produce the effect of him not, in fact, being there at all.

As Orpah had been finishing her duties, the dining parlour door had opened and a young man, who was certainly not a Pullan, had walked in with an air that was almost proprietorial. Dressed in a serviceable brown linen doublet and hose, he'd shown no surprise to find Seeker there, and idly cracked a hazelnut taken from a dish on the sideboard before turning his attention to him. 'You'll be Captain Seeker, then.'

'And you are?'

The man had raised an eyebrow, affected amusement. 'Oh, it's to be like that, is it? Fair enough. I'm Lawrence Ingolby.'

'Sir Edward Faithly's secretary.'

'That's right.'

Seeker had seen Ingolby's type before — cocksure, dismissive of authority, could stir up trouble just for the sake of it. The type who could strip away a veneer with a few well-directed words. Such men could be dangerous, but they could also be very useful.

As Ingolby had been selecting another nut from the dish, Matthew Pullan had come into the room. 'I see you've met Lawrence, then, Captain. Too clever for his own good. Perhaps a spell in the New Model would have sorted him out, what do you think?'

Seeker had appraised the long, thin, pale man who was grinning at the commissioner whilst passing him a goblet of burgundy. He had indeed encountered a handful of his sort in the army. 'Oh, the likes of him usually made general, if the first three days didn't kill them.'

Pullan had laughed, but Ingolby had looked a little abashed, and Seeker had wondered whether he might not be so cocksure after all.

'Where are Sir Edward and Lady Emma, Lawrence? There's nothing amiss?'

Ingolby shook his head. 'All's well. They're on their way down, in the carriage. I rode on ahead — wanted to look in on Septimus, you know, see if he was . . .' His voice trailed off, but he raised an eyebrow at Matthew as if that should finish the sentence for him.

'And is he?'

'Oh, aye. He'll be over shortly. Just getting into his best bib and tucker.'

A rapping on the street door had then sent Ingolby hastening to answer it. Whilst he was out of the room, Pullan said, 'More than half of that's for show. He's not as bad as he would have folk think. His mother was a slattern and he never knew his father. In a village like this, folk don't let you forget such things. But his mind's as sharp as your dagger there. This place is too small for him.'

'You might say it was too small for you, too, Matthew, but you came back. You could have risen high in the army.'

'To what end? My war was over. Anyway, I was needed here, and you can't stay away for ever.'

There was silence between them for a moment, then Seeker said, 'And what about Lawrence Ingolby? Why does he stay?'

The commissioner had tilted his head to the side. 'Loyalty, maybe? Scared to cut himself from the only roots he has. Scared he'd fail.'

'Do you think he'd fail?'

Pullan had laughed. 'Lawrence? No, Lawrence wouldn't fail. Lawrence watches, he listens and he learns. Lawrence'll do all right.'

Seeker had been about to question Pullan further on the secretary when Ingolby had reappeared, escorting his master and mistress into the room. Sir Edward Faithly was tall and gaunt, and did indeed walk with a pronounced limp. He was perhaps forty years of age, his features hard and brittle. His eyes were those of a man diseased. He nodded towards Seeker. 'Captain. I'm told I am to expect a visit from you tomorrow morning.'

'Commissioner Pullan will inform you of the Council of State's instructions, Sir Edward. I have a personal message to impart to you from the major-general himself, that won't take long.'

Edward Faithly laughed. 'I don't doubt it, three Yorkshiremen, you, me and he. We don't waste time. At least Cromwell had the sense to send us one of our own to keep us under heel, and Lilburne's no upstart land-grabber like some of them.'

'No one will be kept under the heel that doesn't need it,' said Seeker.

Faithly moved his mouth a little as if discarding words he didn't like the flavour of. 'And who's to judge the need, eh, Captain? No doubt Pullan will inform me of that too. But your message will have to wait, whatever it is. I'll be at the trier's court at the Black Bull tomorrow. The Reverend Jenkin will not stand trial before your Master Turner without my wife and I be there to witness it.'

The woman beside him, who had hitherto appeared not to be listening to the conversation, spoke at last. 'I don't see why I should be there.'

Her husband laid a hand on her shoulder. It was a light touch, but Emma Faithly flinched all the same. His fingers played a moment with the gold chain at her neck from which a heavy jewel hung. It was a strange thing, and

Seeker had not seen its like before. As Edward Faithly fingered the chain, Seeker saw that it was no precious stone set there, certainly not the ruby he had taken it for at first glance in the half-lit room, but a fragment of scratched red glass. The red was dull against her pale skin and the heavy grey silk of her dress, and had not sufficient lustre to catch the auburn of her hair. Now that his attention was on Emma Faithly, Seeker found it difficult to move it away from her. She didn't fit in this room, this situation, somehow. She must have been a little over thirty years of age, yet there was something ageless, something elemental about her, something born of the moors. She was almost as slight of build as Gwendolen Sorsby, Bess Pullan's ward, yet whilst the younger girl might have been made of porcelain, everything about Emma Faithly – her eyes, her bearing – spoke of impermeable Yorkshire granite. It occurred, fleetingly, to Seeker, that she was a match, a perfect balance to Matthew Pullan, yet here she was, a guest in his house and the wife of someone else.

Edward Faithly pressed the tips of his fingers a little further into the flesh of his wife's shoulder, and Seeker saw Matthew Pullan's fingers dig into the palms of his own hands. 'Oh, I think you must be present at the trial, my dear. My family endowed almost everything in that church and had the appointment of its vicars for generations. I would not like that Septimus should be abandoned to his fate and we not be there.'

If such were Septimus Jenkin's friends, thought Seeker, then the vicar of Faithly surely was without hope. Emma Faithly said no more to her husband, and passed wordlessly by Seeker, the lustrous pewter silk of her skirts brushing the floor, to take up her place on the settle next to the fire. As she passed, Seeker caught scents of something wild, of wood spices, and green moss and fresh earth. He watched her compose her hands as she sat, find a flame in the hearth on which to focus. She somehow possessed this place just by being in it.

Silence followed Emma Faithly, and in its wake, Seeker turned his attention once more to her husband. 'Since you are not to be at home tomorrow, then, Sir Edward, I'll give you the major-general's message now.'

Faithly looked a little taken aback by Seeker's bluntness. Seeker pressed on. 'It concerns your brother, Sir Thomas Faithly.'

Something like wariness crossed Edward Faithly's features. 'What of him?'

'What do you know of his whereabouts?'

Faithly's face relaxed. 'Less than you, I'll be bound. I haven't seen or heard from my brother in thirteen years. All I know of him is what is known by common rumour, that he is of the court of the King in exile, abroad somewhere.'

'Are you certain of that?'

'I told you: all I know is what comes here by common rumour.'

'Well,' said Seeker, 'not so common rumour has it that

your brother has disappeared from Charles Stuart's court, and may be heading for Yorkshire.'

Edward Faithly was trying to maintain his former confidence, but he could not control the colour in his face, which even in the golden candlelight visibly blanched.

Seeker pressed home. 'The major-general would have me remind you that your brother is a traitor to this nation. I'll not need to lay out for you the penalties for giving succour to traitors. You understand me?'

Edward Faithly looked him directly in the eye. 'I understand you perfectly, Captain.'

'Then you will also understand that whilst you are here, my men are currently making a search of your house for any trace of your brother or communication from him.'

Faithly's face turned quickly from white to puce. 'This is outrageous! I am a justice of the peace!'

'And I, by the power of the major-general, as you will find in the papers I brought today to Commissioner Pullan, am the Law,' said Seeker.

Faithly regarded him with unconcealed loathing. His voice was hoarse and filled with contempt. 'Then the Law will leave this place empty-handed, Captain, for you'll find nothing of my brother in Faithly Manor but his portrait.' He then walked, as straight as his twisted leg would allow, to stand behind his wife.

Lawrence Ingolby's face was still a study in astonishment at the exchanges of the previous few minutes, but he had not yet been able to remark upon it when Bess Pullan's kitchen maid showed in the man who tomorrow would face trial of his fitness to be a minister of God. The name 'Septimus Jenkin' had conjured up in Seeker's mind visions of a worthy but ineffectual preacher, his best years behind him, who had escaped the worst censures of the Commonwealth through sheer dullness. But before Jenkin even opened his mouth, Seeker saw that the man just arrived was neither dull nor worthy. Tall and handsome, he was about Matthew Pullan's age, but with an air of danger in his eye and a curve of his mouth that made Seeker think of some shady scion of the Stuarts. Had a bastard cousin of Charles Stuart woken unexpectedly sober one day to find himself a clergyman, he would have looked like Septimus Jenkin. His best days were not quite behind him, but Seeker could tell when a man was on the cusp – in a year or two the fair, handsome face would begin to run to fat, the eyes, already dark-circled and showing a hint of bleariness, would become puffy and their whites yellowed with drink. In five years he would be a mere raddled memory of what he was now. In ten he would likely be dead. As yet, though, the veins on his nose had not yet begun to crack and splinter, and Septimus Jenkin was holding on to the advantages God had given him.

The newcomer appeared a little wary of Seeker. 'I did not think the army troubled itself over the running of a trier's court, Captain. Am I condemned already?'

'Under the new governance of the major-generals, the army will trouble itself over whatever it is required to trouble itself over, but I am not here for your trial. And whether or not you are to be condemned depends upon the Committee of Ejectors, not me.'

'And who is on this committee?' asked Lady Emma, never lifting her eyes from the fire.

Matthew Pullan heaved a sigh. 'Of local men, Abel Sharrock, John Clough and Jude Morley.' The sexton, the cobbler and the smith. 'And then there's the trier himself, Caleb Turner. You'll meet him tonight. A man of few charms, by all accounts.'

'But very godly, no doubt,' said the vicar.

'Not so godly he hasn't got himself a pretty little wife in tow. You'll like her, Septimus,' said Ingolby.

Jenkin turned towards Ingolby, interested, but Bess Pullan, with Gwendolen in her train, had also entered the room by this point. 'Reverend Jenkin's in enough trouble as it is, Lawrence. If he's half the sense he was born with, he'll go nowhere near the trier's wife.'

And then Abel Sharrock had arrived, and they had learned they'd have to wait another day to cast eyes on Mistress Turner.

The two unwanted settings were cleared away by the confused maid, and they sat down to the supper, nine of them. Matthew took his place at the head of the table, Bess hers at the far end, with Gwendolen just around the corner to her right. The girl was in near darkness, almost as if fearful of being seen. She too, Seeker noticed, wore a strange ornament about her neck. Hers, though, was no piece of old scratched glass such as adorned Lady Emma's neck, but a fair-sized amulet of some sort, that looked to be of fine silver mesh. What manner of keepsake the amulet held, he could not tell. Lawrence Ingolby had been placed to Gwendolen's right, and immediately set to entertaining her with sly nonsense whilst clearly keeping an ear to the talk around the table. Seeker, at his own request, was seated opposite Sir Edward Faithly, that he might observe the man more closely. At the other side of the table, between her husband and Lawrence Ingolby, was Lady Emma. It was Matthew Pullan who had handed her to her place, and Seeker found himself watch Pullan's hand lightly let go of the woman's as she sat, a touch between them that seemed to linger after their hands parted. Seeker thought it impossible that others hadn't noticed it. He glanced to Sir Edward, to see whether he also watched the pair, but the justice of the peace appeared to have no interest in his wife and the Commissioner of Faithly, intent as he was in replenishing his wine glass.

Had it not been for Faithly's presence at the supper, Seeker would have been happier eating with his men in the kitchen, and had told Bess so quite pointedly. Bess had responded, in no uncertain terms, that no officer in Cromwell's army would take his supper in her kitchen whilst the likes of Abel Sharrock was waited on hand and foot next door. And so it was that Seeker found himself seated uncomfortably close to Sharrock. For all his Puritan principles, the constable gravedigger was fat, and in the warmth of the parlour, where the heat of the fire was heightened by the press of the company, he was already perspiring, beads of sweat appearing on his bald pate to be dabbed at intermittently with his linen napkin. It was Bess who had seated him beside Seeker, 'and see that you keep him in check', she'd muttered to him whilst pointing Sharrock to his place. The constable appeared well pleased with his positioning, and lost no time in broaching the subject that most interested him.

'You bring papers from York, they tell me, Captain. From the major-general. The new orders, I suppose?'

'Aye,' said Seeker. 'For the commissioner.'

The attention of the room was now on Matthew Pullan.

'Go ahead,' said Seeker. 'It's the law now, no secret about it.'

So Pullan told them of the new penalties to be imposed upon Royalists, the new tax to be levied, of a tenth of their wealth, even on those who'd sat quiet the last thirteen years. If Edward Faithly's face had blanched at talk of his brother, it was even paler now. His face hardened as Pullan recounted the litany of new measures, the confiscations of arms, bonds for good behaviour, restrictions on movements that would fall on any who had ever shown support for the Stuarts.

'The Council of State surely cannot think this will make dormant Royalists loyal to Cromwell?' asked Lady Emma. 'As well poke a slumbering bear.'

'Better a dead bear than a sleeping one,' replied Seeker. 'These orders are to make plain to any who think to rise again that they will lose everything they have.'

Septimus Jenkin now leaned into the light. 'Aye, but will they care, Captain? This England that Cromwell is making is not the England of free men.' He left his seat and went to the head of the table where he picked up at random sheets Matthew Pullan had been reading from. 'Local officers – village constables – to be encouraged to inform on magistrates, justices of the peace, even, that they don't consider well enough affected to the new ways. No race meetings nor cockfights nor bear-baitings to be held, no gatherings of former Royalists in men's private houses nor in public places even, for fear that should a handful find themselves in the one place they will have nothing to do but plot to overthrow Cromwell. Answer for your movements, don't gather with your friends,' he cast a contemptuous glance towards Abel Sharrock, 'let men who can scarcely read look into the heads of those that do and report on what they fancy they have found there.' Jenkin threw down the sheets. 'What England is this?'

'An England that will be at peace,' said Seeker.

'Peace!' Edward Faithly's voice was rank with bitterness. 'All suspected Royalists are to give a bond for the behaviour of every last man in their household, down to the meanest stable boy. And should that stable boy forget himself so far as to take a tumble in the hay with a milkmaid, the whole bond will be lost as surely as had the master taken aim at Cromwell himself. Men of property are to engage themselves for huge sums. Entire families could be ruined by the whim of a drunken footman.'

If Edward Faithly had thought to make his point with a flourish, he was disappointed. Into the silence that followed his outburst came the steady voice of Bess Pullan. 'Then I daresay they'll have to mind their footmen better, won't they?'

'You're a hard woman, Mother,' said Matthew, laughing.

'These are hard times,' she replied, attending to her plate.

They all followed suit, and nothing else was said for a few moments until Edward Faithly spoke again, directing his question to Seeker.

'And what of their wives?' he asked.

Seeker paused, a piece of bread halfway to his mouth. 'Their wives?'

'Aye, Captain. Are we to give bond of security for the virtue of our wives?'

Across the table from him, Lady Emma did not pause in the slow swallowing of her soup, but Seeker noticed that in her left hand, the piece of bread she held was crushed almost to dough. He was still searching for an appropriate response when Lawrence Ingolby stepped in smoothly.

'And what's the money for?' he asked. 'From the fines and the bonds?'

'It's to pay for the militias.'

Ingolby laughed. 'Your wages, then?'

Jenkin swallowed down more wine. '"The Army is a beast that hath a great belly and must be fed".'

'What's that, Septimus?' asked Lady Emma.

'Just something a friend wrote.'

Edward Faithly was now doing nothing to hide his distaste at finding himself sitting down to sup with such as Seeker. 'Aye, a beast that feeds off those that sit at home, minding their business, praying not to be taken notice of by some yeoman who likes the look of his horse, his house, his wife?'

Seeker put down the hunk of bread he'd been dipping in his soup. 'Every time some halfwit adventurer has slithered out of the sea from Paris or Cologne or wherever else Charles Stuart's rag-tag court has pitched up, too many of those, such as you talk of, give off sitting quietly at home and minding their own business and take it into their heads to ride out and proclaim him King. They gather others round them, disturb the peace of honest men and women, threaten the good order of towns and villages for miles around and the lives of those whose duty it is to keep it. They are fantasists who would lead us all into bloody civil war once more, and it is time to bring these constant irritations to an end. Such men have given up their right to the freedoms of other Englishmen, and if they come at last to learn that they do not have a God-given right to the halls and manors they sit in and the lands they live off, they might think twice before riding out to disturb the peace of the state again.'

Seeker wondered whether here, in the North Riding, it could be possible that Faithly had never had such truths made plain to him. 'You would not be wise to think that having fallen from your horse thirteen years since will always indemnify you against everything your father and brother did, nor everything that your brother might do.'

There was, around the table, an audible drawing in of breath. Only Bess seemed unmoved by what had been said, whilst Abel Sharrock was almost beside himself with right-eous indignation.

In the end it was Lawrence Ingolby who spoke, half-amused yet deadly serious. 'They're to put an end to much else besides cock-fighting and the like, these new laws of yours. Every Royalist that ever was to register with his commissioner at home, with a new registry in the City of London should they make their way there; every foreign traveller coming in from the continent to do the same. Every movement to be traced, recorded, authorised. As well lock them up and throw away the key.'

'As well indeed,' said Seeker, who noted that for all his affected disinterest, Lawrence Ingolby had taken the time to read the major-general's orders given to Matthew Pullan very thoroughly.

'And what about the rest of us, that like a drink of ale with our friends sometimes, that would pass his leisure hours laying a penny or two on his favourite fighting cock, a shilling or so on a fine filly over the gallops? No more gambling – taverns to be closed, market fairs put an end to.

No joy to be had in this world, Captain.' Ingolby drained his goblet and refilled it from the jug in front of him.

The constable, Abel Sharrock, was at last able to make an intervention. 'You've a deal too much leisure, Lawrence Ingolby, it seems to me, whatever it is you claim to do up there at the manor.'

'What I do is Sir Edward's business, not yours, Abel Sharrock.'

'Well, the day might come when it is my business, and then we shall see if he would have done better to keep a closer eye on you and others around here.' Sharrock had given a contemptuous glance towards Lady Emma in saying this. 'Whores and drunkards holding sway over the godly!' In a second Matthew Pullan was on his feet, followed by an unsteady Septimus Jenkin, who knocked a pewter water bowl clattering to the floor in the process. Pullan urged the vicar to sit again and turned his full attention on the sexton.

'I'll tell you this once, Sharrock, and not again: you're in my house only because you were to accompany this trier, who has not come. There is no other reason I would have you seated at my table, and if you insult any of my guests again, you'll be out on your ear, constable or no constable.'

Sharrock's face became an outraged snarl. 'I say nothing that isn't rumoured over half the North Riding. You'll answer for it, though, all of you. You'll answer like anyone else for your godlessness.' He nodded towards Jenkin. 'Him first, but the rest of you will follow, and then we'll see whose table I shall not sit at.' Sharrock stood up and pushed his bowl away, before stepping over the edge of the bench and making for the door. Something of the moment of his departure was lessened by the snagging of the edge of his new black cloak on a loose splinter in the bench. He tugged at it, pulling up the weft of the cloth so it wrinkled all the cloth around it. In frustration, Abel snapped the caught thread and strode for the door.

No one said anything until Bess Pullan, looking down at his place, tutted. In his irate departure, Sharrock had slopped half of the creamy mushroom soup over the side of his bowl so that it had spilled down onto the oak table, where it was already congealing.

'Good madeira wine and the last of the cream I put in that,' said Bess, annoyed. 'Such as Abel Sharrock has never supped before, and he didn't see fit to eat it.' She took Abel's discarded shoulder-napkin and wiped up the mess from the table top, before calling the girl Orpah to come and take the bowl away and to feed its remaining contents to the pig.

Thomas leaned against the far corner of the workshop almost laughing with relief. So intent had he been in observing the comings and goings to and from Matthew Pullan's house, so entertained and intrigued by the supper scene of which he had stolen a few perilous glimpses, it had not occurred to him that Sharrock would leave by the back yard rather than the front door as any other guests at such a gathering would have done. Once he had realised, it had been all he could do to dash from his position beneath the small side window of the Pullans' parlour across the yard in time to slip through the door of what he had at first thought to be a common log-store, but soon discovered to be some sort of apothecary's workshop. There had been no apothecary in Faithly nor anywhere near in Thomas's youth, only the strange woman Tansy Whyte, whose herbs and salves had healed the people or killed them, just as those of the best of apothecaries the world over would also do. Hunkering down in the furthest corner from the door, his woollen cloak pulled up over his head, Thomas heard Sharrock stomp past, muttering and threatening to spill his outrage to his harridan wife. What had they left this place to, himself and his father, as they had ridden out of Faithly to fight in the King's cause? Had it been that gravediggers might sit at a rich merchant's table and make threats to the justice of the peace, Thomas's own brother, and insult his wife? No, though that was what Thomas's father had said would be the end of it all, if the King were defeated, and now it had come to pass.

Edward looked ill, though, worse even than Thomas had been led to expect. Perhaps Thomas should pity his brother, but he had used up all his pity, all his human sympathies, long ago, as he'd watched better men by far, their own father amongst them, die in mud and gore in a cause his brother had not lifted a finger for. And what of Matthew

Pullan? Where was the fervour of the old Puritan foe, the older childhood friend? For all that Matthew's side had proved the victors, the commissioner was tired, a tiredness Thomas thought he recognised. Maybe he'd learned the same lessons as Thomas had. Or maybe it was just because of Emma. Maybe that loss had been enough.

Only Bess looked the same. Older, a little bent, but the same nonetheless. Thomas had no doubt she could administer as sharp a slap now as he had often felt in his boyhood, heir to Faithly Manor or no. Bess would have no truck with the scrumping of apples, the tormenting of pigs, the insolence of a mere boy masquerading as charm. It had been half in his mind to walk into the house, saunter into that parlour and make his bow to old Bess Pullan, just to see the look on her face.

He might have done it, too, though there was still a point to his plan that should really have been carried out first, if it wasn't for that captain. The captain was unexpected, a complication. He'd been warned already of the trier's court that had come to sit in the village; how badly awry had Septimus Jenkin's life gone, that he should face a panel of such worthies that were to sit in judgment on him tomorrow? About as badly as the lives of most in this, his homeland, Thomas thought. But the captain, no, he had not known of the captain's coming to Faithly, and that would require elucidation before Thomas could proceed quite as he had planned. Certainly he would not be walking into Matthew Pullan's house tonight, to make his bow to anyone. He would carry out his next task as had been planned, and then he would consider how to deal with the matter of the captain.

FOUR

Spilled Milk

Gwendolen's bedchamber was hung with herbs. Bess had seen to it that she slept in sheets of the best linen, on a feather bed finer by far than anyone else in the house had to lay themselves down on. Gwendolen slept on a pillow of crushed lavender and rosemary. She kept the window of her small chamber open by night, so that she could hear the owls as they swept, hunting, over their nocturnal world and imagine that she heard other beasts creeping about the moor. The night brought scents of moss and clover and peat and honeysuckle, so that Gwendolen's senses were filled with the things of the earth. More often than not, on a good night, the tinctures Tansy had taught her to make warded off the bad dreams, and she would sleep until the cock crowed and Orpah's weary trudge made its way across the yard. But not tonight.

Tonight Gwendolen had woken after only a few hours of restless slumber, a pain in her stomach as if it would split her in two and a nausea rising so that she scarcely had time to reach the ewer on her wash-stand before half the contents of her stomach voided themselves down the front of her new muslin nightgown, that Bess had brought her only last week from York. She tried to shout out, but could not make a sound issue from her throat, other than a hideous, irresistible retching.

Bess had woken early, before cock-crow, and lain waiting in the last of the night-time for dawn to send the first sliver of light through the shutters of the little room beside the kitchen. The fine bedchamber upstairs that she had shared with her husband was Matthew's now — she had insisted on it — he was the master of the house. He hadn't argued long — they both knew she could hardly manage the stairs any more. She thought of the nights she had risen from that bed, woken by the sound of weeping from Gwendolen's chamber. Digby had never heard it, even when Gwendolen had been a little girl and crying out loud at her unnamed terrors, nor Matthew neither, for Matthew had been taught by war to disregard sounds of anguish in the night. But Bess had heard, for she had learned to listen for them, and on countless nights she had crept from her own bed to go and comfort the child. As the years had passed, the distress had subsided, but these last months it had returned, replenished and unreachable. Bess wondered how many hours Gwendolen had wept alone through the darkness for that there was no one to hear her. It was a truth Bess could not turn her face from as she saw the days of her own life hasten to their end: she had failed the child.

She forced herself to consider the coming day. Today, the trier's court would begin its sitting, grievances would be aired, grudges repaid, lies told. Bess could feel the tension, the fear of it rising from the street outside, from the houses and cottages, from the moor, coming to this house, her house, on the last of the night air to curl through the shutters and seep into the walls, infuse the very floorboards that they stepped on. Bess had no care for all that; she bore no ill-will to her neighbours – well, not to most of them, at least – but whatever might befall them they had brought upon themselves, one way or the other. Bess's care was for those in this house, under this roof. The cock crowed and she summoned a silent prayer, as she did every morning, before rising from her bed and reading her portion of scripture.

Bess was already busy in the kitchen by the time Orpah arrived. The girl had seen the trier, 'And I do not like the look of him, no, not one bit, Mistress Pullan, and I would not like to come before him.'

'Then play the fool, girl. If they think you're simple, no one will pay heed to what you have to say.'

'But I'm not a fool, Mistress Bess.'

'I know that, child, but you're slow and clumsy enough. Better when people pay you no heed, always better.'

Orpah nodded. She'd lived in this village long enough to know the truth of what Bess said. 'I'll just get Hilda milked, then.'

'Best you do, before she comes wandering in here looking for you.'

By the time Orpah returned with a jug of milk from the freshly filled pail, the jannocks were made and Matthew sitting at the table waiting on his breakfast. Bess could see the tension of the night before – of having the Faithlys here, and listening to the outburst of Abel Sharrock – had not yet left him. Nothing would be gained by speaking of it. 'Where's Gwendolen?' he asked, as Bess set a jug of ale down in front of him.

'She'll be out at her berries by now, I daresay,' said Orpah.

Matthew looked up from beneath troubled brows. 'She'll not be at her berries,' he said. 'I've spoken to her of it, told her she's not to go to the woods alone any more – or with Tansy.'

'You spoke too late,' said his mother. 'I had Maud Sharrock in here yesterday, casting all sorts of aspersions in front of the captain.'

'Seeker's not interested in women's gossip,' said Matthew. 'It's not what he's here for.'

'Is he not?' said Bess. 'How long before he's not? How long does it take for idle gossip to become accusation, fact? How long did it take in Norfolk, with Matthew Hopkins?'

'This isn't Norfolk, Mother, and Matthew Hopkins is long gone. Damian Seeker's no witch-finder.'

Bess turned away to look out of the window across the yard towards the moor track. 'With this Committee of Ejectors at the Black Bull there'll be a whole village of witch-finders. If Abel Sharrock should take it into his head to whisper to the trier . . .'

Matthew put down his tankard. 'If Abel Sharrock should take it into his head to do any such thing, I'd soon stop his mouth for him.'

Bess nodded. 'Aye, well, see that you do.'

Orpah, who had been attempting not to overhear the conversation between her master and mistress, suddenly said, 'Oh!'

Bess turned around. 'What's the matter, child?'

'Gwendolen has left her cloak,' she said, nodding towards the back of the kitchen door. 'And the morning so cold. She will catch a chill for sure.'

Matthew stood up, wiping his mouth. 'She's maybe not gone out at all. Best you get upstairs, Orpah, and see that she's not overslept.'

The clumsy clatter of the girl mounting the wooden stairs, the tentative then louder knocking on the door of Gwendolen's bedchamber, were soon replaced by a shriek of horror, and wailing.

Seeker and his men had risen early, and were up on the moor before the mist had risen from the surrounding dales. The heavy silence was broken only by the sound of their horses' hooves and the occasional call of a solitary bird. Seeker could feel the tension in his men, as if they rode watched by some unseen presence. No trace of Thomas Faithly had been found in their search of his brother's house the previous night, and when the mist lifted, Seeker would set them to searching the nearby woods. When the mist lifted on this bleak, open place, there would be nowhere else for a man to hide.

The horses crossed the track as if their feet remembered it, and it was not long before Seeker saw, looming out ahead of them, hard-faced and double-gabled, as bleak a house as he had ever come across. Stone and slate, and never a rose nor creeper to afford relief to walls that might have glowed honey in the sun, should ever they have seen it. Faithly Manor was grim and grey as death. Seeker wondered that any man should want to hold onto this, or having once left, ever think of returning, but then he remembered that Edward Faithly had had no choice – the convenient fall that had stopped him fighting for the Stuarts against Parliament made him as suspect to the Royalists on the continent as he was to the authorities at home. Edward Faithly was as exiled as surely as were those in whose cause his father had died.

By the time they dismounted in the courtyard, Lawrence Ingolby was standing in the front doorway at the top of a broad flight of stone steps, waiting for them. 'I thought your men had had a good look over this place last night.'

'They did. And they'll do so again if I think it necessary. Meantime, I've business with Sir Edward.'

'He's getting ready for the trier's court,' said Ingolby.

'Then I'll get on with it,' said Seeker as he moved past the man and into the great hall of Faithly Manor. Sir Edward was already there, evidently waiting for him, seated in a large carved oak armchair by the fire, which had just been lit. The grey light seeping through the mullioned window panes was not as kind as had been the soft candle glow of Bess Pullan's dining parlour, and harrowed out the man's features even more.

'You will excuse my wife's absence, Captain. We had not expected you at this early hour.'

'I daresay you can relate to your wife what I have to say.'

'I daresay I can, Captain. But as you know, I am to attend the trier's court today, so you had better state your business.'

'Given your family's support of the late Charles Stuart—'

'Ten years since,' interrupted Sir Edward, 'and I did not fight.'

'Because you could not, and that alone saved you this estate on your father's death. On the authority of the Council of State, and under the governance of the major-generals, I am here to examine your accounts, and to recommend the figure in which you should be taxed according to the new orders. One tenth of your wealth.'

Edward Faithly's face hardened, and he pushed himself out of his chair, bringing his face towards Seeker's. As he did so, the mastiff that had been lying at his feet also stood and began to bare its teeth, until a motion of the hand and a curt command from Seeker put it into submission. This appeared to anger Sir Edward still further. 'This new directive is nothing but the envy, writ large, of petty men whom fortune has put in the seat of power.'

Seeker remembered the times he and his father had been hunted like vermin over the taking of a rabbit or a pheasant from a rich man's land. 'That those you speak of have been placed in the seat of power means they are no longer petty men. You should have known that before now.'

'We'll see,' said Sir Edward. 'But today I am bound to observe the doings of other petty men. Ingolby will show you my accounts. Now,' he said, hobbling towards the stairs, 'if you do not object, I must see what is keeping my wife. She will need time to prepare herself properly for this trier's court.'

'Your wife is to be questioned?'

'No,' said Sir Edward, with a thin smile as if Seeker were somehow simple, 'she is to be seen.'

Lawrence Ingolby wasted no time in providing Seeker with the accounts and papers he asked for.

'You're going to the trier's court as well, I suppose?'

'Aye.'

'Are you asked to speak for the Reverend Jenkin?'

'Me? No. Septimus can speak for himself.'

'As long as he's sober,' said Seeker.

Ingolby gave him a wary look. 'Septimus isn't daft. He'll be sober. It's what the rest of them have to say I'll be listening for.'

'Such as?' asked Seeker.

Ingolby shrugged. 'Who knows? But Abel Sharrock and his cronies have axes to grind, and I don't plan that they should grind them on my neck.' He laid the most recent ledger on the table. 'Is that it?'

'Yes,' said Seeker, 'for now.'

It suited Seeker to examine the estate papers without the assistance of the ever-watchful clerk. It was early in the afternoon that he finally finished. The fortunes of the Faithly estates had suffered badly during the war, and after it too, although it was clearly the result of plain bad management rather than ruination by any fighting or the billeting of soldiers upon the land, for there had been none. Four years ago, the estate had been dragged back from the brink of near ruin. Records began to appear in a different hand – Lawrence Ingolby's, Seeker deduced – and those records showed a significant investment of capital in the form of a large mortgage – in the name of Matthew Pullan. Better management since then meant Edward Faithly could just afford to pay the tenth of his wealth demanded by the new law, and it gave Seeker some satisfaction to draw up the figure for collection by Matthew Pullan in his role as local commissioner. Seeker was less satisfied to find no reference whatsoever to the fugitive Thomas Faithly, or anything that might give any clue as to his whereabouts. Once he had seen Pullan again, he would join his men in their search of Faithly Woods – although it seemed unlikely the renegade had returned home – and then they would be on their way back to York, where he would write his report for Thurloe.

When Seeker rode back down to the village, the curious eyes that had watched his arrival the day before were directed elsewhere – all village life and interest was centred on the trier's court at the Black Bull inn.

The girl Orpah was in the Pullans' yard, hanging out

white linens – a woman's nightgown and underthings, and bedsheets. The girl's hands were red raw with scrubbing and cold.

'Is the commissioner home?' he asked her.

Orpah shook her head. 'Master's at the Bull. Speaking for Reverend Jenkin.'

'And your mistress?'

Bess Pullan appeared in the kitchen doorway. 'Better things to do with my time.'

Seeker raised an eyebrow. 'Than speak for your vicar?'

'Than waste words when that trier had his mind made up before he ever clapped eyes on Septimus Jenkin. I've heard of your Mr Turner – the vicar was finished here as soon as his name appeared on Caleb Turner's list.'

'You've not much faith in justice, mistress.'

'I would know justice well enough, Captain Seeker, if I saw it. Were you wanting something?'

'I'm just here with some papers for the commissioner.'

'Well, you know where to leave them,' she said, stepping back to allow Seeker into the house. As soon as he entered it, he became aware of a strong smell of vinegar, masking something else. Gwendolen Sorsby was huddled in a blanket in an armchair set by the kitchen hearth.

'Your ward's not well.' It was a statement rather than a question.

Bess's brow furrowed. She seemed to grow smaller, draw in on herself. 'She was up half the night, half-dead on the floor this morning with vomit and flux, and not a soul heard her. Nearly carried Orpah off, finding her like that. Me too, by the time I got up there.'

'She'd be better off back in her bed,' said Seeker, nodding awkwardly towards the narrow stairs.

'As I've told her,' said Bess.

The girl pushed herself up out of the chair, a little unsteady but quite determined. 'I don't need my bed, Captain. I've been telling Aunt Bess these last few hours. Whatever was ailing me I've got rid of. I need to be in my workshop. I have compounds to see to, things that must be distilled, that will not keep . . .' Her voice was rising in her anxiety.

Bess put a hand on her shoulder to calm her and direct her back to her seat. 'Your tinctures and compounds will keep, my girl. You'll stay there where I can have my eye on you.' Then a thought seemed to strike her. Her eyes searched Seeker. 'You were not ill last night, nor them up at the manor?'

He shook his head. 'No.'

'And Lawrence?'

'Hearty as a horse,' he reassured her. 'There was nothing wrong with your food, mistress. There's been none of the rest of the household taken ill?'

'No,' said Bess. 'Only Gwendolen.'

'It'll be something she's picked up in the woods, I expect. Don't know what half those things are she brings home.'

Bess turned a furious face on Orpah. 'You don't know half of anything, you fool girl! If you're so keen to have

your opinions heard, you take them down to the Black Bull
and give them to the trier, for they're not wanted here!'

Orpah's face paled before becoming suffused with a bright
pink which crept rapidly up her neck to disappear beneath
her cap. Tears were pricking her eyes, and she could hardly
master her voice enough to say, 'Sorry, Mistress Pullan.'

Bess looked almost as abashed at her own outburst. 'Yes,
well. Talk's dangerous. Too much talk.' She rubbed her
hands on a drying cloth and went into the hall. Seeker was
still trying to understand the meaning of the exchange he
had just witnessed when she called sharply, 'Well, Captain?
Have you papers for Matthew or not?'

Matthew Pullan's business room, off the main hall and
with a window looking out on to the back courtyard, was
not large, but well ordered. Ranged on a shelf behind the
desk was a set of ledgers, which brief examination showed
to be accounts relating to the transactions of Pullan's business as a wool merchant.

Lying on top of the desk were the instructions Seeker had
brought with him from York yesterday. Alongside them,
in a ledger of business brought before the commissioner,
Seeker read the story of the battle that had been quietly
waging in Faithly these last few months. It was a battle
that had begun innocuously enough, so that many might
not have noticed it, but it had grown incrementally more
vicious, so that now it seemed to underlie everything that
happened in the village and the surrounding moor. Petty
disputes over boundary walls; the course of streams; the

weight of a loaf; the ownership of a wandering sheep
– all such things as bind a community with its grudges
throughout the generations – had progressed to complaints of a different tenor, and those complaints formed
a pattern. The dammed or diverted stream, it would be
recalled, figured in old tales from times of superstition,
when supernatural properties had been claimed for it. The
next accusation against the same defendant might refer to a
dispute over a beast followed by a sudden illness in the sheep
or milch cow concerned. The measuring of a boundary
would, by chance, have occasioned a suspicious sighting of
two persons who really should not be seen together. Unruly
public houses upon the moors were mentioned, the fears of
the godly brought to mind. But then the accusations, insinuations, began to reach a little higher: there were concerns
that some Royalists caught fleeing after the spring rebellion
had been on their way to Faithly Manor, 'or anywhere else
in Yorkshire', muttered Seeker; there was talk of card games,
and dice. And had the Reverend Jenkin not been seen to
sway and slur his speech on the day of the Thornton Fair?
It was said he had danced. The flock of Faithly was straying,
and like to be lost: young girls were suffered to walk abroad,
unaccompanied by their elders, at all hours of the day and
night. Who was to say what influences, malign in body
and spirit, such wandering girls might give themselves over
to? No names were named. As yet, no names. The commissioner was urged to think on it; the commissioner was
urged to consider; the commissioner was urged to ask him-

self whether this might not be an indication of . . . Seeker could himself have recounted the accusations that followed: popery, treachery, drunkenness, debauchery. And then a final throw of the dice, for it was all that was missing: the children of the village were fearful of Tansy Whyte, for that they thought her a witch. As was known, and had been known by the whole village for many years, Tansy Whyte was supplied with her food and her fuel by the commissioner's mother, and he should surely think on it.

Seeker read over the accusations a second time: aside from that last, there was nothing in them that would not be found amongst the papers of any commissioner the length of the country. The war had bred fear in the people: questions over the instability of the Protector's regime bred fear, concern for their immortal souls in a world beset by evil bred fear. In their desperation to counter things they did not understand, the people turned on those they did: old resentments raised their heads and gave themselves new names. In the insinuations made to the Commissioner of Faithly, time and again, the names of the complainers were the same: Abel Sharrock, Jude Morley, John Clough. The sexton, the smith and the cobbler. Today, though, those men had another name: 'Ejector'. At this very moment, all three sat alongside the trier Caleb Turner as the Committee of Ejectors pronouncing judgement on Septimus Jenkin.

Seeker closed the ledger and sat back in Matthew Pullan's chair. The pattern of the complaints was one he had seen and heard of before, beginning ten years ago and spreading northwards. The trials held then had been adjudged not by a trier, but a 'Discoverer', whose name had been Matthew Hopkins, and whom those with something to fear, which had become a great many souls, had called 'the Witch-finder'.

Seeker let out a sigh of frustration. From the tenor of the papers in front of him, it was clear that Abel Sharrock and his associates were determined upon the removal of more than their vicar; they would be coming next for Matthew Pullan, by any means at their disposal. Only last night he had told the Reverend Jenkin that the trier's court was no concern of his, but Seeker knew that the panic engendered ten years since by Matthew Hopkins could not be allowed to rear its head in the North Riding now. He took his cloak from the back of his chair and went to call his two men to attend him to the Black Bull.

Passing through the kitchen, Seeker saw Gwendolen emerge from her workshop and begin to cross the yard. She had a jug of some liquid in her hand, and though still pale, her face had begun to regain a little of its colour. He considered the future that might lie ahead of the girl in this place. The commissioner treated her as a sister, but perhaps Bess Pullan meant to marry her to Lawrence Ingolby, who seemed almost as a son to the old woman. He looked away. Something in the girl summoned thoughts he kept locked away of his own daughter, only a year or two younger now than Gwendolen Sorsby, and where she might be. In London those thoughts could be buried, obscured in the morass of other things calling his attention, but here, on the moors, where he had once been a father, silencing them took more strength than he could summon.

He was almost at the door when a sharp cry from the courtyard was swiftly followed by the sound of glass smashing on cobbles. Seeker was through the door in time to see Orpah run from the dairy, closely followed by her hobbling mistress. Gwendolen Sorsby lay on her side on the ground, knees drawn up and hands clutching at her stomach. Agony was etched on her face.

'What's happened? Gwendolen?'

Seeker ignored the panicking women whilst he checked the girl's mouth and eyes before gently slipping his arms beneath her and lifting her up. Before he had even got her back in the house she was retching and vomiting, her face turned a dreadful yellow. 'Where is the nearest doctor to be found?' he asked as they laid her down on Bess's bed.

Bess, face grey as stone, appeared not to have heard him.

'A physician?' he repeated with urgency.

'Dr Hollerenshaw, over at Thornton,' she said distractedly.

Seeker cursed to himself. Six miles at least. 'I'll fetch him.'

'Shall I fetch Tansy?' he heard Orpah ask her mistress as he pushed past them out of the room.

'What?' said Bess, hardly hearing. 'Aye. Tansy. That would be best.'

Within minutes, the map of the moor that had engraved itself on Seeker's mind as he had travelled it as a boy was playing out beneath his horse's thundering hooves. Acheron seemed to sense his master's being as one with this place, and responded to Seeker's urging at the first touch, the first suggestion. Bog, track, pass, ford disappeared beneath them as they flew towards Thornton.

The place was smaller, and quieter, than he remembered from the market days and hiring fairs that he had marvelled at as a boy. The inn was there as it ever had been though, all unchanged. He had no time to scan the faces of aged men sitting outside at their dinner for younger ones he might once have known.

'The physician's house?' he demanded, bringing Acheron to a halt in the road.

'There,' said the oldest of the three men, pointing to a large dwelling near the church.

Seeker was about to wheel round when the man stopped him. 'But you won't find him there today.'

'Where then?'

'Faithly,' the old man replied, chewing his food carefully. 'Trier's court.'

Since early morning, from his vantage point halfway up Faithly Ridge, Thomas Faithly had been watching the comings and goings in the village. As he had glimpsed the gathering in Bess Pullan's parlour the night before, and seen there one of Lilburne's militia captains, he had cursed his timing and his luck. Since then, he had learned the name of the captain: Damian Seeker. It was not the first time

Thomas had heard that name. One or two disappointed heroes, returning to Charles's court from failed missions and near scrapes, had brought back with them the name of Damian Seeker. It had seemed to Thomas, in the early hours of the night, that his plan could not proceed, not now, at least. But then a few hours of cold, uncomfortable reflection, along with the events of the morning, such as he had been able to comprehend them, suggested that his timing, and indeed his luck, might not be so bad after all.

He thought longingly of the clothing he might find amongst his brother's belongings at the manor, but the time was not yet right, and a day or so more in the guise of a Flemish peasant must be his lot. Even then, a Yorkshire farmhand's clothes would have been more to the purpose, but those were not to be got, it seemed, as easily as he had supposed. The lifting of the early mist had enabled him to see the movements about the places he had an interest in – Pullan's, the Black Bull and the track up to his own manor house – but with that mist had gone the cover he had hoped to make use of. The departure of the Seeker, at some speed, across the moor in the direction of Thornton, had been an unexpected bonus, and it seemed that everyone else for miles around was taken up with the spectacle of this trier's court. He had not been surprised to see his brother's carriage trundle and bump its way down the track towards the inn this morning, for he knew Edward must have been waiting a long time for this day.

And in that carriage had been Emma Hart, too, or Faithly

as he must learn to call her now, turning a moment to the carriage window, a stray tendril of auburn hair falling from her grey velvet hood. Thomas had not been able to properly make out her eyes from here, those grey granite eyes that he had never quite managed to charm, but he would have sworn that his brother's wife, in that brief moment, looked directly at him. That had been well over an hour since, and soon afterwards he had seen Seeker emerge from Pullan's stable yard and spur his horse up onto the moor towards Thornton. Thomas had waited as long as he could, but time was against him – he might not have a better opportunity than this. Checking once more that there was no one within sight, he emerged cautiously from his hiding place and began to make his way down onto the moor track, towards Faithly Manor.

FIVE

The Trier's Court

Matthew Pullan had never before seen the Black Bull as it was today; not even on fair days, before war and the Protectorate had put an end to them. Those who could not get into the taproom thronged the yard, jostling for whichever position might best afford them the chance of witnessing proceedings. Matthew shouldered his way through the eager ranks of his neighbours to take his place, as local commissioner, on a bench just below the dais on which the trier and his ejectors were to sit. Edward Faithly, as justice of the peace, was already there, Lawrence positioned behind him. Matthew looked searchingly at Lawrence, who glanced upwards, to his left, where Emma was taking her seat on an upper landing that had been got up for the occasion as a balcony of sorts. He watched as she drew down the hood and undid the clasp on the fine velvet cloak he knew Faithly insisted upon when she was to be seen abroad. Beneath, though, she had dressed herself in one of the simple grey woollen gowns that she favoured. Matthew felt a surge of pride at the act of rebellion. Once seated, she composed

her face and looked directly ahead of her, as if determined
not to acknowledge what was about to transpire below. Of
the trier's wife there was no sign.

Matthew turned to Edward Faithly and gave him a curt
nod. The heat and stench in the room were already oppres-
sive. Faithly brought out a handkerchief. 'The air is so
bad and close in here a man can hardly breathe, and bad
humours everywhere.'

'Not everywhere,' said Lawrence. 'Look at Abel Sharrock
– have you ever seen him look so pleased with himself?'

Both Sir Edward and Matthew followed Lawrence's gaze
to the entrance from the outer hallway just as a shepherd's crook, in a passing approximation of a mace, was
thumped up and down on the wooden platform of the dais,
demanding silence for the entry of the panel of ejectors to
the taproom over which they would now hold court.

At their head was Abel Sharrock, surveying the throng
of his neighbours and betters like a slaughterman coming
to market. He was overheated already, and almost salivat-
ing with anticipation. Matthew's stomach was awash with
disgust. Behind Sharrock were another two villagers –
Morley the smith and Clough the cobbler – both fervent
in their Puritanism and redolent with grudges. Any hopes
for a fair trial for the vicar rested with the trier himself, but
they were not great hopes, and they dissolved into nothing
when Matthew had his first sight of the man who walked
at the end of the procession. There was no warmth in the
face of Caleb Turner, no trace of anything good. Other

men might be lean, spare of build, have faces more akin to a bird of prey than to a man, and yet carry in them the light of humanity; Caleb Turner did not. There was something in the eyes that surveyed the gathered men and women of Faithly that spoke of disgust, and cruelty even.

'"Let me have men about me that are fat",' Matthew murmured.

But behind him, Lawrence Ingolby was more prosaic. 'Dear Jesus,' he said, 'Septimus is done for.'

Once the trier and his fellow ejectors had taken their places, Septimus Jenkin was summoned to stand before them, like a prisoner brought to the dock rather than a minister of God. Septimus had dressed himself too well for the role he was to play today – he should have come as penitent, supplicant, he should have come in humility, but he had not. A fine lace collar and matching cuffs, gifted to him some years ago by Sir Edward's mother, adorned a suit of much better quality than anything any of the men sitting in judgment upon him could have hoped ever to wear.

'Well, well,' said Sir Edward.

'He's throwing it in their faces,' murmured Lawrence. 'He's telling them he's better than they are, whatever they might say.'

'He's a fool,' said Matthew. Septimus Jenkin, who had been lifted from this very village and given a scholarship to Oxford, who might have expected high preferment had the Church of England not fallen with its King, had not had the sense to abandon that church. Septimus was going to have his moment, and even Matthew, for all such rich displays were tasteless to him, would admit that he cut a fine figure. Nevertheless, the effects of the sleepless nights of the last few months since Sharrock's insinuations had begun to gain currency, and the slight tremor in his hand, could not well be hidden.

The cobbler-ejector began a seemingly near-interminable invocation on the Lord to attend to the trier's labours and to leave any dissembling sinner exposed. When the prayer finally ended, Matthew looked again at Caleb Turner. He could see, by the way Turner was running his tongue around his mouth, that he was readying himself to begin. And as Turner began to address the gathering, Matthew heard the tones of Cumbria, roughened as if by gravel and honed to a studied contempt.

'By order of the Council of His Highness the Lord Protector, I am empowered to eject scandalous and inefficient ministers and schoolmasters from positions which they are unfit to hold.' He moved his eyes from Septimus Jenkin to where Matthew sat. 'It has been brought to my attention, by men of honest and worthy repute, that the present authorities in this place have failed to prosecute their duties.' Matthew felt the blood rising in him, and there was much stirring and murmuring amongst his neighbours as many eyes turned to Abel Sharrock. 'Any shortcomings on the part of the local commissioner or justice of the peace are the business of the major-general, who will attend to them in due course, I have no doubt. My duty, which I have been called by the Lord to perform, is the investigation of accusations that have been made about this man, Septimus Jenkin.' He lifted his hand and pointed at Septimus, a thing quite unnecessary as everyone in the room knew who their vicar was.

'Septimus Jenkin, you are brought before this committee to undergo trial of your fitness to preach the word of God, to minister to his people and to carry out the schooling of the children of this parish. Before I commence, do you have anything to say in your defence?'

Septimus stood very straight and spoke clearly. 'No, for I do not know of what I am accused.'

Turner appraised him a moment, as if he had been addressed with the utmost defiance. 'Oh, but hear a moment and you shall know, and then you may wish you had a better answer.' The trier turned now to Abel Sharrock. 'Constable, you will read out the accusations.'

Sharrock, whose face was already reddened by the clamorous heat built up in the taproom, glowed an even deeper scarlet and unrolled the parchment the trier had handed him. Out of the corner of his eye, Matthew could see Lawrence Ingolby smirk. 'This'll be interesting,' said Lawrence.

Clearing his throat once, and again, Abel Sharrock began to read, but he had not had half the learning, nor a quarter of the advantages of the man who stood accused, and stumbled again and again over words of greater complexity than a common gravedigger was called upon to know. The trier's face registered his growing impatience, so that by the time

Abel was attempting a third time to get to the end of the first charge, Turner snatched the scroll from his hands and thrust it towards the cobbler. 'You do it,' he spat.

Cobbler or no, John Clough read out the charges against Septimus Jenkin without difficulty, and with a degree of satisfaction that was not edifying to witness: Septimus used the banned prayer book of Laud and the liturgy of the discredited church of Charles I; Septimus, contrary to the diktats of the Protectorate, celebrated Christmas, Easter, the feast days of saints; Septimus owed his place to the patronage of a notorious Royalist; Septimus obscured the word of God by the unnecessary parading of his learning. Clough was about to proceed to accusations relating to Septimus's conduct as schoolmaster, but here the trier held up his hand. 'Let us first hear how the accused answers for his failings as a minister of God.'

Jenkin lifted his head and looked at Caleb Turner without exhibiting any fear. He acknowledged the charges against him and began to defend himself. His admission of the celebration of Christmas was too much for Abel Sharrock.

'Condemned out of his own mouth!' put in the constable, unable to contain himself.

The trier silenced him with a sharp look, and then told Septimus Jenkin to continue.

And so Septimus did. 'To your third charge I acknowledge that I hold my place of the beneficence of Sir Anthony Faithly. Call him a Royalist if you will, but when he showed me that kindness, we were all Royalists, and we all remained so: you, I, everyone in this room, until such time as Oliver Cromwell that is now His Highness Lord Protector, and others of his like, came out in arms and told us we must be otherwise.'

A palpable shock went through the room. Caleb Turner's jaw twitched but he held his temper. For all the vicar's words shocked him, Matthew could not help murmuring to Lawrence, 'He goes down, but he goes with spirit, does he not?'

Sir Edward Faithly contented himself with a smile.

'To your charge that I have learning,' continued Jenkin as if nothing untoward had been said, 'I—'

'We need hear nothing further.'

'Oh, but I would speak further, all the same, for there is something I have long wanted to say. The first learning I got was in the schoolroom in which I now teach. Amongst my schoolfellows was John Clough, now cobbler, who sits to your left in judgement on me. I am sorry, John, that you do not value learning as once you did. The day I won the scholarship to Balliol College that you had had such hopes of, condemned you to your father's cobbler's last and me, eventually, to find myself standing before you today. I pray it had never been, for I valued our friendship more than I ever did my place in the eyes of men.'

As John Clough sat back, over twenty years of ire and hatred going out of him, Septimus Jenkin turned to pick up his fine hat from the bench behind him. 'And now if you will excuse me, Mr Turner, John, Abel, Jude, I will go. I know your judgement on me before you ever pronounce it, and I will have quitted my place before Mistress Thatcher calls you to your supper.'

The taproom began to murmur, at a loss, deprived of their show and, a few, a little shamefaced. But Caleb Turner revived their interest with a word. 'No!'

'No?' enquired Jenkin, his back half-turned now to those who had come to eject him.

'No.' Turner smiled a crisp smile and it chilled Matthew Pullan's blood. 'You shall not go. There are other accusations to which you will answer.'

Jenkin stopped as he was. Matthew Pullan saw him look over the gathering of men and women he had known all his life. Matthew knew every face, as did Septimus, but what he looked upon now were strangers of whose existence he had not known until an hour ago. He wondered, when it came his time to witness, as he had been told it would, what words this trier would use to try to make him condemn his friend.

Caleb Turner spoke low and deliberately to Abel Sharrock. 'Tell Mr Jenkin for what he is to answer, Constable. I warrant you will have no need of the document to remind you of the charges.'

This was Abel Sharrock's moment and he drew himself up as far as he could and began to speak; as he did so, Matthew realised the constable was not looking at the accused minister standing in front of the dais, but at himself. Abel, indeed, had no need of the document, for he had evidently rehearsed what he was about to say with great care. 'It is alleged and attested, by witnesses of most excellent repute, that you, Septimus Jenkin, vicar of this place, have consistently failed to call to account those of your flock who have sinned. It is alleged and stated that you failed to investigate accusations of witchcraft made, on more than one occasion, against the madwoman Tansy Whyte.' An audible intake of breath went round the room, but there was no time to pronounce on Abel's accusation, because Abel had not finished. 'Further, it is witnessed and stated that you dismissed calls to question the girl Gwendolen Sorsby about her wanderings in the woods and her consortings with the alleged witch Tansy Whyte.' Matthew felt his fist clench, but made himself stay seated as Abel continued. 'It is alleged and stated that, in years past, you failed to act against the known fornicator and adulterer, Digby Pullan' – at this, there were outright expressions of shock, which turned to utter commotion when Abel Sharrock added, 'or to confirm informations of bastardy resulting from such fornication.'

It took both Matthew and a farmer sitting in front of him to hold back Lawrence Ingolby. 'I'll kill him,' said Lawrence. 'I swear before God, Matthew, I'll bloody kill him.'

The trier had heard Lawrence's oaths, it was certain, but Matthew could see he was enjoying too well the effect of Sharrock's diatribe to intervene, yet. Abel, growing in confidence, went on, for he had one final, explosive accusation to make. 'It is further alleged that you have failed to investigate accusations of the diabolical crime of incest within this very village.' There was instant commotion, and the trier was forced to bang his hammer again and again on the desk before him to restore order.

'I will have quiet or I will clear this room! Constable, you will continue.'

Sharrock licked his lips, smiled at Matthew and went on. 'It is alleged by common report that the girl Gwendolen Sorsby is the natural daughter of Digby Pullan, notorious adulterer, and that Bess Pullan, mother of the commissioner, has permitted the most horrid and despicable practices to go on under her roof.' The shock of these words reduced the room to silence. Abel opened his mouth as if to say more, but got no further, for now it was Matthew Pullan who lunged at him, sending the place once more into uproar, and upending the jug of ale that had been set there for the ejectors' use over Abel's fine Sunday clothes.

Eventually, Lawrence Ingolby managed to restrain Matthew, but beat his hammer as he might, the trier could not get the court to silence. And then Orpah Bigley burst into the taproom, shouting for Matthew Pullan. 'Master, please! You're to come away!'

Abel Sharrock, purple with indignation and struggling to recover his dignity, yelled, 'Orpah Bigley, what do you mean by this show of yourself?'

The girl looked around like a startled deer. 'Master must come!' She sighted Pullan at last. 'It's Miss Gwendolen, and the captain has gone over the moor for Dr Hollerenshaw and— Oh no!' She had spied the physician, sitting on a bench below the trier's platform.

The red anger drained from Matthew's face. Ignoring Abel Sharrock's outrage and shaking off Lawrence Ingolby's hold, he went to take hold of the girl.

'What has happened to Gwendolen?'

Orpah tried to summon some coherence. 'She's taken ill again, master, like last night, but worse, and like to die if the doctor don't come, and look, here he is and the captain gone over the moor to fetch him.'

Matthew was momentarily frozen with shock, but Lawrence Ingolby was already hauling a protesting Dr Hollerenshaw to his feet.

'But the court!' spluttered Sharrock.

The constable's voice brought Matthew back to his senses. 'Court be damned,' he shouted as he forced a path out of the crowded room.

SIX

Tansy

Despite the opened window, the heat in the small room was stifling and the air rank with all the odours of illness, flux, vomit and an insidious presentiment of death. Gwendolen was worse, much worse, than when he had left her that morning. Her hair was plastered to her forehead, her face and eyes, when they were not clenched shut in pain, a sickening yellow and her lips cracked and bleeding. Matthew had rarely felt so helpless. His mother was trying to calm her and cool her with damp cloths, whilst Tansy Whyte smeared balm on her lips and attempted to coax her to swallow a foul-looking infusion of green herbs. Whatever she swallowed down came back as bile. Something of the terror he had seen in Orpah's eyes in the courtroom was written on his mother's face.

Tansy glanced over at him and shook her head once. Matthew laid a hand on his mother's shoulder and took the cloth from her. 'Here is the physician come, Mother.'

'What, already?' she asked, bewildered.

Hollerenshaw ushered Tansy aside and stooped to look at Gwendolen.

'Has she boils?' he asked Bess. 'Or lesions?'

The old woman shook her head wordlessly.

'Let me see the spewings.'

Tansy, her face contorted in a contempt Matthew had never before seen on it, held out the bowl of foul liquid towards the physician, who took half a sniff before recoiling, his handkerchief over his nose.

'A pestilence,' he declared, stepping backwards. 'A mark of God's displeasure on this place, this house, you may be sure. There's little you can do but pray that the rest of you be spared. She'll be dead by nightfall.'

Gwendolen, by some act of strength, forced herself up on her pillows, only to be taken once more by an agonised retching of her long-emptied stomach. The physician, taking fright, started from the room with his white collar pulled up over his mouth. Before the front door banged shut after the man, Pullan heard him say, 'Put a guard on that door, Captain, and let none in that house wander from it, for there may be pestilence there.'

A moment later, Pullan saw the frame of Seeker in the doorway. The soldier looked over to the girl who had settled back on her pillow and appeared to be calm. 'Not like any pestilence I know,' he said.

Tansy had come in again behind him, still muttering about the physician and drying her hands on a linen napkin. 'No pestilence. Not here. Destroying angel's come for Gwendolen.'

And so it was; within an hour of Seeker's return, Gwendolen had slipped beyond her senses, beyond pain even; within three she was dead.

It was almost two in the morning when the household around Seeker fell to an uneasy rest. Bess had refused to have the physician called back, saying they needed no further prescription of the judgement of God. Tansy had gone into Gwendolen's workshop and brewed a decoction of honey and camomile, which the old woman consented to take. Orpah would not go to her own home, and lay now at her mistress's side in the fine chamber upstairs to which Matthew had carried the old woman. Matthew had declared he would watch through the night over Gwendolen, laid out in clean linen strewn with lavender and lemon thyme in the small, scrubbed room in which she had died. Only Seeker, and Lawrence Ingolby, who had insisted on staying at the Pullans, remained talking quietly by the light of the kitchen fire.

'Tell me about Tansy Whyte,' said Seeker.

'Tansy?' Ingolby was instantly on his guard. 'What Abel Sharrock said in that court today was nothing but an evil lie.'

'I wasn't in the court today, and I don't know yet what was said there, but I've seen enough of the constable not to take him at his word. That's why I'm asking you to tell me about Tansy Whyte.'

'Right,' said Lawrence, somewhat surprised and a little mollified. 'Well, Tansy lost her wits fourteen years ago when her good-for-nothing husband went away to the fair at Helmsley and never came back.'

'Not so witless that she wasn't sent for when the girl fell ill.'

Ingolby shrugged. 'There's no physician in Faithly, as you saw. Tansy is the midwife who attends the women in childbed, and it's she who cleans and dresses the dead. Maud Sharrock would have folk think she's a witch, but Tansy's no witch, just a healer, harmless. Tansy and Gwendolen had nothing but kindness for one another. What has Tansy to do with this?'

'Where does she live?' said Seeker, reaching down his cloak from the hook on the door.

'What?' said Ingolby, screwing up his face.

'Where does Tansy Whyte live?'

'In the cottage over from the churchyard. You're not going there now?'

But Seeker was already gone.

The moon was three-quarters full in a cloudless sky and the moor lay out beyond the village like a slumbering beast. Seeker looked behind him at Faithly — one street of mis-shapen dwellings, stone, wood and thatch, only the church and the Pullans' house being slate-roofed. Wisps of smoke snaked into the air from the kitchen chimney of Pullan's house, where he knew Lawrence Ingolby would wait for him. Only the inn, at the far end of the village, and the sexton's cottage over in the churchyard, showed any light.

Maud Sharrock had been chased from the Pullans' door when she had come to solicit news of Gwendolen.

Tansy Whyte's dwelling looked to be little more than a hovel, a poorly thatched pile of stones with one door and no window. Smoke curled from a hole in the roof – Tansy was not sleeping.

He knocked softly on the door.

A tremulous voice. 'Who's there?'

'Captain Seeker, Tansy. There's no need to fear, but I'd have a word with you.'

There was a soft rustling and the door creaked open in front of him. She stepped aside to let him into the one room of her dwelling.

The meagre light of the fire in the middle of the room revealed shapes, cast shadows. In this light, and closer, with no one else to claim his notice, Seeker saw that the woman was younger than he had imagined, hardly forty, and that she might have been pretty, once. A straw pallet against the wall and an old deal chest serving as table, dresser, stool or all three, were all the furnishing in the place. An empty tripod stood over the fire; a couple of pots and ladles hung from the low beams of the roof. Something about the beams, even in the near darkness, took Seeker's notice. He reached up a hand and ran the tip of a finger along one. Grooves, each one of them had cut into it hundreds of grooves. He looked more closely – some were fresher than others. Tansy was watching him.

'Days,' she said. 'Days since my Seth went. I keep the tally.'

Soon there would be no space left on the beams, and what would Tansy do then? It was hardly a way to live. Seeker could not see how Tansy Whyte, on her own, with no husband, no child, no animals, no land, could live at all, were it not for the charity of her neighbours. Whatever her poverty, the place was as clean as such a place could be kept, and Seeker settled himself, cross-legged, on the rushes across the fire from Tansy's bed.

The woman ran her tongue over her bottom lip, looked frightened, but no more frightened than was her habit.

'What did you mean, Tansy?'

She looked away from him. 'Mean by what?'

'When the physician said Gwendolen had been struck by a pestilence, and you said it was no pestilence. You said the destroying angel had come for Gwendolen. What did you mean?'

The hand-wringing grew more urgent, the eyes more darting. 'Nothing. Meant nothing. Full of nonsense. Tansy's just a fool, wits gone. Meant nothing.'

Seeker stretched over the hearth, stopped the wringing of her hands. 'I know you meant more than nothing, Tansy. Now, I will know the truth of that girl's death, and you will tell me what you know. Who is the destroying angel?'

She continued silent a moment and then looked up at him, direct, eyes clear. 'You will find the destroying angel in Faithly Woods. Lovely to look at, so pretty. But it'll poison you. Every bit of it'll poison you and you'll die, just like Gwendolen died. No one survives the destroying angel. Not ever.'

It came back to him now, a snatch of his mother teaching his sister. 'They look just like the mushrooms of the field, do they not? But see, their gills and stalk are all white. Destroying angel, they're called, and you don't touch those, don't even touch them.'

Seeker's voice was low. 'Tell me how you know.'

Tansy shook her head at the memory. 'The way she died, that's how I know. Destroying angel toys with you, laughs at you. Makes you ill, pain, vomit, flux, and then it leaves you, goes away, takes a rest, gathers its strength whilst you think you're getting better. Gwendolen thought she was getting better, didn't she? But she wasn't. Not really. Destroying angel was just waiting for the final fight. It comes back for you, and it always wins. Worse pain, worse sickness, empties you then sends you senseless, like you're sleeping, beyond reach. That's when it finally takes you. Dead. Like Gwendolen. Dead.' She sat back, repeating the word to herself.

Seeker thought back over the last hours, what he had heard of the night before and what he had seen for himself. It was all as Tansy had said. 'But why would she have taken this mushroom? Did she not know the woods?'

Tansy nodded. 'Gwendolen knew the woods, knew every-thing in it, better than me. She'd never eat the destroying angel, not by herself.'

'You're saying someone poisoned her.'

Tansy's eyes lost their focus. Too quickly, Seeker thought.

'I don't say anything, Captain. I'm just Tansy, and my wits are gone.'

She'd closed herself off, and there was no more to be had from her. Seeker had heard what he'd needed to about the destroying angel but he left her hovel nonetheless frustrated. The other matter he'd wanted to question her on would have to wait for tomorrow, but he was determined he would have an answer to it before he left Faithly. He would know from Tansy what it was in that amulet that had hung around Gwendolen Sorsby's neck, and why it was that, at the moment of the girl's death, Tansy had taken it.

Lawrence Ingolby was asleep in a chair by the kitchen fire by the time Seeker returned to the Pullans' house, and did not stir as he passed. Seeker walked through the sleeping house to the parlour.

The shutters had not been closed and the place was swathed in a clear blue light from the moon. In the stillness and quiet of the night, Seeker could envisage those who, only the night before, had gathered together in this room. Ochre light from fire and candelabra had bathed them in warmth and suggestions of colour. The aromas of the food, the scents of men and women, got up in their best clothes, perfumed and not, had created a tableau of movement, sound and life, a carefully shifting, living babble. But now, here, in the cold blue stillness, he pictured them again, seated where they had been, frozen in his mind's eye.

He called back to mind, slowly, one by one, their movements and their words, what he had seen, heard and what
he thought he had seen. He saw the great tureen Orpah
Bigley had struggled to the table with before setting it in
the centre. The ladle dip in nine times, nine times pour a
thick mushroom soup into which Bess Pullan had put the
last of the cream and her son's good madeira in the bowls
set in front of the diners around the table. He recalled a
glance at Gwendolen Sorsby and saw her, swathed more
in shadow than in light, lift her spoon to her mouth and
swallow. Just as he had swallowed. Just as they had all swallowed. But not one other of the people at that table had as
much as taken ill. Gwendolen Sorsby, he was certain, had
met her death at this table, but he did not know at whose
hand, how they had managed it or why they had done it.

Seeker went then into Matthew Pullan's study, lit a candle
and drafted a report on the girl's death to take to Lilburne
at York. The death of the young girl troubled him, but
once he had completed his search of Faithly Woods for any
sign of the fugitive Sir Thomas Faithly, he would be gone
from here. He had been in the north too long, away from
London too long. He was as cured as he was ever likely
to be of the attachments in London that Thurloe had sent
him north to cure him of, and he was determined he would
stay away no longer. Seeker was resolved to make clear to
Lilburne, on his return to York, that someone else should
be sent to investigate the death of Gwendolen Sorsby.

When he finally reached his pallet in the stable loft of

Pullan's yard, Seeker saw that a paper had been laid out on it for his inspection. There was enough of moonlight through the opened shutters of the loft, looking out to the expanse of the moor beyond, to see that it was the report he had asked one of his men to obtain of the first day of the trier's court. Removing his boots and cloak, he sat down to read what he could of it. He read it twice and wished he had never seen it. Hidden things in the life of this place were being uncovered in that court, secrets kept for years, and others lately born. The accusations of bastardy and incest, set forth by Abel Sharrock, and that had so enraged Lawrence Ingolby and Matthew Pullan, were linked to that of adultery on the part of Digby Pullan, the five years' dead father of Matthew and husband of Bess. And now Bess Pullan's ward, Matthew Pullan's foster sister, had been murdered. Seeker would have liked to have set flame to the paper, but instead he put it away. He slept little in the ensuing hours of the night, and by the time the first light of morning began to creep through those same open shutters, Seeker knew that he would not be riding for York today: there was some darkness here and a young girl had died because of it, and he must sit out this court and see what the public shaming of so many in this village might tell him.

He would attend the trier's court in the morning.

SEVEN

Return to the Trier's Court

Lawrence had tried to talk him out of going to the trier's court at all today, but Matthew was determined that he would have his say, and give the lie to the filth that had been peddled yesterday by Abel Sharrock. Lawrence had eventually given up arguing with him and sent a note up to the manor to let Emma know what he was about, before agreeing to set out once more with him for the Black Bull. There was nothing could be done to lift the desolation of the house they left behind them in any case. Matthew was hollowed out with shock and grief. From the day his father had brought Gwendolen to them, he had felt an overwhelming love for his foster sister, and had sworn to protect her from all that was bad in the world. And he had failed in that as he had done in so much else that mattered to him. As well he and Lawrence being at the court as sitting with Bess, staring at an empty grate, whilst Orpah wept her eyes dry. The anger unleashed in him yesterday was all he had to offer, and he was determined that it might have its day.

Lawrence had been concerned about Seeker's late-night visit to Tansy and had gone to see her early. Matthew had told him not to worry himself over it – whatever the cause of his visit, Seeker would have meant the woman no harm. Lawrence had insisted on seeing her before they left for the court, all the same. Of Seeker himself there was no sign – he had breakfasted early and ridden out to Faithly Woods, still searching for Thomas Faithly, no doubt. A fool's errand, to Matthew's mind: there was nothing here any more for Thomas Faithly.

As he and Lawrence approached the Black Bull, it seemed, if it were possible, that there were more people trying to crowd into the trier's court today than there had been yesterday. A mass of villagers, arrived too late to get into the taproom, milled around outside the inn. They fell silent as Matthew and Lawrence drew closer, looking anywhere but at him lest they catch his eye.

'Cats got your tongues, or what?' Lawrence said.

None of them replied. As Lawrence ushered him, Matthew heard him turn to the villagers and say, 'I see. Well, one word, one word of Abel Sharrock's ravings in that court spoken out and about by any of you, and none of you need bother coming to Commissioner Pullan's house looking for work or a few shillings to tide you over, nor up to the manor either: you'll be out on your ear. Is that understood?'

Matthew glanced over his shoulder. One or two had

raised their heads and Lawrence nodded at them. 'I warn you, any of you thinks different, better say it to me now.'

It was an ostler who finally had the courage to speak. 'None of us thinks different, Lawrence.'

'Good,' Lawrence muttered, starting up the steps behind Matthew. 'And since you don't bother to ask, I'll tell you anyway: Gwendolen Sorsby's dead.'

The courtroom was even more of a stir today than it had been yesterday. Lawrence had almost caught up with Matthew when Maud Sharrock somehow managed to push her way through from where she'd been standing and start pawing at him, her face curdled in false sympathy. Ingolby was clearing a path through the crowd to get to them. Matthew pushed the woman's hands away from where they clutched at the front of his doublet. 'Get this woman away from me, Lawrence, for God's sake!'

Ingolby leaned past the person in front of him and took hold of Maud's arm. 'Best shift yourself, Maud. You'll get better trade out in the street.'

'Trade?' Maud's chest swelled in indignation. 'In the trier's court!'

Ingolby leaned down and Matthew just caught his whisper close to her ear. 'Aye, and in your face, too, you old witch. You don't know what we might have caught in that house last night, Matthew and me. I'd get out of here whilst I can still stand up.'

Maud's pig-like eyes widened in horror, and she turned

to push her way back through the room, shrieking, 'Abel! Abel!' as she did so.

Sir Edward was again already there. He offered Matthew only brief acknowledgement, but no word of sympathy. Just as well: Matthew couldn't have stomached it from him in any case. He didn't look at the justice of the peace at all as he again took up his place as commissioner, and Lawrence, as would have been expected, took his behind Sir Edward. Emma wasn't there, of course – Edward might have managed to force her here once, but he would not do it again, not after what she had had to sit through yesterday. Matthew saw Lawrence look at Abel Sharrock, on the high bench next to the trier's place, challenging Abel to try shifting him again as he had done the day before, but the sexton affected to have papers to shuffle. It took all Matthew's self-control to prevent himself from ascending the dais and crushing the man's throat with his bare hands.

It was close to the appointed time for the court to recommence, and Matthew was beginning to wonder if the vicar had somehow got away when Septimus finally appeared. He was a deal more haunted today, yesterday's composure having dwindled and almost gone. Matthew tried to recall when first it had appeared, that occasionally desperate look in the vicar's eyes, the shake in his hand, the old, habitual smile coming less readily to his face. He'd have had a bishop's hat by now, Septimus, if Matthew and his fellow Puritans hadn't tried to cleanse the church, if Laud hadn't fallen. He'd learning enough, and charm enough, and looks enough that in another time he'd have left Faithly the day he got that scholarship to Balliol and never thought of this godforsaken place again. But the Puritans had come, and Laud had fallen, and England wasn't a place for pretty, clever men any more. England was a place for men with guile, and for all his brains and his charm and his looks, Septimus lacked guile, and that's what would finish him.

The vicar turned his eyes towards them. 'You should have called me to her, Matthew,' he said.

From the bench, Abel opened his mouth to admonish the vicar not to speak from the stand, but Lawrence stepped in. 'Your court's not started yet, Sharrock.'

Matthew swallowed, ignoring the constable. 'There was no time.'

'She's with God now, though, Matthew.'

'Aye, Septimus, I know it. Whichever route she took, she's with God now.'

It took a few moments after the vicar had arrived for all who had come to see the trial, or to gawp at the commissioner's grief, to manage to squeeze into the room and find themselves a stool to stand on or an inch or two of window ledge to balance on. Whatever distinction had been intended between man and woman, all had been thoroughly jostled and mixed. Matthew was no stranger to the stench of his neighbours, but before this court was done for the day he knew it would be overwhelming.

At last, the place started to settle and quieten, in anticipation of the arrival of the trier. Abel Sharrock had hired a new constable for the day – from his own pocket, it was said – to escort the trier in, for fear that giving up his own seat to fetch him he should never get it back again. And so the puffing up of Abel Sharrock's chest, as if that would somehow add height to his frame, and the setting of his face into a masterwork of self-importance, alerted Lawrence to the imminent arrival of Caleb Turner. Those who had crowded the passageway started to shuffle back, and the assistant constable, employing the staff he usually used to herd his sheep, cleared a path towards the makeshift dais. Like everyone else, Matthew turned his eyes to the doorway in which the trier stood, waiting. And like most of them, probably, he saw what the trier could not: a few yards behind Caleb Turner, with a jostle of people between them, Damian Seeker had just emerged at the top of the steps to the inn.

His feet were damp after his early-morning walk in the woods. He'd tied Acheron to a tree and gone in on foot to the place Tansy had described to him. It hadn't been far – near enough to the edge of the woods on the village side that anyone coming up from there to gather the mushrooms might have been there and back in half an hour. It hadn't been long before he'd come across where the destroying angel grew either. It had been there, in abundance, in a small clearing just a few yards from the edge of the wood. White and lovely and as deadly as a scorpion's sting. Seeker kept his gauntlets on to gather half a dozen, inadvertently crushing some of the slender stalks between the heavy leather cladding of his fingers. He'd dropped what he'd gathered into a small leather pouch, to take to an apothecary in York, and paused for a moment to wipe the fingers of his gauntlet on the early-morning dew of the grass. The heavy, earthen smell of the woodland floor that had hung around him as he'd ridden back across the moor left him now, faded to nothing as he was enveloped by the fug of the overcrowded inn.

It was evident that the second session of Septimus Jenkin's trial had not yet started. Up ahead of him, Seeker could just see the top of the black-brimmed hat of the trier waiting behind Sharrock's hired officer to make his entrance to the taproom. Beyond, there was hardly a space to be had – people balanced on window ledges or stood on benches or barrels for a better view. At the far end of the room, the local ejectors had already taken their places, and beneath them Sir Edward Faithly sat, Lawrence Ingolby behind him. Seeker had not thought to see Ingolby here, after the events of the night, but he was not surprised to see Matthew Pullan: the man he had known eight years ago in London had not been one who would let an accusation such as Sharrock had made in here yesterday go unanswered. He wondered what further poison Sharrock and this trier planned to unleash upon the village of Faithly today.

Matthew Pullan had noticed him, and Seeker returned his nod of acknowledgement, but Lawrence Ingolby had not, so fixed was his gaze upon the trier. The young secretary had none of the awestruck reverence and fear that gripped most of the onlookers. In fact, the openness of the gaze and the slight half-smile playing on Ingolby's lips made Seeker realise the man was trying to stare the trier out. He wondered what devil might have taken hold of Ingolby that he should do such a thing. It was not often that Damian Seeker didn't know what to make of a man, but he could not read Lawrence Ingolby.

Ingolby held the look even once the trier began at last to move towards the dais, but Seeker found his own attention shift from the young secretary to the man in the black cloak and broad-brimmed black hat before whom the crowd was parting. Caleb Turner was not tall, in the general run of things, but even from behind, himself having to stoop through the doorway into the taproom, Seeker could see that the trier carried himself with a degree of assurance born of confidence in his authority. The looks on the faces of the people shrinking back a little as he passed confirmed the power this man could exert to disrupt their lives. But it was something else that riveted Seeker's gaze to the man's back — a movement of the head, the particular sway of a shoulder as he walked, the flick of a hand to some mote of dust on his cloak. Seeker felt the tension rise within him from his stomach, his heart begin to race. He had seen it all before. His hands shook as he began to push past the people who had started to fill the gap again in the trier's wake. It was him. It was him. Seeker was almost certain. He could hardly master the breath heaving through his chest.

But it was not until Turner put his foot on the first of the three wooden steps leading up to the dais and turned his head to the side to glance back the way he had just come, that everything in the taproom of the Black Bull changed.

A spasm of shock went through the trier's body. Those who missed it might yet have caught the look of terror on the man's face that soon followed it, seen the colour drain from it. Seeker felt tension radiate from every inch of his body, and he realised that others had begun to notice it too. He didn't care: he was barely aware of anyone else in the room save the man ascending the dais. As Turner saw him, that tension fell away, like chains unbound: Seeker released his shoulders and lunged across the space between them to fix on the trier's pristine plain white collar and haul him up off the steps. For the first time in almost twelve years he was looking into the eyes of the man he most loathed on earth.

Turner's face was alabaster. 'Seeker,' he said, 'I—'

The voice was enough to unleash the white heat of rage that had taken control of Seeker. If the man said anything else, he didn't hear it. All he heard was the sound of his fist smashing into the trier's jaw. As the exquisite pain of it came firing back up his own arm he did it again. The second blow sent the trier keeling over sideways, catching his head on the edge of the ejectors' desk before he slumped to the floor. Seeker bent and hauled him up by the collar again to face him. 'Where is she, Hungerford? I swear to God I'll finish you here if you don't tell me right now where she is.'

A few yards away, Lawrence Ingolby wrinkled his brow.
'Well, I didn't see that coming,' he said, beginning to move
out from behind the commissioners' bench. 'Come on,
Matthew, best get ourselves over there before he kills him.'

Felicity Turner stared at the small, fat woman standing
before her. Maud Sharrock was breathless and gabbling,
and it was a moment before Felicity understood what she
was saying. Even once she did understand, she would not
believe it. She wanted to put her hands over her ears, over
the woman's mouth so she would not hear it.

'No, but mistress, you must come. Mr Turner is laid
downstairs and Dr Hollerenshaw thinks like to die if not
by some miracle. Abel is praying mightily already, but you
must come and offer him your comfort. Only think if he
should die and you never went to him!'

Felicity felt as if she was frozen, as if her jaw would
not move, as if her tongue was rooted to the floor of her
mouth. She moved her lips, mouthed the words, 'I cannot,'
but could not force the sound out.

The fat woman grew ever more anxious, her face redder.
'Nay, but you must come. Come to your husband. 'Tis
your duty as a wife, surely, to comfort him in his last
moments?'

Now Felicity found her voice. 'Will he truly die?'

'Aye!' Maud threw up her hands in exasperation. 'That's
what I am telling you. Come, in all Christian charity, come!'

'But the other man,' said Felicity, 'the soldier . . .' She would not name him.

'Under guard in the cellar, a double bolt and three padlocks on the door. Took four of them to get him off the trier. Lawrence Ingolby got himself a black eye for his trouble, though well deserved, no doubt. Matthew Pullan is gone to write to the major-general at York, and will get this Seeker's own men and two from the village to escort him back, to be dealt with there.' Maud shook her head. 'The judgement on Septimus Jenkin not pronounced, either, and so many folk come to see it. Now come to your husband, Mistress Turner, before the Lord takes him for sure!'

There was no option, but Felicity had to shake off this woman first. She smoothed her hands over her lap. 'You are right, Mistress Sharrock. It has been a great shock, and I will go to Caleb. Of course I must go to him. But you must leave me a moment to myself. I feel the need of the Lord; I must seek the Lord in prayer, first, to ready me for what is to come.'

Maud was wrong-footed now, Felicity could see that. She pressed home. 'You go down, now, Mistress Sharrock, and let them know I am coming.'

'But surely I should accompany you?'

Felicity reached over and touched the woman's hand. 'The Lord accompanies me. You must tell the trier I am on my way. I will be with him soon.'

There being nothing else for it, Maud Sharrock reluctantly left her. Quickly, Felicity looked at her image in the glass in her chamber. The years had been kind to her. Life with Caleb had had its costs, but hard work and poverty had not been amongst them, and she was not as worn out as she might have been. The occasional grey could hardly be seen in the white-gold of her hair, and her skin was soft still. She left off her white linen cap and pulled the brush through her hair to smooth it. He had liked her hair loose, she remembered that.

The woman Sharrock was not lingering on the stairs as Felicity had feared she might have been, and all attention was taken by the trier laid out and breathing his last, or otherwise, in the taproom. Once downstairs, she passed the end of that corridor as swiftly and silently as she could. The steps leading down to the cellar were to the back of the inn, and nobody remarked her save the kitchen boy who was hastening towards the taproom with a basin of water. She hesitated at the top of the cellar steps. Only one man was on guard there, the man Ingolby, if his swollen eye was anything to go by. Caleb had spoken of him last night, after the first day's trial, and she knew her husband did not trust him, but there could be little time before the soldiers arrived to escort their captain back to York, so she did not have long.

Ingolby looked up at her, squinting a little with his one good eye. 'Mistress Turner, I think you are lost.'

'Not lost. I . . . I would talk with your prisoner.'

He half snorted. 'I don't think so. If Matthew Pullan and I had not dragged him off your husband when we did, you would be a widow now.'

'I am to be a widow anyhow, if Mistress Sharrock is to be believed.'

The man shifted his posture from where he had been leaning, almost casually, against the cellar door. 'Aye, well, if there's one thing in life you can be certain of, it's that Maud Sharrock is seldom to be believed. Your husband'll mend all right, but he won't be pretty.'

Felicity's voice was toneless, almost inaudible. 'What does the physician say?'

'William Hollerenshaw? Same as Maud, like as not, and just as worthless.'

Felicity bit her bottom lip. There was so little time, but she was more inclined to believe the word of a physician than of this cocksure clerk, and if the snatches of rumour that had reached to the North Riding about Seeker over the years were even half true, Caleb was as good as dead anyway.

'I want to talk to him. To Seeker.'

Ingolby stood up straight now. 'I'm telling you, Mistress Turner, that's not a good idea.'

'Tell him my name.'

Ingolby started to shake his head but Felicity was descending the stairs now, repeating, 'Tell him my name. I would have you tell him my name.'

Ingolby held his hands out to stop her, but she reached the door, started banging on it. And shouting, 'Damian. It's me, it's Felicity. Damian, you must tell him to let me in!'

EIGHT

Felicity

The banging ceased and Seeker sensed that Lawrence
Ingolby had stopped trying to hold her back. For a moment
there was silence and then she said, 'Damian, please, tell
him to let me come in.'

The voice shook him. All those years, all those miles,
all the long nights of quiet torment, struggling to conquer
the memory of her, of what had happened. And now there
was only that one door between them. Seeker looked at his
hand. His knuckles were stained with Hungerford's dried
blood. He should have mastered himself better. He should
have waited until he'd had the man alone. They'd never
let him near him now, always supposing Hungerford did
recover his senses. So it would have to be her.

'Let her in,' he said at last.

There was shuffling and grumbling from Ingolby, and
then Felicity's voice, 'You heard him, let me in.'

A sigh. 'He's not safe, Mistress Turner. Have you seen
the state of your husband, or that taproom?'

'He won't touch me.'

Still Ingolby hesitated.

Seeker spoke again. 'I won't lay a finger on her. You have my word.'

And then, at last, was the sound of the key turning in the lock, of bolts being drawn back, and the door opened. Lawrence Ingolby was standing in front of her. 'All right, but I'm staying between you. Say your piece, Mistress Turner, but I wouldn't bother praying for him if that's your plan. A man that fights like that is way past prayer.'

He saw her move to pass Ingolby. 'You cannot stay,' she said.

'What?' He spluttered a laugh. 'I'm not daft, even if you are. He could kill you.'

'I won't touch her,' Seeker repeated. 'Bind me hand and foot if you like.'

'I'm not in the habit of carrying chains and padlocks when I go out of a morning.' He turned then to the trier's wife. 'I'll go, but I'll be just outside that door, and if your husband comes to hear of this, I'll deny it to my last breath. Understand?'

'I understand,' she said. 'And he won't come to hear of it.'

Still Ingolby hesitated, then he shrugged. 'Why should I care if you don't? Go on then.' He stood aside to let her pass, then stepped out of the cellar and drew the door to, about halfway.

Now it was just the two of them in the dank cellar, eight foot square, cold and dimly lit, what light there was coming from the torch above Ingolby in the stair wall. Dim light was kind to a woman, and it was kind to her; she didn't seem to have aged as other women might, and her hair was still almost white-blonde, and lustrous. But the poor light couldn't hide the vanity in her that he had once thought grace, or the hardness he had once thought strength. She reached a hand out towards him.

He steeled himself. 'Don't,' he said.

'Damian, I just wanted—'

'I've no interest. Tell me where my daughter is.'

'Damian, you have to understand, it has not been easy for me . . .'

He almost laughed; she still had the power to take his breath away. 'Not easy for you? Felicity, are you serious?'

'Yes, Damian. I have had—'

Now he did laugh. 'Dear God, you haven't changed. Not easy for you? Am I truly supposed to care how it has been for you?' He shook his head. 'You made your choice over eleven years ago and we have all had to live with it.'

She took a step closer to him, pushing her hair back from her face in a gesture he remembered.

'Don't waste your time, Felicity. Every word, every movement you make is a code for something else. Eleven years, and I've learned to read codes, to read people. All I want from you is to know where my daughter is. What have you and Hungerford done with her?'

'It was Caleb . . .' she began.

'Caleb.' He considered it as if he had heard it for the first time. 'Interesting choice of name, but call him what you will, it's Thomas Hungerford you cast me off for, and Thomas Hungerford who walked into that room today calling himself Caleb Turner. How long has he been "Caleb" and you "Mistress Turner"?'

She'd stopped calculating now, and settled for honesty as her only option. 'Caleb saw how the wind was blowing, he had to make a choice, one side or the other.'

'We all did,' he said. 'But he wouldn't fight like any honest man, is that it? He must needs sit in judgment on other men's lives, and none to know the truth of his own?'

She bridled at that. 'Caleb is a gifted preacher.'

'Oh, I remember,' said Seeker. 'I remember when he came to our village and he preached and preached, and his name was Thomas Hungerford, and he preached that well you fell into his bed.'

She was trembling now, less with fear than with anger, the anger he remembered when her pride was piqued. 'Was it wrong to want to better myself?'

Her clothes were of a better quality than she had ever worn when she had been his wife, and no one had served her hand and foot and doffed their cap respectfully to her then as they did now to Mistress Turner, but whatever it was he had loved in her he couldn't see any more.

'And did you?'

'Did I what?'

'Did you better yourself, Felicity?' He said it in such a way that she would not doubt what he thought the answer should be.

'I was better, even then, than you could have hoped for.'

He shook his head. 'No you weren't, just I didn't know it. But I've known women since you, Felicity, and I've learned. I've learned what a woman can be.'

He saw that rattled her a bit. 'You have a wife now?'

'What I have is none of your concern.'

She shook her head. 'You were never like this, Damian.'

'You don't know what I was like, in my mind, my heart. I was a fool for you and you never saw anything else. Now everyone sees what you didn't, and I am no one's fool. And I'm not your fool now, Felicity, so you will tell me where my daughter is.'

She straightened herself. 'You left her with me.'

'Should I have taken a child from her mother?'

But yes, he knew, he had known almost straight away, before he had ever reached Fairfax's army encampment, before he had ever become a soldier for Parliament, that he should have done. He should have taken Manon from her and left her with his own people.

She didn't answer him.

'I went back,' he said. 'A few weeks later I returned to the village but you were gone, you and Hungerford and Manon with you, and no one could tell me where you went, other than that your new husband had stolen money from the meeting house and with it your father's horse.' He hadn't managed to hide the bitterness in his voice, the memory of the hurt. He had not realised it could come to an end so easily, that life they had had. A hundred years or more the people of their sect had travelled the north in the kinder seasons, finding work – woodcutting, carpentry, labouring – before returning in the winter to their own place. He could picture it now, their cottages around the meeting house in the clearing, the elders who had tended the beasts through the winter. They had looked for the light of God within themselves and lived according to their own laws; they had had no need of pastor or prayer book, of magistrate or judge, the Seekers. Marriage had been by public proclamation in the meeting house. Divorce, too, as he had learned a few months after the arrival in their midst of the travelling preacher, Thomas Hungerford.

Even in the darkened cellar he could see her cheeks flush. 'We had need of the money, and the horse. Caleb was not able to labour as my father wished him to, and without work we could not make our way.'

'So you stole money and a horse and you left your old names behind when you rode away and took my daughter with you.' He sat down on an upturned barrel now, his head in his hands. 'I thought you were dead, all of you, or gone to America. I have spent the last eight years since I was sent to London trying to hunt down a Cumbrian man called Thomas Hungerford travelling with his wife and daughter.' His voice was bitter. 'I, who can find the smallest rodent in the darkest cellar of a London hovel, couldn't find my own daughter on these wide open moors.'

She leaned against the wall, remembering. 'You came close enough more than once. Someone would arrive in whatever village or town we had thought to settle in and ask too many questions. We changed our names a good few times – Walker, Barlowe, Langton – it was necessary, but still it wasn't enough. Until Thomas became a trier.' She had become more and more the Felicity he had left in the village, forgetting now herself that the man of whom she spoke would have them call him Caleb. Soon she would get to the point of her visit. He saw her take in a breath, drum her fingers slowly by her side, and then it came. 'Damian, I have come to ask you to tell no one of this.'

'What?' he said, not looking at her.

'I don't want you to tell anyone of our past – yours, and mine, and Caleb's. If you tell them, it will all be finished for him, and what would become of me? What would they do to me, even in this village?'

Seeker was almost struck speechless with disbelief, and when he found words, he could not mask the disgust in them. 'What, you think I should lie for you now? Woman, you have lost your senses.'

'No,' she smiled, 'no, I have not. You will lie for me, Damian, and you will lie for Caleb, too, or you will never see your daughter again.' Then she changed her expression, changed her shape almost, adopted the meek, blameless pose of the trier's wife. 'In any case, which one of us do you think they would believe?'

Before he could answer, a commotion of boots and clanking weaponry above announced the arrival at the inn of his own men. The door of the cellar swung open and

Lawrence Ingolby pointed at Felicity Turner. 'Right, you, out!'

Bobbing the most fleeting of curtsies to them both, the demure trier's wife left the cellar and went back up the stairs without further word, to tend to her stricken husband.

NINE

York

As Lilburne read Matthew Pullan's letter, the colour on his face changed from the hues of hearty autumn to deep winter, and his features hardened accordingly. He held up the letter, as if to speak, before putting it down again without having said anything. Eventually he looked at the two soldiers who had brought Seeker in. 'Leave us,' he said. The men lost no time in obeying him, evidently relieved that their escort duties were over.

'Sir—' began Seeker.

But the major-general held up a hand. 'No, Seeker. No.'

He stood up and began to pace around the chamber of his governor's quarters in York Castle. Once or twice he paused, looked at Seeker a moment and then resumed his pacing. Eventually he came to a halt behind his desk, and looked out of the window on to the river below. At last he spoke, with what seemed a great effort at containing himself. 'I'll ask you once, Captain, and I'll have the truth. What was the cause of your violent assault upon the trier, Caleb Turner?'

Seeker stared straight ahead of him and kept his voice as even as he could. 'What I already told Commissioner Pullan, in Faithly. The man's name is not Caleb Turner, but Thomas Hungerford. He is a thief and an adulterer and not fit to sit in judgement on other men.'

Lilburne clenched and unclenched his fists at his sides and turned around slowly to lean across his desk. 'There are witnesses, from one end of Yorkshire to another, who will testify as to the man's identity, and to that of his wife whom you have also, I understand – though I can scarce credit it – slandered. For ten years, ten years, Seeker, Caleb Turner has preached and sat on ejectors' panels all over the north, removing the unworthy and the ungodly from their pulpits and schoolrooms, for the better upbringing of children and the edification of the people.'

'And eleven years ago his name was Thomas Hungerford.'

Lilburne slumped into his seat in an attitude of despair. 'And what of Thomas Faithly? It was him you were sent up there to look for.'

'I have found no sign of him yet, sir. But I have not finished my investig—'

'Oh, yes you have, Seeker! You finished your investigation in Faithly the minute you stepped into that court and took a swing at the trier – or near enough killed him, if this report is to be believed. The man who, on the orders of the Lord Protector, is there to try the local vicar on his fitness to keep his place, and you lay him out like a butcher's boy in a common brawl! As if this is not quite enough, you calumniate the virtue of his wife into the bargain?' Lilburne closed his eyes and ran his hand across his forehead. 'These are not the actions of a man in his right mind, Seeker. Why is it you are so certain this man is not who he says he is? What is this trier to you?'

Seeker had had ample opportunity, on the long ride back to York, to consider how he would answer this question, which he had known Lilburne would surely ask. There was but one answer to it. Fixing his eye on the window beyond the major-general's shoulder, he began to speak, to tell him what, in eleven years, in all his time marching and fighting in the New Model Army, in his years at Whitehall in Cromwell's guard, in the service of John Thurloe and stalking the streets of London, he had not told one living soul. 'Eleven years ago, a preacher named Thomas Hungerford came to my village in the North Riding. He spoke of freedom of worship, and much else. The man was a Ranter then, and told the people that nothing was forbidden them, no depths of sin they were not permitted to plumb, that they might know it and overcome it. When he left, he took with him my wife, who went willingly enough, and my child. Sometime afterwards, having adopted and abandoned several aliases, he took the name Caleb Turner. The woman who calls herself Felicity Turner is the mother of the daughter I have not seen in eleven years. That is what this trier is to me.'

Outside, greylag geese called to each other at the King's Fishpool and the sounds of the castle went as on any other day: boots marched over flagstone, orders were shouted, carts trundled across the yard, kitchen boys scolded. But here, in Lilburne's chamber far above the confluence of the Ouse and the Foss, there was an absolute silence. It was Seeker who eventually broke it. 'Believe me or not as you will, sir, but that is all the truth I know.'

When the major-general spoke, his voice was low and there was a trace of kindness in it. 'Does Thurloe know?'

'I've never told him.'

They both knew that that didn't mean Thurloe, who knew secrets from the darkest and most far-flung corners of Europe, didn't know.

'I think it likely he does not,' said Lilburne at last, 'for if he did, he'd never have sent you back up here. But what's to be done, that's the question: what's to be done?'

The major-general made a steeple of his hands, and appeared to look through it at a problem of great weight. At length he collapsed the steeple and said, 'Well, you can't go back to Faithly, that's certain.' He drummed his fingers on his desk, his thoughts seeming to follow the rhythm. He came to a decision. 'There is much information to be collated on the Royalists of Yorkshire for the new registry that is to be set up in London, and more coming in every day. Until such time as Thurloe calls you back to White-hall, you will be charged with gathering together, filing and reporting upon what has come in.' He threw out a dismissive hand. 'You know the sort of thing better than I, for it is Thurloe's stock-in-trade – suspicious movements, communications, activities. I have directed these papers to be housed in King's Manor, and I have put in place the bones of a secretariat to deal with them, but they need the firm hand of one who knows what he's doing. Go up there and tell them to find you space.'

'Sir—' began Seeker, but Lilburne was not finished.

'Aside from your duties at King's Manor, you are, in the meantime, to remain within the city walls. I will give orders for you to be quartered in one of the guardhouses above the bars.'

So Lilburne didn't trust him not to return to Faithly of his own accord; he was to be contained where they could keep a watch on him. That was a problem to be dealt with later, but there was another, more pressing. 'What about Hungerford?' he asked.

'Hungerford? The trier? He'll live, I'm told, although it'll be a good few days before he can take to his bench again, the state you left him in.'

Seeker held firm. 'I meant, sir, what's to be done about him?'

Lilburne took a deep breath. It was clear what he had to say was not pleasant to him. 'Nothing, Seeker. Nothing will be done about him, other than to persuade him to lay no further charges against you, which, if what you have told me is true, should be an easy enough thing to manage.'

Seeker almost forgot himself. 'But the man is—'

Lilburne held up a hand. 'The man is the face and voice of the reform of the North, and has been these ten years.

He has done his work in the name of the godly of the Commonwealth, and now of the Lord Protector. He has put unsound vicars and teachers from their places all across Yorkshire, Cumbria and Northumbria,' the major-general's voice dropped a measure, 'and in doing so he has built up grievances and resentments amongst Royalist sympathisers and adherents of the old church that can only be contained because the people are on our side, and believe themselves to be on his side in these matters. If we should tell them now that the man is a fraud, an adulterer and a thief, what do you think would happen, not just in Yorkshire but all over the country, in the associations of the other major-generals? There's not a panel of ejectors would be safe to walk into a courtroom. Secure the peace of the Commonwealth? Set the Commonwealth alight, more like. No, Seeker. Whatever your personal grief, yours alone it must remain, and no further retribution can be seen to befall Caleb Turner than that which you have already inflicted upon him.'

Walmgate Bar. Lilburne wasn't taking any chances, thought Seeker as he mounted the steps of Fishergate Postern and then the wall. Walmgate was in full view of the castle, and at the same time at the opposite extremity of the city from King's Manor, where he was to put in order the information coming in for the Registry of Royalists. Seeker would have to walk from one end of York to the other, cutting diagonally across the whole city, to get from his billet to his place of work each day, and right the way back again.

A good mile each way through the thrumming city, lined with eyes that missed nothing. Lilburne would know within a quarter-hour if he ever veered from his path, or attempted to slip out of the city and head northwards, out towards the moors and Faithly.

None of the men on the wall questioned him, and the soldier on guard duty at the western entryway to Walmgate Bar simply stood aside as Seeker approached. Inside the guardroom a fire had been lit, and a pot with some kind of poultry in a broth simmered over it. The two guards at their supper stood to attention when he came in, but he told them to sit back down and get on with their dinner. 'I'll be billeted here a while, but you'll take your orders from your usual officers.'

'Yes, Captain. The chamber above is ready for you.'

'Right,' he said, setting his foot at the bottom of the narrow wooden stair. He glanced at the pot over the fire. He hadn't had a decent meal since Bess Pullan's supper. 'And bring me up some of that broth, will you?'

The chamber was big enough to house a dozen men at least, but it was clear Seeker was to have it to himself. They'd be cramped down below in the guardroom tonight, and for a few more to come. But that wasn't his concern. He looked out of one of the two small windows at the back of the room, down on to the barbican. A good few nights he'd spent out there, not so very far away on the other side of that barbican; that had been his first real taste of life as a soldier, in Fairfax's army, besieging the Royalists in York. Almost thirty thousand of Parliament's men, in the end, circling the thirteen thousand souls within those walls, and those thirteen thousand would not give up. He'd thought he'd known stench before then, he thought he'd seen vermin, and then he'd led a burial party at Heworth Hall, where four hundred of his comrades were billeted. The sights of the sick and wounded, as he'd picked his way through their number to find the dead for burial in the convent garden, had haunted his dreams for nights afterwards, until they became the commonplace. He'd learned then that the morale of the besieger could dip as low as that of the besieged. When news had come of the approach of Prince Rupert's forces at the head of the royal army to relieve the city, it had seemed all would be lost. The miracle of Marston Moor had taught him that all was never lost; it had also taught him that to survive in battle, a man had to kill, and kill, and kill again.

By the end of that day, that battle of Marston Moor, Seeker had been a different man from the one who had walked away from his own village without a fight, leaving his wife and child behind. He had made himself something else. Eleven years, and the different life he thought he had made for himself in those years was slipping from his grasp, disappearing, and everything he had tried to forget had returned to stare him in the face and tell him it must finally be answered.

The bell of St Nicholas somewhere to the east rang the hour, and the other bells of the city behind him took up the challenge. He heard the order called for the portcullis to be brought down for the night, shutting all comers out of York until the morning. The sound of the young guard coming up the stair with his supper roused him from his reflections. Thinking on past mistakes had never got him anywhere; it was what he did next that mattered. As the soldier set a tray bearing a bowl of chicken broth, a loaf of bread and a tankard of ale down on the deal table near the hearth, Seeker lit another candle to counter the growing darkness sweeping over the city. He lifted his satchel and removed from it the pen, ink bottle and two sheets of blank paper from the sheaf he had brought from the castle clerks' room. He laid the sheets side by side and across the top of the first wrote *Gwendolen Sorsby*, and on the second, *Caleb Turner*.

As he ate, he considered the name at the top of each sheet of paper. The first he put to one side, that he might properly consider the second. Beneath the words *Caleb Turner*, he wrote: *Parishes of Ejected Ministers, Seasonal Pattern of Travel*, and *Felicity's People*. The records relating to the trier's courts for the northern counties were held at King's Manor, along with papers relating to civil matters. If he could discover the routes on which Turner and Felicity travelled, he should be able to hazard a guess at where they returned to in the winter months and set out from in the spring. And that, he suspected, was where he would find Manon.

Still looking at the near-blank papers, he attended to his supper. Whatever bird had been used in the broth had surely died at a great age, and whoever had boiled its carcass with a few beans and onions was no cook. He doubted Bess Pullan would have fed it to her pig. As he lifted another spoonful of the watery offering towards his lips, he stopped. He saw Bess Pullan tut as she wiped Abel Sharrock's spilled soup from the table top; heard her tell her kitchen girl to feed the rest of the creamy confection of mushroom and madeira wine to the pig. And yet the pig had lived to truffle heartily, as all who had sat at the table had lived, all aside from Gwendolen Sorsby, poisoned that night by the destroying angel.

Abandoning his soup, he took again the sheet of paper with Gwendolen's name at the top of it. He pictured the girl, remembered the progress of her death, how the poison took hold and then appeared to retreat and Gwendolen to recover, before it returned, its strength redoubled to take her to her death. To those who knew, it was the clear pattern of the destroying angel. And through all her obfuscations, there was one thing Tansy had been clear about: Gwendolen would have known the destroying angel from any edible mushroom – she would not have taken it by accident. She must have unwittingly taken it in some hidden form – the soup. But why, if it was in the soup, had they not all succumbed? What Gwendolen ate had come from the same tureen that they had all supped from.

Seeker stood to stretch his back, and went over to the window to look again out over the barbican and at the straggle of houses that led from the city south-eastwards, many still bearing the signs of their burning during the siege. The burning aside, it was not so different from that shorter straggle of houses, little more than a street, that made up the village of Faithly. A village full of tension, animosity and secrets tumbling after one another to be exposed. He went back to the paper and began to write down the names of everybody who had been present at Bess's supper, and of those who should have been present. Matthew Pullan, Bess Pullan, Sir Edward Faithly, Lady Emma Faithly, Lawrence Ingolby, Septimus Jenkin, Abel Sharrock, Gwendolen Sorsby, Orpah Bigley, Damian Seeker. Absent: Caleb Turner, Felicity Turner. Seeker put his pen down and sat back, the thing suddenly plain to him: the killing of Gwendolen Sorsby might very well have been a mistake, and another amongst those twelve have been the intended victim that night.

He began to consider the names, one by one. Matthew Pullan: he could not see that anything in Matthew's Leveller past or his spying on his fellow Levellers for Fairfax had any bearing on the small community on the moors, and he appeared to have carried out his duties as local commissioner in as even-handed a manner as was possible in such times and in such a place. Of Pullan's mother, Bess, Seeker knew little enough, other than that she was a wealthy merchant's widow, that she was no great respecter of persons and that she left her friends and neighbours in no doubt as to where they stood in her regard. 'Like nearly every other woman in Yorkshire,' he murmured to himself, moving on to the next name on his list: Sir Edward Faithly. As justice of the peace, Faithly would have enemies enough amongst the petty criminals of the surrounding moors and villages. There'd be others, too, who'd have their gripes: the destitute and the vagrant, denied poor relief or sent to the workhouse on his whim, the immoral and the insane hurled together into the house of correction. But Seeker could not see that any so helpless or so desperate could have attempted to effect his poisoning at Bess Pullan's supper. And then there was Lady Emma. There was a composure, a stillness to the woman that seemed to put almost everyone around her at a distance, but Seeker was not certain that it was not the stillness of the ocean before a storm, of the greying sky before a blizzard. Only the proximity of Matthew Pullan seemed to summon any warmth in her, a glimpse of light. A man such as Matthew Pullan should have been married long since, but Seeker knew he never had been, and he wondered if Emma Faithly was the reason for that.

Seeker put down his pen. Motives, grudges from the outside, might be found against any one individual at the dinner, but he thought it more likely that one of these people had set out that night to murder another at that table. If Lady Emma was unfaithful to her husband, the cuckolded husband or one or both of the adulterous lovers might just as well serve for murderer or victim. Or Jenkin might be looking for revenge on those who sought to try him, or Abel Sharrock, who was clearly loathed by every other person in the room — with cause, as the next day's trier's court had shown – might have become overwhelmed with the grievances he so plainly bore. But there were easier ways to kill a man such as Sharrock. And then there was Sir Edward's steward, Lawrence Ingolby, a man, Seeker was certain, who was privy to several people's secrets and possibly some of his own. As for the girl Orpah, he could see no reason why anyone should want to kill her, and it could not be certain that a kitchen girl would sup what the guests supped.

And finally, there was himself. Many over the last eleven years had wished him dead, but Seeker had always thought a knife in the darkness or musket or cannon ball in the midst of battle would be his parting with the world – nothing so subtle as a poison in a soup. There might well have been those at the table with secrets they would not wish him to discover, but in Faithly that night, those who had most cause to want him dead had not come. Had Maud Sharrock's blabbing tongue not told Caleb Turner and his wife that Damian Seeker was in Bess Pullan's house he would have met them there, face to face, in that dining parlour. But they had known he was there, and they had not come. Caleb and Felicity. And then there was another who had not been there, who had never been meant to be there, but who had caused Damian Seeker to travel north to the moors in the first place: Sir Thomas Faithly.

Seeker's eyes stung. The answers to his questions, the truth behind what had happened to Gwendolen Sorsby, would not be found in York. They were up there still, in that village, along with the truth about his own daughter. He snuffed out the candle and stretched himself on a bed beneath the north window of his chamber, but he did not sleep.

TEN

King's Manor

In the days that followed at King's Manor, the routine nature of his work also allowed Seeker better to channel his emotions and his rage to a place where they would be ready when he required them. The public attack on Turner, the loss of self-control, had been ill-advised, but that could not be helped now. The memory of it, the feel of Turner's jaw breaking under his fist, the sound of the man's yelping and the sight of him crumpling to the floor still gave Seeker a great deal of satisfaction.

The morning walk across the city, from the Walmgate in the south-eastern corner to Bootham Bar in the north-west, enlivened Seeker and sharpened his mind. Michael, the clerk appointed to assist him, was young and quick-witted, and was always ready to work when Seeker arrived in their garret room high up on the attic floor of King's Manor. He quickly became adept at classifying reports on known and suspected Royalists as they came in, and in arranging and prioritising them for Seeker's inspection.

From every angle, every perspective, slowly but surely,

they were grinding the Royalists down. Financial penalties for long-forgotten loyalties, and threats of more; confiscations of land and arms; the enforcement of morals and exacting of bonds; the limitation on gatherings; the restriction on travel and surveillance of what travel was allowed was wearing out all but the most desperate and deluded. One was as dangerous as the other, and Seeker wondered into which camp Thomas Faithly fell.

None of the reports on suspect activity in the North Riding that he called up hinted at collusion in any planned return to Yorkshire from the continent of Thomas Faithly. Indeed, little since the failed spring rising appeared to give cause for concern. The mention of his old adversary Lady Anne Winter's name in one or two reports from Northumbria caused him to smile in spite of himself. It was but six months since the lady had been banished from London to Bamburgh, where it was thought she might do less harm. 'The Barbadoes would hardly be far enough,' he muttered to himself, but at least they were having the sense to keep an eye on her. Aside from Anne Winter's name, there was nothing to take Seeker's especial interest, and that suited him well, as it allowed him to devote the rest of his time to the matter of Caleb Turner.

Seeker kept the papers relating to his investigation into Turner in a small oak cabinet beneath his desk. These papers he had retrieved from the document store himself, the librarian looking only mildly curious when first he had asked for them, but not so curious as to press Seeker on the matter. The young clerks and older secretaries who buzzed in and out of the place were careful not to get in his way, or even to catch his eye.

Late on the morning of his fourth day at King's Manor, Seeker lifted from the oak cabinet the records of decisions of the trier's courts all over Yorkshire and Cumbria, going back for two years, and with them a map.

On the first morning of their association, Seeker had noticed that his clerk had a very fine writing hand. 'Can you draw as well?' Seeker had asked him.

The boy had beamed. 'Give me the materials, and I can draw anything you like, Captain!'

'Good,' Seeker had said. 'Get yourself down to the requisitions office and tell them you want pencils and charcoal and good drawing paper. And then get back up here and draw me a map of Yorkshire and Cumbria.' Utilising old maps and texts stored in the manor library, the boy had lost little time in carrying out his commission, and yesterday, when Seeker had finished going through the documents relating to the trier's courts, he'd handed Michael a list of names – towns, villages, parish churches – that he wanted marked on the map. The last name on the list was Faithly Moor.

Now Seeker spread the map out on his desk and studied it, looking especially at the thin lines, with dates, that he himself had drawn between the places Michael had marked upon it. The late-morning sun was beaming strongly through the window behind him, sending dust dancing in slow spirals as if the thing he looked upon were already old and faded and of little use to his present purpose. He could not make out any pattern.

Seeker got up and opened the casement window. He looked out over the abbey gardens, taking in the fresh breeze coming up from the Ouse, trying to clear his mind. It was not difficult to see why Lilburne preferred to station himself in the castle, at the south-eastern corner of the city, rather than here, just beyond its north-western gate. Here, at King's Manor, the major-general would be surrounded, as Seeker was, by reminders of the transience of power. This very building had been home to the Benedictine abbots of St Mary's, they and their abbey long since swept away by King Henry, who had taken this place for himself, and put men in to rule here as presidents of the Council of the North. But the kings and their presidents had also been swept away, by Cromwell and the men who were now his major-generals. Outside, beyond Seeker's window, were the ruined symbols of an even greater power: the remnants of the rule of Roman emperors, remembered now only in crumbling walls and the gaping stone cists of their graves. Those open, empty graves made more of an impression on Seeker than did any of the grander ruins of this place.

The ringing of the minster bells brought him back to the concerns of the present, and he turned away from the window. Such reflections achieved nothing, and men who dwelt on the ultimate futility of their present actions achieved nothing.

He returned to the map on his desk, again searching for the pattern that he knew must be there but couldn't yet see. Michael came and went and the business of King's Manor went on around them. An hour passed, another, and then Seeker had it: by the time the bells of the minster rang out for three he had traced the route of the trier Caleb Turner – or of Thomas Hungerford and his wife Felicity, as he still thought of them – and at last found the pattern he had been looking for. He lunged for a pencil left lying on Michael's table and marked arrows on the lines whilst the pattern was still clear in his head, and then he saw it for sure: the unfortunate places where, as autumn had passed to winter, Caleb Turner had held his final trier's court of one year, and the places where the following spring he had held his first of the next one, formed a pattern that always returned him to somewhere between the Vale of Pickering and Gisborough Moor. It was a vast area of hill and moorland, but it was a start. Somewhere, within the area he had marked with Michael's pencil, was the place to which Seeker was certain Caleb Turner and Felicity must each winter return, far from any who might have known them of old. Somewhere there they had left his daughter. Seeker's head swam. He had to find a way of getting back to the North Riding.

He was still sitting at his desk, trying to formulate a plan, when Michael arrived from the mail room, carrying several letters. The boy was somewhat out of breath from his hasty ascent of the stairs. He handed the topmost letter to Seeker. 'This has been sent to you from the castle, Captain. They say it arrived just this morning, in the mails from Whitehall.'

Seeker recognised the seal as that of Thurloe's department. He had been waiting a long time for the orders he was sure were in this letter. He turned it over in his hand and then laid it down on his desk. 'So,' he said to Michael, 'what else have you got there?'

The boy held out to him a packet. 'Letters, that the keeper of the record stores gave me to bring to you. He said they had become separated from the rest of the documents relating to the trier's courts, and were only come upon again this morning.'

Seeker took the pile and began to sift carefully through it. Each letter had been written from a locality subsequently visited by Caleb Turner, and painted an England bubbling under with resentments and spite. They were written by men such as Abel Sharrock, and, after due expression of religious conviction, were torrents of invective that scarcely concealed searing envy and ambition. It was happening all over England, not just in Yorkshire. 'Did I really fight for the Republic in order to put power into the hands of men such as these?' a fellow officer had asked when confronted with just such letters. But the letter Seeker held in his hand now was of a different order completely to the mass of others. This letter, calling for the trier to be sent to Faithly to look into the fitness of Septimus Jenkin to continue in his living, had been written not by Abel Sharrock, but by

Sir Edward Faithly. Seeker put the letter down on his desk and thought again of the way Emma Faithly had looked on the night of Bess Pullan's supper, and of Sir Edward Faithly's determination that she would witness, and be seen to witness, the trial of Septimus Jenkin. The muddied waters of what had happened that night seemed to be becoming a little clearer: Edward Faithly had been determined to see Septimus Jenkin's fall. Why he had been so determined that his wife should also be there was a thing Seeker did not yet fully understand. Perhaps it was simply that he might demonstrate his power over her.

Seeker set the letter aside and picked up the one from Thurloe; it could not be put off any longer. He broke it open and began to read. As he had expected, word of his assault on Caleb Turner had reached London. Thurloe made no comment, asked for no explanation, simply said, 'In consequence of this information, I require you to return to London as soon as Major-General Lilburne can appoint another to your duties.' It was the order Seeker had wished for for months, and it had come a week too late.

'Is there a reply, Captain?'

'What?'

'A reply, sir, to the letter from Whitehall.'

Seeker took a flint from a drawer in his desk and sparked it to the unlit candle by his inkstand. Once the candle was well lit, he held the edge of Thurloe's letter to the flame and watched it burn. 'No,' he said at length, 'no reply.'

He dropped what remained of the letter on the floor and

finally stamped out the flame. Michael, whose eyes betrayed his disbelief, had had the presence of mind to lift the ewer of water that stood on a small side table near the window. At a sign from Seeker he doused the smoking black mess.

Seeker dismissed the boy and asked that he should not be disturbed. As Michael disappeared into the anteroom and closed the door, Seeker leaned back in his chair, to think. But he didn't need to take time to think, for he knew what he was going to do. He'd known even before he'd broken the seal on Thurloe's letter what he would do: he'd be gone from York at first light, but it would not be the road for London that he took. He put the letters relating to the trier's court in the cupboard under his desk where he had already stored all the other documents relating to Caleb Turner, and locked it. Rolling up the map he had had Michael draw for him, he put it into his satchel and bound the fastenings. He took up his cloak and hat once more and left his room in King's Manor, telling Michael as he passed that he was finished for the day.

ELEVEN

The Merchant Adventurer

There were things Seeker would need if he were to slip out of York unnoticed. The time and the place of his leaving would present him with little difficulty, but by the time the alarm of his absence was raised at King's Manor, and communicated to the major-general at York Castle, Seeker would need to be travelling northwards in the appearance of something other than a captain in the militia. He had not always been a soldier, and, occasionally, reversion to the guise of his old trade had served him well over his time in Thurloe's service. There was a joiners' yard on Coppergate, run by an old comrade of his, where he would be given the clothing and tools he required to dress the part of journeyman carpenter, and where he would not be questioned.

The street was as busy as usual, and nothing out of the ordinary, but then something up ahead took Seeker's eye and made him look again. It was fleeting, the back of a man as he disappeared down the passageway leading to the Merchant Adventurers' Hall, but it was enough. Seeker quickened his pace and let himself be led by sound; over the rhythm of the river burbling past the gardens of the hall, and over the rumbling of wheels and horses trundling along Coppergate and Fossgate, he could hear the sound of money. As he turned down the passageway and then ascended the stone stairway to the front entrance of the Merchant Adventurers' Hall, that sound grew from a vague hum to a ceaseless babble. Here, all the wealthy merchants of York who made their fortunes in overseas trade gathered to do their business and protect their interests. Here, wool, hides and finished cloth were bought and sold, records of ancient rights kept secure in iron chests and coin stored. And over the smell of bales of cloth, of carded wool, over the smell of damp even, from when the Foss rose time and again to threaten the undercroft of the hall, Seeker didn't just hear money, he could smell it.

An officer of the Company, noticing his approach, stepped in his way and asked his business, courteously enough.

'I'm after a man named Lawrence Ingolby, who's just come in here.'

The Company officer inclined his head briskly. 'I shall make enquiries in the Great Hall. You can wait there if you like,' he said, indicating a sturdy oak seat in the entrance hall.

'I don't,' said Seeker. He nodded towards the double doors a few steps ahead of them. 'That'll be the Great Hall, I take it?'

He headed for the double doors, not waiting for the other man. The hubbub that had been audible in the entrance hall rose now by several degrees, the high ceilings of the huge double-naved Great Hall amplifying the noise rising to its rafters and sending it back again as something unintelligible. Everywhere there were merchants, some richly clothed, some merely respectable, and all appeared to be earnestly engaged upon business. Where men were not grouped in twos and threes in conversation, they were huddled around one of several sets of scales, carefully watching the rise and fall in weights and coin. None even seemed to notice Seeker's entrance. He scanned the groups, tried to keep track of the flow of movement all around the room. There was no sign of Ingolby anywhere. Seeker was about to give the thing up as a mistake, a trick of the light, but, as he made to leave the hall, a movement in brown amongst the more sumptuous clothing took his eye, like a country hawk flitting low through the room. It took a moment for Seeker's mind to register what he had just seen. By the time he realised that Lawrence Ingolby had passed within ten yards of him, the hawk was gone.

Seeker cursed and started pushing his way through to the door of the hall. Outside, there was no sign of Ingolby in the courtyard, and once he had made his way through the passageway and out onto Fossgate, Sir Edward Faithly's man of business was nowhere to be seen. He cursed again and stormed back up to the hall. Again, the Company officer was alert at the entrance. 'Captain, is there—'

Seeker held up a hand to stall him on his way past. Back in the hall he scanned the place until he had a picture of where Ingolby had been, and made for the two men standing there. 'Who was Lawrence Ingolby talking to?'

A grey-faced man in a good suit that had seen better days stepped forward. 'To me, Captain. What's a'do?'

'What did he want?'

The man shrugged as if the matter could hardly be of less importance. 'Wanted to know where Ben Scrope lived.'

Seeker took a breath and mustered his patience. 'And who is Ben Scrope?'

'Old servant of William Sorsby's. Lives with his daughter now on Goodramgate. Near enough ninety, I'd say.'

'And the Sorsbys?'

'All gone, them, years since.'

'No, Jack,' said his companion, 'there's a young lass, lives up Faithly way, with Matthew Pullan's mother, up on the moors. She were sent up there after her mother . . .'

The men were still arguing over whether there had been such a girl or not when Seeker left, cursing Lawrence Ingolby a third time: given all the questions that had run through his mind these past few days, he could not reconcile himself to leaving York without knowing what the steward of Faithly was doing here asking about the dead girl Gwendolen Sorsby's family.

As Seeker made his way back up Fossgate towards Colliergate, he could almost imagine himself watched and followed. More than once he turned round to think he glimpsed the ghost of a movement, a shape passing into a doorway or the end of an alley. He needed to be back in

London, a man cloaked in anonymity, not here in Yorkshire where whispers of the past stalked him at every turn. But London would have to wait a while longer, until he had set that past in order and recovered what Yorkshire owed him.

It was just as he reached the end of the Stonebow that Seeker heard his name called from the opening to a nearby passageway. The voice was familiar and he turned towards the sound, but not quickly enough. As if from nowhere a heavy club swung through the air towards him, catching him a blow across ear and jaw that sent him reeling into the corner of the wall. His head ringing from the blow, Seeker slumped to the ground. For a moment, he could not think, the intensity of reverberation about his skull drowning out all but the flaming pain shooting through his jaw. He was aware of voices around him and an arm touching him as he attempted to push himself up.

'Easy, Captain. I have you.'

He managed to make his eyes focus a moment on a large butcher, with arms like the slabs of meat he hefted.

'Easy there.' The man made an effort to raise Seeker from the ground, but to no avail. 'You'll have to help me there, Captain. Lean forward now and push up on your feet.'

With an immense effort, Seeker did as he was bid. His eyes opened, only to shut again, and he could not tell if the blood on the butcher's apron was that of some beast recently butchered or his own. The warm smell of it almost turned his stomach. Once the butcher had him propped against the wall he called for a stool to be brought, and one was produced from a nearby booth. Seeker heard himself murmur that he had not the time to sit before he felt himself slump once more down the side of the wall.

It took ten minutes, a deal of sound advice from the butcher and much fussing over the application of a poultice by the butcher's mother, before Seeker could hold his head up properly and keep the same object in view for more than half a minute. A jug of ale was brought from a nearby tavern and Seeker drank from it gratefully, but he refused the offer of a pasty from the cook shop over the way. His lurching proximity to the butcher's bloodied apron made him doubt that he would ever consume flesh again. He was insisting he was fit to stand when two soldiers, come running down from Monkgate, appeared. The younger of the two stared in disbelief at Seeker while the older, a sergeant, found himself addressed by the butcher's mother.

'He's a big lad, but he'll not listen to sense,' she said.

A smile briefly threatened the man's lips.

'Who did this, Captain?'

Seeker tried to speak but was forestalled by a carter held up in his delivery of coals.

'It was a small fellow, swathed in black, hood down round his face did it. Ran off down Stonebow.'

There was much assent to this, followed by an awkward silence when the sergeant asked, 'And no one went after him?'

Eventually, a chandler who'd come out of his shop across the road spoke up. 'Well, it was a bit of a shock, seeing as it's . . . him.' He nodded in Seeker's direction, as if no further explanation were needed.

Another joined in. 'Never saw a big man felled so quick. There was venom in that swing.'

By nods of the head and a great deal of murmuring it was agreed that Seeker's attacker had indeed been possessed of an almost demonic strength. Through the murmur, another two soldiers appeared, and the sergeant sent them down the Stonegate in pursuit of the assailant.

'William, fetch the cart,' ordered the butcher's mother.

'The cart, Mother? What for?'

The old woman clouted her huge son about the ear. 'To carry the captain along to the surgeon's, of course!'

Moves were made to fetch the cart, but Seeker finally succeeded in raising himself from his stool. 'No.' He lurched towards the sergeant and gripped hold of his bandolier. 'Goodramgate. That collier's cart,' he said. 'Get me up to Goodramgate.'

It was a good ten minutes later that the bewildered collier brought his cart with its strange cargo to a halt outside a mean-looking house on Our Lady Row on Goodramgate. 'This is where old Ben Scrope lives,' said the collier, 'though the old fella can hardly lift a pipe these days, never mind a club to go battering militia captains with.'

Seeker ignored the man and put out an arm to grasp that of the mortified young soldier deputed to help him off the back of the cart whilst his sergeant rapped on the door. The woman who answered was herself a worn-looking grandmother, but confirmed that yes, she was Benjamin Scrope's daughter and that yes, her father was at home, for where else would he be at the age of ninety-two?

The house Seeker was shown into was one room deep, with a rickety set of stairs leading to another room above. The small window let in little enough light, the upper floor overhanging the lower by a good foot and a half. The air was as it usually was in such places. The light from a greasy lamp mingled with that from the smoking fire to show a very ancient man happed up with blankets, propped up in a box bed set into the wall.

'Your father was servant in the household of the Sorsby family?'

The woman nodded. 'All his life, near enough. Came to me three years since, and he's had more visitors today than in half a year,' she muttered. 'He'll be worn out with it.'

'When did your last visitor leave?' demanded Seeker.

'Not ten minutes since. Thought that was him back with more questions when you come to the door. Here,' she said, peering at him more closely in the ochre light, 'you take a seat on that bench before you fall over it.'

Seeker took the seat gladly, wincing as even the movement of sitting sent reverberations through his body to his head and jaw. 'What was this man's name?'

The woman pursed her lips, then turned to the old man. 'What were that fellow called, Father? Inkerman, Imberley?'

'Ingolby,' came back the surprisingly strong voice. 'His name was Lawrence Ingolby.'

Seeker turned with care and addressed the old man. 'And what did Lawrence Ingolby want?'

'Wanted to know if Bess Pullan had been here last time she were in York.'

'Bess Pullan?' Seeker leaned forward. 'Be certain, Grandfather. He did not come on the business of Sir Edward Faithly?'

The old man looked bewildered. 'Why, no. How should such as me know him?'

'Aye, but Father,' interjected the man's daughter, 'he did say to me he were Sir Edward's man of business, whoever Sir Edward is, I don't know, but that he had come to see you on another matter.'

'Aye,' said the old man, almost angered to have been doubted, 'and that other matter were of Mistress Pullan.'

Seeker took a moment to consider this, but could not see what its relevance could be. 'And had she? Been here of late?' he asked at last, holding to the edge of the bench as his vision began to swim in the smoky closeness of the air.

'Aye. Brought us a nice lot of provisions too. A good woman, Mistress Pullan. Always was.'

'She often came here then?'

'Whenever she were in town, early spring and late summer, even after my old mistress died.'

'That would be old Mistress Sorsby, the girl Gwendolen's grandmother?'

'Aye!' The old man's face brightened. 'Do you know Gwendolen, Captain? Gift from God, that child. How that house did miss her when she went! There was no need for it, we could have looked after her! But then, the mistress was prone to fret, and—'

'Hush, Father!' scolded his daughter. 'The captain isn't here for all that.'

'No, I don't suppose he is,' he said sadly. 'But I would like to know how she is, all the same – that young fellow didn't seem to have much news of her when I asked him.'

Seeker glanced at the old man's daughter, whose eyes shot him a warning. 'Well,' he lied at last, 'the girl does well. But I need you to tell me what you told Lawrence Ingolby.'

The man raised a grey eyebrow. 'Just what happened, Captain, though why it should interest you or him, I don't know. Mistress Bess had been a very great friend of my old mistress, and generally called in on me when she was in town. She come here a few weeks since to ask after me, and brought provisions and all sorts of tonics Gwendolen had made for me, and I gave her the things Rosemary there found in my old chest.'

Seeker turned back to the woman. 'What things?'

'Things my father brought here with him when he came to live with me after Francis Sorsby, Gwendolen's uncle, was drowned coming back from Amsterdam three years since. Old master and mistress – the child Gwendolen's grandparents – were long gone, and the creditors took the house. Father had nowhere else to go, so he come here. Now, he had but a box with him of his own things, apart from the clothes in a sack over his back. Old Bible, a few coins, his tobacco pouch and a clock old Master Sorsby had brought him from Hamburg before I was ever in this world. And there were an old gaming box in there, too, and I don't hold with gaming, Captain – cards and chequers and the like. Many's a good man gone wrong and a good woman suffered over the heads of gaming.'

The old man in the bed looked sheepishly at Seeker. 'A couple of shillings, now and then, never lost the coat off my back.'

'Not for want of trying,' grumbled his daughter. 'Anyway, when I was having a good clear out in the spring, Father's box fell down in the cupboard and the gaming box fell out and broke, 'cept it wasn't a gaming box at all – no cards nor chequermen nor any such thing, but an old locked book and a necklace. Old painted wooden beads. Gwendolen's, he said, and the book her grandmother's private accounts book, that she'd always kept locked. Father said he hadn't wanted strangers coming upon it when the creditors sold the Sorsbys' house, or neighbours ogling over their business, and so he'd taken it away here with him when he'd left, to keep it from the creditors.'

Seeker shut his eyes against a pain that was slicing across his forehead, and marshalled what the woman had just told him. 'Did you read this book?' he asked the old man at last, when the pain had subsided a little.

'Not me,' said the old man. 'Saw it once or twice, when she was writing numbers in it. I've no notion what it was for – I never could read, nor our Rosemary neither.' He pointed to a Bible on the stool beside him. 'Just like to have that Bible by me, and have Rosemary's lad read to me from it from time to time. Anyhow, it were just before Mistress Bess come to visit last time that Rosemary come upon the book, and she thought it more fitting that Mistress Bess should have it than we, her having been such a friend to Mistress Sorsby, and so we gave the book to her.'

'And this is all you had to tell Lawrence Ingolby?'

Ben Scrope nodded vigorously. 'All I could tell him, for I knew no more. And he knew even less, if you ask me – didn't even seem to know why he wanted to know if Bess had been here.'

'Hmm,' said Seeker, who couldn't think past the pain in his head and jaw to guess on the matter himself. 'And where did Ingolby go when he left here?'

It was Rosemary who answered. 'Old Star inn, Stonegate. I offered him a bit of supper with us, but he said he had a dinner waiting for him there.'

Seeker turned to his sergeant. 'Send one of the men to the Stonegate, Old Star inn. Tell them to detain Lawrence Ingolby until I get there.' He began to rise unsteadily to his feet. 'However long that might take.'

Ben Scrope's daughter waved a hand towards Seeker's jaw. 'Him that did that, was it?'

'No,' said Seeker, turning painfully. 'It wasn't Lawrence Ingolby who did this to me.' It hardly made sense to him, but the last thing he remembered before being felled by the wooden club was hearing the voice of Caleb Turner.

TWELVE

The Old Star Inn

Of all York, it was the Stonegate that Seeker liked best. It put him in mind of London: a hotchpotch of buildings, each too busy with its own business to concern itself with line or style, contending with one another for space over the narrow street. Inns and taverns squeezed shoulder to shoulder with the printers', stationers' and booksellers' shops whose workers and patrons formed their trade. All had grown up in the service of the minster that loomed hugely over it, as if threatening to suck all into its maw. The Stonegate was less a place for profit than for the ideas and mischiefs of men, and Seeker understood its every nook and cranny. His duties in York were not what they had been in London, but he would look in, from time to time, to a printer's workshop or a bookseller's back room, 'just to keep my hand in, just to keep them on their toes', as he told his sergeant.

He had also once or twice cut through that way at night, to stop by the end of the narrow snicket of Coffee Yard, where the aromas of the coffee house took him back to another coffee house, on Birchin Lane, deep in the city of London. There, in Birchin Lane, in the conversation and silences of the old soldier whose place it was, Seeker had found the closest thing to friendship he had ever known. He thought also of a young woman, in a cold London attic room, who had loved him once. He had known from the beginning that a love between himself, who must enforce order and the law, and Maria Ellingworth, whose brother's writings did little but trouble the peace of London's citizens and aim at fomenting rebellion, could hardly prosper. Maria had never once let him think that she would consent to abandon her brother, but she had never understood that Seeker could not abandon that which anchored him – his place in Cromwell's service, his devotion to the state – either. And then he thought of the other woman – Dorcas Wells – who had promised she would wait for him. Dorcas had seen more of life, understood more of the world than Maria, in her garret in Dove Court with her lawyer brother, ever might. Dorcas understood Seeker, and asked little from him whilst offering all she had. She was a better woman than he could have had cause to hope for, and yet she waited there for him, in her tavern in Bishopsgate. He was a long way, now, from Dove Court and from Bishopsgate. He had thought that Yorkshire was his past, but there were things he must accomplish here before he could ever return to London.

Tonight, on the Stonegate, Seeker didn't turn left down Coffee Yard, but right, towards the Old Star inn. He was grateful for the narrow passageway that led off from Stone-gate to the courtyard of the Old Star – the walls helped keep him upright as he lurched from side to side. One of the men from Monkgate Bar was standing guard at the bottom of a wooden stairway leading to an upper porch of the inn. Seeker sat down heavily on a bench in the courtyard, its occupants having cleared it on his approach. He let out a weary breath and addressed the young soldier. 'I suppose you're about to tell me he's up those stairs.'

'Yes, Captain,' said the boy with more confidence than was merited. 'We've put him in a private room.'

'Well get him down, you fool!' bellowed the sergeant. 'How's the captain supposed to get up there?'

The boy gulped and ran up the wooden steps, reappearing only a moment later in front of a studiedly bemused-looking Lawrence Ingolby, who had another guard behind him. Ingolby's face broke into what might have been a genuine grin. 'Well, Captain, this is an unexpected pleasure.'

'I don't doubt it,' said Seeker. He nodded to the bench opposite him and addressed the guards. 'Put him there and go and stand guard at the back door of the inn. You can mind the end of the passageway, Sergeant.'

The sergeant looked doubtfully from Ingolby to Seeker. 'If you're certain, Captain.'

'I am. This one's a thinker, not daft. He won't try anything.'

Still unconvinced, the sergeant sent his men to do as Seeker had bid them and went to take up his own position at the street end of the inn's passageway.

'I might not try anything, but someone obviously has,' said Ingolby, raising an eyebrow at Seeker's evident injuries. 'Shouldn't you be getting that seen to?'

Seeker was dismissive. He remembered the first time he had seen the Old Star, years ago when Fairfax's army had used it for a hospital, and a morgue. He'd seen men die here, out of their minds with fever, or their blood seeping from mangled bodies onto the cobbles of this very yard. A dunt on the head with a wooden club wouldn't even have got them a corner of wall to lean against. 'It's nothing,' he said.

'If you say so,' said Ingolby. 'But it's freezing out here and there's a nice big fire blazing in there and as good a drop of ale as you'll get in York, so whatever this is, can't we do it inside?'

It had indeed grown cold, and Seeker could feel himself beginning to shiver. 'All right,' he relented, 'but what this is is between you and me for now, and not for other ears.'

'Aye, well, I have very little truck with other ears anyhow,' said Ingolby, offering a hand to help Seeker up.

The seats by the fire were cleared for them, and whilst Ingolby ordered ale, Seeker took a spiced caudle. The inn was busy and noisy enough that they wouldn't be overheard.

'What are you doing in York?' Seeker asked when the innkeeper had left them.

In the shifting glow of the fire, a shadow of wariness flitted across Ingolby's eyes before he said, 'Needed a new suit, winter coming on and all.'

'Ben Scrope's no tailor,' said Seeker.

'Ah.'

'You're right, "Ah." Now I'll ask you again, what are you doing in York?'

Ingolby took a moment, evidently considering how he should proceed. He ran the tip of his tongue over his bottom lip and a decision was made.

'I came to find out what had happened the last time Bess was here in town. Matthew said his mother always visited an old servant of the Sorsbys, Gwendolen's grandparents, when she came to York, so I went there.'

'But you had to ask at the Merchant Adventurer's where it was that Ben Scrope lived.'

Ingolby puffed out his cheeks in surprise. 'Thought I'd got out without you seeing me. Anyhow, I had to go there because Matthew didn't know where Ben Scrope lived nowadays, but he knew a couple of old traders he thought might, and he couldn't ask Bess.'

'Why not?'

Ingolby was uneasy. 'Because she's not . . . she's not been her right self since Gwendolen died. She's a husk, empty, like Gwendolen took what was left of life with her. She hardly speaks.'

Seeker had seen the beginnings of this decline in Bess Pullan himself when the girl had died. And yet it didn't explain why Lawrence Ingolby had come to York.

'What does it matter what happened the last time Bess was in York?'

Ingolby looked as if he was wondering how far he could trust Seeker. 'Might not matter anything at all,' he said at last, 'but when Bess came back to Faithly after that visit, something had changed.'

'How?' asked Seeker.

'She . . .' He was hard put to find the right words, and started again. 'She was nervy, suspicious of anyone that came near the house. Wouldn't let anyone from outside the household near Gwendolen, had to have her by her all the time — watched her like a hawk. That's why Gwendolen took to wandering the woods and moors so early in the mornings, before Bess was up and about. There were arguments, too, blazing rows with Matthew.'

'About?'

'Bess wanted to send Gwendolen away to her niece in Bristol, to make a "lady" of her, she said. Matthew wouldn't hear of it. It was a daft idea, at any rate; I mean, what would a girl like Gwendolen have done in a place like Bristol?'

'And nothing came of the idea?'

'No, nor of sending her to a second cousin in Carlisle either. They were daft, half-baked ideas, and Matthew wouldn't have it.'

'And Gwendolen?'

'Gwendolen?'

'What did she have to say about it?'

Ingolby shrugged. 'I don't think she was ever told. She was in her own world, half the time. Didn't really notice what was going on around her. Didn't really trouble herself over the same things as the rest of us.'

'Had Bess ever spoken of sending Gwendolen away like this before?'

Ingolby shook his head. 'It was out of the blue, the very day she got back from York.'

'Had something happened in Faithly whilst she'd been away?'

Ingolby looked puzzled. 'Like what?'

'Anything between Matthew and the girl?'

Ingolby put down his ale. 'Betw——' Then when he saw Seeker's meaning, he began to rise from his seat. 'Now wait a minute. All that filth Abel Sharrock was peddling . . .'

Seeker had read the report of the first day of the trier's court and drawn his own conclusions as to what Abel Sharrock was implying. 'Was there any truth in it? Was Matthew's father, old Digby Pullan, also Gwendolen's father? Was there something between Matthew and Gwendolen?'

Lawrence Ingolby's face was twisted in anger, and he could hardly grind out the words. 'No. Digby was an old goat, but he took his pleasures far away in taverns and stews. Gwendolen was a Sorsby through and through. And Matthew had no interest, none, in her as anything other than a sister.'

Seeker was about to assure him that he believed him, but Lawrence wasn't finished yet. 'And he wasn't my father, either. Wish he had been, but he'd not have gone near my mother with a broom handle, and trust me, if she'd had any chance of winkling money out of the likes of Digby Pullan she'd have been shouting it from Faithly Cross. Which she wasn't.'

Seeker held up a hand. 'Peace. But I had to ask.'

'Aye, well,' said Lawrence, calming only slightly and taking a long draught of his ale.

'So,' continued Seeker, 'what had changed when she was in York?'

Ingolby looked him directly in the eye. 'I think Bess discovered something when she was here that made her think Gwendolen was in danger, and that was why she tried to send her away. Maybe Matthew should have listened to her.'

'Why would he, if she wouldn't tell him the truth? Anyway, what of this account book Ben Scrope says he gave her?'

Ingolby was surprised. 'Told you about that, did he? Well, I've never seen her with it, and Matthew never mentioned such a book. Mind you, neither him nor me knew she had any such book until today, and he still doesn't. I can't see what difference an old account book would make, anyway. Sooner I get back to Faithly, the better.'

Seeker leaned closer. None of his men was in earshot, and any of their fellow drinkers would have had trouble hearing what they said above the babble of voices in the taproom. A scruffy-looking fellow drinking alone by the hatch had glanced over at them once or twice, but looked away when Seeker glared at him. 'And how do things stand at Faithly? The trier?'

Ingolby laughed. 'Well, he stands. Leastways, he did stand, finally, about three days after you laid him flat. Hollerenshaw did what he could for his jaw.' Here Ingolby winced. 'Rather him than me. But fair play to him: he stood up, packed up and made off.'

And so Caleb Turner was not laid up, incapacitated, almost forty miles away. 'What do you mean, "made off"?' asked Seeker in a low voice.

'Got on his horse and legged it.' He shrugged. 'Or the horse legged it. Either way, he's gone, and there hasn't been sight nor sound of him since.'

Seeker ran a finger through some ale that had spilled on the table top. 'And his wife?' he asked, without looking up.

'Ah,' said Ingolby, warming to his tale, 'that's the best bit – he left her behind. Jack Thatcher at the Black Bull threw her out when he saw her husband had taken all the money with him.'

'And where is she now?' asked Seeker, a strange unease beginning to stir in him.

'Where is she now? Well, actually, that's the best bit. Maud Sharrock has had to take her in, seeing Abel had made such a song and dance of being the trier's right-hand man.' Ingolby, now shaking with mirth, had to put down his tankard. 'Poor Maud doesn't know which way's up. Abel's insisting the trier'll be back, though it's plain as day he's no more idea where the man's gone than I do, and Maud's having to fetch and carry for her ladyship, whose "ladyship" Maud is beginning to question. They'll be at a fine old fetch by now, I should imagine. I'm sorry to be missing it.' He lifted his tankard once again to his mouth and took an appreciative draught.

Seeker pictured Felicity, stranded in the sexton's tiny cottage, the hard dirt floor, a straw pallet in the corner if she was lucky, hardly a shaft of light getting in at the small window, woodsmoke and stinking tallow candles and at the mercy of the man's porcine wife. She would not like that, not one bit. But the longer Turner was away, the fewer were Felicity's options. Seeker knew, though, that it was not a question of how long Maud Sharrock would put up with Felicity, but how long the woman who had once been his wife would tolerate Maud and her cottage.

'It wasn't Abel Sharrock,' he said.

'What?' said Ingolby, still smiling at the thought of Maud's discomfort.

'It wasn't Abel Sharrock that called the trier to Faithly. It was Sir Edward.'

Ingolby put down his tankard. 'Sir Edward?'

Seeker had expected mockery, denial, argument, but what he saw was Ingolby's smile disappear and the shock of hearing something he understood instantly to be the truth.

He gave Ingolby a moment. 'You don't seem surprised.'

Ingolby moved his mouth, scrambled for some thought to express. Found none.

'Did you know of this?' said Seeker.

'No.'

'Nor even guess?'

Another flat 'No'.

'And yet it does not surprise you?'

Ingolby took a drink, as if to give himself more time. 'I can see that . . . that he might have done, that it is possible he could have done it.'

'And why might he have done it? I've looked into it, and even if the man has never avowed his Royalism, he's a supporter of the old church and no Puritan.'

Ingolby sniffed, sat up a little straighter. 'You would have to ask him, I imagine.'

'He's not here,' said Seeker, 'so I'm asking you.'

Ingolby looked at the table a long while and pursed his lips. 'Well,' he said eventually, 'I'd say Edward Faithly did it because he's a vicious, twisted bastard. Septimus must have got something over on him, sometime in the past, and Sir Edward's getting his revenge. He enjoys that, revenge. It's what gets him up in the morning.'

'Oh?'

Ingolby looked startled, then pointed to his empty tankard. 'I've had too much of that, blabbering nonsense.' He stood up as if to leave. It was clear that he knew more than he was telling, but Seeker's thumping head told him he hadn't the strength to play mind games with the clever secretary tonight. There were other things, though, that he did want to know.

'Sit back down,' he said. 'You can maybe answer me this instead: why would Sir Edward Faithly's secretary be travelling to York on Matthew Pullan's private business?'

'I . . . Matthew, that is, it was Matthew that released me – if you like – into Sir Edward's service, but it was on condition that I should be free to work in his business too, from time to time.'

'Released you? From what?'

Ingolby shrugged. 'My position, my obligations to him, and his mother.' He could see that Seeker still didn't understand. 'My mother,' he began, 'was what you might call unfortunate in life. Well, some would call her unfortunate, most would call her a trollop, or worse. I know Digby Pullan wasn't my father, but she couldn't have told you who my father actually was, even when she was sober. And she could hardly remember my name when she wasn't. She was hounded out of every village and town she fetched up in. Only piece of luck she ever had was that she finished up in Faithly.' Ingolby laughed, a half-laugh with more bitterness in it than humour. 'Lucky for me, anyway. They found me in a cave, do you know that? That's where I was born, a cave up in the woods. Sir Anthony Faithly was out hunting one day and one of his dogs went astray, and that's where they found us. He was all right, Sir Anthony – let her have an old shepherd's hut up on the moor. When I was old enough, Septimus made sure she sent me to school – wouldn't give her anything out of the poor box, otherwise – and when Digby Pullan fetched up in the schoolroom one day asking for a likely lad with a good head for numbers, Septimus pointed at me. Bess went that very day and told my mother I was coming to live with them. Burned my clothes, scrubbed me raw in a tub in the yard, gave me old stuff of Matthew's to wear and I never looked back. Old Digby Pullan taught me all I know about keeping a minute and casting a set of accounts and drawing up a letter for a man of business or the law, and plenty else besides. Matthew kept me on after Digby died.'

'But not for long.'

Lawrence spread out his hands. 'Sir Anthony Faithly and Thomas, the older brother, were long gone by then, and Edward was running the estate. Matthew found out what a mess the place was in, that Edward was up to his ears in debt. He'd held on to the estate because he'd stayed put when his father went off to fight for the Stuarts. Paid a pretty penny to save it from forfeiture when the Republic came about. Things were going from bad to worse, the estate was running into the ground, and it does no one up round Faithly any good when the estate's on its knees. Matthew sent me up there to try to sort things out, keep an eye on things.'

Seeker had traced much of this in his examination of the estate papers at Faithly Manor – only stringent discipline of finances in the last three years had staved off what might otherwise have been ruin. Seeker had also seen the extent of Matthew Pullan's wealth. 'Matthew could have bought and sold that estate twice over – why didn't he just get it for himself if he was so concerned about it?'

'Matthew was what you might call radical when he was younger – a bit of the levelling tendency to him. I'm not saying he was, mind – a Leveller . . .' Seeker said nothing, and Ingolby continued. 'But he's not the type to look to be lord of the manor.'

'And Sir Edward doesn't mind having you there, Matthew Pullan's man, "keeping an eye on things"?'

Lawrence gave a contemptuous grunt. 'Sir Edward's in no position to mind.'

'Because he's reliant on loans from Matthew Pullan to hang on to his family's house and land?'

'That's about the size of it,' said Ingolby, draining the last of his ale. 'Can I go now?'

'Back to Faithly?'

'No. To finish my supper. I've been trudging about this town all day, trying to find where Bess went.'

'And did you?'

Ingolby shook his head. 'Apart from Ben Scrope, I only know that she went to an apothecary.'

'That would be usual enough, wouldn't it, on her visits to the city?' said Seeker.

'If it had been her usual apothecary, yes, but it wasn't, so I went to see what she'd been there for.'

'And?'

Ingolby screwed up his face in a picture of incomprehension. 'Something I've never heard of before – snakeroot.'

Seeker frowned. 'What is it? A poison?'

Ingolby shrugged. 'No idea. The apothecary didn't either. Said he thought he'd seen a picture of it once, in an old herbal. It had come in from the Levant, last century he thought, but he didn't know what it was for or where it could be got nowadays at all.'

Not for the first time since he'd come north, Seeker regretted that his neighbour, the apothecary Drake, was not to hand here as he was in London. 'And is that you finished with all your investigations?'

'I've one more thing to see to,' said Ingolby. 'I want to go and ask after Bess at the lodging house on Trinity Lane, over by Micklegate, that she stayed at whenever she and Gwendolen were in town without Matthew. "Respectable place for respectable gentlewomen," she always said. I'd have been there by now, if your men hadn't taken hold of me and told me you'd had a better idea.' He frowned. 'I doubt I'll learn much more than I already know, but might as well give it a try, seeing as I've come all this way.'

Seeker nodded. 'Right.' He steadied himself against the edge of the table as he rose. 'Ten o'clock tomorrow morning. Trinity Lane. And don't think of leaving this town without with my say-so.'

Despite the support of the table, Seeker felt his legs sway and buckle beneath him. The last thing he heard before crumpling to the ground was the voice of Lawrence Ingolby shouting to the soldiers to come quick.

It was a good three hours later that Seeker finally found himself alone again. They hadn't taken him back to his billet at Walmgate Bar, but to King's Manor, where on Lilburne's orders he was put in a comfortable chamber near his own offices. His clerk, Michael, had been told to sleep on the floor of the room, and to summon Lilburne's own physician, a wealthy native of the city whose home was on nearby Gillygate. The physician, after examining Seeker and despatching Michael with a script to the apothecary, concluded that the surgeon would not be necessary, and that the captain should on no account shift from his bed for the next two days. Seeker summoned the grace to thank him and was glad to see him leave.

The first of the preparations Michael bore back from the apothecary he dissolved in a beaker of canary wine before handing it to Seeker with instructions that he must drink the whole. 'Is there laudanum in this?' said Seeker suspiciously.

'Only a little, Captain, but the major-general's physician is very clear that you must take it.' Seeker swallowed down the wine and readied himself for the next medicine, a limp-looking decoction of chamomile, feverfew and willow whose odour was utterly repugnant. He shook his head. 'I wouldn't let my horse drink that from a trough.'

'No, but Captain, you must take it, for it is that that will take away the pain in your head and help you to sleep.'

Seeker swallowed reluctantly, and braced himself for the last preparation, a pungent treacle, which but for the hovering boy he would have spat out. Their foul taste notwithstanding, the medicaments were not long in taking their effect, and as the pain in his head began to ease, he felt sleep come on.

The night was stormy and his sleep a restless one. October winds rattled the windows in their casements and sent strange howlings down the chimney piece. Michael, to whom the comfort of a warm bedchamber was something of a novelty, slept on, but Seeker found himself waking at unwonted times. At some point between dusk and dawn, a troublesome dream was brought to an end by the thud of something heavy against his window. The boy not having stirred in his blankets, Seeker got himself up from the bed and over to the window. The clouds sent scudding across the sky by the forceful east wind now covered the moon, now unveiled it; the gardens and ruins of St Mary's Abbey became stark in the pale blue light before being plunged once more into darkness. Seeker could see no mark on the window from any bird that might have hit it, but the branches of a huge oak by the ruins of St Leonard's hospital off to his left were creaking and snapping in the wind, sending wooden debris flying manically through the air. Seeker's head was a fug of sleep and drugs as he looked out on to the gardens and many organic forms took on all manner of shapes that God had not intended. The open stone burial cists that he knew and saw in daylight to be clear and empty, were now abundant with menace. He had to screw shut his eyes and open them again to be certain that he had not seen a figure raise itself up from one of them and extend a talon-like finger towards him. Another cloud across the moon and the spectre was gone. Seeker felt a chill go through his whole frame and gladly sank down once more on his bed.

Sleep was a long time in returning, and his mind roved over the question of Caleb Turner – was it truly his voice that Seeker had heard call his name? And why had Turner, even if he had come to York to silence Seeker, left Felicity in Faithly? Did he mean to return to her, and if not, what might she do now? And all the while, every time he closed his eyes, images of a black-hooded man swinging a club, and Gwendolen Sorsby putting a spoonful of creamy mushrooms to her lips, filled his vision. Before he at last slept again, Seeker resolved he would take no more medicines.

THIRTEEN

The Pricke of Conscience

The gales had blown themselves out by morning, and despite Michael's protestations, Seeker refused to swallow any more of the apothecary's brews. He needed a clear head for whatever the day had in store for him, and had no wish to invite back last night's visions.

Outside, a fresh breeze off the Ouse blew away the vestiges of the lingering miasma of the sick room, and Seeker breathed it deep. The ground in the abbey gardens was strewn with snapped branches and pieces of masonry, loosened by a century's neglect and now at last fallen. Birds flitted from the heights of the old Roman tower and the tumbled walls of St Leonard's hospital to peck at worms in the moss around the ancient graves of the monks. Best place for them, Seeker thought, buried deep. Not like those other, more ancient graves, stone cists, set in and not beneath the ground, their coverings long gone, the bodies in them also gone. Against his will Seeker found himself drawn towards the burial cist that had taken his attention in the storm of the night. Nothing sinister about it now: whatever he thought he had seen could only have been an owl, or fox, or other night-time creature briefly illuminated by the moon's light. And yet he felt the need to take a look all the same. First, he stood by the cist and looked up. The window of the chamber in which he had passed the night could be seen clearly from here. The loose clod of earth on the ground directly beneath it was just that, earth, and Seeker discounted it. He bent down to examine the tomb itself. Lying in the bottom, amongst the blown twigs and leaves, was a thin strip of black cloth, tied around a sharp stone. Seeker brushed away the debris that had blown over the top of it, and saw something beneath which made him take a step backwards. In thin, but clearly shaped letters, scratched into the ancient stone, was the legend 'Damian Seeker V.X.MDCLV'. The message was simple, and had been left plain for him to see: it was a warning that he would die today.

Seeker had been threatened with death often, but those had been times when the possibility, the likelihood, of death had been honestly offered and clearly understood. This ghostly threat, this shadow opponent, was something different. Half of York must have known where he had been taken to after his collapse at the Old Star – Michael, the physician, the sergeant and three men who had borne him from Goodramgate to Stonegate and then from the Old Star up to King's Manor. Any who had seen him taken from that inn, any who had seen him borne through the streets. Tens, hundreds of individuals perhaps, and amongst them all, that unseen one who wished him very ill.

The call of a crow from the gables of King's Manor reminded Seeker of the business he must attend to. He turned and walked back, his sense of balance all but returned, and if any thought anything untoward in his gait, they quickly turned away lest their curiosity be noticed. He returned to his chamber, where there was no sign of the boy Michael, no doubt gone out to fetch Seeker a late breakfast. He wrote a note bearing only six words, over which he took a great deal of care, and appended to it his signature. It was addressed to Chief Secretary Thurloe, and Seeker placed it, sealed, on his table for Michael to post later in the day. As he unlocked the door of his offices once more, Seeker reflected upon those six words: 'I ask that you trust me.' He pictured Thurloe opening it in Whitehall, the things that would be set in motion. He had not reached the top of the stair to the courtyard of King's Manor when he turned around, went back to his rooms, threw the note to Thurloe on the fire and watched until it had burned to ashes.

The boatman who ferried him across the Ouse from Lendal landing to Barker Tower evidently had the measure of his passenger's humour and did not attempt conversation. By the time Seeker had turned on to Trinity Lane to find Lawrence Ingolby already waiting outside the lodging house at Jacob's Well, his mind was clear: whatever it took, Major-General Lilburne would give him permission to return to Faithly Moor.

'How's the head?' enquired Ingolby, composing his face into an approximation of concern.

'Still attached,' said Seeker, before rapping hard on the door.

A shutter opened in the overhanging casement above them, and an unseen maidservant enquired of their business. Seeker stepped back into the street and looked up. 'Army business. Fetch your mistress, girl.'

It was a very short time later that the heavy timber door in front of them opened out, and the landlady, a respectable-looking woman of middle age, bade them come in.

'Outside'll do fine,' said Seeker, ignoring Ingolby's exaggerated foot-stamping and remaining under the wooden canopy jutting out from above the door. 'You had a woman named Bess Pullan staying here, a few weeks back.'

The landlady nodded. 'Mistress Pullan and her ward always lodge with me when her son's not with them.'

'Mistress Pullan was alone this time, though?'

'Yes.'

'Did she tell you why she had come to town?'

'She always comes at this time of year, to buy new boots and the like for herself and for young Gwendolen for the winter.'

'And was there anything unusual about her visit this time?'

The woman thought. 'Well, she didn't stay as long as she usually would, but perhaps that was because she didn't have her ward with her for company. She got her business done quickly and didn't stay to pay the social visits that otherwise she might.'

'So what was her business — boots and the like aside?'

The woman made a show of trying to remember. 'She carried out her usual charitable visits, there was an old family servant of a dead friend up on Goodramgate—'

Ben Scrope.

'Yes,' interrupted Seeker. 'We know of that. What else?'

The landlady shook her head. 'Nothing, but that on the last morning, the day after she had been to visit the old fellow, she went to All Saints' church, on North Street.'

Ingolby frowned. 'Never heard her talk of that before. Bess isn't given to touring churches.'

'No,' conceded the landlady. 'It was unusual, but well,' she looked downwards and then addressed herself to Ingolby, 'Mistress Pullan isn't well, as you must know. I could see it in her these last couple of visits. She's failing. The elderly often take to churching when they're ailing. I don't think she had much comfort of it, mind — she looked worse when she got back than when she'd left. Them windows, I suppose — they'd put the fear of death on anyone. She'd her bags packed and a carter called within the hour, and off home. There's nothing amiss, I hope?'

'Oh, there's plenty amiss, but not your concern.' Seeker put his helmet back on. 'We'll be on our way.'

Seeker had already turned away, and the woman was about to close the door, when Ingolby asked her, 'What did you mean, about the windows?'

'At All Saints?' she asked.

He nodded.

'Pricke of Conscience,' she said, shuddering. 'End of the World, earthquakes, fires, monsters from the sea. Horrible. Bones of the dead, rising from the ground. Demons leading the damned down to Hell.' She addressed herself to Seeker. 'You'd have done better to have smashed them up after the siege. Best forgotten, all that sort of thing. A lot better.'

Seeker had never been a destroyer of windows, a puller-down of statues, but after his experiences of the night, he wondered if the woman might not be right, if such superstitions might not be as well done away with altogether.

Ingolby was unnaturally quiet on the short walk to North Street.

'You didn't know she was ill,' said Seeker.

Ingolby shook his head. 'No.' He cursed himself. 'I've known that woman all my life, and didn't see it. But now, well, aye. She's been failing a while, I suppose.'

'And has Matthew any idea, do you think?'

'Matthew?' He sniffed. 'Matthew's the same as me. Bess is doing what she always does, so he doesn't see what's under his nose. Too much else on his mind to notice his mother's dying right in front of him.'

'Like what, for instance?' said Seeker.

Ingolby was taken off guard. 'What? Oh, business, commissioner duties, that sort of thing.'

Seeker was unconvinced but moved on with his enquiry.

'And what of Gwendolen? Would she have known? About Bess?'

Ingolby's features took on a gentler set than Seeker had

observed in him before. 'Aye, Gwendolen'll have known. She had a sort of – sense – about these things, you know? Like animals do, dogs and that.'

Seeker nodded.

'Gwendolen was always making things up for Bess in that workshop of hers, always fussing round her. I thought Bess only took them to please her – Gwendolen could be that strange sometimes, it was best just to go along with her.'

Seeker stopped him. 'What do you mean?'

Ingolby shrugged. 'Well, she would be happy one minute, and then, if she thought she'd done something wrong, there was no consoling her. Sometimes you could make a joke with her, others . . .' He shook his head. 'I loved Gwendolen, Captain, like she was my own sister, too, just like Matthew did, but there were times I didn't understand her. Bess did, though, and they were that close. Huh, but Gwendolen would never have done out in the world. Bristol? Carlisle? What was Bess thinking of?'

Seeker nodded towards the spire of All Saints, which was now in view. 'Perhaps we'll know better by the time we're done there.'

They went in by the south door. Ingolby had lost all his cocksureness since the fact of Bess's illness had been made plain to him, and he came to a halt at the bottom of the nave almost as a penitent. Stone colonnades ran down to the chancel, supporting the high, hammer-beamed roof, and making flanking aisles to the north and south. 'What

Septimus wouldn't give for a church like this,' said Ingolby at last.

Seeker pictured the stark little drystone church that stood within its own churchyard on a slight rise at the top of Faithly village. Bare walls. Simple benches. Plain windows. Nothing to the craftsmanship of the masonry, carpentry and glasswork on display here. Seeker looked at the capitals of the columns supporting the roof – the work of different ages. And the beams of the roof itself – fine work, the work of master craftsmen, but he did not like it. Pairs of angels supported each hammer beam, the traces of their gaudy reds and blues and golds still to be seen in the paintwork that had yet to wear away. 'As many centuries' worship in Faithly as here, I daresay; as much faith there too,' he said at last.

'You think?' said Ingolby. He began to walk slowly up the south aisle, his gaze moving from the ceiling above him to the stained-glass windows to his right. 'Saints. Angels.' He laughed. 'You won't find many of them in Faithly.'

'Look closer,' said Seeker, joining him before a window that seemed to show angels leading different ranks of citizens to their proper place in the world. 'Look who's at the top – bishops, popes, priests, then emperors, kings, lawyers. Look who's at the bottom.'

Ingolby leaned in and looked closer. 'Labourers. Craftsmen. The workers.' Again he laughed. 'You and me, Seeker. That'll be why Matthew got rid of the ones in Faithly.'

'Got rid of what?' asked Seeker.

'Windows,' said Ingolby. 'Painted windows. There were some in Faithly church. I remember from when I was a boy. Nothing to this, but they were all right – took your mind off the sermon. Old Digby wasn't bothered one way or the other, but Bess had brought Matthew up a good Puritan, and Matthew levelled those windows good and proper. Sir Edward was none too pleased – said his ancestors had paid for half of those windows – were in most of them, Bess says. "Vanity," she told him, and out they came. Abel Sharrock never had as much fun with his shovel as he did that day.'

Seeker cast his mind back to the ardent young Leveller Fairfax had first taken him to meet in a London gaol. He could well picture that young man – whom Fairfax had given the choice between informing on his comrades or seeing that they were left to stew and worse in prison – smashing painted windows and tearing down crosses. The war and the struggles that had followed had changed Pullan as it had changed him, but it hadn't completely wiped out what either of them had once been.

Seeker watched Ingolby as he studied the window a while longer then moved on. Saints and more saints, and multiple images of the mother of Christ. 'Nothing so terrifying here,' said Ingolby, leaving off his examination of the east window of the church and turning in to the north choir.

Seeker had lingered a moment, though. 'Bess was right,' he muttered, noting the coat of arms that would have been those of the window's donor, and the images of laymen and women portrayed beneath. The donor's family, no doubt, there for a posterity who might otherwise forget they had ever been. 'Vanity of the rich.'

Ingolby came to a halt before a set of window panels in the north wall. 'That's it,' he said, almost wary. 'That's what that lodging house landlady was talking about.' He puffed out his lips and shook his head. 'Horrible. Just horrible.'

Seeker came to stand beside him. '"The Pricke of Conscience",' he said, at last. 'Did your mother never tell you that tale?'

'I think I told you about my mother,' Ingolby replied glumly.

'Aye, you did. Your grandmother then?'

'She was worse, they tell me.'

Seeker smiled. 'Fair enough. Well, my grandmother told it me. An old, old poem, about the end of the world, the last days. Floods spouting up hideous roaring monsters from the sea, earthquakes, fire, everything burned, men and women hiding in holes in the ground. The dead rising up, being led to heaven or hell.'

Ingolby nodded as his eyes followed Seeker's tale across the coloured panes of glass. 'Sounds like a lovely woman, your grandmother.'

Seeker laughed out loud. 'She was all right. Kept me on the straight and narrow, anyhow.'

'For which we must all be thankful, I'm sure,' said Ingolby, moving on to examine the next window. 'This one,' he said after a minute. 'This is more like Bess.'

Seeker considered the three panels Ingolby was standing in front of. Yes, that was more like Bess Pullan. 'Corporal Acts of Mercy,' he said. 'Feed the hungry; give drink to the thirsty; welcome the stranger; clothe the naked; visit the sick; relieve the prisoner.'

'That's only six,' said Ingolby. 'Shouldn't there be seven?'

'Aye,' said Seeker. 'Bury the dead.'

Ingolby snorted in derision. 'Abel Sharrock again. But Bess didn't need a window to tell her to do those things.'

'No,' acknowledged Seeker, remembering the old woman's wary welcome and insistent hospitality, 'she didn't. So what was she doing here? If all she'd wanted had been to pray, there are churches a lot nearer Trinity Lane than this.'

Ingolby shook his head. 'Bess didn't come here to pray. Says you don't need a church to pray in. The world's God's church.'

There was nothing to be learned here. 'Come on,' Seeker said, indicating it was time for them to leave. He'd given enough time already to the wanderings of a dying old woman. And the ornate church, with its memorials to human vanities, its obsession with death, was closing in on him. He felt himself watched, felt the hair prickle on his arms and the back of his neck in a way that owed little to the cold, stone-flagged building.

They'd reached the bottom of the nave and were headed for the door when a black-clad figure appeared from a small vestry. Ingolby merely inclined his head to the man and carried on walking, but Seeker stopped. 'Are you rector here?'

The man nodded. 'Can I help you, Captain?'

'Maybe,' said Seeker. 'A woman called Bess Pullan came here one day, a few weeks back. Upright, dark-featured woman, gaunt, though. Seventy or so. Came from the North Riding. Do you remember her?'

The man took a moment to think. 'Mistress Pullan. Yes, I remember her.'

'Had she been here before?' asked Seeker.

'No,' said the rector, 'not that I knew of.'

'What was she doing here?'

'I cannot tell you. She didn't say.'

Seeker studied to mask his frustration. 'I didn't ask what she said she was doing. I asked what she was doing when you saw her.'

The rector shrugged. 'Looking about her. I thought she had perhaps come to see the windows. She asked about what good works we do here.'

'And what did you tell her?'

The rector waved a hand towards the Corporal Acts of Mercy window. 'We take that as our guide.'

'And what did she do then?'

The rector coloured a little and Seeker's mind cleared. 'She gave you money.'

The rector coughed. 'A goodly woman.'

'How much?' said Seeker.

Another cough, but Lawrence Ingolby had come to join them, a new interest on his face. He leaned a little towards the man, but spoke to Seeker. 'I'll tell you how much. About five pounds, give or take, is that right?'

Seeker looked at him.

'Bess had taken a little more than that for purchases she planned to make when she was here – clothing, some new furnishings. She didn't bring much back, but the money was gone all the same.'

The rector was a little on the defensive now. 'I didn't ask for it, but she was most insistent. For the care of the sick in body and mind, she said. A goodly woman.'

Seeker looked around him. 'This is no hospital.'

'We give succour in the parish. Where it is needed.'

'In this parish.' Seeker turned towards Ingolby. 'Where did the Sorsbys live?'

'Gwendolen's family? Over near King's Staithe. Fine old house. All went to the creditors when Gwendolen's uncle drowned.'

'So nowhere near here.' He turned back to the rector. 'Did you know the Sorsby family?'

This time the man didn't hesitate. 'No, I didn't. I've only been here five years. I believe that family had flourished and withered before I ever arrived.'

'Hmm, no more to be had here then.' Seeker continued towards the door and then stopped one more time. The sensation of being watched was almost overwhelming. He looked around him. Looked upwards. 'That,' he said at last, pointing to a hole at the southern end of the west wall. 'What's that?'

'That?' the rector broke into a smile. 'That's the squint. Emma Raughton's squint.'

'Who's Emma Raughton?' asked Ingolby as Seeker gave a disparaging grunt.

'Madwoman,' said Seeker before the rector had a chance to reply. He knew the legend. 'Said she'd seen the Virgin Mary, who came and told her things. Mad and dead two hundred years since.'

The rector bristled a little and stood straighter. 'Emma Raughton prophesied the death of King Henry V in France, and that the Earl of Warwick would serve as Protector for the young King.'

Seeker was dismissive. 'That'd be the same Earl of Warwick who was a regular visitor to her here? Handy for him.' As the rector struggled for a reply, Seeker pointed up to the squint. 'She lived up there then, Emma Raughton?'

The rector's cheeks were now blazing. 'Her old anchorhold's still there. A ramshackle wooden structure out the back, up wooden stairs on the outside. She was able to live there and see the mass through the squint without being pestered and ogled at.'

'And do you have some demented prophetess up there now?' asked Seeker.

The rector was visibly shaking now. 'No,' he said. 'We do not.'

'Oh?' said Seeker. 'Then who's that been watching me since I first set foot in here?' He turned and strode outside, Ingolby and the rector hurrying in his wake. The anchorhold was ramshackle indeed, and the wooden steps little more than a ladder that looked like it would barely hold Seeker's weight. He had nonetheless set a foot on the bottom rung when a man suddenly rushed past him from behind the back of the structure and bolted up the side of the church towards North Street. Seeker immediately gave chase, barging past Lawrence Ingolby and almost knocking over the churchman as he did so. He had a fistful of the man's coat collar and had him slammed up against the wall of the church by the time Ingolby caught up.

One hand pressed hard against the scrawny fellow's chest was enough to keep him in place. Whoever else he might be, this man was not Caleb Turner. 'Why are you following me?' Seeker demanded.

The man was so terrified he could not make any sound that was comprehensible. It was only when his desperately roving eyes found Ingolby that he managed to gather himself. He raised a shaking hand and pointed towards Edward Faithly's secretary. 'Him,' he managed to say at last. 'I was following him.'

'Me?' said Ingolby in perplexed outrage. 'Why would such a rag of a man be following me?'

Seeker relaxed the pressure on the fellow a moment to allow the man to answer, but just at that very moment the sound of a gun cracked somewhere not much distant, and the whistle of the ball was hardly in his ears before he felt it graze his jaw on its way into the wall in front of him. Instinctively, he spun round, relinquishing his hold on his captive as he did so. Ingolby, who had sworn profusely, had now recovered his wits sufficiently to run in the direction the gunshot had come from, and Seeker was quickly after him. They hared up North Street, towards the Ouse Bridge, men and women going about their daily business hastening out of their way. Halfway towards the bridge, Seeker directed Ingolby to make for the riverside whilst he himself started up the alleyways and lanes towards Micklegate. Long before he reached the bar, he knew it was hopeless. The man, if a man it had been, for neither of them had seen the shooter, had melted into the city or got out already through the gate. Seeker left instructions with the guards at Micklegate Bar nonetheless, refused attention to his bloodied jaw and ran back down to North Street and All Saints church. Ingolby, bent double and out of breath, was already there. The man who had been following him was nowhere to be seen.

Seeker stormed towards the rector, who was now standing outside the door of his church. 'You didn't get him?'

The rector was trembling. 'The man you had hold of?'

'You went after him?'

The rector nodded. 'Down Tanner Row, but I couldn't chase him beyond that. By the time I got to the end, he was gone.'

Seeker looked him up and down. He was a poor enough specimen, and many wouldn't even have bothered to give chase.

'All right,' he said. 'Did you know him?'

'No. Never saw him here before.'

'Nor anywhere else?'

'Nowhere.'

Seeker let out a deep sigh and looked very close in the rector's face. 'If you see him again, you send word to me at King's Manor, understand?'

The rector nodded vigorously and Seeker went to join Ingolby, who was now sitting on the ground, his back against the church wall, examining the squashed lump of lead he had just removed from it with his knife.

He held it up for Seeker to see. 'Mine or yours, do you think? Of course, could have been meant for that fellow who was trailing me.'

Seeker took the ball and shook his head. 'This was meant for me.'

Ingolby squinted up at him. 'How can you be so sure?'

'Somebody left me a note,' Seeker growled. He was convinced now that it had been Caleb Turner outside his window at King's Manor last night, and he that had left the scratched warning on the old burial cist. The trier had been toying with him, determined to show that he was cleverer than Seeker. Cunning and cowardice were two sides to the same coin for Caleb Turner. 'Come on. I need to get this nick seen to before it gets infected, and you've got some explaining to do.'

'Me?' Ingolby protested.

'Yes, you. Now move it.'

FOURTEEN

The Walls of York

Seeker deposited Lawrence Ingolby in the guardroom at Walmgate Bar and instructed him to stay there until he got back. To Ingolby's protests, Seeker gave a curt, 'Do as I say: it's for your own good.'

The wound on his jaw still stung from its dousing in vinegar, but at least it was clean and the apothecary on Fossgate had assured Seeker the poultice he had put on it would staunch the blood and hasten healing. A message from Lilburne had been waiting for him when he'd arrived at Walmgate, with orders to report before nightfall to the major-general. The grey was deepening, but Seeker reckoned he had an hour yet before he would have to be at the castle.

He headed for Stonegate, and the Old Star inn. Lawrence had been uncharacteristically quiet on their way from All Saints church to Walmgate Bar. As they were climbing the stone steps to the guardhouse of the bar itself, he suddenly turned to Seeker and said, 'I've seen him before somewhere.' He screwed up his eyes. 'Long time ago, but I know him from somewhere.'

'Who?' said Seeker.

'The man who ran from the church,' said Ingolby.

Eventually, Seeker had told him. 'He was at the Old Star inn.'

'What? When?'

'Last night. By the hatch. Watching us. Watching you.'

'And you saw him?' Ingolby had been outraged. 'Why didn't you question him there and then? He might have wanted to kill me, or anything!'

'Might have done,' Seeker had answered casually, 'but I thought at the time it was me he was after and I wanted to wait till he'd shown his hand and I'd found out what he was up to.'

'Well, he's shown his hand now, hasn't he?' said Ingolby, still indignant.

The soldiers in the barrack room of Walmgate Bar regarded Lawrence with open suspicion.

'You'll be one of his agents, I suppose?' said one. 'Come up from London?'

'Agents? London? Do I sound like I'm from London?'

'Could be from anywhere, the way they train them up.'

Ingolby looked from one to the other of them as if they were slightly deranged. 'I have no idea what you're talking about.'

The younger of the two soldiers leaned towards him, his voice very quiet. 'The captain. He runs spies in London.

Not a rat slithers up a drain there but he knows where it comes out.'

'Pity he didn't know the doings of Yorkshire rats better,' muttered Ingolby. His voice took on a hint of derision. 'Anyhow, Seeker running spies? The size of him alone – that's not a man that blends into the shadows.'

'Huh,' grunted the older man. 'By the time Seeker's on the scene his spies have come and gone and your luck's well and truly out.' He considered a moment and then qualified his assertion. 'If it's you he's after, at any rate.' He looked at Ingolby with renewed interest. 'So, what you done?'

'Me?' protested Ingolby. 'Nothing. Just had the misfortune not to get out of the way quick enough when he crossed my path.'

'Aye, that'll do it,' said the older man, before leaning closer to him. The stench of stale tobacco and sour cheese when he spoke made Ingolby recoil. 'But know this, if you have got anything to hide, he will find you out.'

Lawrence was glad when it came time for the Walmgate guards to change their watch. The two just in off the walls were too concerned with getting warm and something in their bellies to pay him much heed. When they did at last turn their attention to him he simply mumbled that he was 'Seeker's man', and, as he had hoped, they left him alone after that.

At the Old Star, Seeker learned a little more about Ingolby's pursuer, but what he learned served only to muddy the waters further, not clear them. The innkeeper knew straight away who he was talking about.

'I remember him all right. Scrawny fellow. Thought he was foreign at first, way he was dressed. Hung around like a stale fart till they carried you out, then tried to get over to the young fellow you were talking to. He was out to bother him, that was plain enough, so I got my boy Dick to tell him to sling his hook. Hanging about, watching young men. I know his sort. I don't allow none of that filth here, Captain.'

More's the pity, thought Seeker. At least then they would have known what he wanted of Ingolby. 'Did he protest?'

A broad smile spread over the innkeeper's face. 'My Dick's a big fella, Captain, just like yourself. Not many'll chance their hand with him. Mind you, he did say something to him.' He opened a hatch through to the kitchens. 'What did he want, Dick, that bundle of rags I got you to throw out last night?'

A large, good-natured face appeared through the hatch, its owner stooping to see through. 'Wanted me to ask the Ingolby fellow about a girl.'

'What girl?' asked Seeker.

'Gwendolen something. Wanted to know if she was dead.'

Lawrence's face went chalk white. 'I swear it, Seeker, he never asked me. The only person in that inn who even mentioned Gwendolen's name to me was you.' Ingolby was visibly shaken. 'I'll have to go back there, though. My pack's there.'

Seeker slung a brown leather satchel and a package that felt like books onto the table. 'No, it's not. Check everything's there before I get back.'

'Back?' Ingolby lifted worried eyes to him. 'Where are you going now?'

Seeker stopped in his tracks. It must have been a good few years since anyone who wasn't on first name terms with Cromwell had even thought of asking him that question. 'To get on with my business,' he said, before going out the guardhouse door and leaving it to bang shut behind him.

Lilburne was already at his supper in his private quarters in the castle. He called for more food to be brought and ordered Seeker to sit down and eat with him. After he'd poured wine into both their goblets he looked at Seeker, chewing slowly.

'Well, Captain. You didn't get that scrape to your jaw keeping to your bed in King's Manor as the physician ordered you to do.'

'Too much to do.'

'Perhaps, but not many folk get shot at in their beds, Seeker. You should have done as I ordered and stayed there.'

'I'm sorry, sir.'

Lilburne grunted and resumed eating. 'So, same fellow that clonked you over the head yesterday, do you think?'

Clearly, a report of the incident outside All Saints church had already reached the major-general's ears. Seeker wondered if word of his recall to London by Thurloe had also come to Lilburne, if that was why he'd been called here. It didn't matter.

'I'm certain of it, sir.'

'You think it was the trier, Caleb Turner? That's the name the men that carried you from the Old Star heard you murmur.'

Seeker felt himself flush and Lilburne continued. 'And all because of the feud over your wife?'

'There's no feud over my wife – I'm done with her. My concern's for my daughter.'

Lilburne pushed away a plate of picked chicken bones and looked at Seeker directly. 'Aye, I'll warrant it is. Of your daughter, though, I have no information, but Turner – that's another thing.'

Seeker waited whilst the major-general chose his words with care.

'As to Turner being your assailant – that may be a possibility if all you've said of the man is true.' Lilburne wiped his mouth and called for his adjutant. 'Bring me the report that arrived today from the commissioner at Faithly. Give it to the captain here.'

In less than a minute Seeker was holding a letter in Matthew Pullan's now-familiar hand. He put down the chop he'd been working on and read it through. 'Aye,' he said eventually, 'I'd heard Turner had cleared out of Faithly.'

Lilburne cocked his head to one side and appraised him

carefully. 'How?' he said eventually. 'I've not long heard myself.'

'Sir Edward Faithly's secretary's in York. He told me.'

Lilburne breathed out heavily through his nose. 'Then why didn't Pullan send me the news by him?'

Seeker shrugged. 'Maybe he's in no great hurry to get the trier back.'

'Hmm. Well, whatever Pullan's reasoning, we can't leave the fellow roaming at will across Yorkshire, that's for sure. He'll have to be found and taken in, put straight or shut up. It's one thing for a trier to be laid out by one of my soldiers, another entirely for him to be seen to publicly abandon his wife and his duties whilst running up unpaid bills. The triers should be one of our chief weapons in the reform of this nation. We need the people on our side, and Turner's behaviour puts that at risk.'

Seeker drained the wine from his goblet. 'Might I speak, sir?'

'Speak away, Captain.'

Seeker glanced over to the adjutant who had remained by the door, awaiting further orders.

'Leave us,' Lilburne said.

When the young man had shut the door behind him, Lilburne sat back in his chair. 'Go on then, Captain,' he said.

Seeker knew this was his chance to get back to the North Riding to search for his daughter. 'I had a letter yesterday,' he began, 'from Secretary Thurloe, recalling me to London.'

Lilburne opened his mouth, ready to say something, but

Seeker pressed on. 'I'd like your permission, sir, to delay my return south until after this matter of Caleb Turner has been dealt with. I want your permission to go after him.'

Lilburne sat back, a look of mild surprise on his face. 'That's a turn-up. Thurloe wrote to me too, and I called you here to tell you I was denying permission for you to return to the south yet. I know you've been waiting on it a while, thought you'd want to be straight off. But I want Turner apprehended, and if anyone has the know-how and the will to do it, it's you. So yes, Captain, you have my permission to go against Mr Thurloe's orders. I've already written to tell him so. You find this trier, and you bring him before me. This is a godly enterprise we are embarked upon, and Caleb Turner is besmirching its name.'

Turner had been in York – last night and this morning – Seeker knew it. Whether he was still here, or had already slipped out through the gates or away by the river was another question. Either way, Seeker hadn't the time to run around the streets of the city looking for him. On taking his leave of the major-general and giving orders to the men of his troop at the castle, he headed not for Walmgate but up through town to Bootham Bar and King's Manor. The boy Michael was still there, working steadily on the papers for the register of Royalists, and tried one final fruitless attempt to make Seeker take more of the treatments left by the apothecary the previous evening.

'Not tonight, lad. Need a clear head tonight. Now, put

that muck away and fetch your pen and inkpot through here.' But as Michael was doing as he was bid, a thought struck Seeker. 'That apothecary – he's no mountebank, no charlatan?'

Michael's eyes went wide. 'No, Captain. He's the best in York – Lord Fairfax himself uses him.'

'All right.' Seeker nodded. 'Well, when we're finished here, I want you to take him this.' He took Michael's pen and ink and scrawled a note in his own hand. The boy, curious, looked over his shoulder.

'What's "snakeroot", Captain?'

'That's what I want to find out,' said Seeker, straightening and folding the paper. 'As soon as you get his reply, you forward it to me – at Walmgate. They'll have instructions where to send it if I'm not there. Understand?'

Michael nodded, and took charge of the note.

'Now,' continued Seeker, handing Michael his pen and ink and stepping back, 'you write this down.' Seeker gave the boy as detailed a physical description of Caleb Turner as he had given of anyone: slim, yet tautly muscled, a little less than middling height, with somewhat lank, greying hair that had once been a light brown coming just to his shoulders, hard grey narrow-set eyes beneath arched brows, an aquiline nose and a down-turned mouth flanked by deep furrows. A hungry look to him. Should he put that? Aye, for it was a quality that somehow marked Turner from others of a similar description. He then ran through the list of aliases he knew Turner to have used in the past, and had

Michael set those down too. 'You get down to Stonegate now. Tell Roper at the Red Devil I want two hundred of these ready by tomorrow morning.'

'Two hundred?'

'I want them pasted up in every street in York, and I want a pile sent on after me.' Seeker left his chamber, Michael following quickly at his heels into the small office where he did his own work.

'Sent on where? Where are you going?'

Twice in one day he'd been asked that question. He must be slipping. He was about to tell the boy 'Faithly Moor', when he glanced down at the ledger lying open on Michael's desk. The boy went to sit himself down when Seeker motioned him aside to plant his own hands on the edge of the desk and lean over, the better to inspect the ledger. He brought his head up slowly, turning to speak to Michael, his finger hovering over an entry three days old.

'Who,' he began, not troubling to conceal his growing anger, 'who told you to put this name on the list? Was it some prank, some schoolboy foolishness to bait me? Who was it?'

Michael, his face now a mask of terror, bent his head in an effort to see around Seeker to what it was that so offended him.

'But . . . it is simply the register of known Royalists currently resident in York.'

'I know what it is,' said Seeker, his voice dangerously

low. 'What I am asking you is who told you to write that name in it?'

Michael was now shaking. '"Lady Anne Winter". It . . . it just came in with the household return, three days ago, to register the new arrival, in accordance with . . .'

But Seeker wasn't listening; by the time Michael stammered 'new regulations', he was halfway down the steps of King's Manor, taking them two at a time.

He was through Bootham Bar and storming through the gates off Minster Yard within five minutes. One of the guards on the gate had stepped forward to stop him but had been pulled back by his colleague, who had realised who he was. Another guard was at the top of the steps leading to the front door of the Treasurer's House.

'Is he at home?' demanded Seeker.

'Who?' asked the man.

'Lord Fairfax, who else?'

The soldier coughed. 'No, sorry, Captain, but her ladyship is at home.'

Seeker's heart sank. Lady Fairfax was not a person he would choose to deal with, and she had made very plain over a number of years that she had no liking for him either. But there was no choice. 'Well, you'd best tell her I'm here.'

A minute later Seeker was standing in the great hall of the Treasurer's House, residence in York of Lord Thomas Fairfax, former parliamentary general, and of his wife. Regarding him with scarcely disguised amusement were two women he thought had no place being in the one room. One of them was the Lord General's wife, Lady Anne Fairfax, whom Seeker had long suspected of Royalist tendencies. The general was not the first man not to be able to manage his wife, and in households up and down the land, men and women who had pledged themselves to one another before ever there was such a thing in England as Royalist or Parliamentarian, had had to make their choices. The other woman was Seeker's old adversary, Lady Anne Winter; Seeker suspected she had never had a moment's pause for thought in choosing her side, and he knew for a certainty she had never done anything to hide it. Anne Winter was a Royalist through and through.

Seeker was so astonished to see her there he almost forgot to make Lady Fairfax his bow. Lady Winter he did not bother with.

Lady Fairfax stood up. 'Captain, it is no doubt a matter of great importance that has you storming into my house at this late hour, but I must tell you that my husband is away, and in any case, he has made plain to the Lord Protector that he will play no part in this, your new rule of the major-generals.'

Seeker stiffened. 'I would not think to advise his lordship on that or anything else. He has done great service to this nation, and none would begrudge him his retirement to private life. It is on another unfortunate matter that I am here, and I would not trouble your ladyship over it were it not a matter of the security of the state.'

'Then you had best say your piece, Captain Seeker.'

Seeker turned to look at Lady Anne Winter, who was watching him with her head cocked ever so slightly to one side, as if she were a bird encountering an insect she had never before come across.

'This woman, your ladyship,' he said, addressing Lady Fairfax, 'is a convicted traitor, and only in life and at liberty through the clemency of His Highness the Lord Protector.'

Lady Fairfax was about to respond, but it was Lady Winter who spoke first. 'Come now, Seeker. Not so coy. You know my man Richard traded for my life.'

Seeker remembered Anne Winter's Rat, remembered how carelessly the man had given up his life in the Stuart cause, with no concern but that she be spared.

'The Lord Protector is under no obligation to make such trades. For anyone. It was understood, and very clearly explained to you, that you were to remain in Northumberland until such time—'

'Until such time as it pleased His Highness's government I should have my liberty to travel at large.'

'And have you had it?' demanded Seeker.

Anne Winter coloured slightly, but only for a moment. 'Lady Fairfax has known me since we were children. Is it not enough that she vouches for me?'

She thought she had him there. She had clearly forgotten who she was dealing with. 'No,' he said. 'In law, it is not.'

Lady Fairfax again rose from her seat. 'Captain, might I remind you—'

Seeker turned to her. 'You need remind me of nothing,

your ladyship. But you should know, as I think you must know, that this woman, scarcely six months ago, conspired with Royalists abroad in an attempt to bring Charles Stuart back to London. Should she set one foot out of line again, the Lord Protector will not have the option of clemency. I caution you, for the good of your husband's unblemished name, and for your own good, see to it that she does not wander from this house until such time as I can take advice from Mr Thurloe.'

Lady Fairfax had gone as white as he had ever seen her. He doubted that the woman had ever before been spoken to in such a manner. She called for her servant to show him out, but just as he reached the door, Seeker turned and spoke again.

'I have one more question for you, Lady Anne, and I charge you to answer me plainly: do you know, or have you any correspondence, of any nature whatsoever, with or regarding Sir Thomas Faithly?'

Lady Anne Winter's face was a blank, still in shock at how he had spoken to her friend, the wife of one of the most powerful and best-loved men in England. 'No,' she said at last. 'I have never heard of the man.'

By the time Seeker had emerged back out onto Minster Yard, darkness had well and truly fallen over York. The narrow, winding streets and snickelways of the city could be troublesome enough to negotiate in daytime; by lamp-light and darkness they became something other, offering endless shadowy avenues of access or escape for all sorts of miscreants. Caleb Turner might be there, somewhere. It would be best, Seeker thought, if he was still lurking in the city, away from Faithly, from the moors, from Manon.

It would have been quicker to cut across the city and return to Walmgate by the Foss Bridge, but there were one or two things Seeker wanted to settle in his mind before he left York. He climbed the steps at Bootham Bar and went out onto the walls. To his right, the shell of St Mary's Abbey rose beyond King's Manor. Closer was the ruin of St Leonard's hospital. All those graves, forgotten or emptied, which had troubled him the night before, were illuminated tonight by the blue light of an almost full moon in a sky with no clouds. A holy place once, perhaps, but more fit for a witch's sabbath now. Bats flitted through the stone corpses of the ancient buildings and owls hooted in the gnarled black skeletons of trees. At the foot of it all, the Ouse slipped quietly past. He'd have to cross it twice to get back to Walmgate, but that could not be avoided: All Saints was on the other side of the river, and if Turner had made his escape from the city, it was most likely through Micklegate Bar that he'd have done it.

The chains were up across the Ouse between Lendal Tower and Barker Tower on the other bank. There'd be no escape for anyone upriver tonight. The boatman grumbled a little to be disturbed at his supper, but set to his oars quickly enough. Further down the river, where lamplight glistened off the water, murmurs of laughter and catches of song came up from the taverns on King's Staithe. Not so cheerless, yet, this world of the major-generals. Landed by Barker Tower, Seeker ascended the walls again. To his left, lights and life were evident in the cottages of Tanner Row and around Toft Green, and the occasional flickering jewel in the darkness suggested candlelight through the coloured panes of All Saints church. The straggling branches of a tree, black in the night, obscured the flimsy wooden remains of that mad, dead prophetess Emma Raughton's anchorhold. At Micklegate Bar, where no memory of any sighting was prompted by his description of Caleb Turner, Seeker left orders that the anchorhold should be searched at first light. He had done all he could do in York; it was time to turn his attention back to Faithly Moor.

FIFTEEN

Fallen Woman

'Now?' Ingolby had been sleeping when finally Seeker had returned to the guardhouse at Walmgate Bar.

'Right now,' replied Seeker. 'Unless you want to take your chances returning to Faithly on your own. I daresay you can outwit your mysterious shadow without my help.'

Shaking himself awake, Ingolby began to stumble up from his pallet. 'No, wait, I didn't say that.' He screwed up his eyes against the light from Seeker's lantern then looked towards the window over the barbican. 'But it's pitch-black out there.'

'There's moon enough to see by. Your horse is waiting outside. Five minutes.' Seeker gathered what he needed from amongst his belongings, then went below to see to his horse.

Five minutes later, as Lawrence grumbled his way down the bar steps, Seeker urged his horse forward and set off in the direction of the Foss bridge. Ingolby began to shout, and Seeker could still hear his shouts of protest two hundred yards away. He slowed on approaching the bridge and let the furious secretary catch up.

'I told you five minutes,' he said, before turning to set off again.

'But why the hurry?' shouted Ingolby in frustration as he cantered after him.

'Once we're out of York,' called Seeker over his shoulder as he urged Acheron over the bridge.

Monkgate Bar was well behind them, and Heworth Hall in their sights by the time Seeker slowed enough for Ingolby to catch up again.

'Well?' panted Lawrence, once he had sufficiently recovered his breath. 'Why are we set out upon the moors tonight? Why couldn't it wait for morning?'

'Because I have orders to find Caleb Turner, and to bring him before the major-general.'

'And you really think he'll go back to Faithly?'

'Not if he's got any sense,' said Seeker. 'But there's something I need to make sure of, someone I must track down before he has a mind to.'

Ingolby screwed up his face. 'Who? Thomas Faithly?'

'No,' said Seeker. 'It isn't Thomas Faithly.' For all he liked the young secretary, and was even beginning to trust him, Seeker was a long way from telling him of his daughter, Manon, and his determination to find her.

They rested the horses and slept an hour or so at a shepherd's hut outside Old Malton before pressing northwards again, to the moors. Ingolby was clearly still not satisfied by Seeker's answer, and as they took an early breakfast of ale and jannocks at an inn near Thornton-le-Dale, he chanced his luck once more.

'Why are you going back to Faithly?'

'I need to talk to Turner's wife.'

Ingolby gave a shrewd smile. 'You know her, don't you? You knew her before all that business of the trier's court. Something to do with her that you went for him in the first place, isn't it?'

Seeker merely continued with his breakfast, and looked out through the small window of the inn on to the road ahead.

'All right.' Ingolby drained his tankard. 'So, not my business.'

'No,' said Seeker, 'but there are other things at Faithly I don't much like the smell of either.'

'Gwendolen's death?'

'Aye, that's one of them, and that fellow hovering about the Old Star inn and All Saints church wanting to ask you if she was dead doesn't help clear things. But I think there's a chance the girl was an accidental victim of Caleb Turner's desire to put an end to me.'

Ingolby considered. 'Well, aye, given what he had in store for you in York I'd say there was at least a chance he tried to poison you in Faithly, although how he'd have gone about it, I don't know. But Gwendolen's death is only one of the things that's bothering you?'

'Matthew Pullan and Sir Edward Faithly. There's something going on there. Why would a man such as Pullan, a Leveller by conviction if no longer by action, bail out a debased Royalist like Edward Faithly by sending you up there to save his estate for him?'

Ingolby looked away. 'I told you, it'd be bad for everyone in Faithly if the estate went to rack and ruin, and Matthew doesn't want to be lord of the manor.'

'Others with his scruples have gained property, and managed it for the benefit of the people. Matthew Pullan could have done the same. A man who ordered the destruction of windows bearing the images and names of Edward Faithly's ancestors clearly bears no love or reverence for him.'

'That was thirteen years ago,' said Ingolby evenly.

'Perhaps, but there was no warmth between those two at that supper of Bess Pullan's.'

'Matthew didn't try to poison Sir Edward Faithly.'

Seeker was learning one thing about Lawrence Ingolby. Wherever he might have come from, whoever he might be employed by, he was utterly loyal to Matthew Pullan. There would be no point whatsoever in voicing his own thoughts that there might be something between Matthew Pullan and Lady Emma Faithly. He moved on. 'And the Reverend Jenkin.'

'Septimus?' said Ingolby. 'Come on, Seeker, the man takes a drink, has an eye for a pretty woman, might resort to the prayer book now and again when inspiration deserts him, but there's nothing evil in him.'

'There's a bit more required of preachers nowadays than the absence of evil. It's plain to see, trier or no, that Jenkin's one of Laud's leavings that should have been swept away long ago. So why should a shadow Royalist like Edward Faithly want rid of him, and why now?'

'Septimus was always friends with Edward's brother, Thomas. I don't think they ever had much time for Edward, and now he can take his revenge.' Ingolby wiped his mouth and stood up. 'Like I told you: he's a twisted bastard who takes pleasure in the misfortune of others. Now are we leaving, or what?'

Back out on the road, Seeker looked over occasionally at Ingolby as they rode, and wondered about his loyalties, his near abnegation of self for those who had raised him. 'What happened to your mother?' he asked after they'd gone on in silence a good long time.

'Drank herself to death more than ten years since.'

'And your father?'

Ingolby stared straight ahead, spoke almost through gritted teeth. 'Never knew him.'

'Aye, but you must have an idea who he was?'

'Why? Not even sure that she did, and if she did she never told me.'

'No chance it could have been Sir Anthony Faithly?'

Now Lawrence laughed out loud. 'Sir Anthony? Just because he happened across her and me in a cave in his woods? My mother was a drab, Seeker. If she'd had any hold on Sir Anthony, she wouldn't have wandered the country looking for a better offer. At least once I was with the Pullans she didn't trail me around with her. She always came back to Faithly, mind. Until the day she didn't, and we heard she'd been found dead in a ditch on the road to Whitby.'

Seeker wondered about the man who'd been trailing Lawrence in York, but dismissed the idea. Then another came to him. 'Gwendolen Sorsby,' he said.

'What about her?'

'Her father – did you ever see him?'

Lawrence slowed his horse a moment and considered. 'Once,' he said eventually. 'I would have been a young lad, and Gwendolen just a baby, when Digby took me to York the first time. William Sorsby didn't pay me much attention, but I remember him, all the same. He died of a fever in Amsterdam not long after. Gwendolen was his, all right.'

'When exactly did she come to live with the Pullans?'

Lawrence puffed out his lips and did some calculations. 'About fourteen years since? Before the war, at any rate. She was only two or three – lost her mother to the sweating sickness and her grandmother not long after to old age, or a broken heart, if folk can die of such things. God knows what would have happened to her if Bess hadn't taken her in.'

'You never saw any of her family after that then?'

They were riding into a north-easterly wind, and that might have accounted for the moisture in Ingolby's eyes, but

Seeker didn't think so. After a silence, Lawrence said, 'We were her family. Me, and Matthew and Bess and Orpah. We were her family.'

It was mid-morning when they came to Faithly. All was quiet. Quieter than Seeker had seen it before. There was no hubbub at the inn or on the street, little sound or movement but that of men and women going about their daily tasks. The trier's court, the great excitement, was over. But still something struck Seeker as wrong.

'Where's Tansy?' he said as their horses' hooves clattered over the bridge.

'She's maybe with Bess. Sometimes she's not down here till near dinnertime. Not many folk arrive in Faithly this early,' said Ingolby, pointedly. 'When that feckless husband of hers came home from the markets or wherever else he'd gone, it was always well gone dinnertime.'

One or two people appeared in doorways as they passed, hurried inside and brought others out again with them. Up ahead, they saw a young boy being sent running from the smithy, in the direction of the sexton's cottage.

'Huh! Abel Sharrock'll be at Matthew's door before we are,' said Ingolby.

'And I'll be across Sharrock's door before I'm across Pullan's,' replied Seeker. 'Tell the commissioner not to go anywhere – I've business to see to at Sharrock's first.'

By the time Seeker was drawing Acheron up at the churchyard gate, Maud Sharrock and her husband had almost knocked each other over in their rush to get through it. The sight of Seeker dismounting brought them to an abrupt halt. Sharrock, whose hat had been put on in such a hurry that it was squint, puffed out his chest and did his best to project his small authority. Maud, behind him now, did a passing approximation of a woman in terror.

'Captain, I can hardly credit you are at liberty and returned to Faithly. I cannot think the major-general has sanctioned this.'

'Credit what you will, Sharrock. Where's your house guest?'

'Our . . . ?' queried Maud.

'Caleb Turner's wife. I have information she's in residence here.'

Now Maud did push past her husband to stare determinedly up into Seeker's face. 'In residence, indeed, and conducts herself as though a guest, though uninvited and all unpaid for, either!'

'Hush, woman!' scolded Abel. 'Harness your tongue. It's the trier's wife.'

'And is it, though?' Her small eyes became beads of jet, her mouth quivered in satisfaction. 'Then where is the trier? Answer me that if you'd have me continue to fetch and carry after her!'

Seeker didn't wait to hear Abel Sharrock's spluttered reply, but pushed past them, through the gate and along the short path to their cottage.

They had left the door ajar in their haste to get over

to Pullan's, and Seeker pushed it wide. Felicity was there, seated on one of the two flimsy wooden seats set either side of the meagre fire. A pot of some dank and foul-smelling broth simmered over it. He saw her hands grip the sides of her stool when he came in, but her face was a practised study of indifference.

'So, Damian, you've returned.'

'Yes, Felicity, I've returned.'

She looked him up and down. 'The tang and the dirt of the moors are on you, but you're in a better way now than when I last saw you, locked in the cellar of the inn.'

'And you in a worse one,' he said. She flinched at that. He might have added that her face, too, showed a smear of grime from the fire; that the steam from the broth had made her hair lank, and that her good white collar and tucker were not as white any more as they should have been, but he didn't. Neither did he comment on her hands, the fingers already red and coarsening from whatever work Maud was having her do.

'So, Hungerford left you then,' he said eventually.

She raised her chin, tried to assert some sort of position over him, reclaim the place of the Trier's wife. 'Caleb will be back.'

'No, Felicity,' he said, 'I don't think he will. Caleb Turner, Thomas Hungerford, any other of the half-dozen aliases he used over the years. I don't think there's any of them coming back.'

He saw the realisation of the truth dawn on her. Her

voice became very cold. 'What have you done? What have you done to him?'

'Not as much as I'd like to, that's for certain. Not what he tried to do to me, at any rate,' he answered. 'But dead or alive, he's burned his boats in Yorkshire. The major-general in York knows all about him, all about both of you. And he knows the way you left here, not a by-your-leave, bills unpaid. Your Caleb's not daft. He won't be coming back for you – he'd never have left you here if he wasn't done with you.'

'You . . .' She sprang forward, fingers reaching for his face, but he caught her wrists and held her away from him. 'It's done, Felicity. He's not coming back. You will listen to me now.'

He heard the door creak open behind him. It was Maud Sharrock, her mouth open, her eyes all astonishment at what she saw. 'Get out,' he said, in tones she could not fail to pay heed to.

Felicity shot him a look of unadulterated loathing, jerked her wrists free and sat back down in her chair.

'Did you know?'

'Did I know what?' she almost spat.

'That Hungerford was coming after me? That he'd gone to York to kill me?'

'Caleb? Kill you? I think you're deranged, Damian. You could crush him with an arm tied behind your back.'

'Man to man's too much for your Caleb. He came upon me with a club first, and then later a musket, from a distance and on a public street as I was engaged on other business. If he'd had a better aim I wouldn't be standing here.'

A look of shock came briefly into Felicity's eyes, soon to be replaced on what Seeker had once thought her pretty face by contempt. 'Do you think if I'd known I'd have let him leave me here, in this?' She surveyed the small sexton's cottage with disgust.

'I don't know,' Seeker replied. 'Maud keeps a pretty clean house from what I can see. He could have left you to a lot worse.'

'Could he?' she said sullenly.

So, there was no doubt: Hungerford had abandoned her. 'And the poisoning? The mushrooms at the supper – was that your work or his?'

She looked at him as if he was talking in a new tongue. 'What mushrooms? What supper? I could not tell you whether the slop dished out in that inn contained mush-rooms or not, and certainly Mistress Sharrock has no interest in such delicacies. Beans and kale and rancid mutton fat are all the diet here.'

'The mushrooms at Bess Pullan's supper that killed that young girl. Was that your doing, Felicity? You know your way about the woods well enough.'

'I had to – what might we have lived off if I had not learned to forage?'

'Our larder was never bare.'

'Rabbit, roots, pigeon, fish. You never knew a sauce or a seasoning until you met me.'

Seeker felt the tension rise in him. It was becoming a conversation about something else. She had always known how to do this. He went closer to her, and bent down so that his face was near to hers. 'I'm not your husband now. I'm a captain in Major-General Lilburne's militia, and you will answer my questions or you will face the consequences.' He stood up, addressed her as he would any other he was interrogating. 'Did you, or your husband, the man calling himself Caleb Turner, have poisoned mushrooms put amongst the food at Bess Pullan's supper on the night before the opening of the trier's court, with the intention of killing me?'

Felicity had gone white, but now some of her impatience returned. 'No,' she said, 'of course we didn't! We didn't even know you were to be there until that ridiculous woman came bustling in, bursting with the news. The last place either of us would have gone near that day or night was Matthew Pullan's house. Caleb had more than half a mind to leave there and then, but he had not yet been paid, and the word was you'd not come about the trier's court anyway. I persuaded him to stay, to take the chance you'd never come near us. When you didn't make an appearance at the first day's sitting, we thought all would be well.'

Seeker could picture the desperate exchanges between them: the cowardly Hungerford wanting to run, calculating Felicity urging him to stay. The image gave him no satisfaction.

'I wouldn't expect you to do it yourself, Felicity. You'd have had someone else do it for you.'

'What? Who? How?'

He didn't know. Anyone, he might have said. Felicity might have persuaded anyone to do anything.

'Has it not entered your head that half the village might have wanted you dead? I doubt Caleb and I were the only ones not happy to hear you'd ridden into Faithly.'

'Aye, well, if there were others none of them followed me to York.'

She had no answer to this, her mind busy calculating as she poked at the paltry fire, to little effect. Her mouth tightened. 'And what is to become of me now, Damian?'

She had no concern now whether Hungerford was alive or dead. Seeker only wasted a moment in wondering whether to feel sorry for the man. 'That depends,' he said.

'Depends on what?'

'On how soon you tell me where you have left Manon.'

He saw a smile begin to creep onto her face, a look of triumph appear in her eyes. 'Manon is where we left her.'

He summoned all the patience he could. 'And where's that, Felicity?'

She looked interested. 'Why do you want to know, Damian? Do you want us to be a family again?'

'I'm her father.'

'And I her mother.' Her features shifted, softened. 'You could take us back to London with you. No one need ever know about Caleb.'

He laughed. 'I would know about Caleb, Felicity. Besides, I don't want you. It took me long enough, but I realised it eventually, and that's not something that's going to change. You won't be coming back to London with me.'

The hope, the gleam of calculation in her eyes went out, like a snuffed candle, to be replaced by anger. 'And so what is to become of me? Am I to be left in this hovel with that harridan shrieking at me, and her husband slobbering every time she turns her back?'

Again Seeker laughed, but the humour was real this time. 'Oh, that would be tempting, to see you here scrapping it out with Maud over Abel's favours. You'd make a good hypocrite of our upright Puritan constable, I'm sure.'

She shook her head. 'I will not stay here.'

'It's of no concern to me where you are, Felicity, once you've told me where my daughter is.'

'And if I told you she was dead?'

It felt like the air itself had stopped, the slender flames in the hearth frozen where they were. He looked at her for a moment, then said, 'I wouldn't believe you.'

'Why?'

Why? Because he still heard her cradle swing in the night breeze, still felt her soft curls against his cheek, the child he had last seen over eleven years ago who, in a few years more, would be a young woman. 'Because you would have told me if it had been so. It was the last interest I had in you, and if she had been dead, you would have told me, to free yourself from me. Where is she, Felicity?'

'Consider again, Damian: the last interest you had in me, or the last hold I have on you?'

He shook his head. 'Do not try me, Felicity, or I'll have you thrown in a hole that'll make this place look like a palace, and I'll leave you there to contemplate your poor choices the rest of your days.'

But Felicity just smiled, untroubled by his threat. 'That'd get you no nearer to Manon, would it? Both of us or neither, Damian. That's your choice.'

He felt nausea rise in his stomach. His head thumped through lack of sleep, and the wound on his jaw was sore and seeping again, opened by his hard ride. It needed cleaning. He had to be on the alert, and with a clear head, to deal with Felicity, and he was running out of the reserves to do so. He went to the door and bellowed for Maud Sharrock, who, as he had suspected, was loitering just outside.

'Fetch your husband. Now!' Maud almost jumped out of her skin, and hurried off towards the Pullans' house.

Less than two minutes later, Abel Sharrock came marching along the path, Matthew Pullan having thrown him out of his house.

'What's ado? What's ado?' he panted. 'Terrorising honest Christian women!'

'Here?' said Seeker in disgust, looking from Maud to Felicity. 'I see none here. But as for this trollop, you will keep her under lock and key in this house until I return from Commissioner Pullan's. She is not to leave this room, and no one is to be admitted to see her. Do you understand me?'

Abel had been rendered momentarily speechless by Seeker's outburst, but Maud had not. Her small eyes gleamed in vindication. 'Have no fears, Captain. The trier's hussy will rue the day she ever looked down her nose at Maud Sharrock.'

Tansy was troubled. She had thought the soldier well gone, and good riddance to him, though she wished him no ill. Now here he was back, and riding in off the moor with Lawrence Ingolby. That could not be a good thing, and whilst she thought the return of Lawrence would do something to restore Bess, the sight of the soldier surely would not. She would think more on it later, what she might do to help Bess, but it was time now to go down to the bridge over the beck and wait for Seth. He would not be pleased to come home and find her not waiting there for him. He liked her to be there, that they might walk through the village together, and the other men see what a fine and loving wife he had. He always said it. It would be today. He would be back today: she was certain of it. She wished she had a looking glass. She would ask Bess if she might have Gwendolen's.

As she stepped from her cottage, she glanced over, as she did each day, anxious, to see whether Maud or Abel were watching for her. She was certain they went in and searched her home when she was not there, and she was always careful not to leave anything about that they might take as signs. Bess had wondered once, aloud and in Maud's presence, how it was that Maud could be so well informed as to the wherewithal of witches. Abel would have had anyone else up in the stocks for that, but it was Bess, and so he could do nothing, and Maud had been a deal more quiet with her accusations after that. But Bess was fading with every day that dawned, and Tansy would have to have an extra care to give Abel no cause to take an interest in her.

It wasn't Abel, though, but the soldier who was coming out of the churchyard gate and looking towards her. He winced as he moved, and his face was the colour of limestone. He glanced at her. There was no threat in the look he gave her, but a plea for help. She nodded and went over to him. 'Gwendolen's workshop,' she said. 'We'll put you right there.'

Once in Pullan's yard she called for Orpah, and the two women soon had him on a stool against the corner of the workshop. Tansy carefully lifted the poultice and examined the wound. She pursed her lips and shook her head, muttering, 'Bad work, bad work,' as she gently removed the stinking linen. She continued to shake her head and mutter as she looked at the hastily stitched wound. She told Orpah which balms to use to begin cleaning it with, and cautioned her to be careful, then hurried back to her own hut. Her small box of bone needles and waxed thread were concealed in a recess in the wall. She had heard tales of women made to swim or burn for that figures with needles sticking from them had been found amongst their belongings. Tansy was careful, though. She wouldn't even use a bobbin for fear it was taken for a human likeness.

Perhaps she should not have left the soldier there alone, in Gwendolen's workshop, but Orpah would keep an eye on him, and a soldier would hardly recognise the half of what was on those shelves anyway, or know what it was for. Only the amulet, maybe. But Tansy had emptied Gwendolen's amulet days since.

There was still no sign of Abel and Maud when she left her hut again, but she could hear the sound of raised voices from the sexton's cottage. The trier's wife, but Tansy had seen what Abel and Maud had not. She had seen the Reverend Jenkin cross the churchyard to the sexton's cottage, a place she had never before seen him enter, when Abel and Maud were not there. He had done it several times, and stayed longer each time. And she had heard the trier's wife sing old ballads, as she hung out Maud's laundry, and cast long glances towards the church. The trier's wife and the Sharrocks: Tansy doubted that sleek cat would be amongst those fat pigeons much longer.

Back in the workshop, she checked on what Orpah had done, and set to work on repairing the stitches. She'd handed the soldier a linen bandage to bite down on, but he refused it, and sat with gritted teeth and his eyes tight closed as she first removed the old stitches then began to put in new ones. The whites of his knuckles as he gripped the edge of the shelf beside him told her all she needed to know of his pain. Tansy worked quickly, but with great care. As she was tying up the last stitch, he let out a breath of relief and thanked her.

She merely nodded, and carried on tidying as he swallowed down the measure of brandy she had sent Orpah to the house for.

When he had finished, he stood and took a while to look around the workshop. He examined the still and Gwendolen's instruments with some interest, and then moved on to her cabinet. Tansy cursed herself that she had not locked it as soon as she'd taken from it what she'd needed for his treatment. He picked up bottles and jars, unscrewed lids, sniffed liquids and ointments. He closed the cabinet and slid open the drawer beneath. Tansy's heart was in her mouth as he drew from it a small, plain book. He turned its pages and then held it out towards her. 'What is this?'

'Gwendolen's,' said Tansy.

'What do these lists mean?'

Tansy shook her head. 'Tansy can't read.'

And then he read it out to her: feverfew, dittany, evening primrose, hemp, St John's wort, peony, borage, balm, melancholy thistle, briony.

'What are these for?' he asked again. 'There are dosages and dates, all over the last year. What was she doing with these?'

Tansy twisted a bandage in her hand. 'Women's troubles. Just for women's troubles.'

He looked at her, a cold look, and Tansy could see he

didn't believe her. 'And snakeroot,' he said, 'why did Gwendolen want snakeroot?'

Tansy turned away. 'I don't know. Tansy doesn't know.'

She heard him close the drawer but he was still holding the book when he walked to the door. He stopped there and spoke again.

'How do you manage?' he asked. 'On your own, how do you manage?'

'Kindnesses,' she said. 'Bess.'

'Since your husband left?'

People had said it to her before, but she knew it wasn't true. 'He didn't leave. I've got to wait for him.'

She could see the soldier thinking then. 'How long have you been waiting?'

She turned away. The trees in Bess's orchard had given fruit fourteen times since the day Seth had gone off to market with Digby Pullan. 'Fourteen,' she said. 'Fourteen winters.'

He said nothing in response, just nodded towards his leather bag. 'In there,' he said. 'My money pouch.'

She shook her head. 'Kindnesses,' she repeated. 'Tansy lives on kindnesses.'

SIXTEEN

Old Wounds

Matthew Pullan didn't mince his words. 'So why are you back?'

'Unfinished business,' said Seeker.

'The trier's gone,' said Pullan.

'Aye, well, it's not the trier my business is with, and anyhow, there's more wrong in Faithly than has to do with Caleb Turner.'

'Oh?'

'Sir Thomas Faithly.'

'There hasn't been sight nor sound of him,' said Pullan. 'Besides, he'd have nothing to gain by coming back here.'

'Perhaps,' said Seeker. 'And then there's the matter of your foster sister.'

Pullan became wary. 'Gwendolen?'

'Aye. I'm not certain it was her that those mushrooms were meant for.'

Pullan's brow furrowed. 'Meant for? But surely it was an accident. Gwendolen gathered the mushrooms herself. She mistook the destroying angel for the common meadow mushroom. She was always out foraging about those woods.'

'Which is why she would never have made that mistake. Someone at your mother's table was supposed to die that night, but I'm not sure it was your sister.'

The colour was draining from Matthew Pullan's face. He sat down slowly behind his desk. Took a moment to try to make sense of what Seeker was telling him, then held up his hands in frustration. 'If not Gwendolen, then who?'

Seeker chose his words carefully. The list of medicines and dosages he had found in Gwendolen's workshop had put a new suspicion in his head. 'I don't know. I have begun to wonder if your sister herself might even have been behind it.'

Pullan reacted with scorn. 'Gwendolen? Poison somebody?' He shook his head. 'I have business to get on with, Seeker – I have no time for listening to your fancies.'

'They are not fancies,' said Seeker. 'There are things going on in this place that make little sense, and it may be that one of them has cost your sister her life.'

Pullan's voice was hoarse. 'What things?' he said.

'Like the fact that it was Edward Faithly and not Abel Sharrock who called the trier to this village, to make trial of the fitness of Septimus Jenkin to be vicar and schoolmaster here.'

He could see that this revelation surprised Matthew Pullan, but only for a moment. A process was going on behind Pullan's eyes of making sense of this information, and this process did not take long.

'So,' continued Seeker, 'why would he have done that?'

Pullan walked from his desk to the window. 'I cannot answer for the workings of Edward Faithly's mind.'

'Perhaps not. But you can tell me about the windows in Faithly church.'

'The windows? What of them?' asked Matthew, his expression revealing no comprehension this time of where Seeker's thoughts were tended.

'You destroyed them, every one of them, before you went off to join the parliamentary army in '42.'

'That's old news. Besides,' his eyes slid towards the door, that was closed, and back to Seeker, 'you've known for years I was a Leveller.'

'No one was a Leveller in '42.'

'Maybe not, but plenty were church-breakers, even then. You must know that. I don't deny that I was one of them, and I'm not sorry for it. Those windows were a testament to idolatry, not fit for a place made for the worship of God.'

'Perhaps,' said Seeker. 'But they were also testament to Edward Faithly's family's standing hereabouts.'

'And?' In the defiant turn of Pullan's jaw, the slight curl of contempt to his lip, Seeker saw the young radical he must have been, setting off to war with no doubt in his cause.

'You're no fool, Pullan, and I doubt you ever were. You must have grown up knowing what those windows meant — a testament to the Faithlys' patronage, their position, their control over the lives and even the souls of the people of this village for generations.'

Pullan was untroubled. 'And you think Edward took it into his head thirteen years later to feed me poisoned mushrooms over the heads of some broken windows?'

'Lawrence Ingolby told me Edward Faithly is a man who enjoys revenge, and many have taken longer than thirteen years to exact theirs.'

'But not Edward Faithly, Seeker. He took nothing like it. And if you think he wants me dead, you couldn't be more wrong. For Sir Edward to enjoy his revenge – and I can assure you he does – it is very necessary that I should live, and see it every day.'

Seeker thought again of the crippled knight whom Matthew Pullan was forced to have to his dinner table, of the manor house that man lived in, that Pullan could have bought and sold and the Faithly estate along with it. And finally, he thought of the woman Sir Edward shared it with. He remembered the look that had come over her face on the night of Bess's supper, whenever Matthew Pullan had spoken.

'How long have Sir Edward and Lady Emma been married?'

Matthew Pullan didn't need to take any time to work it out. 'It'll be fourteen years come March,' he answered flatly.

Just after Matthew Pullan had ridden off to join Parliament's forces. Seeker saw it at last. Emma Faithly was her husband's revenge. Matthew loved her. He was slumped now in the chair behind his desk.

'It's not Faithly's estate you sent Lawrence Ingolby to keep an eye on, is it?' said Seeker. 'It's to protect his wife.'

Pullan took a deep breath and nodded. 'Aye, and I'll tell you this. If you ever find that someone has murdered Edward Faithly, don't waste your time travelling the country, asking questions. It'll have been me.'

Bess was waiting. Orpah had told her the captain wanted to speak to her. No surprise there: Lawrence had had her well warned. Lawrence, that everyone thought so cocksure. They were wrong. Like a startled doe he still was, like that first day Digby had gone over to that schoolroom and fetched him back. Lawrence, skin and bones and half-stitched-together rags under the grime, wondering what it was all about. And here he was, so many years later, still the same, cleaned up and grown up, though not filled out much, if she was being honest, standing before her in that good brown woollen suit she'd had made for him, still wondering what it was all about. He'd wanted to ask her, she could see that, but he hadn't had the words, or if he had, hadn't had the courage to use them, because he loved her.

'Get on back up to the manor, lad,' she'd said at last. 'I'll be fine: nothing the captain can do to me.'

Once she'd got Lawrence gone, she'd waved away Orpah's suggestion that she should meet the captain in her bed-chamber. 'No good you getting up and getting cold in your bones, mistress. And I'd stay the whole time. So's there'd be no talk.'

Bess had laughed at that, a laugh that took the breath and half the strength out of her. 'Talk! Oh, Orpah, my girl, who shall look after you when I'm gone, eh?'

The fool girl had had tears in her eyes at that. Bess had already told Matthew, though. 'You keep her on when I'm gone, and you get that dim-witted lad at the smithy to marry her. No more sense than she has, but he's got a kind heart.'

It took a while, all the same, getting up out of bed and getting dressed. She'd insisted, too, on her black woollen gown and her weekday bib and tucker and her second-best cuffs. The gown hung loose at her back, even after the hooks were tied. Bones, she thought. All I am now. She had to take Orpah's arm, though – there would be no getting through to the kitchen without it.

'But the fire's on in the parlour, mistress. Captain's waiting there. Master told me to make sure you went in there if you got up, on the settle, comfy and warm.'

Bess snorted. 'Near fifty years ago I came into this house Digby Pullan's bride, and even his son won't tell me I can't conduct my business in my own kitchen. The captain'll see me there or he'll not see me at all. And you bring me some turnips for peeling.' She nodded to herself, pleased to have thought of it. 'The Devil makes work for idle hands.'

'But the master said . . .' implored the girl, with real tears in her eye now.

'You never mind what the master said. It's me you've to

answer to, Orpah Bigley, or you'll be back at your mother's before suppertime, and never a character from me.'

'Yes, Mistress Bess,' the girl sniffed, as she lowered Bess gently into the cushioned carver chair she'd set at the end of the long kitchen table. She was still trying not to sob as she fetched a bowl of turnip roots and a knife for Bess to do the peeling. She dropped them clumsily on the table and hurried off in the direction of the parlour to fetch the captain through, as Bess had told her to. Bess regretted for the hundredth time that she was forced to be so harsh with the girl.

When Seeker came through, Bess told Orpah to leave them. After the girl had closed the door to the yard behind her, Seeker tilted his head. 'She's still upset about your ward, then?'

'And will be a good long time. But that's not what all the sniffing's about, not today at any rate.'

Seeker waited.

Bess concentrated on the root she was trying to peel, then put it back in the bowl. 'I've been harsh with her. Too harsh, but for her own good.'

Seeker smiled. 'You think she'll learn better that way?'

Bess managed a laugh, a shorter one this time. 'Orpah, learn? It's a wonder that girl ever learned her own name. No: she's too soft, and she's too soft on me. I won't be here for ever, and I don't want her missing me.'

'I think you've maybe left it a bit late for that, Mistress Pullan.'

'Hmm.' Bess fussed with her cuffs, avoiding the soldier's eye. She never had been able to take a compliment, especially from one like him, that evidently didn't go in much for giving them. 'Well, you've not learned much since you were last here, by the look of you, and if half what Lawrence has told me is true. Think you'll keep out of trouble back here in Faithly?'

'That depends who offers it.'

Bess had tried her best, but she was wearying, and couldn't keep up her performance much longer. She could see he knew it too, but at least he'd spared her pride. She knew by the set of his face that he was coming to the point.

'So, mistress, Lawrence Ingolby has told you what went off in York?'

'What he thought fit for me to hear, at least,' she said.

'And did he tell you what he was doing there in the first place?'

Bess straightened her shoulders, which she could feel begin to slump. 'Not my place to ask after Sir Edward Faithly's business.'

He wasn't fooled, she saw. 'Aye, but he wasn't there on Sir Edward Faithly's business, was he? He was there on Matthew's.'

'Then you'd best speak to my son, hadn't you?' she said, taking hold again of a small turnip and trying to grip the knife hard enough to make a nick in it.

'I already have. Matthew sent Lawrence Ingolby to York

to find out what had scared you so when last you'd been there. He thinks you learned of some threat to Gwendolen, some harm that was coming her way. Is he right?'

Bess put down the knife and stared up at him, her lips pursed. 'What does it matter if he was right or not? Harm came anyway, didn't it? And now it's done with.'

'Is it?'

'Well, she's gone, isn't she? I'm no Anabaptist, Seeker, but soul or not, dead is dead. There's no more harm'll come to Gwendolen.'

She saw him watching her. He looked almost shocked at her words. Almost, but then she suspected he'd heard a lot worse.

'Even so.'

'Even so what? What more do you want of me? I've Matthew's supper to see to, and a hundred other things besides, with Gwendolen gone and that girl more work than she's worth.'

'You learned something in York that sent you hurrying back here, and threatening to pack Gwendolen off to sisters in Bristol and Carlisle and who knows where else. What were you trying to get her away from?'

Bess pushed the basin of roots away from her, summoned her will again. 'Matthew. I wanted her away from here and far from Matthew.'

He hadn't expected that. 'Why?' he said at last.

'Why do you think? Abel Sharrock would hardly have finished shovelling the dirt over me over in that churchyard before he was making insinuations, outright accusations maybe.'

'Of what?' asked Seeker. But he knew, he was just determined to make her say it.

She twisted her lips. 'Fornication. Incest. Whatever filth he could fling at them.'

'Why?'

'Why? Have you been in the south too long? To make trouble for Matthew, of course; to smear his name and hound him from here, so that that puffed-up puddock might take his place.'

'Incest?' said Seeker. 'So there was truth in what Abel Sharrock hinted at – your husband was Gwendolen's father?'

This again. Bess felt the anger rising in her. 'No, Digby was not Gwendolen's father.'

'And there was nothing between Matthew and Gwendolen?'

Again Bess struggled to control her temper. 'I'll not have Abel Sharrock's filth talked in this house, not by you nor anyone else!' Her whole body was shaking with rage and she took a moment to calm herself before speaking again. 'Matthew loved that girl as a sister, and if you think it could have been otherwise, then you don't know my son at all.'

The soldier appeared a little abashed, and she saw he took more care over what he was to say next. 'But you are certain that your husband could not have been Gwendolen's father? I've heard it more than once that he was an adulterer.'

'Yes, yes he was,' she said wearily. 'But he wasn't Gwen-

dolen's father. She was the very picture of William Sorsby
– never saw a child look so like her father. She'd the col-
ouring and grace of her mother, but the rest was William
and he was the image of his own mother, even the way
Gwendolen smiled was the same as them.' She smiled herself at this. 'You can mask some things, Seeker, but there's
smiles'll go through families for generations. Gwendolen
wasn't Digby's child, but that would have made no difference once Abel Sharrock had started on them. That's why
I wanted her away from here before the trier's court and
before I was gone myself.'

'Right,' he said. And to her horror, she saw that he didn't
believe her. He crouched down in front of her and looked
closer into her eyes. 'You didn't need to go to York to learn
any of that, Bess: you must have known it long ago. Four
things I'd have you tell me, and then I'll leave you in peace
and I won't trouble you more.'

'Four things? You don't ask much.' Her heart was
thumping. She didn't feel old any more: under his un-
wavering scrutiny she felt young and scared. 'You'd best
get started then, hadn't you?'

'Where's the amulet, that Gwendolen wore around her
neck?'

'The amulet? I gave it to Orpah, a keepsake.'

'No you didn't. Tansy took it. What did she do with it?'

Bess felt flustered. His eyes missed nothing. 'Tansy just
took it to clean it, after she died. Then she gave it back
and I gave it to Orpah.'

'She's not wearing it now, though, is she?'

'I should think not,' said Bess. 'Finest of work. Digby bought it in London, Goldsmiths Row. I should think Orpah Bigley wouldn't wear it for digging roots and feeding pigs!'

'Fair enough.'

One dealt with.

'Why did you want snakeroot from the apothecary's in York?'

She was ready for that one. Lawrence had told her enough for that. 'Heard it was good for aches and pains. Couldn't find it.'

'You didn't go to your usual apothecary, though.'

Bess shrugged. 'Will Marsden's set in his ways, doesn't hold with new cures. Behind the times.' He wasn't convinced, she could see that. It didn't matter. 'What's your next question, Captain?'

'What was in Elizabeth Sorsby's account book, that Ben Scrope gave you the last time you went to visit him in York?'

Bess felt her breathing come harder, but she rallied herself. 'What do you think?' she asked. 'Accounts.'

'Of what?' he said.

Bess made the effort to shrug. 'How should I know? I'm no businesswoman.'

'Can I see it?'

'No. No use to anyone now. I burned it long since.'

'I see,' said Seeker.

'And your last question?' she said.

This was the one he'd most wanted to ask all along. She could see it in his eyes.

'Why did you go to All Saints church on North Street?'

She felt her jaw go slack and such a coldness creep over her as she'd never known.

'Well, mistress?'

Bess thought of what she had read in the account book, of what she had seen at All Saints. She looked up at Seeker, but her eyes felt clouded over and she couldn't see him properly, as if she had already begun to fade away from this life. 'Gwendolen's dead,' she repeated, 'so what can it matter?'

SEVENTEEN

Faithly Manor

Maud had not known whether to crow in triumph or to protest at being deprived of her prey. Abel had at first been unable to speak, only managing an incoherent blustering until such time as he could finally articulate his outrage.

'You cannot! The trier! This is against all good law and decency. The major-general shall know of it! The commissioner himself put her into my care!'

'I've no doubt he did, Sharrock — better sense than to have her under his own roof. But never fear, Constable, you'll have your money for her board and lodging. Put your claim in writing.'

'But the trier!'

'The trier's done with her, Sharrock, and he's done with Faithly.' And without waiting to hear what else the constable might have to say on the matter, Seeker turned Acheron and spurred him onto the track to Faithly Moor and the manor.

Her wriggling and the pressure of her head beneath his jaw threatened to dislodge Tansy's fresh bandage. 'Keep still, Felicity, or I'll let you tumble.'

'Untie my hands and I can hold on myself.' She had been glad enough to be taken from the sexton's cottage, but less pleased to have her wrists bound and a rope passed round her waist and secured to Acheron's saddle.

'I'd as soon trust a viper,' said Seeker. 'Now, keep still or you'll walk after me at the length of that rope instead.'

He could feel her fume, sense her master her temper. 'Where are you taking me? Are you taking me to York?'

Seeker laughed, despite the discomfort of having to hold her close as he reached around her for the reins. 'York? You? You'd be down a snickelway and off before I was off my horse. No, Felicity, I'm not taking you to York.'

'Where then?'

He ignored the question for one of his own. 'You didn't tell them Turner has abandoned you, did you?'

He felt her stiffen. 'It was none of their concern.'

'Oh, but it was. Do you think Maud Sharrock would have let you stay in her house if she didn't think you were the trier's wife? Do you think Abel could have justified keeping you there, without a scandal? Do you think people would have carried on doffing their caps to you, dipping their curtsies, once they knew you weren't the trier's wife? No, you didn't think that, because you're not stupid. That's all you had, Felicity, that you were the trier's wife. Now you're just another fallen woman on her own who'll have to work for her bread.'

They rode on in silence for almost two minutes before she made her muted reply. 'You never did know me, Damian, did you?'

Sir Edward Faithly's amusement was written all over his face, and he made no attempt to conceal it. 'There are a multitude of bedchambers in this house, Captain. The lady could surely be more comfortably accommodated.'

'Her comfort's of no concern to me, Sir Edward. I want her under lock and key.'

'All the private bedchambers have locks, I can assure you, Captain. The lady's virtue would not be in peril.'

'The lady's virtue is not my concern either,' responded Seeker. 'I want bolts and padlocks. You have both in your cellars, as I've already seen. A window too high and narrow for her to get out would also be good, but if your cellars have no such windows, then she can do without. It's the bolts and padlocks that matter.'

Emma Faithly had been observing the exchange with a mild curiosity. 'The whole house is a prison, Captain. I doubt the trier's wife can be in need of such tight fastening.' There was a quality to her voice that Seeker had noticed at Bess's supper; it seemed to encompass in it the quiet power of the moors, of the vast grey skies. It gave her a substance that made others around her, her husband in particular, seem trivial. Giving Felicity a last, unreadable look, Emma Faithly picked up her book and without showing any further interest in the arrivals to her house, ascended the wooden stair at the far end of the room, to the gallery and the darkness beyond.

Faithly made no acknowledgement of her leaving, instead glancing over at Felicity. It was not the look Felicity was used to getting from men; Faithly had no real interest in her, other than as an element in some entertaining diversion he was working to understand. 'She doesn't appear so very dangerous a person to me, Captain Seeker. What are her crimes?'

Seeker also looked at his former wife, a dismissive look that made her flinch. 'Those are yet to be established, though they will be, in time. But there is information I require of her, and I need her person secured until such time as I am ready to extract it. I have the authority of the major-general, Faithly. I'm not asking.'

The amused look vanished from Sir Edward's face. 'No. That's not the way of this commonwealth of Cromwell's, is it? An Englishman is no longer to call his home his own.'

'What? With your family's history? You're lucky you're still allowed through the front door,' said Seeker, already turning away and prodding Felicity in the back, in the direction of the basement stairs.

Seeker took his supper in a corner of the manor kitchen, and the servants worked warily around him. Lawrence Ingolby appeared periodically, to issue instructions or check stores. 'Rack and ruin,' he muttered to himself. 'Rack and ruin.'

'What's up?' said Seeker from his corner.

'Oh, that's where you've fetched up, is it? Thought you'd be up in the great hall.'

'Doesn't do to be overfamiliar.'

'What? With the enemy? Is that what the Faithlys are?'

'With anybody,' replied Seeker. 'What's gone to rack and ruin?'

'This whole place. I'm away less than a week and the place is more of a mess than York Shambles. Papers interfered with, boxes going missing, stores not tallying. Another couple of days and the roof slates would have been disappearing.' He glared at the now motionless manor house servants. 'Useless, the lot of you!'

A middle-aged stable hand, also in for his supper, stood up. 'Come now, Lawrence, that's not fair. You know we can't keep him in check when you're not here.'

'Aye, well,' said Ingolby, relenting slightly, 'you might try now and again.'

'What's gone missing?' asked Seeker, understanding enough to keep his voice low.

'Nothing important,' said Ingolby, glaring at the other servants slowly resuming their tasks, then he murmured, 'I'll be in my own quarters in half an hour.'

'Right.' Seeker nodded.

As Ingolby was heading back to the stairs, the cook called over to him. 'And what about that woman, Lawrence, that woman kept down in the cellar: should I fetch her down some supper?'

'You'll go nowhere near her,' said Seeker. 'If there's any

fetching and carrying down to her to be done, I'll be doing it.'

Lawrence poured out a tankard of ale for each of them. Seeker looked around his quarters with approbation, if not a little envy. 'You do all right for yourself, then.'

Ingolby's indifferent shrug was belied by an accompanying grin. There was a sturdy oak bed with a heavily curtained canopy; velvet drapes embellished with the white rose of York. Oak panelling, two comfortable wainscot armchairs sat either side of a healthy fire, and against a wall, a large carved linen chest bearing the same rose design. The Faithlys had held this house and land since long before the Tudors, never mind the Stuarts.

Ingolby stretched his arms back and sighed contentedly. 'I'd rather be at Bess's, but still, it's not bad for a lad born on a cave floor. Could have been worse, I suppose – might have been a ditch, if her luck hadn't been in.' He took a long draught of his ale. 'Talking of luck, your Mistress Turner doesn't seem to be having much this weather, does she? Husband made off, incarcerated with Maud Sharrock and then freed only to end up locked in a cellar halfway up Faithly Moor. What's the woman done, for pity's sake?'

'Not much pity about it. Anyway,' snorted Seeker, 'you're too young, and I haven't the time.'

'Not my business then. Fair enough. But how long do you plan on keeping her down there?'

'Not a minute longer than it takes for her to decide to

tell me what I need to know. Don't suppose there are rats down there, by any chance?'

Ingolby let out a whistle. 'Whoo, Seeker – you're a hard man. No, no rats, no. I've got a nice little pack of terriers that see to all that. More use than most of the servants up here. More use than Sir Edward, too, if truth be told.'

'The truth. That would be good. So tell me, Lawrence Ingolby, does he harm her?'

Ingolby's eyes flashed instant wariness. 'Who?'

'Sir Edward Faithly. Does he beat his wife?'

Lawrence lost any air of dissembling. 'No. If he did . . .'

'Matthew Pullan would have killed him,' Seeker finished for him.

'I – don't – Matthew . . .'

Seeker spared him. 'He's told me. Matthew Pullan's all but told me, and it doesn't take much working out when you see him and her in the same place – Matthew and Emma, that is – he put you up here to keep an eye on the woman he loves.'

Ingolby took a minute to process what Seeker had just said. 'Matthew told you that?'

Seeker made a dismissive gesture. 'Good as. But what he didn't tell me was how it all came about. I know Sir Edward's marriage to Lady Emma was to spite Matthew Pullan, but no more than that. You can fill in the gaps.'

Ingolby looked into the fire, evidently considering what he would say.

'I was only, what, twelve, thirteen, maybe. Been in Digby

Pullan's service a couple of years. Digby was an old rogue, and liked his pleasures – as you've heard – but Bess was always a good Puritan, and brought Matthew up the same. She tried with me too, but, well, truth be told, Seeker, I was never that bothered one way or the other. It was when the war was starting. When the King put up his standard at Nottingham, old Sir Anthony Faithly and his son Thomas got on their horses to rally to it and thought all the men hereabouts would follow them. Some hope! Sir Anthony was all right – did all right by me, but folks have long memories hereabouts. The Faithlys had worked the people like beasts for generations, mill dues, tithes, rents going up every year, and they thought the folk of Faithly would happily die with them for the sake of their titles and their King and their rotten religion.' He paused to swallow down a good measure of his ale. 'I'll say one thing for Abel Sharrock and his sort: they'd as soon a' fought for the Pope of Rome as rally to the Faithlys' banner.'

'And Matthew Pullan?'

'Matthew rode round the moor, rode for miles, gathering men and whatever horses, weapons they could lay their hands on. Mustered them all back here in Faithly, to go and join with Lord Fairfax. But before they left they destroyed the windows of Faithly church, and a few others.'

'Did you join with them?'

Ingolby gave an ironic smile. 'What do you think? No, I stayed stood by Digby Pullan like he told me to. I wasn't daft, even then. Smashing something to pieces doesn't get rid of it, not if it's been there hundreds of years. People remember, and they're not always going to be folk who think like you do. Digby knew that. Matthew should have done too, but he was so taken up with the cause that he didn't care. He thought Edward was too weak and the rest of them too busy with the King in any case to retaliate. He hadn't reckoned on Edward's spite. Or on Emma.'

Now they were coming to the point.

'Edward Faithly watched the whole thing, the church-breaking. Him and Septimus, side by side.'

'Did they try to stop it?'

'Septimus was too astonished. Matthew was his friend, and he hadn't reckoned his Puritanism could override their friendship. And Sir Edward knew when he was beat. There was nothing going to stop that crowd. He just sat there, on his horse, watching. When it was over, he got Septimus to help him down and went crunching across the broken glass till he got to where the pieces from the biggest window had fallen. He bent down and picked up a piece that was bright red. He walked right over to Matthew and held it up right in front of his face. "I will gift this to my bride, in remembrance of you, on our wedding day".'

Seeker thought of the strange red glass pendant Lady Emma wore about her neck. 'Lady Emma's necklace.'

Ingolby nodded. 'Emma's father lived over Lockton way. Hardly two pennies to rub together, but lived off his lineage, very keen on that, Sir Robert was. Anyhow, Matthew Pullan and Emma had fallen for each other when they were both very young, but Sir Robert wasn't too keen on his daughter marrying trade. Not until his rents dwindled and so many leaks appeared in his hall roof you'd have been as well stopping outside. Not just that, but he'd debts he'd no hope of repaying. Digby Pullan's money just about had him ready to agree to Matthew and Emma's marriage when the drums started beating down in Westminster. When Matthew declared for Parliament, Sir Robert said no daughter of his would be a "roundhead's strumpet", I seem to recall his words were. Well, the day Matthew smashed those windows and rode off to Lord Fairfax's army, Edward Faithly went off in the other direction, to Lockton. Sir Robert couldn't believe his luck — Edward had never as much as glanced at Emma before, and here he was now ready to pay off her father's debts and make her lady of Faithly Manor.'

'And Emma?' said Seeker.

Lawrence sighed. 'What do you think? She's got spirit, Emma. She was having none of Edward Faithly and she told him that straight. You think Bess can speak plain? Bess and Emma under one roof would have had the thatch alight! But she was seventeen years old and at her father's mercy. Sir Robert pointed at her mother and her little brother and sister and asked her if she wanted them out walking the roads, because that was her choice: marry Edward Faithly or consign her family to destitution. Told her they'd be long dead before Matthew Pullan ever came back for her.' Lawrence looked down at his hands. 'It was no choice, was it?'

No, thought Seeker, no choice. 'And that was in 1642?'

'Yes, just after Matthew left.'

'And they've no children, Sir Edward and Lady Emma?'

Ingolby shrugged, a man of the world. 'Sir Edward doesn't seem much bothered, if you know what I mean, about man or woman – not much interested. And just as well, for marrying him is one thing, anything else is another. Emma sleeps down a different corridor from him.'

Seeker thought of the lack of interest with which Faithly had appraised Felicity. What Ingolby said seemed likely enough. 'Matthew Pullan was in London in 1647. Are you saying he stayed away from Faithly five years?'

'Five years?' Ingolby shook his head. 'No. He came back at the end of the first war, in '46. Home the conquering hero, and all that. Thought Sir Robert would have to let him marry his daughter now.'

'You mean he didn't know she was already wed?'

Lawrence pursed his lips. 'Digby wanted to send word to him, but Bess wouldn't let him. Said Matthew was such a hot-head he'd either come back and kill Sir Edward or he'd never come home again. She was probably right.'

'So what happened?'

'When Matthew got back to Faithly, he didn't even get off his horse. Just leaned down, gave Bess a peck on the cheek and told her he was off over to Lockton to fetch Emma from her father's. And that's when Bess had to tell him. So he wheeled round and up over the moor and came hammering on this door instead, demanding to see Emma. Sir Edward went and stood her in that casement above the main door. Opened it far enough so Matthew could see her, and made a show of hanging that red glass pendant round her neck. Emma was in such a state of shock to see him again after all that time she nearly threw herself out of that window. Took three of the servants to pull her back in. Matthew went stone mad, but Edward wouldn't let him in. Eventually, he had to turn round, ride back out those gates. He went down to his father's stables to change horses and rode off without setting foot back in his own house. I suppose that's when he went to London.'

Yes, thought Seeker. Like so many others, Matthew Pullan had sought to lose himself in London. He had recognised something in Pullan when first he had met him, in that prison cell and later, too, amongst the Levellers, in the Bull tavern in Southwark, and now he knew what that thing had been: a man to whom his own life no longer mattered.

Lawrence continued. 'It was only when Digby took ill that Matthew came back to look after Bess and Gwendolen. And me, I suppose. He wanted to move them away from Faithly altogether, but Bess said she was going nowhere and neither was Gwendolen. I'd a' gone, for sure, but no one was asking me. So Matthew stayed, and took over the running of things, and him and Sir Edward have brooded at each other over the moor ever since.'

'And yet Sir Edward allows you to be foisted on him, to run his estates and look after his wife.'

'He'd no choice. Between the money he paid out to cover Emma's father's debts – just for the sake of spiting

Matthew – the fines he had to pay for his father and brother's Royalism and his own bad management, this place was on its knees. Matthew's money keeps it going, it's mortgaged to Matthew. Lady Emma's about the only thing in here he doesn't own. Sir Edward knew it was either that or be turned out of his own house, but he'd have been in his rights to take Emma with him, and Matthew wasn't going to let that happen. So Sir Edward saves face and the roof over his head, Lady Emma has her own apartments and I keep an eye on Matthew's investment, and on her. Sir Edward's not a well man, and when he dies, both house and wife will come to Matthew anyway, one way and another.'

'And meanwhile, she just waits.'

'Emma?'

Seeker nodded.

'Aye. She waits. Never saw a woman so able to wait for something. And every day she grows more determined.'

'Well,' said Seeker, thinking of the disease-ridden Royalist who sat coughing by the hearth in the great hall, 'I doubt the day's very far off when she won't be waiting any more.'

'No,' conceded Ingolby. 'It isn't. For which God be thanked.'

Now he knew the truth of it, of Ingolby's loyalty to Matthew Pullan and of Matthew Pullan's love for Emma Faithly, Seeker did not wonder that Pullan's placeman should want Sir Edward Faithly dead, only that he should talk quite so openly of it. But time was getting on, and there were other matters to discuss.

'So, what's gone on whilst you've been away?'

Lawrence was more at ease with this. He threw up his hands in a gesture of bewilderment. 'I don't know for sure. It started before I left for York. The second day of the trier's court, just after Gwendolen had died and you came into the court and laid into the trier . . .'

Seeker sighed with impatience. 'Yes.'

'Well, when I finally got back up here – latish, by the time all the fuss had died down – I found someone had been in my office, mucking around with my papers.'

'Servants?'

Lawrence shook his head. 'None of them would dare.'

Having seen the awe in which even grizzled old stable hands seemed to hold the young secretary, Seeker didn't doubt this.

'And was anything missing?'

Lawrence shook his head. 'Not then, not from there, at any rate.'

'But?'

'Well, food's been going missing from the stores, and that's not the servants pilfering, either. For all I rail at them they're an honest lot, and there's none of them would risk dismissal over a round of cheese or a measure or two of wine. But there are some papers missing, too, or so Sir Edward says. By the time I got back here from York he'd turned my office upside down looking for them.'

'Estate papers?'

Lawrence looked up warily from under his fringe. 'Aye. More or less.'

'Speak straight or we'll be here all night.'

'Well, the papers that have gone missing were tied up together in a box, a chest, actually. A Nuremberg chest that's been there a hundred years, with a special locking mechanism, the like of which you'd need the man that made it to tamper with.'

'And what sort of papers were these?'

Ingolby made a face. 'Letters.'

'And?' Seeker was growing impatient.

Ingolby turned up his palms in a gesture of helplessness. 'I only caught sight of them the once, and Sir Edward nearly had my head off me for it, but . . . but, well, the writing on them, it looked like Thomas Faithly's. I know his hand from some of the old family documents – they were all in a mess, but I catalogued them when first I came here.'

Seeker spoke low and with great deliberation. 'You didn't, by any remote chance, see what was in them?'

Ingolby shook his head. 'It was only the top one that I got even half a look at. All I could make out of it before Sir Edward chased me for my life was the line at the bottom.'

'And?' said Seeker, wondering that someone had not strangled Ingolby before now.

The secretary swallowed. 'What I think it said was, "by

my own hand, in the town of Edinburgh, this seventh day of July, year of God sixteen hundred and fifty-one".'

'What?' Seeker was on his feet so quickly he almost knocked over the joint-stool he had set his tankard on. 'Thomas Faithly was in communication with his brother before Charles Stuart invaded with the Scots? Sir Edward gave no intelligence of this.' He leaned down towards Ingolby. 'This estate should have been forfeit!'

Ingolby, who was very pale now, nodded. 'I know. But that whole business was done and dusted, the Scots invasion crushed and Charles Stuart packed off back to the continent trailing Thomas Faithly in his skirts before I ever came to work at the manor or had sight of those letters.'

'And do you think Sir Edward knows you managed to read that much?'

Lawrence shook his head. 'I don't think so – he'd have shifted them before now if he did.'

Seeker began to pace the length of the room, thinking. 'And who has the key to this Nuremberg chest and its mechanism?'

'There are only two keys,' answered Ingolby. 'Or at least there were. Sir Edward has one.'

'And the other?' pressed Seeker.

Ingolby raised an eyebrow. 'Old Sir Anthony Faithly took it off to the wars with him when he rallied to the King's standard. It hasn't been seen since.'

'Hmm.' Seeker had paused by the window, and was looking out over the darkness of the moor towards the village. 'Well, it obviously has, and by someone who's been in this house at some point in the last five days.'

As Seeker made his way along the oak-panelled corridor from Ingolby's rooms, between Lady Emma's apartments and the main stairs that descended into the great hall of the manor house, he considered whether Matthew Pullan might have attempted to hasten Edward Faithly's demise, and taken the opportunity of his mother's supper for the trier to do so, all with such fateful results for his foster sister. There was no point discussing it with Lawrence Ingolby, for even if Ingolby had handed Pullan the knife to slice the destroying angel into a bowl, he'd have denied to his dying breath that Matthew Pullan had anything to do with the poisoning.

At the far end of the great hall, Sir Edward and Lady Emma were seated disconsolately at either side of the huge hearth, she stony-faced, he drunk and disappointed. By what? Seeker wondered. He could hardly be surprised that his wife didn't love him. Perhaps just that his revenge had brought him no satisfaction? But Seeker had a loveless wife of his own to see to before he could give any more time to the Faithlys. He turned right at the bottom of the main stairway and headed for the small door that led to the servants' hall, and from there to the cellars.

He pulled back the shutter in the door of the cellar in which he had secured Felicity, and held up a lamp. She was huddled against a pile of hempen sacks in the corner.

Wrapped around her was a heavy sheepskin blanket that one of the servants must have given her despite his warning – for he had not – and the pewter tankard and dish beside her were empty. She was asleep, or making a good show of it. He had not allowed her a candle, and the light of his lamp cast a warm yellow glow over her sleeping form. Despite the sheepskin, he wondered whether she might be cold. She looked younger now than the woman who had spoken to him so scornfully earlier in the day. She had always looked lovelier in her sleep, like the woman she might have been. Seeker felt something clench deep in his stomach. He watched a moment longer, then made himself close the shutter and walk away.

EIGHTEEN

Comings and Goings

Tansy woke early. Before she had even pulled back her door to see, she could feel the mist rolling down from the moor. The damp chill of it was seeping through her thin woollen shift already. She shuddered as she pulled the shift over her head and began to rub herself with one of the coarse cloths cut from a blanket Bess had ceased to have a use for long ago. Let them say what they liked about her: no one would say Tansy was not clean.

But perhaps she was a fool, witless. They did say that. The children made fun of her, called her names, dared each other to come rapping at her door in the darkness. She had helped their mothers birth them, every one. Cradled them, every one. But never one of her own. And perhaps that would never be, now, if Seth did not come home.

She dressed hastily, pulled an old comb through her hair, which in truth was more knotted than it should have been, and pulled back the door of her dwelling. The hen, Betty, was grown old, but still gave an egg now and again. Tansy would not wring her neck, though, not even when she finally stopped laying. Bess would have Orpah come instead, and take her away and kill her, in the Pullans' yard. Tansy had to be careful. Dead birds, feathers, they might be taken as signs by those keen to find them. Chicken's feet were bad, especially. And Bess would return her the carcass's worth in food tenfold, at any rate.

But Tansy didn't get as far as Betty's roost. The dawn light had only just started to inch its way over the eastern ridge; the path to the favoured roost was well trodden, and Tansy didn't think of looking where she put her feet, which were still bare. When her toe hit the stone, hard, it was all she could do not to cry out. She did not, though, for fear Abel would appear at the churchyard gatepost in his night shift, to ask who she communed with at such an hour whilst godly folk kept to their beds. So Tansy bit her lip, and bent to examine what it was that she had struck her foot upon. As soon as her fingers touched the stone, she knew. It didn't matter that the light was dim, she knew by the feel of it. She gathered the stone up quickly and scuttled back into her cottage, mindless now of Betty's eggs, and pulled the door to, hastily, behind herself. Seated by the hearth, at first she did nothing more than run her fingers over the long-familiar rounded contours of the smoothed limestone. She took a spill from the embers of the fire and lit a rush lamp the better to see the stone. There could be no doubt about it, none. Tansy could hardly breathe. She wrapped her thin fingers around the stone and held it to her breast. Then, she stood up and turned and turned, around and around the glowing embers of the hearth, her head tilted upwards, her eyes tight shut, moving to an unheard music. They had called her fool, they had laughed at her all these years, for that she had never given up believing that Seth would come home. But here was their sign, their special token in her hands. The rhythm of her joy filled her as she spun. If Abel Sharrock could have seen her, he would have hauled her out there and then to burn her in the street, but Tansy cared nothing now for Abel Sharrock.

Seeker's mood was not good as he swung himself up into Acheron's saddle in the courtyard of the manor house. His morning interview with Felicity had not gone well. A night without light or warmth, and only stale bread for her supper, had done little to soften her resolve; still she would tell him nothing of Manon, insisting she must first have assurances for herself. There were indeed things he was prepared to do for her, not for her own sake, but to rid himself of her, but he was not going to tell her that until he was certain she was ready to tell him everything he needed to know. A filled purse, a false character and a passage to Massachusetts, or some other such new world that would no longer collide with his, were what Felicity could hope for from him, but she did not know that yet, and seemed still to believe that she might gain much more. With every hour that passed Seeker knew the time to find his daughter safe might be running away. But there were other lines of enquiry he could pursue whilst Felicity stayed mute.

Despite the earliness of the hour, Lawrence Ingolby was already up and feeding his terriers at their kennel. Seeker appraised the darting, fierce little pack, then allowed himself a grim smile. There might be no rats in the cellars of Faithly Manor, but an early shadow on their marriage came back now to cheer him. Felicity had a virulent dislike of dogs.

Sir Edward Faithly had been in flat denial that the papers taken from his Nuremberg chest had been letters from his brother, the blatant lie only making Seeker the more determined to find the one brother and expose the other. The dawn mist had started to clear a little, but still he felt the damp chill as he set off down the track towards Faithly village. The moor, which a few weeks earlier would have been a carpet of purples and pinks, was grey in the morning light, and silenced by the lingering mists. Up to his left, the rocks of Faithly Ridge, above the woods, were veiled in such a way that they looked like the precipice of some ancient fortress. Below them, at the edge of the wood, he caught a movement out of the corner of his eye, which he thought at first must be a tardy fox or bold deer, but when he turned, unthinking, to glance more directly its way, he saw that it was no fox or deer, but Tansy Whyte disappearing quickly into the wood, well swathed in shawls, and holding to her chest a bag which he supposed she must use for the gathering of herbs. Seeker watched her until the mist enveloped the opening in the trees through which she had gone, before he continued on his way down to the village. He'd have his men search that wood again today.

Jack Thatcher at the Black Bull was not pleased to see Seeker, still less was his wife, whose dread seemed inspired rather by the mood into which the soldier's appearance sent her husband than by the soldier himself. Hettie Thatcher was one of those women who noticed nothing of the outside world, so busy was she spinning on delicate threads around her husband's humour.

'Have you brought reparation?' the innkeeper said to Seeker when the pot boy had hurriedly drawn back the bolt on the door at Seeker's bidding.

'Reparation? For what?'

'Loss of trade,' grumbled Thatcher. 'That trier's court was the best business I ever did; better than any fair day. It would have gone on two days more at least, if you had not put an end to it by laying out the trier. Two days' trade, and then the trier's bill unpaid. Who is to make me reparation for that?'

Seeker looked about him, the dirt and meanness of the place more evident now that it was not thronged as it had been in the days of the court. 'You water your ale, you don't keep regular hours, and,' he nodded towards a door he knew led to a small yard in which cockfighting took place, 'you allow prohibited activities to take place on this property. You are lucky you have not been shut down already, and would have been, I daresay, did not Abel Sharrock have his take to turn a blind eye.'

Thatcher sniffed importantly and wiped greasy hands on his apron. 'The constable is an upright man.'

Seeker grunted. 'Abel Sharrock'll keep, and so will you, for now. I'm here about the trier, Caleb Turner as he called himself.'

'"Called himself"?'

'He went by other names too.' Seeker tried them on Thatcher, but the innkeeper denied having heard of Turner by any of those. He knew nothing of where the trier and his wife might have come from – he had no interest in what bills they might have left unpaid elsewhere, only his own – and he had not heard them speak privately, for he was not a gossiping woman and had been run ragged with preparing for the court and the crowd that was there and their unceasing demands, surely Seeker had seen it?

Aye, Seeker had seen it. Jack Thatcher had no interest in his customers or guests in the inn other than what money he might make from them. The pot boy looked terrified at the idea that he should have been permitted anywhere near the trier, to say nothing of his wife. The chambermaid, likewise, denied ever having overheard their conversation, although, she added shyly, she had helped Mistress Turner, in pressing her pretty clothes and mending for her a button. Useless, they were all useless. Perhaps Seeker had been in Thurloe's service too long, to think that a man's first duty was to spy upon those around him. The pity of it was that Maud Sharrock had not worked at the Black Bull. She had been hovering about it often enough, though, before Turner had left Felicity to get by on her wits, and if any woman was made to listen at a keyhole, it was Maud.

Seeker stood up, warned Thatcher to shut up his cockpit and keep more honest hours, thanked his ghost of a wife for the ale and sausage she had brought him, putting more coin into her hand than was required, and left.

More of the village was waking and seeing to its business by the time Seeker walked out of the Black Bull. Any who saw him feigned not to have done, and turned to some pressing business out of his line of sight. They had feared the trier, but at least they knew what the trier had come to Faithly for. Seeker's attack on Caleb Turner, though, had been beyond their comprehension, and none of them could quite be sure why he had returned to their village, or whether they themselves might be next. If they kept quiet, he might do whatever he had come to do and leave them alone again.

Passing Pullan's house, Seeker saw Orpah out feeding the pigs. She gave him a cheerful wave, and then cast her eyes downwards as if fearful she had done the wrong thing. He crossed over and called her to him.

'Yes, Captain,' she said, still gripping her bucket as if for support.

'The necklace Bess gave you, that was Gwendolen's,' he began. 'The silver one, with an amulet?'

She was following him very closely, and concentrating hard. 'Yes, Captain. It was the one she always wore, and Mistress Bess said I might have it as a keepsake.'

'Do you still have it?'

She flushed. 'Of course. And I keep it safe.'

'Can you tell me what is in it – in the amulet?'

Now the colour crept up her cheeks and tears started to appear in her eyes. Her lip was trembling.

'Orpah? What is it?'

'Oh, I'm sorry, Captain. I know it was Miss Gwendolen's, and I should have treasured it, but I didn't like it, and I asked Tansy to throw it away. Then when Mistress Bess gave me the amulet, I wondered if I should have kept it.'

'Kept what, Orpah? What was it that you asked Tansy to throw away?'

The tears were running down her cheeks now. 'It was just a horrible old gnarled bit of root. I'd never liked it and it frightened me, and I never knew why Gwendolen wore it.'

'What kind of root was it, Orpah?'

'Peony, she said it was, but I don't know why she kept it,' she sniffed. 'And the flowers so pretty, too, but the root is ugly, and I didn't want it.'

Seeker reached out an awkward hand to touch the girl on the shoulder. He had reduced her to tears for no good purpose. 'Never worry, child. No one will chastise you for that you didn't care for a dirty old root.'

A sound from up across the other side of the street took their attention. Septimus Jenkin was shutting up his schoolroom door and affixing a message to the front of it. He was dressed for riding, and had saddlebags slung over his shoulder.

Orpah, a little reassured, took the opportunity to hurry back towards the pigs, who were now in the orchard, and

Seeker crossed over to the churchyard. The case against the vicar of Faithly, halted by Seeker's assault on the trier, had crumbled altogether on the trier's flight from the village. 'You don't hold school today?' Seeker asked, indicating the note on the schoolroom door.

'I have business at the manor, and so I have given the children a holiday.'

'What business?' asked Seeker.

'Oh,' said Jenkin lightly, 'something Sir Edward would have me see to.' He smiled and then continued, hesitant, 'Do you return to the manor, Captain?'

'Come dinnertime, perhaps,' said Seeker.

'Then perhaps I shall see you there,' said Jenkin. 'And now I must borrow a horse from Matthew's stable, for I fear I will be late for my appointment.'

Seeker watched the vicar cross the road to let himself into Pullan's yard, taking Orpah by surprise so that, shrieking, she dropped her buckets, giving the pigs a second breakfast that had been meant for others. Seeker smiled to himself and went to bang on Maud's door. When the sexton's wife appeared, somewhat apprehensive, Seeker asked her if she knew where Turner and his wife had come to Faithly from.

'Where they come from?' asked Maud, perplexed. 'But surely they do come from York, sent, like you, by the major-general?'

Seeker had a glimpse into the vision in Maud's head, wherein Caleb Turner sat in state in York Minster, waiting to be summoned to pronounce his justice on such as Septimus Jenkin in places like Faithly. He shook his head. 'Turner does not live in York. It isn't known where they live, or indeed whether there is one place they return to at all.' Instructions were sent in multiple copies to postal drops at market towns throughout Yorkshire and Cumbria. The trier would collect them from whichever town he was nearest to, inform the next town or village on his list of his intention to visit at an appointed time, and appear there to hold his court at that time. 'For all we know, he and his wife may simply progress from place to place. What I need to know is whether they ever spoke, in your hearing, of somewhere they returned to.'

Once they had dispensed, and that quickly, with the pretence that Maud was not a woman to listen at keyholes, it was established that she had not overheard them speak of a return to a particular place, but that there was a person who was the subject of more than one hushed and hurried conversation that Maud had not been able but to chance to overhear. She leaned closer to Seeker, who had to bend to hear her urgent whispers, although there was no one else at that time in the sexton's cottage, Abel Sharrock being engaged elsewhere. 'They spoke of a woman, or a girl perhaps, I know not which. I could not catch the name, for it was strange and foreign-sounding.' Then her eyes became wide as a thought struck her. 'You do not think it might have been a witch, with such a name?'

Seeker reined in his frustration. 'Mistress, you have only this minute told me you did not hear the name.'

'No,' said Maud, shaking her head, firm in the rightness of her cause. 'I said I could not catch it. I heard it, all right. Something foreign, diabolic.'

Manon, thought Seeker. What use to tell this woman it was the name the Welsh gave for queen? He repeated the name, out loud, and Maud became excited, like a cat that almost has its paw on the mouse. Her tongue protruded a little from the corner of her mouth. 'Aye,' she said, 'Manon, that was it for certain. Sounds like some familiar of the Devil, does it not?'

Seeker breathed deep and leaned down to look right into her small, expectant eyes. He summoned his every reserve of patience. 'What did they say of this Manon? You must tell me exactly, mind.'

Maud became frightened. 'Is it a witch?'

Seeker resisted the urge to slam his fist down on the table beside her. 'No. It is not a witch, but if you do not tell me now what they said, I will have you called out for one.'

That was enough. She spilled out everything she had heard, her words tripping over themselves as if trying to run from the room. 'They said she was a difficulty. He said it, at any rate. She – this Manon – was insolent and did not labour hard enough for her bread. He said it was time she was married, and she – the wife, so called – complained that that would leave her with all to do by herself. He said he knew of someone to take her and they would be well recompensed. There. That was it.' She nodded, pleased with herself. 'I'd warrant this Manon is a servant, or perhaps a spinster sister.'

Seeker could feel the blood pulsing through him so hard he thought it might burst from his veins. 'You heard nothing more? Think, woman.'

Maud became prim. 'No, but I asked her — Mistress Turner, if such she was — of it when she was in our house. She denied ever having spoken of such a thing or person, but I had caught her in a lie and she knew it.'

Seeker had had all he would have from Maud Sharrock, and left her cottage in such haste that he did not bother to close the door behind him. Felicity's time was up. He would dip her in pigs' blood and set Ingolby's terriers at her throat if that's what it took to make her speak, but her time was up.

Pulling on his helmet, he pushed past Abel Sharrock coming up the path as he went to untie Acheron. A shape moved from the side of a tree in the churchyard, and he saw it was the wraithlike wife of the innkeeper. She took a hesitant step towards him, then stopped, as if terrified by the expression on his face.

'What is it, woman?' he said impatiently. 'I have things to do.'

'I know, Captain. I'm sorry. It's just, my sister is mistress at the Lion Inn on Blakey Ridge. Her husband keeps the inn there.'

'I know it,' said Seeker. 'What of it?'

'One of those names you said to Jack, that the trier used. Hungerford.'

'Yes?' said Seeker, completely still now.

'I have heard her talk of a man called Hungerford, with his wife and daughter, who pass there often. She does not like him, for he puts the other travellers ill at their ease, but he always pays, and leaves the child there to work for her keep whilst they travel on. I know the trier and his wife had no daughter with them, Captain, but it was just that the name struck me . . .'

And the name was enough. Seeker took a moment to tell the woman she had done right, before putting his spurs to Acheron's flank as he had not done since they were in the heat of battle. He noticed nothing, then, not Abel coming out of the church, nor Maud Sharrock gaping at him from her door, not Bess Pullan, bent and shivering, setting light to a brazier in her yard, not the empty space by the bridge end where Tansy should have taken up her vigil for the day.

Dismounting at the manor stables, Seeker threw the rein to the stable lad. There was no sign of the horse Septimus Jenkin had gone to borrow from Matthew Pullan to ride up here with, but that was no concern of Seeker's. He ran into the servants' hall, shouting for Lawrence Ingolby to be brought.

'I'm here, man,' said Ingolby, emerging through the doorway at the top of the stairs. 'What's ado?'

'Bring your dogs,' said Seeker. Then a thought struck

them. 'They are not out with Sir Edward and the Reverend Jenkin?'

Ingolby frowned. 'Septimus? Septimus isn't here.'

'Oh, aye, Reverend's here, Lawrence,' corrected the cook.

'Is he? Where? He's not with Sir Edward – I've just left him.'

'No. He came to offer comfort, he said, to pray with that woman.'

'What woman?' asked Lawrence, his face already greying.

'The one the captain there put in the cellar.'

As he ran down the steps into the cellars of Faithly Manor, Lawrence Ingolby at his heels, Seeker could hear the plaintive cries of the cook become fainter and fainter, 'But I thought there could be no harm. Seeing as it was the Reverend . . .'

Seeker knew before he reached the bottom step at the end of the corridor. He knew before Ingolby put a light to the torches set in the wall. He knew before he looked, that when he came to the end of that long, cold, stone passageway, he would find the door to Felicity's prison swinging open, and that prison empty.

'Blakey Ridge?' said Ingolby, buckling on his sword as he ran after Seeker to the stables. 'Are you sure?'

'Near certain. Jack Thatcher's wife told me her sister at Blakey Ridge sometimes spoke of a couple using one of Turner's aliases who'd leave their daughter there from time to time. It fits the pattern of Turner's movements I've been able to trace. That's where Felicity'll be headed,' said Seeker. 'Come on, if you're coming.'

'Oh, I'm coming all right,' said Lawrence, who'd been giving Seeker a strange look. 'I knew Septimus could be a fool when it came to a pretty woman, but I didn't know he was this much of a fool. He'll be lucky if Turner doesn't burn him at the stake after this.'

'There'll be nothing left to burn,' muttered Seeker, pulling Acheron's saddle from the rest where the startled stable boy had laid it when he'd set to rubbing down the horse.

'But what's he thinking of? Well, I know what he's thinking of, but even so— Damn him!' cursed Ingolby. 'He's given her my horse.'

They were both mounted, Ingolby on one of Sir Edward's favourites in place of his own, and making their way from the courtyard when a horseman came galloping up from the village at a fevered rate. Seeker charged on, taking with him two of the soldiers the major-general had sent up to Faithly whilst Seeker had been in York, to continue the search for Thomas Faithly. Ingolby, however, reined in and waited for the horseman to arrive. Seeker glanced over his shoulder and saw that the man was a soldier, but Lilburne's commands would have to wait. Ingolby took the packet the man had carried from York, and directed him to the stables and then towards the kitchens. By the time he was ready to follow on, Seeker was nowhere to be seen. Lawrence merely laughed and geed up his horse, calling to

Sir Edward's two best deerhounds, who could track and bring down anything, and setting out after Seeker onto the moor in the direction of Blakey Ridge.

Coming out of the woods, having returned the stone to where it had always been kept, Tansy Whyte watched Seeker's party follow the captain north-westwards, and satisfied to see the soldiers gone away from Faithly Woods, allowed herself a smile.

NINETEEN

On Blakey Ridge

A light drizzle had started before they'd reached Adderstone Rigg, and by the time they were threading their way past the Bridestones, the rain and wind were lashing through them. Lawrence had never liked the Bridestones: huge sandstone lumps, like clouds petrified and upended on the moor. They'd hidden there once, his mother and him, when she'd had to make herself scarce from Faithly a while, before he'd gone to live at the Pullans'. There'd been no shelter, whatever the fool woman might have thought.

Now they took the Old Wife's Way and then skirted the Hole of Horcum onto Levisham Moor. All the way, Seeker pressed on, always looking ahead, scanning the landscape before him, never letting up as his horse's hooves negotiated woodland track and thundered over moor as if it had never had another purpose. Lawrence had tried asking, just once, why it mattered so much that Septimus Jenkin had made off with the trier's wife, why the captain didn't simply let them go, to discover their fates elsewhere, but

Seeker had given him one withering look, as if Lawrence were a fool, before urging his mount onward. Lawrence was glad to have Sir Edward's horse after all — he wasn't certain his own could have kept pace with Seeker's much beyond Muffles Rigg.

By the time they'd forded the Seven at the bottom of Rosedale and begun to make their way up onto Staunton Moor, there was such a tension coming off Seeker it made Lawrence wonder at the rain even landing on him. He could see it in the other two soldiers, too, the tension, and before long, he felt it himself. The sound of a grouse in the heather, growling like a small cur worrying at a bone, before it flew off, laughing, became something sinister, and there was a prickling on his skin as they mounted at last to Blakey Ridge, a sensation, a feeling that whatever awaited them there was something unavoidable and fundamental.

Seeker saw the inn from a good way off. It sat high up on the ridge, amongst the burial howes and the waymark crosses, a refuge and a beacon for weary travellers crossing the moors. It was not a good place for Felicity to have come to — no riding party could leave the Lion inn and travel any distance unseen. How could she have hoped to escape from here? Once the choice had been made to return here, there could be no escape. And still she had made that choice: she had come for Manon, just as he had come for

Manon. Nothing could be hidden here, and all would be exposed for what it was.

They must have been a mile away yet when he saw them: two figures on horseback emerging from the stable block behind the inn. He thought there were two figures; certainly, it was two horses, but whether one of them carried more than one rider, he couldn't tell at this distance. He realised then. They'd been keeping a lookout, too, of course. He'd half-expected it. Even Jenkin would have had the sense for that, or Felicity, more like. It didn't matter, though – they'd left it far too late.

It was Felicity on the lead horse, he could see that now, and she knew better than to make for Castleton, as others might have done. Easier riding it might be for her horse, but for Seeker's too, and she would know that. She headed westwards, towards Farndale, and as her horses mounted the moorland path beyond the inn Seeker saw for certain now that there were two riders, not three. He shouted to Ingolby to make for the inn with his dogs, and to make sure that no one left it, and then ordered his own two men to come with him.

Their horses made good speed and it wasn't long until they were past the inn and headed out towards Blakey Moor, and close enough to see that the two riders ahead of them were a man and a woman: Jenkin and Felicity. He had not thought her capable of doing it: she had left Manon behind. Seeker felt something shift in him, like a stone dropping through him; he almost pulled Acheron up, but then she turned and saw him, and called something to Jenkin, and Seeker urged the beast on.

Whatever she had called, Jenkin appeared not to have heard, or not to want to listen to, and Felicity called to him again, more urgently this time. Seeker was gaining on them every minute, but he couldn't yet hear what she said. And then he realised that they were changing their course, reining the horses south-westwards. They were leaving the track that skirted the moor and heading towards the edge of the ridge down into Farndale.

It didn't make sense: they had not the horsemanship, nor indeed the mounts, either of them, to make a safe descent down into the valley at any sort of pace. It was madness. They would have to pull up, for there was nowhere for them to go. As he closed the space between them, they did pull up, and he saw that it was more than madness, it was desperation. Felicity first, and then Jenkin, abandoned their horses and they began to run. The ground was rough and boggy and the thing hopeless, and yet, with her skirts pulled up and tucked in at the waist, Felicity made good progress. Seeker had a vision, back twenty years, of a young girl, long-legged, barefoot and careless, running laughing through woodland ahead of him. He had caught her that day, amongst the bluebells and primroses. If he had not, they wouldn't be here now, in this place, none of them. For a moment, today, he wanted to let her go, to let her carry on running to whatever she was hoping for, but there was more at stake now than Felicity. He could not be certain that Manon was at the inn, and if he let Felicity go now, he might never find his daughter again. He spurred Acheron on as far as the horse could safely go, then swung himself down to meet the ground, shouting to his men to go after Jenkin.

It felt good, he realised, to be out in the open, running, giving chase. His chest opened up and his body seemed to remember how to run on heather and peat, his feet how to plant themselves, and how to descend steep inclines without mishap. His men were less sure-footed, but not less so than Jenkin, in his good velvet suit, whom they were easily gaining on.

Seeker was momentarily distracted by the aggrieved cry of a lapwing as it flew up in front of him, its wingtips spread out like a Spaniard's black lace fan, and in that instant he lost sight of Felicity. He stopped, briefly bewildered, and then saw, in horror, where she had gone. Felicity had disappeared over a dip and run along a bracken-fringed ridge to come to a halt on a granite ledge, cleaved down the middle by a rush of water that had gouged a drop at least twenty feet down through the rock. He stopped, holding his breath, thinking she must also stop. But she didn't. She looked back at him, once, then turned her head away, to stretch out her arm and grab at a clump of heather at the edge of the fissure, near to the top where the gap was narrowest.

'Felicity!' he shouted, but she ignored him and he began again to run. Behind him, he could hear Jenkin also shouting, and it angered something in the depths of him. This was not Jenkin's fight; this was not Jenkin's wife.

The ground became ever more difficult as he tore up the distance between himself and Felicity. He stumbled once, and another time his foot caught in a divot that a hair's breadth to the left would have had him turning over his ankle and rolling down the side of the ridge, but he powered on. Ahead of him, he could see Felicity measure with her eyes the distance between the ledge on which she stood and the sister ledge on the other side of the torrent. Wet stone glistened on both. Whilst Seeker himself might have made the leap, he knew she could not.

'No!' he shouted, as she brought her weight back tentatively, preparing to jump. Everything else left him: gone, meaningless. All that had happened, that had brought them here, dissolved to nothing, and all that Seeker saw was that barefoot, laughing girl of the woods about to dash herself to death on the granite of Gill Wath Falls.

He couldn't hear what he shouted over the sound of the tumbling water, and he couldn't hear if she made him any reply at all as she gripped again at the clump of heather above her and swung herself back once more. But he felt the roar go through him as he lunged for her, only just reaching the waistband of her skirts. He pulled her back in the very moment that her hand let go its hold, and he pulled her to him as her foot slipped, clasped her to him, gripped her in his arms as they fell backwards against the bracken. She struggled against him, but only for a moment, and then she stopped and gave the thing up. Her breath began to calm, and yet he gripped his arms more tightly round her, and pressed his lips against her hair, and whispered her name.

TWENTY

The Lion Inn

Lawrence looked over at the girl. She was like a cornered hind. He had left the dogs at the door, but nothing he had done or said had been enough to convince her that he was not the huntsman.

Inside, the inn was a burrow of rooms, low beams, small doorways, big fireplaces, but it had taken him less than five minutes to find her. A creaking above his head had put the lie to the landlord's contention that there had been no one in the inn but himself, his wife, Mistress Hungerford and the well-dressed man she had arrived with only an hour earlier. By the time Lawrence had understood that 'Mistress Hungerford' was the woman he knew as the trier Caleb Turner's wife, the nervous glances of the landlord's wife had already led him to a doorway he'd assumed to be a cupboard.

Lawrence didn't even know who it was that he was looking for – just someone else, most likely the daughter Seeker seemed to think Felicity had returned to the inn for, and without whom she had now left it. To the landlord's continued protests, Lawrence had wrenched open the door. He'd been only briefly disconcerted to find it was no cupboard, but a steep and narrow wooden stair that lay behind it. The steps were too narrow for his feet, but he'd gained the top of them in five great strides and found himself in the middle of a long, partitioned attic housing several beds in various states of decrepitude. Stayed in worse, he'd thought as he'd carefully made his way round the partitions between the beds where travellers spent the night on their way over Blakey Ridge. It was in the smaller room to his left that he'd found her, crouching in the corner of a small cot, in her stocking-soled feet and with a faded blue cloak clutched around her, from fear, or cold, or both. Lawrence had taken a step towards her and she'd shrunk back, so he'd stayed where he was. 'I mean you no harm.'

She'd considered him. 'Are you the Seeker?'

'Me?' Lawrence had laughed a little. 'No, I'm not the Seeker.'

To his surprise, she'd shown no relief at this, but had seemed to sink further back into the corner.

'But he's coming,' he'd added hurriedly. 'He'll be here soon.'

'Has he gone to fetch my mother back?' she'd asked.

Even in the meagre light from the one small window in this half of the attic, Lawrence could see that, with her white-blonde hair and pale blue eyes, the girl bore a resemblance to Felicity Turner. 'Aye,' he'd said with a sigh, 'he has.' He'd reached a hand out towards her again.

'Shall we go and wait for them downstairs? It's freezing up here.'

He could see the hesitancy in her eyes, the uncertainty as she pulled her cloak more tightly around herself.

Lawrence stepped away a little. 'He asked me to come in here and look for you, the Seeker, make sure you were safe.' Not quite true, and yet he couldn't help thinking, as he looked at the girl, that that was the reason Seeker had sent him in here.

Still hesitant, she eventually nodded – what choice did the child have – and very tentatively took Lawrence's hand.

Back down in the main parlour, he had the innkeeper's wife bring them each some of the mutton stew he could smell cooking in the kitchen beyond, and he himself built up the fire and made sure the girl was settled in the large oak chair beside it. Lawrence, who was rarely at a loss for something to say, regardless of who was seated in front of him, found that every question, every comment that occurred to him, died on his lips under the girl's distrustful gaze. He settled on prodding the fire every so often, between mouthfuls of stew and draughts of the landlady's gratifyingly good ale.

Lawrence was just beginning to drift into sleep when the sounds of riders coming down from Blakey Moor began to reach them. He went instantly to the window, but the girl, although wide awake, sat rigid in her seat, her face taking on a pallor that the warmth of the fire had not long chased from it. 'Is Caleb with them?' she asked at last.

'Caleb? Your father? No, he's not with them.'

She said something else then, about her father, but Lawrence was listening to the voices of the horsemen outside as they went past into the stable yard, so he didn't properly hear her. He saw Septimus first, dejected, his hands tied as his horse was led by one of Seeker's men, the other coming behind them. Then he saw Mistress Turner. She was a good deal more dishevelled than he was used to seeing her. Less the fine trier's wife and more . . . something else, that Lawrence could not quite put a name to. She was like an animal caught, but her eyes were still animated from the chase. Her cheeks, which even at Maud's and after that in the dungeon of Faithly Manor, had exhibited a delicate pallor, were slightly flushed, her hair disordered and tumbled from its pinnings, her clothes crumpled and mud-smeared. Felicity Turner, he noted, did not have her hands bound, but rode only a little in front of Seeker, and Seeker himself had the look of a man who has just seen death up close, and is not yet certain that he has escaped it. The confidence that Lawrence had felt as they'd ridden out from Faithly that morning, that this was just a chase, an adventure, a distraction from the mundanity of his life, dissipated, and he realised he did not really know what they were doing here, or what might happen next.

Whatever that next thing might be evidently did not bode well for Septimus. The vicar was more dejected than Lawrence had ever seen him, even than when he had come that second time before the trier's court. His fine clothes were mud-spattered and torn, his hair somewhat more matted than he was used to have it. He had aged ten years in fewer hours, and bore the look of a man who knows his time is done. What else Lawrence noticed was that Felicity Turner didn't as much as glance at Septimus, not even once – she'd lost whatever fleeting interest in him she might ever have had. Seeker gave some cursory instruction to his men regarding Septimus, and then, after helping the woman dismount, guided her wordlessly towards the door of the inn. When it opened, Felicity came to a halt just a yard inside. Behind her came Seeker. He looked at the girl for a moment, and must have seen, as Lawrence did, the expression on her face change as she, in return, looked at him. And then Seeker said, his voice terrifyingly quiet, 'Get out, Lawrence.'

Seeker could feel his heart thumping and his hands shaking. She was sitting there, in a large chair close to the fire, six feet from him, watching. Only six feet, and all those lost years lying between them. Like a wall he didn't know how to breach. As he looked at her, took in the shock of the three-year-old child now a girl of almost fifteen, his mind went to another place, a low-ceilinged, cruck-framed cottage that he had built with his own hands, and the mid-wife coming towards him from where Felicity still lay in childbed, holding out his daughter. He'd felt terror, and the world had shifted for him. He would not have believed, then, that he could ever have walked away from her, from them. He would not have believed that the promises he'd made that day would not be kept, that he wouldn't have fought for her, for Felicity, that he wouldn't have stood his ground against Thomas Hungerford. Eleven years. She wouldn't even know who he was.

'Manon,' he said, so quietly he was not certain she would hear him.

She nodded slowly.

He looked to Felicity, but she was lost to her own troubles and offered him no help. He walked across the room to where the child sat, and crouched down before her, longing to reach out and take her hand. Her head was lowered and he could see she was trembling. He waited until she looked up at him.

'Manon,' he said again. 'Do you know who I am?'

She swallowed. 'Are you my father?'

He nodded and said, 'Aye, Manon, I am.'

For a moment she said nothing, and he thought his heart would stop. And then she looked down at her hands and up again at him, tears creeping over the rims of her eyes and beginning their course down her cheeks. 'I thought you would never come.'

Seeker could hold back no longer. Now, on his knees, he put his arms around her and pulled her close into his embrace. 'I am sorry,' he repeated over and over again. 'I am so sorry.' He felt her fragile frame pressed against his chest, the thin arms tighten around his back; he felt the sobs heave through her as her arms pulled tighter, and he felt his heart might cave in on him. After a minute or so, he pulled back a little and lifted her chin with his finger, so that he might properly see her face. With his other hand he brushed the hair back from her forehead. 'It is you,' he said, nodding, almost wanting to laugh. 'Truly, it is you.'

She took some deep breaths and pulled her head back to look at him. 'They said you had forgotten me, and I thought you would never come.'

Felicity stepped past them and crouched down at the hearth. She was damp and cold and could not think right until she got warm. Still Septimus and the other soldiers had not come in. Septimus had been a gamble, and he had got her this far, but she no longer had any use for him, nor interest. She wished him no ill, but he should make his decisions better, she thought.

Felicity looked at Damian and their daughter. Manon was fourteen years old, her face so open, so hopeful, so childlike. But she wasn't a child any more, not really. Caleb had been right. Soon men would start noticing her, and what could Felicity, on her own, have done when they did? And the girl made her feel older, made others treat her so. She looked again from child to father. Manon had her colour, her pale blonde hair, the blue of her eyes, her grace; but she had something of her father's height, and though blue, the expression in those eyes was all his. It would not be long before her expression was no longer open, or childlike, and she would judge Felicity as he had judged her. She told her daughter to go to the kitchens and leave them a few minutes.

'Must I, Mother?'

'Yes. Go now.'

As Manon loosened her arms from her father she looked at him with an unspoken question.

'I won't leave you,' he said.

Manon nodded, a little reassured, and went.

'Will you not?' said Felicity after the girl was gone. 'Will you not leave her again, Damian?'

His voice was hoarse. 'I will give her the choice,' he said. 'To go with me or with you, but I will not leave her against her will.'

She took a step towards him, reaching out a hand and then pulling back, remembering the cellar in the Black Bull in Faithly, when he would not let her touch him. But the man who had not let her touch him in the Black Bull was not the man who had clasped her to him out on the moor. Damian: he had not changed so much. There was a deal of grey in his hair where once there had been all black, more lines on his face, and a silver scar against the weatherbrowned skin of his cheek that must have come at some point in the war, she supposed. His eyes were still clear; short, thick dark lashes against the white. Caleb's eyes had been yellowing, too much wine that he had got used to, as place after place sought to gain the favour of the trier. Caleb, who had started out a fishmonger's apprentice in Carlisle, a thieving apprentice, and fled across the Pennines to make himself something else, had been feted and feasted, rigid Puritan that he was, by those who feared him.

People feared Damian now, too. She could see that. Some had feared him in their village, if truth be told, but she had liked that, and she had never feared him, never had cause to, not until that day in the cellar of the Black Bull when she had seen what she would not otherwise have believed: that she had no hold over him any more.

But then . . .

'Could we not try?' she said at last.

'Try?' he repeated. 'Try what?'

'To be a family again. You, me and Manon, as we used to be.'

He was looking at her intently, his lips very slightly parted, as if she were speaking in some tongue he could not understand.

She took another step towards him, hearing her own voice become desperate. 'We might even have another child – I am young enough. We could have a son.'

He was shaking his head as if she were a madwoman. 'Please, Damian.' She ran at him, and he tried to hold her off, but only for a moment and then took her wrists in his hands to make her look at him. She felt the fingers, strong but gentle, and she bent her head to brush her cheek against his skin. 'Please, Damian. You loved me once, and I know you have not forgotten!'

'And what did you do with my love?'

'I was a fool, and if I had those days back again I would

never betray you as I did then, not with anyone, not with the King himself.'

She felt his grip loosen and he actually laughed, a gentle, mirthful laugh that she remembered. 'Oh, I think you might. They tell me the young Charles Stuart is very good-looking, and that he has a way with women that a poor carpenter cannot hope for.'

'But he is not you, Damian. Do you not think I have learned to know what it was I had? What I have lost?' She was inches from his chest. She could see the rise and fall of his breathing. She wanted to put her head against him and feel his arms tighten around her as they so often had. She could almost feel the warmth of his breath on her skin. She put her freed hand up to his face and touched the scar beneath the stubble. 'You loved me once.'

Again his hand came up and caught hers and gently removed it from his face. 'But not any more, Felicity. Believe me, in this place, at this moment, I am sorry for it, but I do not love you any more.' His eyes were kind, as she remembered them, the darkness in them molten, and she felt her stomach lurch. 'Please, Damian,' she repeated. 'Out there, at the Falls . . .'

He shook his head. 'I cannot.'

'There is someone else?' She felt the certainty of it like a blow to the stomach. She repeated it, to herself. 'There is someone else. And you love her.'

'Yes,' he said, dropping her hands and turning away, taking some steps towards the mantel above the hearth, putting distance between them. He stood with his back to her a few moments, his hands clamped to the mantel, the tension across his shoulders, the struggle within him plain to see. Felicity hardly dared breathe. But then, when he turned to face her again, he was once more Lilburne's militia captain, and she knew she had lost him. 'If Manon wishes to travel with you, I will give you a pass for her and you both; if she doesn't, for you alone, with an escort to Liverpool. I will direct you to an agent there, to whom you will pass this.' He held out a paper towards her.

Felicity had to read it twice before she fully understood. 'This asks that I be given sufficient funds to pay for myself, and Manon, if she is travelling with me, for passage to Massachusetts, and that I am given . . .' Her voice faltered over the amount of money.

'It will be enough to set you up respectably in Boston, or some such place. You're a skilful seamstress, I remember that. And as you say, you are still young, and I don't doubt you will soon find another husband. But for the love of God, Felicity, choose better next time.'

She looked up, holding up the paper. 'But why are you doing this?'

'Because I can't have you in London – there's enough mischief there without you thrown into the mix as well – and you're finished in the north. There'll be a lot of folk with a grudge against Caleb Turner, and they'll not forget in a hurry what his wife looks like.'

'But what if I don't like Massachusetts?'

He shrugged, almost grunted. 'You're out of options, Felicity. It's that or nothing.'

She accepted that. He was probably right, and there was no use in arguing any more. They were back on surer ground now. She studied the paper again. 'But where did you get such money?'

'More than eleven years in the army, and my wants aren't much. Uniform, horse, blanket under a roof does me.'

He'd said nothing of a wife. If she cost him nothing, perhaps she was someone else's wife. And he'd said nothing of other children born to him either. 'And you're an officer now.' She smiled and shook her head at the strangeness of it. 'But why do you keep this money with an agent in Liverpool, Damian? What's that about?'

'My business,' he said, 'none of yours.' He went over to the door and called for Manon to come back in.

He didn't soften it for himself, she'd give him that. He told the child straight. The choice was hers: she could go with her mother, to America, or she could come away with him. It wouldn't be an easy life with him; she could not call him father whenever they were out in the world, amongst other people, but she would be cared for, and she would be loved.

Manon looked from him to Felicity and back again. 'I already told her, before, when she arrived with that man Septimus. He talked about the Seeker, and I had heard Caleb say that people called my father by that name. I told them I was waiting for my father.' Seeker wondered what pain, what loneliness his child had faced all these years, that she was so ready to trust in him. She looked at her mother now. 'You'd travel better without me, and fare better without me anyway, Mother. You said it often enough.'

Felicity's heart lurched again, and she took a step towards her daughter. 'But I didn't mean it. Caleb—'

Manon shook her head. 'Past time for blaming Caleb, Mother.'

Felicity was frozen. She watched Manon walk towards her as if the girl were some player in a dumb show, a tableau. The touch of Manon's hands on her shoulders was a ghost touch, and she hardly felt the girl's lips light on hers before they were gone. 'I'll go now and ready my things, Father,' she said to Damian, and then she went through the door.

Felicity felt the strength go out of her. It wasn't a fourteen-year-old girl she saw walk from the room, but a chubby three-year-old who had snuggled in her lap and kissed her and reached for her hand, who had laughed at her father and pulled at his beard and cried for him for days and weeks after he'd gone away. Felicity wanted to reach out and pull that little girl back onto her lap, into her arms, but that child was gone and she would never come back. She slumped to the floor and sobbed against the corner wall.

Damian was watching her, but she did not cry for effect, or comfort even. She cried to empty herself because that was all she could do. She heard him breathe deeply, but he made no move towards her. He watched a minute, two perhaps, and he might have said something, but she didn't hear it, and anyway, there was nothing he could say. Manon had not closed the hatch as she'd gone through to the kitchen, and eventually, he too went through it and was gone.

It had been too late, by the time the thing with Manon and Felicity was settled, and Jenkin brought back and properly secured, to set out on the road back to Faithly. They would never make it before darkness fell. Ingolby had protested that surely Septimus did not need to be shackled, for what had he done that was wrong, save go off with the wife of a man who wasn't coming back for her anyway? Seeker told him to mind his own business better, and he would mind his.

'Aye, but everybody's business is your business, it seems to me,' Ingolby had countered.

'And that's why Septimus Jenkin'll stay secured until I say otherwise,' Seeker had responded.

After a good supper, Seeker asked Manon to sit with him outside. She came quietly, a little nervously, and sat next to him on a bench near the front door. They looked down over Blakey Ridge as the setting sun beyond Farndale swathed the endless sky in blues and pinks and white gold, and colours Seeker hadn't names to give to, and that London had never seen.

'Are you certain,' he asked her after a while, 'that you want to come away with me, south, to London?'

'I'm certain of it, Father. I've waited so long for you to come back.'

He couldn't look at her. Eventually he said, 'What did they tell you of me?'

She worked at her hands in her lap. 'That you had left because you didn't care for me, or for having a family. That you wanted to go to the war and make your fortune and have your own way.'

Seeker nodded. He had expected at least this. 'And yet you still waited for me to come back to you?'

The face that looked up at him was urgent, and angry. 'I knew it wasn't true. I remembered. I tried to remember – a feeling of you, holding me. Your voice.'

'When you were so little?'

She nodded, but the tears were coming now. 'I couldn't, not really. But I told myself I could. And then my grand-mother told me . . .'

Seeker leaned forward. 'Your grandmother?'

'Aye, Father. Grandmother Paxton.'

He sat back again. Felicity's mother. Not his. He should have realised.

'Well, we went to see her, to stay with her, the once. But she didn't like Caleb, for Grandfather's sake, and so we had to move on.'

'Your grandfather is dead?'

Manon nodded.

'I'm sorry for it,' he said.

Manon acknowledged his sympathy and continued. 'Grandmother Paxton wanted to keep me with her,' she said. 'She said you'd be back for me one day, and if I was with her, you'd know where to find me.'

Seeker didn't know what to say. Another thread that he'd thought broken, that had never been broken. Another tie, still binding him, and he had not known it.

'Grandmother said Mother had done you very wrong. She said you'd come back for me.' She swallowed. 'Sometimes, when they left me here, or other places, I thought they'd never come back for me. I used to pray that you would instead. But then you didn't come, and I thought maybe Grandmother Paxton had been wrong.'

'I looked, tried to find out where you were. I should have come back myself, much sooner, carried on looking myself,' Seeker said. 'If I'd known how things were for you — I would have come.'

She didn't say anything for a moment, and then looked back up at him. 'But you've come now, haven't you?'

'Aye,' he said, reaching over to touch a stray hair fallen from her cap. 'I've come now.' A sheep came wandering along and, inspecting Seeker with some disdain, broke the moment. Manon laughed. 'Are the sheep so forward in London, Father?'

'Sheep and everything else. All forward and no back. Never take the time to look at anything right.'

'Different from here, then?'

'Oh, just a bit,' he said, smiling. 'Are you certain now? You wouldn't believe the noise and the dirt and the rushing about, and hardly a space to yourself.'

'Are there no quiet places at all?'

'Some, but you must know where to find them.'

'Well, you'll know then,' she said with confidence.

'How so sure?'

Manon waved a hand back to the inn. 'The man who keeps grumbling . . .'

'Lawrence Ingolby?'

'Aye, that one. He says you know everything. I heard him telling that Septimus, the vicar.' She raised an eyebrow. 'Says he's a vicar, anyway.'

It was like watching the sun come from behind a cloud, or the bud of a flower open to the light, the way Manon gradually became more assured in his presence, let him see her humour, the first hints of the sharpness of her wit. Seeker let her give her assessment of Septimus, and of Lawrence, and then he asked her, carefully, slowly, what she knew and had heard said of the people of Faithly, before Felicity and Turner had gone there, and after Felicity had returned. Her answers were clear enough: they had not known Seeker would be there; they never knew of a Thomas Faithly that she had heard any mention of, and the first Manon had heard spoken of Gwendolen Sorsby was when her mother had returned earlier that day and said that in Faithly a young girl had poisoned herself with mushrooms, and that was what happened if you let yourself be ignorant about plants.

He could see now that Manon was tiring, and that the events at Faithly were nothing to her. 'Get off to your bed, now, for we have a long ride ahead tomorrow, to Faithly, and another the next day, to York.'

She got up, obedient, and took a couple of steps towards the door before stopping, checking that they were not observed, then turning to hug him quickly around the neck, before running into the inn. Seeker sat there a good while longer, as the sun finally went down and the air cooled sharply. He stood up at last and went to arrange with his men the taking of the night watches.

It was about three in the morning that Seeker rose to take the third watch. The man he was replacing fell gratefully into the space in the bed he had just vacated. Before he went down to take up his post by the way-cross above the inn, Seeker looked into the corner of the attic room where Felicity and Manon had lain down for their last night together. Their candle had long been snuffed out, but there was enough moonlight coming in at the small window for him to see that Felicity was no longer there, and that Manon slept alone.

A sound from the courtyard outside took his attention and he went softly to the window. The world illuminated by the bright white moon was grey and black and indigo. The moor was bare and open, as God had made it, and nowhere for man to avoid His eye. Nor woman either. He watched as Felicity led a horse across the cobbles and out up onto the track that would take her west and south, towards Liverpool, if she had the sense he credited her with. She already had her letter, and the money he had given her to last her on the road. She was going without her escort, and she was going without further entreaty or goodbye to her daughter, or to him. She was also going, he saw with a trace of amusement and no little pride, with Sir Edward Faithly's horse. She would do all right, Felicity. When they had cleared the cobbles of the yard, she took hold of the pommel of the saddle and mounted the horse. As she was about to cover her head with the hood of her cloak, she turned around and looked directly at him. Seeker raised a hand and she nodded, before pulling up her hood and setting the horse quietly away. Seeker watched them go, for as far and as long as his eye could see, and then for a good while longer.

TWENTY-ONE

The Exile's Return

Lawrence Ingolby glanced a few times at Seeker as they rode. He'd asked once why the girl hadn't gone with her mother, and such was the force of Seeker's telling him to mind his own business that he didn't ask again. He wondered if the girl was truly the trier's daughter, for whilst she looked enough like the wife, she was nothing like Caleb Turner. Ingolby's other speculations about her parenthood he kept to himself, and it was hardly worth asking Septimus Jenkin for his views on the matter either, for fear they would be overheard. The child was on the horse that Felicity Turner had stolen from the manor stables, Ingolby having assured Seeker several times that it was a docile beast, and he himself was having to make do with a nag from the inn.

Septimus rode ahead on the horse he had taken from Pullan's yard only yesterday morning. He didn't sit as straight as usual, his fine riding habit doing nothing to hide the slumped shoulders of a man who had been taken for a fool. 'Cheer up, Septimus. Better discover what she's like now than halfway across the ocean.'

Septimus looked gloomily over to where Seeker rode. 'I daresay I'll never see the ocean, nor anything else but a scaffold looking out from Faithly Cross.'

Ingolby could find nothing to cheer him, save to say, 'I don't know what he's got planned for you, Septimus, but he'd hardly hang you for running off with the trier's wife.'

They were fording Harcoft Beck at the time, and Lawrence wasn't sure he caught exactly what it was the vicar said in response, though it sounded very like, 'But I have done more than run off with the trier's wife.'

It was mid-afternoon, and the day bright after the early mists when the gables of Faithly Manor came into view, the woods beyond a canopy of yellows, reds and tawny browns against the clear blue autumn sky. Seeker, who kept the young girl riding to the far side of him, away from Lawrence and the vicar, seemed strangely fixated on the woods, and on the limestone rock face above them. Septimus cast several anxious glances that way himself. Lawrence hadn't gone into the woods since he'd heard Tansy tell Seeker of the destroying angel on the night of Gwendolen's death. He was glad when the hooves of his old horse clattered under the stone archway and into the manor courtyard.

Dismounted, Seeker ordered his men to secure Jenkin in a cell in the cellars of the manor, to keep a guard on him and to allow him to talk to no one. One guard – the man who'd arrived from York the previous day and still awaited Seeker's response – would be sufficient on Jenkin. The others were to make a search of Faithly Woods.

'For what?' asked Lawrence before he could stop himself.

'The paper brought here yesterday gives strong cause for suspicion that Thomas Faithly, who disappeared from the continent several weeks ago, has returned to England, and if I'm right, this is where he'll have been making for.'

Lawrence couldn't hear whatever else Seeker might have been telling his men, but he did see the captain at one point brandish a paper at them, one that he was fairly certain had been brought the previous morning from York and delivered to Seeker's hand by Lawrence himself. Lawrence cursed that he had not had the sense to read the letter before he'd handed it over.

The gamekeeper was summoned, to act as guide to the soldiers in their search. As if guessing the idea that was formulating in Lawrence's mind, Seeker pointed at him. 'And you will stay here. No one is to leave this manor house today until my return.'

'Your return?'

'I've things to see to in the village.'

As they rode out under the archway of the manor house, down onto the track that skirted the moor, Manon looked at her father and could not help but smile. His authority over the vicar had been a proper authority, not like Caleb's, but a soldier's authority. They'd all run to do his bidding, his own men, the stable hands; even that steward, who had no respect for anything, had thought better of questioning him. He must have felt her eyes on him, for he turned and caught her with a smile that made her warm to her stomach.

'Shall we race, Manon?' he said, with a dark twinkle in his eye.

'Oh, yes!' she replied, not waiting for him but urging her horse on to fly down the moor. She glanced once or twice behind her where the huge black cavalry horse could somehow not quite catch her slighter mount. 'You're letting me win, Father.'

'Me?' he laughed. 'Never!' and he dug in his heels and flew past her thirty yards to wheel around and wait for her at a turn in the road.

She brought her horse to a stop just before his, and took a moment to catch a breath. She hadn't seen a smile so wide nor eyes so dark and sparkling as those looking at her now, not in almost twelve years. She'd told herself she remembered it, but she'd known in truth that it had gone, that memory. She'd made it a dream, a promise to herself of some better life. And even that promise had begun to slip from her grasp, until the moment he'd walked through the door of the Lion inn, this huge man, this soldier, with his scarred face and the dirt and damp of the moors on him, and something in his eyes that sparked the memory that had been lost. Whatever her fears, her anger and her hurt, she'd known then that this was her father and he had come back for her, her promise.

'How did you know I could ride?' she said, when she had got her breath back.

'Oh,' he said, 'I could tell by the set of you, when I lifted you up onto that horse. I could tell by the way the beast moved at your bidding. Your mother never could ride like that. Was it him taught you?'

'Caleb?' She was dismissive. 'He was scared of horses. Mother said I must have got it from you.'

They rode on in silence a little while, until she saw a village come into view below them. There was another question she had to ask him, and she was afraid of the answer, but she knew if she did not ask him now, when they were by themselves, she might lose her chance.

'Why must I not call you "Father" when there are other people around?' She saw him take a heavy breath and bring the big cavalry horse to a halt again. She pulled up her own mount. 'Will they not like it? The Lord Protector and the others you serve?'

Her father puffed out his cheeks and took a minute to think of his answer. 'I think the Lord Protector would like it very much. He has daughters of his own, and they are more dear to him than any kingdom. And the others, well . . .' he threw up a hand in helplessness, 'I doubt they would believe that one such as you could be mine. But it's not the people I serve that are the problem, Manon, it's those I serve them against. The Lord Protector has many enemies, and in serving him I have made his enemies mine. They would give much to have their revenge upon me, and have often tried, but they have failed to revenge themselves upon my person.'

'You are a very large and well-armed person, Father.'

He laughed. 'Yes, I am, as many have found to their cost. And so they would have their revenge another way, I think, if they could. They would harm those I love, so I must keep that secret. Down to my very dog.'

'You have a dog, Father?'

'Oh, yes.'

'Where is he?'

'He is in London, looking after some of my friends while I am away. He has a warm kennel by the gardeners' hut in a place called Lincoln's Inn, and no doubt grows fat on scraps from the kitchens there.'

'And will I see him?'

'Oh, yes, I'll make sure of that.'

But then another fear struck her.

'But if I'm to be a secret, how can you take me to London?'

He reached across and lifted her chin gently so she was looking right into his eyes. 'I'll not abandon you again, Manon. You'll come to London, and although you'll not live with me, you'll be loved and cared for, and I will be with you often.'

'And the dog?'

He raised his eyebrows in surprise that she should even ask the question. 'Why, most certainly the dog!'

'I'll be back to fetch her in the morning,' Seeker said. 'Don't let Abel Sharrock, nor anyone else outside this household, anywhere near her.'

'The child will be safe here,' Matthew Pullan assured him. 'You'll have no cause to fear for her.'

'I know that, I'd not have brought her here otherwise. How's your mother doing?'

Pullan lifted a stone weight from his desk, seemed to examine it, put it down again. 'I don't think it'll be long till she follows Gwendolen to the churchyard.' He looked up at Seeker. 'Are you going in to her?'

'I'll see her before I leave for York,' said Seeker, 'but it'll keep.'

He left Pullan, and looked in on the kitchen, where Manon was already helping Orpah to prepare Bess's supper. She smiled at him, so trusting, no doubt in her mind that he would be back in the morning, that he would do as he had promised her.

'But why can't I just stay up at the manor, amongst the servants, until you've finished your business there?' she'd asked.

He'd considered how best to put it.

'Have you ever seen a bag of weasels?' he'd said eventually.

'Of course, Father.'

'Well, that lot up at the manor are just like a bag of weasels, and I don't trust a single one of them.'

The paper that had come to him from York the previous day and that he had not looked at until after Manon had been found at Blakey Ridge and the business with Felicity arranged, had given cause for concern about Septimus Jenkin that had nothing to do with his flight with Felicity. In fact, it suggested that it was Septimus Jenkin, and not Sir Edward, that Seeker should have been questioning about the whereabouts of Thomas Faithly. Seeker went over to the churchyard.

Abel Sharrock was standing at his shovel, paused in the clearing of some ground near a large grave at the far side of the churchyard. As Seeker drew nearer he saw the name 'Pullan' engraved across the top of the granite slab. 'Saving myself some time,' said Sharrock, nodding across the street to where the shutters on the downstairs chamber where Bess now kept to her bed remained closed. 'Not long till I'll be opening this up again.'

Seeker was minded to take the shovel from him and break it over his head, but he was confident that Matthew Pullan would, in time, deal with Abel Sharrock.

'The keys to the church and schoolhouse,' he said, holding out his hand. Abel leaned towards him, an unpleasant enthusiasm in his eye. 'Looking for evidence? Of where he might have gone?'

Seeker struggled to keep the impatience out of his voice. 'I've already got Septimus Jenkin locked up in a cellar at Faithly Manor. The keys.'

'Well,' said Abel, his face alive with excitement, 'if you'll give me a moment to clean the dirt from my hands and get myself properly attired . . .'

'Fetch me the keys then get back to your work,' said

Seeker. He looked at the cut the sexton had just made in the turf above Digby Pullan's grave. 'Do your digging somewhere else in this churchyard.'

Visibly enraged at the slight, Abel bit back a riposte and went to fetch the keys. He thrust the old iron bunch into Seeker's hand without having made any attempt to remove the soil from his own. 'I'll have them back as soon as you're finished. The plate in there's counted, every bit of it.'

'I don't doubt it,' said Seeker, going towards the church.

The church of Faithly was an ancient place, bare and cold, but to Seeker had more of God in it than the wild imaginings of a place such as All Saints in York, or indeed the ornate magnificence of the minster. Those places might inspire awe at the majesty of God or the artistry of man, but somewhere like this — bare plasterwork, plain windows, unadorned walls and roof beams, honest and pure, stripped of all vain frippery — was more fit to meet a god who had made himself man.

He could see the marks on the tracery of the triple-lancet east window where, earlier, coloured panes must have been smashed by Matthew Pullan, and stubs on the simple capitals beneath the roof beams where the heads of angels might once have looked down upon the people of Faithly. It must have been fine work, all the same, for all that Matthew Pullan and others believed such things to be vanity, distracting the people from the worship of God.

The pulpit was plain, rough work — Seeker did not think much of the skill of the carpenter who had put that together. Apprentice work, at best. The plate, good but simple pewter, that Abel Sharrock was so concerned with, was set out upon the communion table, with a cloth over it against the dust. It should have been locked away, Abel or no.

As his eye scanned the church, Seeker could discern no trace of any habitation by Thomas Faithly. But Jenkin's connection with Thomas Faithly had suggested to Seeker that other things might well be hidden here. He walked around the altar table to examine the doors to the small aumbry, set into the wall beneath the window and still intact and locked. None of the keys on the bunch he had from Sharrock would fit it. Seeker took out his favourite dudgeon dagger, that he had got from a dead Scotsman, and made short work of the lock. Behind the doors, where the communion cup and cloth should have been, there was instead a packet, tied with cord and bearing the seal of the Faithly family. It took him less time to open the packet than it had the doors to the aumbry, and only a little longer to read and understand what the letters inside it were: those that Lawrence Ingolby had told him had gone missing from the Nuremberg chest at Faithly Manor.

There were only three letters in all. By the light of the south window, he read them again, to make sure he was not mistaken. It was as Ingolby's one glimpse of the contents had suggested: they were letters from the Royalist Thomas Faithly, in exile with the Stuarts, to his brother. They had been written years ago, and spoke of plans for an invasion and uprising, long since defeated, against the Commonwealth. That they had been in Sir Edward Faithly's possession, and not handed over to the authorities, would be enough to lose Edward Faithly every brick and yard of turf of the manor he was now master of – they should not have been his to mortgage to Matthew Pullan. That Septimus Jenkin clearly knew of these letters explained why Edward Faithly had been so keen to bring the trier to Faithly to expel the vicar. Seeker cursed in irritation. It would have saved a lot of time and effort if Septimus Jenkin had simply told him of this in the first place.

Lady Emma and Sir Edward were sitting to their dinner when Seeker arrived back at Faithly Manor. Lawrence Ingolby was hovering, as ever, watching from the fireplace as if waiting to pounce should Edward Faithly treat his wife to as much as a disparaging remark. Seeker thought Emma Faithly looked well capable of looking after herself.

'Well, Captain,' said Sir Edward when Seeker entered the hall, 'this is a disappointment. There have been such comings and goings and swappings of prisoners that I am sorry to see you arrive at our door empty-handed. It has been more entertaining here these last two weeks than on many a fair day.'

'Never trouble yourself over that, Sir Edward,' said Seeker, taking the goblet of wine Lady Emma had poured and was offering to him. 'There's plenty more diversion coming your way.'

Just as he finished speaking, the door from the kitchens, and the steps leading to the cellars below, opened, and one of Seeker's men led a manacled Septimus Jenkin into the great hall. A fleeting look of fear crossed Edward Faithly's face before he recomposed himself to the half-bored, half-amused look he had been studying to affect since Seeker's arrival. 'Well, this is a poor show, Captain. The Reverend Jenkin performs better when he is properly costumed and in his proper setting, either that or in his cups. As is plain for us all to see, he is currently neither. Besides, it is hardly an honourable thing, when your trier could not complete his case against him, to bring him in chains to my dining hall.'

Seeker put down his goblet. 'You're not going to waste my time by pretending you're glad the trier wasn't able to hound the Reverend Jenkin from his pulpit, are you, Sir Edward?'

He wasn't a man for theatre, but Seeker was enjoying this moment. The looks exchanged between Septimus Jenkin and Sir Edward Faithly were a small compensation for the dance these two men had been leading him. Lady Emma looked at her husband in disbelief. Only Lawrence Ingolby appeared as if he might be enjoying what was beginning to unfold.

Sir Edward was the first to recover. 'This is a slur, Captain. I have been accused of many things by those of your sort, but never of disinterest in the Church of England as it was once established, nor of disloyalty to my friends.'

'I'm assuming by "my sort" you mean the officers of this

Commonwealth, those who fought for Parliament and the liberties of the people, and who serve the Lord Protector in upholding the safety of the state. That's my sort, true enough, Sir Edward. As we'll be discussing, for it will be necessary to return to it, the safety of the state.'

Edward Faithly's habitual composure was a little shaken. His hands, also, had begun to shake. Seeker could almost see him holding his breath, wondering what would come next.

Lady Emma stood up. 'Can Septimus not sit down with us, get something to eat?'

'He's been fed,' said Seeker, continuing to watch Sir Edward, who was watching Jenkin. 'And he'll stand where he is.'

'Why have you brought him here?' asked Sir Edward eventually.

'I've brought him here because I thought he might be interested to hear why you wrote to the authorities in York requesting that the trier Caleb Turner be sent to Faithly to make trial of the fitness of your vicar and schoolmaster, the Reverend Septimus Jenkin, to remain in his post.'

Jenkin himself, constrained by his guards, tried to take a step towards Edward Faithly. 'It was you who brought this trial upon me?'

Faithly had started to push his chair back and was half out of it before he saw that the vicar couldn't reach him. He sat back down again slowly. His voice was cold. 'I deny it.'

Seeker slammed a paper down on the table in front of him. 'The letter to the major-general asking for the trier to be sent here is in your hand. I knew as soon as I came across it amongst other documents in York that the hand was yours. I could get Lawrence Ingolby to fetch some scrap of paper with your writing on it from amongst your papers here and make comparison, for proof, but I don't need to. I'll ask you again, and I'll have a better answer this time: why did you want Septimus Jenkin hounded away from this place?'

Faithly took a moment to calculate. 'I . . . the drinking, the women . . . I felt he had fallen from the standards required of a man of God . . .'

Lady Emma turned in astonishment to her husband. 'What have you ever cared for the word or true worship of God?'

Edward Faithly's face became a sneer. 'Spoken like a true Puritan, my dear. What a worthy wife you would have made to Matthew Pullan.'

Lawrence Ingolby went to stand at Emma Faithly's shoulder and touched a hand to her arm – whether of reassurance or restraint Seeker could not have said. Ingolby's eyes told another story, of such a loathing for her husband that Seeker was not certain, should he ever hear that Edward Faithly had been murdered, that it was to Matthew Pullan's door he should, in fact, go first.

'I'll have the truth,' said Seeker.

'Or what? I have heard you have your methods of getting men to talk.'

'And some are not what you might think,' said Seeker,

lifting from a sack he had set upon the floor the packet of letters he had found locked in the aumbry of Faithly church. Again, the looks on the faces of Edward Faithly and Septimus Jenkin mirrored one another – he couldn't tell which was the more frightened, but Jenkin would keep for the time being. For now, Seeker concentrated his attention on Edward Faithly. Faithly's eyes flew to Lawrence Ingolby, who merely shrugged.

'Nothing to do with me, Sir Edward. Those letters disappeared whilst I was away in York.'

'But only I had the key,' Faithly almost spat.

'Well, that's not entirely true, is it?' said Seeker. 'Someone else has the key to the Nuremberg chest you kept these in.'

'I have never given it to anyone,' said Edward Faithly through gritted teeth.

'No. But someone else did. Someone else had a key to that chest.'

'Yes,' said Faithly, exasperated. 'My father, who took it with him when he went to fight for the King and was killed doing so.'

'And was attended by your brother, who wasn't. Killed, that is.'

Edward Faithly had now gone quite pale. 'I told you. I have had no contact with my brother for years. If he has disappeared from the court of the king in Germany or Holland or wherever it might be, I know nothing of it: you'd do better to look in a Flemish brothel or a Cologne bierkeller than in my house.'

'No, Sir Edward: I do better to look right here. I don't doubt you know nothing of your brother's plans. I'd wager you want nothing less than for your brother to return, and claim Faithly Manor in your stead. Thomas Faithly was your father's heir, after all.'

Edward Faithly began to relax a little. The curl at the corner of his upper lip might have been the beginning of a smile. 'But my brother is a declared rebel, a traitor to the Commonwealth and to the Lord Protector, as you well know, Seeker. His rights to this estate are forfeit.'

'As would yours be, if you were found to be involved in his disappearance from the Stuart court and any reappearance here, in England.'

'Which I have already told you I am not,' said Faithly, a vein in his forehead beginning to throb.

'Aye, you're right,' said Seeker, letting Faithly take the moment to begin to relax, 'not now. Not this time. Not like before.'

Faithly's eyes shot immediately to the letters.

'That's right,' said Seeker. 'April 1650. You were in correspondence with your brother then, weren't you, when he was at Breda with Charles Stuart that now calls himself King. When the Scots were there, entreating him, enticing him. And then a year later, when Charles was in Edinburgh, you gave assurances to your brother that the pretended King would find a warm welcome here, that you would rouse your tenants and neighbours to rally to his standard, should he lead an army over from the northern border with the Scots.'

Edward Faithly was swallowing hard. His eyes darted from the packet of letters to Septimus Jenkin to his wife, as if in one of them would he find the way out of his predicament. 'My letters to my brother are not in that packet.'

'No,' conceded Seeker, 'but I don't doubt he has kept them, and by your words you confess that there were such letters.'

'You don't know what was in them.'

Seeker laughed. 'Oh, do I not, "one such as me", eh? Let me tell you about "one such as me", Sir Edward. I may look unlettered but be assured, I am not. I have read many hundreds of letters over the years, letters that are but half of a correspondence, and I have learned to see through their wording to that of the letters to which they were written in response. You made promises to your brother and he thanked you for them, and made promise of great recompense and preferment in the service of the Stuarts in return. The loss of Faithly Manor to him would have been nothing to you in comparison with what you were promised in these letters.' He held up the packet so that Faithly should be in no doubt that he knew what was in it.

Edward Faithly had sunk lower in his chair, his face a scarlet fury.

'I did nothing,' he said, like a youth caught in a lie by his father.

'He's right there, much though I hate to say it,' interjected Ingolby. 'Sir Edward did nothing to rouse anyone when Cromwell was marching up to deal with the Scots at Dunbar. Then four years ago when the K— that is, the traitor Charles Stuart came down over the border at the head of them, Sir Edward here locked his doors and sat by the hearth there. Might as well have stuck his fingers in his ears. He did nothing to help Charles Stuart, or his own brother either, for that matter. I'd a' known and so would Matthew.'

'Aye, no doubt,' said Seeker. 'But Sir Edward's cowardice won't save him this time.' He turned to the man still visibly fuming at the end of the refectory table. 'That you conspired with your brother to bring Charles Stuart back to England with the intention of putting him on his father's throne will be enough. You'll be imprisoned, or banished. And even if you don't lose your estates, they'll be in the hands of your wife, or any who might hold a mortgage on this place.' He took a moment to let that information sink in. 'It's not for me to judge, but I doubt you'll be Lord of Faithly Manor very much longer once this information reaches the major-general.'

Lady Emma, who was leaning forward in her chair, so interested was she in the tale unfolding before her, furrowed her brow, puzzled. 'But what has all this to do with Septimus?'

Seeker indicated the packet of letters which he had placed on the table. 'The letters showing your husband's collusion in his brother's traitorous plans five years ago, bound together here, were in this packet which had been placed in a locked cupboard in Faithly church by Septimus Jenkin, who had stolen them from the Nuremberg chest in the Faithly strongroom.'

Lady Emma looked from Seeker to Septimus Jenkin and then back again.

'He did it with the help of the key that your father-in-law, Sir Anthony Faithly, had taken from here when he went off to war, and which Jenkin got from his son Thomas.'

Septimus Jenkin, who had gone very pale, asked if he might sit down.

'Bring him a stool,' said Seeker.

'Well, I'm still none the wiser,' said Lady Emma.

Seeker went into his bag and handed her a sheet of paper that was crumpled from having travelled many miles that day, and the day before. She looked at it and then looked up, still puzzled, and handed it back. 'It's a drawing of Septimus. Not a very good one, I'll grant you, but it's definitely Septimus.'

Seeker told one of his soldiers to show it to the vicar, whose chin slumped to his chest. 'Yes, it is, isn't it? But that paper was drawn in York, to the description given by a soldier who was one of an escort ambushed in the West Riding nearly three weeks ago. That escort was transferring a group of captured Dunkirkers from Whitby to Halifax. They were stopped on the way by the sight of a burning effigy, that they took at first to be a man, hanging from a tree. The purpose of the ambush seems to have been to effect the escape of one particular prisoner, who was taken from the transport and seen to ride away with the man fitting the description of the one on the paper. It was Septimus Jenkin who held up that transport, and I have reason to believe the man whose escape he assisted was Thomas Faithly.' He turned to Jenkin. 'That's about the size of it, isn't it, vicar?'

But Septimus Jenkin said nothing, rather continued to stare at his own hands.

'Thomas Faithly must have communicated with you from the court, and again from York. Some castle servant or some such, paid to smuggle a letter out. They'll be found, though. Your moment had come at last, hadn't it? Your chance to act, to honour the old Faithlys? The ambush was the night before Bess Pullan's supper. No wonder you looked so worn out.'

Lady Emma had got over her shock and was now thoroughly intrigued. 'But if this is the case, Captain, where is Thomas?'

'Well?' he enquired of Jenkin, but Jenkin, his face defiant now, remained mute.

'Huh,' muttered Seeker. 'It would save time if you just told me, but I'll find him anyway. My men are currently searching Faithly Woods.'

'And then what?' asked Edward Faithly.

'And then you can all tell your stories to Major-General Lilburne in York.'

'All?' asked Lawrence Ingolby, thoroughly affronted.

'Stand easy,' said Seeker. 'I mean the vicar here and Sir Edward and his brother. I daresay Lady Emma will need you here, for the running of the estate, until such time as Matthew Pullan decides what to do with it.'

'Matthew?' asked Emma. 'But what's it got to do with Matthew?'

Ingolby took a deep breath. 'I'll explain later.'

Sir Edward reached out for the bottle of wine on the table in front of him, but Seeker moved it away. 'You've had enough for tonight.'

Just as Sir Edward was about to remonstrate, there was a loud banging on the front door, which soon opened to reveal the men whom Seeker had sent to search for Thomas Faithly in Faithly Woods. In between them, his wrists bound by rope, was a third man, who was most certainly not one of Seeker's men. On their captain's command, the soldiers brought him further into the light.

Septimus Jenkin had swivelled round on his stool, but his face fell, and took on a look of utter confusion.

'I don't believe it,' murmured Lawrence Ingolby.

'Who is that?' asked Lady Emma.

But Edward Faithly just started to laugh, in disbelief at first and then uproariously. 'Oh, Captain, this is entertainment indeed. You present that as the heir to Faithly Manor?' He shook his head. 'Oh, this is too good. That is not my brother.'

Seeker knew it wasn't. The man before him was nothing like the handsome young Royalist who still smiled down from a portrait on the wall of the great hall where his younger brother had until tonight held sway. The man before him was older, a scrawny, unkempt thing, and Seeker had seen him before, for only three days ago he had chased him from the steps of the anchorage of All Saints church in York. It was the man who had been trailing Lawrence Ingolby to the Old Star inn and around the city, asking questions about Gwendolen Sorsby.

Seeker looked to Ingolby, but Lawrence was staring, open-mouthed, in dawning recognition, at the man between the two soldiers. Slowly, his lips started to move. He said something, to himself at first, and then Seeker could see his lips begin to form the last three words once more, to repeat them. 'It's Seth Whyte,' he said. 'Hellfire and damnation! It's Seth Whyte.' Tansy's husband.

TWENTY-TWO

Seth

Seeker slumped down into Lawrence Ingolby's finest arm-chair and let out a heavy sigh. Septimus Jenkin had been returned to his cell, and Seeker had left his two best men standing guard over Sir Edward Faithly in the great hall.

'You're running out of places to keep them,' Ingolby had said, attempting humour, 'or are you putting Seth in with Septimus?'

'I doubt if Seth Whyte's guilty of much more than stupidity,' said Seeker. 'Your room'll do for now.'

'What?' Lawrence had protested. 'I mean,' he said, lowering his voice and looking sideways at Seth, 'have you seen the state of him? He's filthy.'

'I daresay the housemaid can find her way there with her mop and bucket when we're done.'

Ignoring Ingolby's further protests, Seeker had told the guards to loose the bounds around Seth Whyte's wrists and then prodded the new arrival in the back, in the direction of the great stairs and Ingolby's rooms in the west end of the house.

'So,' he said, once he was settled and had put a light to Ingolby's fire, 'tell me.'

Despite Ingolby's objections, Seth Whyte wasn't on closer sight quite as filthy as might have been expected of a man who'd spent days on the road and then hiding out in Faithly Woods. His hair and face he could have washed in any stream, but Seeker doubted the clean and freshly laundered-smelling shirt, much better than the one Seth had skulked around York in, was the prodigal's own work. That would keep, though.

'Tell you what?' asked Seth suspiciously.

'Oh,' said Seeker, stretching his booted feet towards the fire, '"everything" would be good. "Everything" would save time. But let's start with where you've been for the last fourteen years.'

'Well,' began Seth, running his tongue along his lower lip, clearly in search of some halfway feasible lie.

Seeker wondered how Tansy had ever got in tow with someone so stupid. He held up his hand. 'Don't bother, I've probably already heard it, whatever rubbish you come up with. How about I tell you what I know first.'

Seth looked almost relieved to have the responsibility of speaking for himself taken from him.

'I've been doing some adding up, you see. I'm quite good at that, you know.'

Seth kept his mouth shut, clearly terrified and clueless as to what was coming next.

'You left, supposedly for the fair at Helmsley, fourteen

years ago, two days before Digby Pullan went on a trip to York. I know the exact day, because Tansy has scratched out the days and the weeks and the months, every one of them. I went and tallied them for myself this afternoon. Digby Pullan came back, six days later, with young Gwendolen Sorsby, not much more than two years old, in tow. You never did.'

There was a slight look of panic in Seth's eyes now, but still he had the sense to keep his mouth shut, and not attempt any protestation.

'No one sees hide nor hair of you for fourteen years, and then, within a week of Gwendolen's death, you show up in York, sniffing around after Lawrence Ingolby, asking if she's dead.'

Seth was sitting rigid in the small wooden chair across from Seeker, like a rabbit paralysed with fear. Seeker leaned a little towards him, making his eyes level with Seth Whyte's. He enunciated his words very slowly. 'What did you do, Seth?'

Whyte started to exhibit genuine panic now. His feet were tapping and his breathing had become rapid. He looked wildly around the room as if searching for a sympathetic audience.

Seeker leaned closer towards him. 'There's only me here, Seth, and if you want ever to leave this room, you're going to tell me what you did.'

Seth Whyte sniffed and shook his head quickly. 'I didn't kill her. I haven't been back here in fourteen years and I never went near Gwendolen. I never went near her, I didn't kill her. It were nothing to do with me.'

Seeker leaned back in his chair. Seth hadn't told him anything he didn't know, but at least he'd got him talking.

He waited a minute, contented himself with watching the other man, who, though calmed, remained very frightened-looking.

'What were you doing at All Saints church in York, Seth? What were you doing at the anchorhold there? You see, I'm not asking you about what you did at the time of Gwendolen Sorsby's death. I'm asking you what you did fourteen years ago.'

Whatever further protest Seth Whyte had been considering abandoned him, and his already narrow shoulders seemed to narrow in on themselves further, as he looked down at his own feet.

'Just went travelling,' he whispered at last.

'After. You went travelling after. With Digby Pullan's money.'

Seth looked up, a spark of defiance at last in his eyes. 'He give it me! Digby Pullan give me that money, I didn't steal it, no matter who says I did!'

Seeker nodded. 'Oh, he gave it to you all right, Seth. No one's disputing that. But I'm asking what he gave it to you for. What did you do for him, eh, Seth? What did you do for him, that first time at All Saints?'

Seth Whyte's mouth started to move uselessly, and he said nothing.

'You see,' continued Seeker, 'I didn't have time that day we first met — remember, at All Saints, North Street, you, me and Lawrence?'

Seth Whyte nodded dumbly.

'Well, I didn't have time that day — as you will no doubt recall — to go up and see what was in that anchorhold at All Saints, looking out through that squint into the church. But you did, didn't you?'

Seth began to shake his head vigorously, and threatened to begin babbling again.

Again Seeker stopped him. 'You went there to have a look in the anchorhold, and I suspect you found the same thing my men found when they went to search there the following morning.' He brought a paper from the bag at his feet, one of the two reports — the other having accompanied the sketch of Septimus Jenkin — that had arrived for him from York the previous day. He moved a joint-stool from beside his chair and set it between them to serve as a table and then laid the paper out on its surface. 'Can you read, Seth?'

Seth Whyte shook his head, never taking his eyes off the paper.

'Shall I tell you what it says, what my men found?'

Seth shook his head, but Seeker picked up the paper and began to read anyway. He had read it before, silently, that morning, when he'd remembered it before they set out from Blakey Ridge, but now he thought his voice might give way on him.

'Having arrived at All Saints, North Street a little before eight in the morning, we found the vicar, a Reverend Locke, reluctant to allow access to the anchorhold. On intimation of our authority, he eventually furnished us with the key. The steps to the upper floor of the structure are in a poor state of repair. As we ascended them, we heard a scrabbling noise from the upper room, and the sound of something being dragged across the floor. We reached the door before the occupant of the room succeeded in blocking it. Inside, we found a woman, a sorry specimen of between about thirty and forty years of age, clean enough and well-enough fed, as it seemed, but wanting her wits. She cowered in a corner, clawing at her clothing and whimpering like an animal. She offered no response to our enquiries as to who she was and what she did there, but no violence, either. We judged best to leave her where she was. On being questioned, the Reverend Locke asserted she had been there long before he had ever arrived in the parish seven years earlier, that she had been in a sad condition then but had worsened with every passing year, and that he knew her name only as Martha. Her keep was paid out of a benefaction made fourteen years previously by an anonymous donor, and added to from time to time by the charitable-minded of the parish.' Seeker stopped reading. The rest was not Seth Whyte's concern. 'Well?' he said. 'Was that what you found?'

Ashen, Seth nodded.

'And had this Martha worsened over the fourteen years?'

Again, by a slow movement of his head, Seth affirmed that she had.

'And will you now tell me what happened, that first time you saw her, fourteen years beforehand?'

Seth seemed to rouse himself, some defiance returning to his face. 'No,' he said, 'not while Bess lives.'

'All right,' said Seeker, 'but what of Tansy, did she know?'

Anger flashed across Seth Whyte's eyes. 'Tansy knows nothing.'

'She didn't send word to you in York, that Gwendolen was dead?'

'How should she have done? She didn't know where I was. I heard by chance of Gwendolen's death at a tavern on King's Staithe, where a merchant who trades with Matthew Pullan was drinking.'

'And yet Tansy knew you were in Faithly Woods, did she not? Did she not bring you that shirt, that smells so fine and fresh of lavender and thyme and other herbs that hang from her ceiling?'

'It was the stone,' Seth said, a little recovered from his fear and his anger.

In response to Seeker's evident incomprehension, he expanded. 'Tansy's father had no great liking for me, so when we were courting, I would leave a special stone at her door, as a sign that we should meet in the woods. She knew the place. I always carried that stone away with me, whenever I left Faithly — lest another man should take it, I used to joke. Though it wasn't a joke. I didn't want Tansy to go with no other man. I've had that stone in my pocket fourteen years. Well, two nights ago I set it at our cottage door, to let her know I was back.' He nodded, proud. 'And my Tansy came to the place the very next morning, to find me, as I knew she would. But Tansy knew nothing of the business of All Saints, or of who killed Gwendolen.'

'Hmm,' said Seeker, getting up and indicating that Seth should do the same. 'Tansy knows more than you think, I'd wager.'

Seeker took Seth Whyte down to the cellars of Faithly Manor and locked him in the cell next to Septimus Jenkin. He'd tackle Seth again in the morning. His refusal to tell Seeker what had happened at All Saints church all those years ago 'while Bess lived' might not survive a night of better reflection in the cellars of Faithly, but Seeker could not be certain of that. Just like Lawrence Ingolby, Seth Whyte was so loyal to the Pullans he would say nothing he feared might cast them in an ill light. Lawrence had fared better for it than had poor Seth − Lawrence who would sleep amongst rich drapes in a warm room. Sir Edward Faithly would also sleep amongst rich drapes in a warm room tonight, but it would be the last time he did so. A guard on his door would see to it that there were no more escapes from Faithly Manor.

When Seeker returned to the great hall, Lawrence and Lady Emma were still up, talking across the dying embers of the fire. Emma Faithly's eyes, that had been as dull as granite in the rain, sparkled now. Each time Seeker saw her, it was as if she had come a little further into the light since that first night at Bess Pullan's. The more Edward Faithly's hold on their world had slipped from his grasp, the more alive to it his wife had become. It was as if the real, living woman was emerging from the crumbling edifice of the past fourteen years of her life. It seemed natural now to Seeker to address himself to her.

'I've sent for a troop from York to carry on with the search for your brother-in-law, Lady Emma. They should be here before dinnertime tomorrow, and when they get here, I'll be on my way to York, with the Reverend Jenkin and your husband. I wouldn't worry about any of them coming across that door again.'

Emma shook her head. 'Septimus – I'd never have guessed he had that in him – plotting against the Protectorate. Thought he'd no interest in much above wine and women. And Thomas Faithly, well – I'm no Royalist, Captain, and never was – but everyone hereabouts knew he was a better man than Edward. At least he fought for something.'

'Aye, well,' said Seeker, 'he made his choices. But for yourself, you may rest easy. There's none suspects you in any part of this treachery, and I'd be surprised if Major-General Lilburne was not disposed to have this place sold outright to Matthew Pullan. As to the rest, I cannot advise you.'

She looked almost amused. 'Thank you, Captain. I daresay Lawrence can advise me – if I should need it. Matthew too.'

'Hmmn,' said Seeker, looking at his travelling companion

of the last several days, 'I know which of the two I'd be best disposed to listen to. I'll bid you both goodnight.'

Returned to his preferred billet above the stables of Faithly Manor, Seeker reflected on the events of the day, and on the information he now held. He was not looking forward to the interviews of tomorrow.

TWENTY-THREE

Truth

Bess was propped up in bed, her nightcap tied tight under her chin and a thick woollen shawl draped over her shoulders. The fire in the room was blazing, Orpah having overridden her mistress's assertion that she did not feel the cold and that a fire in a bedchamber on such a morning was an outright sin. Bess did not mince her words on the subject of Seth Whyte. 'As useless and shiftless a man as ever set foot on God's good earth.'

'Tansy doesn't think so,' said Seeker, leaning his back against the window sill and almost blocking out the light from the window whose shutter Bess had insisted he open.

'Tansy,' she tutted. 'Tansy doesn't know her own mind, never has. Mind you, she always said he'd be back, said my Digby had told her he would. Digby indeed! What should Digby have known of the doings of Seth Whyte? I told her, time and again, Seth was gone for good. I thought it no kindness to her to pretend otherwise, but she never listened to me. Master Digby had told her Seth would be back one day, and she should wait for him.' Bess pursed

330

her thin lips and shook her head, as if thinking it still nonsense. For all her show, Seeker could see the speech had taken some effort. He poured a beaker of cordial from the earthenware jug Orpah had left by her bedside and held it to her lips. The old woman managed a couple of sips before turning her mouth away and sinking back into her pillows. 'Gwendolen's,' she said. 'Gwendolen made that.'

Her skin was taut across her bones and her face a deathly yellow. Her breathing came hard.

'I can come back later,' he said.

She shook her head, forced herself to rally. 'No, you've plenty on hand up at the manor and in the woods, if half the gossip spilling out of the Black Bull last night is to be believed. Orpah's near upside down with it.'

Seeker smiled. 'Not just Orpah, but it's not your concern.'

'No?' Weak though she was, the piercing look she gave him put Seeker in mind of Cromwell's favourite hawk.

'Major-General Lilburne'll take care of Septimus Jenkin and the Faithlys. It'll be down to your Matthew to deal with the rest.'

This seemed to satisfy her, almost.

'And Seth?'

'Well, that's the question, isn't it? There's things about Seth's disappearance fourteen years ago I don't understand yet,' said Seeker. 'Not much I can lay on Seth, for now, other than giving me trouble running around York. Nothing to do with the Faithlys, at any rate – I left instructions for him to be released at first light. A night's stewing'll not have done him any harm. But I daresay I'll be having more words with Seth Whyte before the day's out, once I get to the bottom of what your Digby has to do with it all. Seth'll have been back down at Tansy's long since, no doubt, so I'll know where to find him when I'm ready.'

His mention of her dead husband had rattled Bess – he could see her knuckles whiten further on the coverlet when he'd said her husband's name. He saw her summon an effort to look indignant. 'Digby? What would my Digby have to do with all this business of Thomas Faithly sneaking back to England? Digby's been dead years!'

'I'm not talking about the Faithlys, I'm talking about Seth and Tansy and Gwendolen.'

She stared straight ahead of her. 'Then I'll thank you to enlighten me, Captain.'

Seeker took a deep breath. 'Seth Whyte disappeared from this village two days before your husband went to York to fetch Gwendolen back here. No one saw hide nor hair of him until he turned up back in York trailing after Lawrence Ingolby, trying to find out if it was true that Gwendolen was dead. And now that he knows she is, he's back here. He's spent the last fourteen years away from here on your husband's instructions and living off money given to him by your husband for a service he performed then. Out of some loyalty to your family, he refuses to tell me what that service was.'

Bess was unmoved. 'Well, I'm sure I can't tell you either, Captain.'

'All right then. We'll start with Tansy: did Digby tell you to look after her, see she didn't go hungry, protect her from Sharrock's accusations?'

Bess was surprised. 'Aye, he did, as a matter of fact. Not that I wouldn't have done it anyhow. It's only Christian, poor soul that she is.'

'And like a good Christian you performed your corporal acts of mercy, feeding the hungry, giving drink to the thirsty—'

But Bess stopped him before he could go further. 'Never thought to hear one such as you talk popery, Captain. Christian charity, that's all I showed to Tansy.'

'Just like in the window,' said Seeker.

'What window?' she snapped, starting to tire of baiting and being baited.

He pulled a stool over and sat down by her bed. 'The one in All Saints, North Street.'

'York?' she asked, as if trying to locate something she had never been quite certain of.

'You know it is.'

She fixed him again with her hawk's eye and sniffed. 'I have no interest in windows and such idolatry.'

'No,' he said, 'I know well enough you didn't go there for the windows. Not for the corporal acts of mercy, nor the Pricke of Conscience either.'

'No,' she said, her face grim, 'but I'll see that one in my nightmares.'

'I know you went there, because your landlady in York and the vicar of All Saints told me you did. And when I went there, I found Seth Whyte was there too.'

Bess couldn't help herself. She flinched and turned to face Seeker now. Watching her, he continued. 'Seth Whyte went there for the same reason you did after he heard Gwendolen had died: he went there to look at the anchorhold.'

Bess turned her face away. 'I know nothing of Seth Whyte's movements,' she said.

'No,' said Seeker wearily, 'I don't suppose you do, or did, at any rate. But something you saw in Gwendolen's grandmother's account book, the one that Ben Scrope gave to you when last you visited him, sent you off to All Saint's church.'

Bess's face was like a stone. She had nothing left to say.

'Where's the book, Bess?'

Bess tried to moisten her dry lips. 'Burned it,' she said eventually.

He could believe that. 'What was in it?'

She sniffed, fussed with her fingers at the edge of the coverlet. 'Private matters. Not for the world's eyes.'

'Aye, but you read it, didn't you?' he said. 'And what you read sent you straight to All Saints on North Street, and then hurrying back here to Faithly, but only once you'd been round half the apothecaries in York asking for snake-root. You see,' he continued, 'I had to come back here in a hurry, too, and I've had to wait for a couple of things I asked for in York to reach me here. They arrived two days ago, just as I had to head off to Blakey Ridge, and I didn't have time to see to them till I got back here.'

'Well, I'm not a woman with much time either, so you'd better get to the point.'

'All right. Before I left York, I left orders for that anchorhold to be searched. I also sent to the major-general's own apothecary asking what snakeroot was for.'

Bess's face became greyer, her mouth slack.

Seeker held between his fingers the note that had come from Lilburne's apothecary in York. 'He tells me it's hard to be got, that it was brought to England in Queen Elizabeth's time, but never took hold, for that the dosage was difficult and mistakes might be fatal. He said used properly, it was thought to cure madness, give relief to the deranged.' He put the note away. 'What my men found in that anchorhold, Mistress Pullan, was way beyond the powers of snakeroot.'

Her head fell to her chest. Her voice was scarcely audible. 'I burned the account book, true enough – it was no use to anybody, but there was a letter with it.'

'With what?'

'Elizabeth Sorsby's account book. The book was a list of payments, month by month, from the same time Gwendolen had come to us until just before her grandmother's death. All they said was "to the church, for Martha's care".' She looked fiercely towards Seeker. 'They'd told me Martha was dead, Captain, I swear it, and I never knew different and nor did Matthew, not until I saw that account book and read that letter.'

'Tell me about it,' he said quietly.

Bess sniffed again, gathered her strength. 'You can see for yourself. I didn't burn it. I've kept it, for Matthew, so he'll understand and set things right after I've gone.' She nodded towards the plain oak dresser by the door. 'In there. Walnut box.'

He got up and opened the doors of the dresser. The bottom shelves stored linen and blankets, but on the top shelf were more personal items, such as Bess had permitted herself to gather over nigh on seventy years. There were pieces of jewellery, plain but of good quality, as befitted the wife of a wealthy Puritan merchant. Seeker wondered if they might one day hang around the neck of Emma Faithly, for he could not see that Matthew Pullan would ever marry another. There was a Bible, bound in black leather. He removed it from the cabinet and placed it carefully on top, that he might more easily reach the walnut box that lay behind it. He lifted the box out and half-turned towards Bess.

'It's not locked,' she said.

There was only one item inside, a letter, folded and addressed to Bess.

'Elizabeth Sorsby must have meant to give it to me before she died, but it was forgotten at the back of that account book. Perhaps it was just as well I never knew . . .'

Seeker opened out the letter, written in an old, rounded

secretary hand, its ink faded to brown now. As Bess watched him, he began to read.

My Dear, True Friend,

I write not that you might forgive me, for I know there can be no forgiveness for what I have done, but that you may of your love and Christian charity care for those whom I wrong as much if not more than I have already wronged you.

I never betrayed my husband but once, and that once was a most dreadful betrayal for it was with his great friend, and your husband, Digby. I make no excuse, for there can be none, but know that I have paid for it in grief many times over since then. The proof of my betrayal was daily before my eyes — for my son, William, was fathered not by my husband but by yours. The boy never knew of it, and my husband never once voiced any suspicion on the matter.

I thought for long enough the grief and shame would be mine alone, and when William married, and soon told me I was to be a grandmother, I thought God had forgiven me. Oh, foolish woman that I was, that thought I might hide my sin from God! My first punishment, that I thought could not be surpassed, was the loss of my dear son at sea when his young wife, Martha, was still with child. The shock of the news almost sent the poor girl from her senses, and indeed it did, for she was never again as she had been before that day. The birth of her child — Gwendolen — only served to make her distraction worse, and it was then that rumour reached me at last that William had known of but kept from me — Martha's own mother had been prey to bleak distress and weakness of mind that some had called madness. Each month that passed gave new proofs that Martha was cursed with the same malady, until such time as it could hardly be longer hidden from the world.

I am grown old, Bess, and more ill than you can know. I will soon stand before my judge and hear my dreadful doom. The good Lord has chosen to blight Martha's wits with this madness, that we might care for her in our charity, but there are those who would read her distraction as something else. Soon I will not be able to shield her from the censure of the world, nor care for her own child myself. What is to become of them in these unforgiving days, afflicted as Martha is, when I am gone and no longer able to protect them? This is why I have done what I had sworn never to do since first I felt the quickening of my son William in my womb — I have asked his father, Digby Pullan, for help. He is to come tomorrow, to fetch Gwendolen and take her to you, whom I trust to care for and love her, for her own sake, more than I would trust any other. Martha is to be taken into the care of All Saint's church on North Street, where she can be looked after away from the eyes of the world, and where I may still visit her. She is — alas — despite all her distraction and delusion — extraordinarily attached to her child, and I fear will make great difficulty over giving her up. Some deception and, I fear, force, will have to be used. Digby has promised to bring with him a man whose strength and silence he can rely upon. I can do no more.

May God forgive me, Bess, for I know that you cannot,
Believe me your loving friend,
    Elizabeth Sorsby, this 14th Day of May, Year of God One
thousand six hundred and forty-one

Seeker lifted his eyes from the page; it was something like what he had guessed, and Seth Whyte must have been the man whose help and silence in incarcerating Martha Sorsby without her child – Digby's own grandchild – Digby Pullan had paid for.

'And you knew none of this?'

Bess shook her head. Seeker could see she was struggling against a tear threatening in her eye. 'I knew Digby had other women when he was away – man like that, I'm not a fool – but I always thought he kept his pleasures away from anything that could touch us.' She smiled. 'I never suspected Elizabeth, nor that their William . . . But none of that matters now.' A great sigh racked her weakened frame. 'How can he have known me so little, my own husband, to think I wouldn't have taken the child in if I'd known the truth? Wouldn't have loved her anyway? Why are men so arrogant, eh, to think that it is always them that'll matter most?'

She didn't appear to be waiting for an answer, and Seeker didn't attempt one, but just waited for her to continue. 'Before he went off to York, Digby told me he'd had word that Martha was dead, taken in a fever. He never told me otherwise, not a hint of it. I already knew Elizabeth was ill. I took in Gwendolen for Christian charity and for love of my friend. It was only as she began to grow to womanhood that I began to fear there was something amiss with Gwendolen – I knew nothing of her mother's family's history, or I might have known the signs sooner for what they were. There were times when she would imagine she saw things – be certain of them – that I knew for certain she could not be seeing for they were not there. Things would become for her matters of great consequence, that really were of no consequence at all. She would be in great distress until these episodes passed. I shielded her from public view at these times, but Tansy saw it, and she knew it for what it was before I did. I think Gwendolen came to know it herself, poor child. Tansy taught her which compounds to make up and take to calm herself, when she felt the darkness or the wildness coming upon her. Tansy insisted on the amulet, with the peony root, to ward off the times of madness, and it seemed to please Gwendolen, though it had a savour of superstition to me.' Her head had been drooping and she lifted it again, the old determination. 'And I thought, in this way, away from the city, it could be managed.' She rounded on Seeker suddenly. 'Matthew knew nothing of it, mind! None of it – no more did Lawrence. They put her changing humours down to the strangeness of women, and I saw to it that Abel Sharrock and Maud and their like were kept well away when Gwendolen was sunk into her darkness, or hearing her voices. I thought all would be well, and that with Tansy's help, even after I was gone, it could be managed.'

'But then the Sorsbys' servant Ben Scrope gave you Elizabeth Sorsby's account book.'

Bess swallowed. 'I found the letter at the back of it that night, after my supper in my lodging on Trinity Lane. I'd never been near All Saints before – I have no interest in stone churches, Captain.' She nodded towards her Bible and Seeker handed it to her. She ran her hand over the front cover. 'The word of God is all my church. Anyhow, next morning, I found my way to North Street. The vicar thought I'd come to look at the windows, but I soon put him straight. Told him I was there to enquire after Martha Sorsby. He claimed to know no such person, and then I heard it.' She closed her eyes.

'What did you hear, Bess?'

'It was like a young dog, a pup, trying to howl. Worst sound I ever heard in my life, and it was coming from right above me.'

Seeker pictured the interior of All Saints church as he had seen it. 'You were near the west door.'

She cocked an eyebrow at him. 'Send your familiar there, did you? Aye, I was near the west door. There was a hole in the wall above me – a squint, the vicar called it. He said there was an animal trapped there, but then she started to cry and it was a sound no animal I've ever known could make. I told him to take me to her or I'd have the major-general and every trier in England on him.'

'And he did?'

'Aye,' she said, biting her bottom lip, 'he did.'

Seeker thought again of the report his men had sent of what they'd found in the anchorage behind the squint, and of what this uncompromising, godly old woman must also have found, and what she must have known it meant.

Bess was staring so hard at the wall opposite her it was a wonder she did not bore holes in the plaster. 'I'd only ever seen Martha once before – at her wedding to William Sorsby. You should have seen her, Seeker – like something out of a fairy tale. Never saw anything so delicate, or so beautiful. I remember thinking, it was as well the Sorsbys had money, because she'd have been no use for work. Never saw her again – not after the child was born. She was always away with her own relatives or some such thing whenever I visited Elizabeth. But I knew her as soon as I saw her, poor wild creature that she was. I'd have known her for Gwendolen's mother even if I'd never seen her before. She had the same face, only twenty years older, the same eyes, same lost look in them, the same desperate soul. She was crouched back in a corner like a frightened hound waiting to be kicked. I went over to her and took her in my arms and held her a good long time. I held her till she stopped weeping. A good long time.'

'And then?'

She looked at him sharply. 'And then I untangled myself from her, told her her daughter was grown tall and loved and lovely, and vowed to her that Gwendolen should never face her fate.'

'And you left her there,' said Seeker.

The old woman had scoured herself almost empty. Her voice was matter-of-fact. 'I gave the vicar all the money I had, told him to get some kindly woman of the parish to help her dress and brush her hair properly and sit with her. And then I left.' She turned now to look at him, summoning the last of her defiance. 'For all it is ramshackle, that hermitage is clean enough, and she is well fed there, and safe. It is all she has known in fourteen years and where else should she go? Some filthy bedlam? She's beyond the help of peony amulets and snakeroot and anything else now.'

Seeker thought of Bedlam as he had seen it, of the creatures incarcerated without hope, if not mad when they arrived turned mad by what they found there, and no peace until death took them.

'But Gwendolen,' he began. 'Why do what you did? A place of safety could have been found for her after you'd gone.'

Bess's mouth tightened. 'You think it, do you? So did I. I thought to send her to my sister in Carlisle, or my niece in Bristol – good women both with husbands powerful enough to keep the curious out and the troublesome away from her. But Gwendolen wouldn't have it, Matthew neither. Should I have said to the child, "But you must go, for otherwise you will be shut up and left to turn animal"?

Should I have said, "You must, or you will be drowned in a barrel or burned at the stake at Faithly Cross"? Should I have said that to the child, Seeker? Should I have left her to those fates? Would you have had me tell her of her mother?'

'But Matthew could have—'

'Matthew?' She turned upon him. 'You know what Edward Faithly has already done for hatred of Matthew. He is justice of the peace here, Seeker. It is Edward Faithly who decides who will be helped in the parish, who sent to the house of correction or to Bedlam. How long do you think before he would have had her carried away in chains? What could Matthew have done against it? Who knew where Abel Sharrock's malice and this new order of the major-generals might have ended? You that rode into Faithly with those very orders in your bag, do you tell me that good men are not being turned out for such as Abel Sharrock the length of this England, for that they are not fervent enough in their hatred of their neighbours? And then that trier come to the village. Who would have protected her then? I remember the witch-finders, Seeker, and who was to say this Caleb Turner was not some Matthew Hopkins by another name?' Despite her failing strength, the hawk in Bess had returned. 'I had a choice to make, Seeker, and I made it. Gwendolen suffered two days, and died in this house with those she loved around her. Never tell me that was a worse fate than her mother's.'

★

Seeker sat on a bench in the Pullans' kitchen, waiting for Matthew Pullan to return from Faithly Manor, where he had gone to give new instructions to Lawrence Ingolby and to assure Lady Emma that as long as the deeds were in his hands, the manor was her home and she the mistress of it.

Manon had almost forgotten herself when Seeker had first arrived in the back yard, running out of the back door towards him, and only recovering her face from its beaming smile as Orpah emerged from the dairy. On the older girl's example, she had lowered her eyes and waited for him to give his instructions. Now, an hour later, once he had finished his business with Bess, he watched them at their work in the kitchen. Manon was quick, if somewhat slapdash, and Bess would surely have had some sharp words for her. Orpah, as ever, was slow, but deliberate now. Without the fear of scolding she was accustomed to live with, she calmly addressed her duties as mistress of the kitchen, and carefully performed those tasks for which she had been so often criticised. As she went about her work, setting out on the table a late breakfast for Matthew's return, an image of watching her before came into Seeker's mind. It was on the night of the supper, the supper in the trier's honour that the trier had not come to, where Gwendolen Sorsby had been poisoned by the old woman who so loved her. In his mind's eye, Seeker saw again Orpah hurry in and out of the parlour, placing trenchers, platters, goblets, candlesticks and salt. But not the bowls. The bowls had already been on the table when first Seeker had entered the room. And how flustered the girl had been, what she had said to him. 'Mistress Bess's been in a hundred times, chiding me for this not being in the right place and that being wrong, and woe betide me if I shift anything if she's already shifted it!'

And then Seeker thought he knew how the thing had been done. Bess was sleeping, and he would not go into her again. They had said their last goodbye. But Tansy Whyte would be up and about, of that he was certain. Setting aside the beaker of ale Manon had poured for him, he got up quickly and left the kitchen by the back way without any word of explanation to the two girls. Tansy was at the front of her run-down cottage, sweeping the path and singing softly to herself. In her hair was the new green silk ribbon Seeker had found when searching through Seth's meagre bundle of possessions the night before.

Her smile of greeting faded as he approached. 'Seth is sleeping.'

'Near time he wasn't,' said Seeker, 'but he'll keep a few minutes.' He indicated that she should sit on the worn wooden bench by her front door and then sat down beside her. Abel Sharrock, crossing the churchyard from his sexton's cottage to the small church, stopped and openly watched them.

Seeker kept his voice low. Sharrock was far enough away that he wouldn't hear them.

'Now, Tansy, I need to speak to you of Gwendolen, and the manner of her death.'

Tansy nodded.

'Gwendolen was poisoned by the destroying angel, was she not?'

'Told you that already,' she said.

'Yes, but I want you to tell me now how it might be done.'

The woman's eyes registered her fear. 'Tansy didn't kill Gwendolen.'

He put a hand towards her to reassure her, but pulled it back when he saw her flinch. 'I know that, Tansy, but I think you know how it might be done. I need to know how it can have been that only Gwendolen took ill and died after eating that soup with the mushrooms in it.'

Tansy glanced sideways at him as if he might be stupid. 'Mushrooms weren't in the soup.'

'There were mushrooms in the soup. I ate it myself.'

She shook her head. 'Destroying angel wasn't in the soup, else you'd all be dead. Must've been in the bowl.'

'But surely Gwendolen would have seen it if it had been in her bowl before the soup was put in?'

Tansy sighed with the impatience of a teacher confronted by an especially stupid pupil. 'You'd rub destroying angel round the bowl, get the juices out, smear the pulp a bit. Gwendolen wouldn't have seen it in the darkness. Bess don't waste no candles.'

No, Seeker thought, Bess hadn't wasted any candles that night. Even for a thrifty Puritan housewife, she had kept her best parlour very ill-lit, that night. She had squeezed the poisonous mushrooms in Gwendolen's bowl and smeared their pulp around it, before setting the bowl exactly in the place she knew the girl would sit. The poor light at that far corner of the dining table had not been to keep the girl from prying eyes, but that Gwendolen herself might not see.

A mumble from inside turned to a long yawn, and then a call for Tansy, who instantly rose from the bench, her hand touching the new green ribbon in her hair. Seeker stood up before her and blocked her path. 'Two minutes, Tansy. Two minutes I need with your man and then I shall not trouble either of you more.'

'Seth is a good man,' she urged, as if fearful.

'Hmmph. An interesting measure of "good" you keep. But if he's not good, I doubt he's actively bad.' He pushed open the door to the hovel.

Seth Whyte's second call to Tansy died in his throat, and, the blanket still around him, he shuffled himself back against the wall of the one small room.

'I know nothing of who might be in Faithly Woods, Captain, I swear it.'

'And I'd swear you know those woods well enough to know someone else's been in there. You'll go in again this morning with my men and you'll show them what you know.'

348

Seth nodded vigorously, whilst still pressing his back against the wall as if in the hope an unknown door in it might open out to him and offer his escape.

Seeker took another step forward to loom over him. 'But I would know what the woman you found in that anchorage in York was to you.'

Seth shook his head, taking fright again. 'Nothing, nothing to me. It were all Digby Pullan. He paid me a purse of money and said there'd be more for Tansy, till her dying day, if I would promise to tell no one.'

'About what you did to Martha Sorsby.'

'Never knew her name,' said Seth. 'Didn't want to. Digby told me, there was a child to be taken from its mother and away from York. The mother was a madwoman and a danger. Paid me fair.' His mouth twisted. 'And I earned it all right. Scratched and bit and kicked and cursed, all to get to the child. I could hardly hold her. Digby knew I was good with pigs, you see, and other awkward beasts. Not a pig could outwit me when it needed tying. Got her bound and gagged, and got plenty of scratches and bruises for my pains. Had the hair near out of my scalp, she did! Covered her up in sacks and rode her to that place in the back of a cart. Vicar gave her something from the apothecary, and we carried her up that stairs to that anchorhold, dead weight that she was, and I untied her bindings and left her there. And that was the last I ever saw of Gwendolen's mother.'

'Until last week.'

Seth nodded. As Seeker's eyes became more accustomed to the gloom of the unwindowed chamber he saw the shifting expressions on the man's face. Indignation at his own past injuries gave way to something like sorrow.

'Nothing wild in her then, Captain, poor frightened beast that she was. And she knew me, too. That was the worst of it. Cried to me for her baby, reached out her hands.' He shuddered at the memory. 'That's why I ran from that place, Captain. I was at the top of the stairs when you and the lad Ingolby started coming down the lane towards the church. Didn't know what to do, so I thought I'd just wait till you'd gone.'

'Hmm. What had sent you back there?'

Seth shrugged. 'Told you – I were after Lawrence Ingolby – wanted to know if it were true, about Gwendolen being dead. I thought I should see if her mother were dead too – if there was anyone else who'd know what I'd done.' He stretched out his hands, pleading reason. 'You see, Captain, Digby had told me I could go back to Faithly once Bess – or Gwendolen – was dead. He didn't trust me not to tell what I knew, but I never told, never told anyone. I always thought it would be Bess first – she always seemed an old woman to me, and I didn't think it would be that long. He promised Tansy would be looked after.'

'And then there was the money,' said Seeker, not troubling to hide his disgust, but Seth flashed back with anger, not shame.

'Easy said by those that have it, but there was more to it than money, anyway.'

'Oh?' said Seeker, wondering what other motivation a specimen like Seth Whyte might have.

Seth shifted uneasily. 'Digby told me I'd be of more use to Tansy away, anyhow. There'd been poachers up at the manor, you see, and . . .'

'And Digby knew it was you.'

'I'd a' swung from a tree if he'd told Sir Anthony it was me. I'd never a' left Tansy, Captain. I was always coming back.'

'See she doesn't regret that you did,' were Seeker's final words to Seth Whyte, as he threw the man's boots and overclothing at him. 'Start today.'

Tansy had no farewell for Seeker as he passed out of her cottage, such was her hurry to get in to Seth and see that he had come to no harm. She was not the first good woman he had known to have a shiftless husband, and he doubted she would be the last. He would not be sorry to be away from Faithly. He was getting to know the place too well, and they him. For all the wide spaces out here on the moors, there was no distance between those who lived on them. The extra men he had ordered would be here by dinner, and then he would be on his way and leave this place to its intrigues and its secrets. Those new soldiers would be left to continue the hunt for Sir Thomas Faithly, but Seeker must get his present prisoners to York, and Manon away from this place, away from the whole of Yorkshire too, to a place of safety and new beginnings.

TWENTY-FOUR

Turncoat

Thomas Faithly watched from his vantage point, cut into the flank of Faithly Ridge, as Damian Seeker rode out of Matthew Pullan's courtyard and set out towards Faithly Manor. He saw that the militia captain was alone, and that he had not taken the young girl he had brought there yesterday away with him. Thomas wondered whether he should change his plans. There were hours yet until darkness fell, and there would be too many risks in attempting to enter the village, and Pullan's house, unseen. Already, the diversion caused by Septimus's foolish dalliance with the trier's wife had exposed Thomas to greater danger and delay than should have been necessary. Two days' delay Septimus's adventure, with Seeker on his heels, had cost him. Nevertheless, Thomas had encountered and overcome many risks before now. He would stick to his original design.

He could hear the voices of the captain's soldiers not so very far away, still hunting the woods. He had heard them say that more had been sent for, and would be here by the afternoon. There might be only two or three hours left of this venture, that had been more than a year in the planning. What his mind had conceived of all that time ago in the King's court in Cologne, after news of the fate of yet another ill-planned and ill-executed plot, would end in success or failure before the sun went down. Thomas Faithly had known then that he would come back to England, and he'd known what he would do when he got here. A wind had got up, and he pulled the collar of the old grey worsted jacket tight. They had served him well, these peasant's clothes, slate grey and moss green, blending into the hill and rock behind him.

Thomas crouched lower behind the two large rocks at the flank of the cave and turned himself sideways, to slip into the crevice in the rock behind them. He had become accustomed, these last few days, to feel his way along the damp passageway as it fed into the first of the limestone caverns under Faithly Ridge. His father had told him of them, that last day, as they rode out together for Nottingham, rallying to the King's standard. He'd found them, he said, when he had followed the sounds of a woman labouring in childbirth, and on finding his way through the crevice in the rock, had come upon mother and child in the depths of the cave. Thomas hadn't believed his father — the old man had always liked to tell a story. But his father had never told Edward that story, nor ever shown him the cave, for Sir Anthony, rightly as it had proved, had never trusted Edward.

Inside, the torch he had lit still burned on the wall, and

afforded him sufficient light to gather up his few belongings, but most importantly, the waistcoat he had worn on the day he had walked from the court of Charles II. He took a moment to shrug off the coarse Flemish farm labourer's jerkin and slip the waistcoat, incongruous in its blue velvet with silver buttons, over the rough linen shirt, before concealing it beneath the labourer's garments once more. His pistol and powder hung from a strap across his body to be hidden by the old buff coat he would button to the neck. Finally, he pulled on his wide-brimmed dun felt hat, low over his brow, then killed the flame of the torch. One last time he groped his way carefully back along the limestone passageway and between its twin guardian boulders, and, assuring himself that Seeker's soldiers had passed safely on, left the cave by the overgrown path and stepped openly out onto Faithly Moor, in daylight, for the first time in thirteen years.

The extra men he'd sent for arrived just before dinnertime. After an early and hastily taken meal, Seeker rode out of the gates of Faithly Manor at the head of the escort taking Septimus Jenkin and Sir Edward Faithly to Major-General Lilburne in York. Where they were sent after that was Lilburne's business, but it would be a long day, if ever, before either of them saw the inside of Faithly Manor or church again.

Matthew Pullan had been to say his piece to Lady Emma. Seeker fully expected the place to be declared forfeit, on account of Edward Faithly's past treachery, and it to be granted, on payment of the requisite sums, to Pullan. Whatever other understanding might have been arrived at between Pullan and Emma Faithly was not Seeker's concern. Sir Edward's declining health, which a spell in gaol could only precipitate, would, he suspected, deprive Abel Sharrock of whatever outrage he might have prepared for the pair.

Emma Faithly was standing at the front door to the manor, watching as her husband was put on his horse. She was every inch the lady of the manor as she observed the scene, impassive. Any who didn't know better might have thought the man whose disgrace she was witnessing was a stranger to her. Seeker wondered what she felt as she watched. Perhaps she no longer felt anything at all.

Lawrence Ingolby was anything but impassive, the departure of the prisoners animating him greatly. He was having a last few words with Septimus Jenkin, who looked resigned to whatever might await him in York. 'Chin up, Septimus, the major-general'll not want you long once he's got hold of Sir Thomas. And wherever you finish up can't be any worse than having to look out on Maud Sharrock hanging out her linens of a morning.' He jerked a thumb towards Seeker. 'Perhaps the captain there'll take you to London with him.'

'London is full of iniquity and idle bellies as it is,' said Seeker, not looking up from attending to his own horse.

Ingolby grimaced, then gave Jenkin, who was already

securely mounted, an encouraging slap on the back. 'See? Told you he was in a good mood. Time'll fly by.'

It was at this moment that Lady Emma began to move down the steps of the manor house and cross the yard towards her husband. Seeker, on the alert, moved quickly to intercept her. She had something clasped tightly in her left fist, and whatever the justice of her grievances, Seeker was determined it would be a living, breathing Edward Faithly he delivered to Lilburne in York Castle, and not a corpse.

'No more farewells,' he said.

'I do not wish him well and I bid him no farewell,' she said, 'but I would give Edward Faithly this.' She opened her hand and held her palm out towards him. In it was not a knife, nor any phial of lethal content, but the red glass pendant that had been the mark of her bondage since the day she'd been forced to marry him.

'Aye, all right then,' Seeker said, taking it from her. He walked across the yard to where Edward Faithly waited, hunched, on his horse, and held the pendant up for him to see. 'Your wife would have me give you this, as a parting gift, but you see, the major-general never did like coloured windows.' He dropped the pendant onto the hard cobbles of the courtyard and slowly ground the glass to pieces beneath the heel of his boot, looking directly at Faithly as he did so. 'Matthew Pullan should have finished the job properly long ago.'

He looked back to Lady Emma and dipped his head briefly to her. She lowered her head in acknowledgement.

Beside her at the top of the steps, his arms folded, his feet planted apart, Lawrence Ingolby was the very picture of satisfaction. He too nodded briefly towards Seeker before following Lady Emma back through the doorway into the hall, and closing the large oak doors securely behind them.

Seeker watched the door close then swung himself up into the saddle, and stopped. Lawrence Ingolby, holding the keys to Faithly Manor, the boy born in a cave.

'Ingolby!' he roared, as he dismounted and began to make for the door. He was halfway up the steps and about to start hammering when it was opened again.

'What now?' said the steward.

'The cave you were born in?'

Ingolby shrugged. 'Yes?'

'Is it up there?' said Seeker, nodding towards the ridge above the woods.

'Aye,' said Ingolby.

'And you can find your way again?'

'Of course,' he said.

Seeker indicated the troops who had not long arrived from York, and were waiting to go out with the game-keeper, to carry on the search for Thomas Faithly. 'You take them, and you show them where it is.' He then called over to the sergeant. 'When you find him, send word after me, straight away, and start out with him directly to York.'

They were less than a mile from the village, and all Seek-er's attention taken up with watching the riding party with

Lawrence Ingolby at its head make haste towards the woods, when one of his own party called Seeker's attention to a figure running up the track towards them. Seeker sent the man on to enquire what the matter was, and he soon returned.

'The woman's name is Sharrock. She claims to be the constable's wife, but says her husband is away to Lockton and not expected back till evening.'

'And what would Mistress Sharrock have us do in this crisis?'

'Her concern is that she cannot get into her neighbour's house.'

Seeker felt his temper deserting him. 'We are not here to pander to the wants of nosy housewives—'

'Yes, sir, but she fears there has been some mischief. It is Commissioner Pullan's house, and she claims to have seen some foreign-looking fellow go in by the back gate, and now the house is all locked up, which she says she never knew before, no one can be seen in the yard and there is no answer at the door.'

Seeker felt his heart crash into the pit of his stomach.

'You, now!' he shouted. 'Down with me to Pullan's. You, remain here with the prisoners. Wait half an hour and if I send no further orders, return the prisoners to the cells in Faithly Manor then bring the search party from the woods down to Matthew Pullan's house.'

Seeker thundered down the track, the soldier behind him. He sent the man on down to the village as he brought Acheron to a halt by the gesticulating Maud Sharrock.

'Who's in there?' he said.

'I couldn't tell. A tall fellow, with his hat down low and swaggering walk. He had a foreign look about him, that's for certain – foreign clothes, though poor stuff. But there were a bulge in his coat like he'd weapons strapped there! And now there's no answer at the door, and the windows shuttered over, and Abel still away at Lockton!'

For the first time, Seeker regretted Abel Sharrock's absence. He knew the man kept arms in his house, and whatever petty politics might drive him now, he was a proven soldier. 'As soon as your husband comes home, you tell him to arm himself and wait across the street from Pullan's door. You understand?'

Maud, plainly terrified at the new seriousness of the situation, nodded her head vigorously and turned to make her hasty way home.

In the village, word of Maud's panic had spread. The street was in silence, two or three uneasy groups gathered in doorways, watching Pullan's, the shutters on most of the houses closed and doors locked. There was little that frightened the people in these providential times so much as the word 'foreigner', but Seeker knew the armed man in Matthew Pullan's house was no more a foreigner than he was.

Having his man dismount in a place where he could see both back and front doors to Pullan's, Seeker went to the front door and hammered on it.

A tremulous voice, Orpah's, called out, 'Who is it?'

'Captain Seeker. Open this door.'

The bolts were swiftly drawn back and the door opened to reveal the nervous-looking kitchen maid.

'Where's Manon?' demanded Seeker.

'With the mistress, and the door locked, like the master ordered.'

'And your master?'

'In his study with—'

But Seeker didn't stay to hear. He was past Orpah in a moment, and forcing the door to Matthew Pullan's study, where he was greeted by the barrel of a pistol pointing at his forehead. The pistol was in Matthew Pullan's hand.

Pullan was seated at his desk, and behind him, in front of the window, was a tall, handsome man who must have been about thirty-five years of age. The man was dressed in the clothing of a Low Countries peasant, but his face was one that Seeker had seen looking down from an old portrait in the great hall of Faithly Manor.

'Sir Thomas,' said Seeker.

'Captain,' replied Faithly. With a sigh of relief, Matthew Pullan lowered the gun.

Seeker looked from Thomas Faithly to Matthew Pullan. 'You've been involved in this all along.'

Pullan shook his head. 'No, Captain, I have not. I've had no communication with or knowledge of Sir Thomas from the day he rode out of Faithly with his father thirteen years ago, until he walked in the back door of this house less than two hours ago.' He gestured towards the pistol now lying in front of him. 'I had no idea who was about to come through that door, or what they might do when they did so.' He took a heavy breath. 'Captain Seeker, in my position as Commissioner for the Peace of this locality, Sir Thomas Faithly has surrendered himself into my custody, and asks that I now transfer him to yours.'

Seeker looked from one man to the other. 'Is this some trick? I have men outside and another six on their way. You'll not escape this house alive, Faithly.'

Thomas Faithly unfolded himself from his position by the window. 'I am done with escaping, Captain, done with fleeing. I've returned to England expressly to surrender myself to the Protectorate and to offer my services to Oliver Cromwell, Lord Protector, in whatever capacity His Highness might have use for me.'

So astounded was Seeker that he could say nothing at all at first. And then he laughed. 'You offer . . .?' He looked to Pullan as if for confirmation of some jest, but he saw that Matthew Pullan's face, like Thomas Faithly's, was deadly serious.

Seeker took two steps towards Thomas Faithly, and ordering him to lift his arms, began to search him.

'The pistol Matthew greeted you with is mine, Captain. I surrendered it to him along with my shot and my person. If you will permit me to divest myself of some of these layers of clothing, I will show you the proof and assurance of my good intentions. I am done with the Stuarts, Captain. I am done with wandering.'

Seeker finished the search for weapons, and finding none, indicated that Faithly should divest himself as he had suggested.

As he waited he said, 'Why? Why are you done with it all, if in fact you are?'

Faithly finished removing his buff coat and began attending to the buttons of his jerkin. 'Because I am an Englishman, and I want to come home.'

Seeker had heard many reasons for men turning their coats – some venal, some cowardly, some ingenious – but he had never heard one put so simply, or with such apparent honesty.

He nodded, but he was not disposed to believe Thomas Faithly yet. 'If that is so, why didn't you surrender yourself as soon as you came in at Whitby? Why go through the farce of being captured as a Dunkirker, and having Septimus Jenkin ambush your escort? Why not just have surrendered to the first Protectorate soldier you saw?'

Faithly paused in his unbuttoning and looked at Seeker. 'I came back to Faithly for two reasons – that I might surrender myself into the hands of Matthew Pullan, the one republican in England of whose honour I was certain, and whom I knew I could trust to give me a fair hearing.'

Seeker nodded slowly. That part of it he could believe. 'And the other reason? Vengeance on your brother, for his cowardice and his treachery?'

Thomas Faithly shook his head with a weary smile. 'I've learned in this life of mine that those things carry their own reward. Edward doesn't need my help to execute vengeance on himself. No, Captain, the other reason I returned to Faithly was because I knew if I didn't come here myself before I could make my surrender, or before I was taken, I might never see it again. Had I given myself up at Whitby, or at York, your Major-General Lilburne would hardly have sent me back here, would he?'

'No,' Seeker conceded. 'He wouldn't have done.'

Faithly nodded. 'And in such a case, I might never have set eyes on these hills and moors again.'

'So much for sentiment,' said Seeker, 'but am I to suppose that gaudy waistcoat is what you plan to tempt the major-general with? I fear you will be disappointed.' Lilburne, unlike so many other of Cromwell's most trusted lieutenants, had been born to land and wealth, and had no interest in a show of quality for its own sake. A blue velvet waistcoat trimmed with silk and set with silver buttons might have interested some who had risen so much higher than they had been born, but it would not interest Robert Lilburne.

Again Faithly smiled, and already Seeker felt he was looking at a better man than his brother, whatever course each might have taken at the outbreak of the war. 'Oh, I remember the major-general from his fighting days, and I would not mistake him for a dandy fancying a waistcoat.' He paused, weighing what he was to say next. 'It was your other master I thought to interest with the lining and stitching of this garment.'

'My other master?' said Seeker warily.

Faithly glanced at Matthew Pullan, still seated at his desk. 'Though we fought on opposite sides, I trust Matthew more than any other man in England. Your name is also known in circles at the Stuart court, Captain, and although I was at first alarmed to learn you were here, I think it may be fortunate that you are.'

'Oh?'

'You are known to be in the service of John Thurloe, Cromwell's master of intelligence, and it is in that capacity that I would entrust to you a document I think will be of no small interest to him. It's for you to decide whether Matthew should witness what I would give you.'

Seeker had come to trust Matthew Pullan as much as he did any man beyond half a dozen in Thurloe's service, and yet that service had taught him trust should be measured very carefully, and dispensed even more so. He turned to the commissioner. 'Will you leave us a moment, Commissioner? But see you don't leave the house – my men are positioned outside, and have orders to let no one leave without my advice.' He glanced at the table. 'Leave the pistol.'

Pullan got up to leave. 'See you don't do anything daft, Thomas,' he said, before closing the door behind him.

Cautiously, Thomas Faithly laid the waistcoat over his arm and held it out towards Seeker.

'Grenade in there, is there?' asked Seeker.

'Of sorts, Captain. And once the pin is out I'd rather be in Mr Thurloe's camp than the other.'

'Hmm,' said Seeker, taking the garment and holding it up to examine it. 'Mr Thurloe chooses his own company, but he's a plain man and he doesn't pick his friends on account of the braiding on their waistcoats.'

'Oh, he'll like this one, though,' said Faithly, nodding towards the garment which Seeker was now turning in the light. 'I can guarantee you that.'

'Right,' said Seeker, his visual examination of the item at an end. He laid the waistcoat flat on Matthew Pullan's desk and got out his small knife. 'Where do I cut it?'

Faithly moved forward and leaned over the desk. 'Here, and here,' he said, carefully tracing two lines with his finger. 'Take care the knife doesn't slip. The document is fragile, and well-worn from much travelling, even before it ever took ship with me.'

Seeker made the incisions into the heavy silk of the material. A couple of minutes' careful work did the job. The letter, when he brought it out at last, was indeed well handled. It was in the hand that Seeker knew to be that of Edward Hyde, Lord Clarendon, Charles Stuart's most trusted and able advisor, and it contained a list of the names of six Royalists, still in England and enjoying their estates, whose loyalty to the pretended King was claimed 'assured'. Two of them, Seeker knew, were already on Thurloe's watch list, but the other four names were of men Seeker had never known to be under any suspicion of disloyalty to the Commonwealth, not since the earliest days of trouble between King and Parliament. 'They know you're watching the first two,' said Faithly, after Seeker had read over the brief document twice, 'so it's the others that they deal with.'

The four whose names remained all lived within an hour's ride of London. More, they had all insinuated themselves into the unreserved trust of circles patronised by Oliver Cromwell.

Seeker looked up at Faithly. 'How far forward is their planning?'

Faithly shrugged. 'I don't know. I was never taken into Clarendon's trust. After my brother's failure to rally to the King's support in '51, I lost all credit with him, and was tolerated as a playmate for the King, nothing more.'

'That's useful then,' said Seeker.

'How so?'

'Men seldom suspect those they regard as fools of working against them. If Clarendon thinks you a fool, he's less likely to think it's you that's stolen this letter.'

Faithly gave an assured laugh. 'Oh, I made sure he wouldn't suspect me, Captain. I stayed at court a good six weeks after I stole it. Long enough to see a poor laundry maid dismissed for her carelessness in soaking a chest of the earl's papers whilst they were being moved from Cologne to the Hague. Several of the documents were ruined beyond recognition, I hear.'

Seeker gave a grunt of admiration. 'I trust you paid her well for her carelessness.'

'Oh, I did, Captain, though she was a very friendly girl, and it was not the first favour she had done me.'

'You'd best clean your tongue before you take any of that talk to the major-general. He'd soon wipe that smile from your face.'

Seeker was glad to see that Faithly had the grace to look chastened. He folded the letter carefully and put it inside the breast of his own jerkin. 'And what do you hope to gain by these actions?'

For the first time, some doubt of his success seemed to flit across Thomas Faithly's face and he looked fearful. 'A chance, Captain, a second chance. To live in my country and to serve it.'

'You'll not get Faithly Manor handed back to you if that's what you have in mind,' said Seeker.

'I know that. But if I can earn the Lord Protector's trust through my service, I may get something. I want to live on this land again, Captain Seeker, alongside its people.'

Seeker appraised Faithly a moment. 'I daresay you do, Sir Thomas, but you haven't chosen the best of times for your return. There are supporters of the Stuarts who haven't said boo to a goose in over ten years that are having to pay fines and account for their every movement. There are men and women under suspicion, many amongst them who've shown themselves a great deal less active on Charles Stuart's behalf than you have been, who're under penalties and close watch.' He pointed to the place where he had secured Clarendon's stolen letter. 'You'll buy yourself some credit by this document, but just how much is not for me to say. For now, and until such time as I hand you over to the major-general in York, I cannot treat you other than as my prisoner.'

Thomas Faithly made a practised bow. 'I would not expect it to be otherwise, Captain. But I'll put my faith in your Mr Thurloe, and whatever uses he might have for a man who has been turned.'

Seeker had had his hand on the handle of the door, about to escort Faithly out of the house and hand him over to the custody of one of the men outside, but something in the last phrase stopped him. He turned around slowly. 'Do I understand you right?'

Faithly raised an eyebrow. 'I hope so, Captain.'

'You would have it believed that you have been taken as a rebel?'

'By all but Matthew, who knows the truth and has sworn not to tell it, and by yourself and whomever else you and Mr Thurloe think to tell it.'

'You are offering to act as an agent of the Commonwealth, to return to your Royalist circles and report back to Secretary Thurloe on what you find?'

'I think that is the best way I can be of use, do not you, Captain?'

Seeker considered it. 'It may well be, but you'll understand the dangers?'

Again Thomas Faithly smiled. 'Well enough, I think.'

'And Septimus Jenkin has no knowledge of your true purpose?'

'No. Septimus is a true Royalist, Captain, and a true

friend to me. But as you have seen yourself, he is a man without cunning and easily led by craftier wits, or a pretty face. I hope he will not be punished unduly for his part in a scheme whose ends he did not understand.'

Seeker gave a shrug. 'You'll both have to be seen to be punished for the deception to work at all. That Jenkin truly believed he was assisting the cause of Charles Stuart makes his case worse, but no doubt if Secretary Thurloe takes you on, you can plead his case.'

'But you won't speak for him?'

'I have enough on hand without wasting my time on foolish vicars. Come on. Time to resume playing your part.'

After Seeker had handed Thomas Faithly over to his men, with orders that he should be heavily guarded, he sent for the party including Septimus Jenkin and Edward Faithly to be brought down off the track, and for those headed for Lawrence Ingolby's cave in search of Sir Thomas to give off and join with the escort in the village.

Matthew Pullan had already fetched Manon from his mother's chamber, and had had his stable hand prepare a horse for the journey. Before Seeker helped her mount, Orpah hugged her and told her she was a good girl, and that she was sure she would always find a welcome in Master Pullan's house, and work there should she need it. Once the full escort party had gathered, Seeker sent them ahead with their three prisoners, the two ill-matched brothers and the dispirited churchman. Pullan wanted a last, private word with Seeker, and Seeker made Manon wait for him. He didn't trust to her safety out on the road without him.

'I wanted to speak to you of Gwendolen,' said Pullan.

Seeker waited.

'You didn't believe her death was an accident.'

'Your foster sister's death was a misfortune, Commissioner, a great misfortune, but it was not an accident.'

Pullan was unflinching. 'And have you discovered who was responsible?'

Seeker thought of Elizabeth Sorsby's journal, of the scenes described by Seth Whyte and by his soldiers of what they had found in the anchorhold of All Saints in York. 'I think there are those amongst the living and those amongst the dead too who are responsible for what befell your sister.'

'And will anyone answer for it?'

Seeker looked towards Bess Pullan's door. 'Not in this world.'

Matthew Pullan nodded. He signalled to Orpah, standing waiting in the kitchen doorway, and she came forward bearing a small sack of evident weight which she handed to Matthew, and he to Seeker. 'My mother would have me pass this to you. She said you would know who it was intended for.'

Seeker felt the weight of the coin bag in his hand and nodded. 'Aye, I think I do.'

Finally, Matthew looked over to where Manon waited, her hand smoothing her horse's mane. 'And, well, she's con-

fused and she's got some fanciful notions in her head . . .'
He hesitated.

'Yes?' said Seeker.

Pullan drew a long breath. 'She said to take care of that lass of yours, too.'

Seeker gave a rueful laugh. 'Aye, you tell her I will.'

TWENTY-FIVE

Trust

Robert Lilburne sat back in his chair, moving his mouth in such a way that Seeker knew he was not yet convinced. 'And do you believe him?'

'Not entirely,' said Seeker. 'He may be telling the truth – I think there's a good chance he's in earnest, but Clarendon's getting cleverer, and it may be that he's sent Thomas Faithly over here to play a double game.' He shrugged as if it didn't matter. 'Secretary Thurloe is alive to all that – he'll have Faithly watched as carefully as any other. If he is telling the truth, he could be of great use to Mr Thurloe's operations. Either way, he's not one to let slip through our fingers.'

'No. I wouldn't want to answer to Thurloe for it if we did. But the sooner Faithly's off my hands and on his way to the Tower, the better. This double-dealing's not how I conduct my business.'

Seeker suppressed a smile. There could be few in Cromwell's service who spoke or acted straighter than Robert Lilburne. He doubted whether Lilburne had dealt anyone double in his life.

The major-general was more interested in his brother Freeborn John's old comrade. 'And Matthew Pullan?'

'Had no foreknowledge of Thomas Faithly's plans, or of the brother Edward's past treachery. He hasn't wavered, sir, and he serves the state well. The constable Sharrock's insinuations are those of a thwarted man on the make.' Seeker didn't feel it necessary to rehearse with Lilburne his final exchanges with Abel Sharrock, the warnings he had issued, the truths he had made plain. Sharrock would be nothing less than dutiful towards his commissioner from now on. 'I've put him in his place.'

'Good.'

Now Lilburne turned to something which he would evidently rather not have to address.

'The trier, Turner.'

'Yes, sir?'

'We scoured York for him and he hasn't been found. No sign of him in the North Riding either, I take it?'

'None,' said Seeker.

'No. Well, if the man has the sense he was born with, he won't show his face north of the Trent till you and I are both dead. He's probably on a ship for Boston or Leiden or some such place he can hide himself and live by another name. We'll not see him here again.' And that, for Lilburne, was the matter of Caleb Turner closed. About Felicity, or Manon, he asked nothing at all. The major-general had greater concerns on hand than the personal cares of a militia captain.

'So, Captain, you will escort Sir Thomas Faithly to London and the attentions of Mr Thurloe and whomever else he thinks fit, and I shall see to his brother, and this troublesome churchman.'

'Jenkin's more hapless than dangerous, sir. He'll learn his lesson all right. Put him in a church in York, under the careful eye of a better man. He'll find himself a rich wife before long and cause you no more trouble.'

'Well, that would save me prison space and manpower, neither of which I have to spare. And the other?'

'Edward Faithly? I'd trust his brother before I trust him, any day, for all Edward never took the field against us. The only interest he cares for is his own, and to do mischief to others. Jail him, fine him and get rid of him. He hasn't the health or the guile to do anything from afar. I doubt he'll live long anyway, but sending him back to Faithly would only mean more damage.'

Lilburne puffed out his lips. 'Another one to clog up my jails with. The Committee of State will have to find some better place for emptying them into – our Caribbean planters have no use for these prisoners that will not work.' He stood up. 'Anyway, Seeker, that's not your concern. I've written to Thurloe to let him know you'll be leaving here within two days, and that I'm sending to him, under your escort, a prisoner requiring his special attention. Once I've finished questioning Thomas Faithly myself, you can be off, back to London.'

★

It was almost dusk when Seeker arrived back at King's Manor, where he had left Manon in the care of his clerk, Michael, on their arrival at York. The boy had blushed as if he had never seen a girl before, and Seeker had leaned in and warned him, a little more menacingly than might have been required, to treat her with all the courtesy he would afford a general's wife.

Once he had assured himself that Manon was safe and comfortable, and had not been importuned, he ordered Michael to bring him the book of requests for licences to travel. He ran his finger down the list until he found the name that he had suspected might be there. When Michael saw where Seeker's finger had stopped, he started to speak quickly, if not to babble.

'I made clear to Sergeant Walker, who carried out your duties here in your absence, that that licence should on no account be granted without your express permission.'

'You did right,' said Seeker. 'Now fetch your pen.'

When Michael had returned with quill pen, paper and inkpot, Seeker began to dictate to him. It was not a long note, and not difficult to draft, as it followed the convention of licences to travel which Michael was already adept at drawing up. It was only the principal name involved, that of Lady Anne Winter, that caused him to pause, pen suspended over paper, and look to Seeker for confirmation.

'Just write it,' Seeker said.

The licence was written, and signed by Seeker, before the seal of the licence office was appended to it.

'Should I deliver it, Captain?' asked Michael tentatively.

'No,' said Seeker, getting up. 'I'll deliver it myself.'

He went into his own private chamber, where Manon was curled up, asleep, on top of the coverlet. He was loath to wake her, and would have spent a contented night merely watching her sleep, but time was pressing, and the sooner she was safely out of York on her way to London, the happier he would feel. He put his hand on her cheek and whispered close to her. 'Time to wake, my pet. It's time for us to go.'

A few minutes later, with Manon shrouded in the long grey woollen cloak gifted to her by Bess, they left Seeker's apartments and walked down into the courtyard of King's Manor, only the bewildered Michael watching them. It was not far off curfew time that they passed under Bootham Bar, but they had not far to go.

Manon had observed the minster from a distance as they'd approached the city, but then been almost overwhelmed by sights as the walls of York had drawn nearer; gradually, as they walked along High Petergate, her steps slowed and then came to a halt altogether. She looked up in awe at the cathedral.

'It's a fine sight, is it not, Manon?' said Seeker.

'But how is it man can build to such heights, Father? How is it such a place does not collapse on those who enter it?'

'The bricks and mortar were well set, by men who knew what they were doing. It's what goes on inside that's dangerous.'

377

Manon gave her father a sideways glance, not quite certain if he was serious. It didn't matter. She grasped his hand all the tighter, and kept close to him as buildings loomed up on every side of her. Just as they reached the minster, her father veered off on a path to the side, taking them behind it and past quiet gardens and silent houses until they came to a narrow street at the back. Halfway along the street, Seeker opened an iron gate and led her into the gardens of a huge house in honeyed brick.

'What is this place, Father?' she said. 'Who lives here?'

'It once housed a great treasury of moneys taken by the church of Rome, in that minster, from the people. That was long ago, before old King Henry Tudor sent them packing. Now this house belongs to a very great man, Manon. And,' he said, after gritting his teeth, 'it currently holds a very wicked woman.'

The heavy panelled doors at the top of the steps to the house were opened very soon after Seeker's knocking. For Manon, to whom the riches of Matthew Pullan's house had been a revelation, the hall of the Treasurer's House of York was no less than a palace. The ceiling was as high as in any church she had ever entered, the floor of marbled black and white tiles such as she had heard her mother speak of, but never seen. The fireplace was of such a size she could have climbed into it and lain down to sleep – her father, too, she was certain. Magnificent brass candelabra hung suspended low from the ceiling, casting marvellous light on an abundance of glittering crystal and plate. For a moment, Manon wondered if her father had taken her to see Oliver Cromwell.

The armed guard who'd granted them access seemed to know her father, as did the well-dressed servant who greeted him. 'I am afraid Lady Fairfax has joined his Lordship at Nun Appleton, Captain, and they're not expected back in York before spring.'

'It's not her ladyship nor the Lord General I'm here for, Robert. Is that woman still here?'

Manon was a little surprised at her father's tone, and wondered for a moment if her mother had found her way to this place.

The servant also looked a little surprised, and began to clear his throat. Before he could answer, there was the sound of a shutter opening above them. Manon hadn't noticed the gallery high up to her right, supported by marble pillars, but now she saw it, and that the middle of its five, multi-paned windows had been opened. She couldn't see who was standing there, because the gallery was in darkness, and the figure stood back a little from the window, but then she heard a woman's soft laughter.

'Oh, Robert, I do fear the good captain is talking about me. I think we should perhaps tell him that I am at home and will see him.'

The window was then pulled shut, as the poor servant flushed crimson and began to mouth some apology, but Seeker forestalled him. 'Never worry, Robert, I've had more than enough of dealings with her.'

379

As Robert retreated to the fireplace to heap more logs onto the firedogs, a rustling to her right took Manon's attention and she turned her head to see a woman in a heavy plum silk dress descend the stairway in the corner. The woman's hair was a deep, dark chestnut, curled into rings which fell from the back of her neck onto her bare shoulders. As the woman paused at the corner of the stairs with her slim pale hand on the dark oak banister and smiled at them, Manon thought she was the most beautiful person she had ever seen. Her father had let go of her hand as they had approached the doorway of the house, but still Manon could feel him tense beside her.

'Captain,' said the woman, descending the final few steps, 'two visits scarce within a week. Surely you are missing me.'

'Oh, you may be sure you are never far from my mind, Lady Anne.'

The lady made him a curtsy, and went to take up her place on a richly embroidered settle to the side of the fire. Manon resolved that, some time later, when her father could not see and be annoyed by it, she would practise to copy that curtsy.

'Robert,' said the woman, 'you might bring a little refreshment for the captain here and his lovely young companion.' She turned her brilliant dark eyes on Manon. 'Come, my dear, sit beside me and warm yourself.' Then she raised an eyebrow towards Seeker. 'The captain feels no heat nor cold nor anything else, but you have the look of a mortal to you, as I am myself.'

Manon's heart was thumping and she was not hopeful as she glanced at her father, but he signalled by a dismissive movement of his hand that it was all right for her to sit down. 'Just ale for me and the child,' he said to the retreating servant, 'she's not used to wine.'

'But she has the look of a lady, all the same, Seeker,' said Anne Winter, touching the soft blonde waves released when Manon had taken down her hood.

Manon saw that her father, who appeared to fear no one, hardly knew what to say to this woman.

'You've applied for a licence to travel,' said Seeker.

Lady Anne looked surprised, then curious. 'Yes, I have, Captain, but permission has not yet been granted. It seems that not even the recommendation of Lady Fairfax is sufficient to countermand your own orders that I should stay put in York.'

Seeker thought it best not to tell Lady Anne his assessment of how far Lady Fairfax herself was to be trusted. 'I daresay the Lord General might have gone over my head.'

'The Lord General, it appears, has no wish to go over your head. It seems Lord Fairfax reveres some of his former comrades sufficiently not to be seen to disagree with them. His view of you, in particular, is unaccountably favourable, and when he learned of your special instructions, he informed me – for he can be quite as direct as yourself at times, Captain – that, "Seeker must have good reason to keep you where you can do least mischief", and that, "No doubt you might travel to London again when it suited him".'

A thought struck her and she looked from Manon back to Seeker. 'Do I take it that this is such a time?'

Before Seeker could answer, Robert returned bearing a tray with a glass of wine, a dish of nuts and dried fruits and two silver tankards of ale, one large, one small. Seeker thanked him, and then told him to leave them a while. Once the servant had disappeared down the stairway leading to the kitchens, Lady Anne said, 'I think you have brought me a person of some importance, Seeker.'

It took Manon a moment to realise the lady was talking about her.

Seeker summoned all his forbearance and sat down on a finely carved oak armchair opposite Lady Anne. 'She is of great importance to those who love her, of very little to the state. Her father has enemies of his own making that he does not wish to become hers. She is to travel to London with an escort I am leading, leaving tomorrow morning. It is an escort of soldiers, with one prisoner whose destination is the Tower of London.'

Lady Anne unthinkingly put a hand out and laid it on Manon's arm. 'Not this child, Seeker,' she said, leaning towards him.

'No,' he said. 'But she must travel in this escort. As you will understand, a military escort of this sort is not suitable for a young girl travelling alone.'

'Of course it isn't, Seeker!' said Lady Anne, her face alive with indignation. 'You cannot watch the men all of the time, and with a child as fair as this . . .'

Seeker didn't want to hear the rest. For all the order of the New Model, he was not going to risk his daughter with a troop of soldiers that he could not watch at every minute. 'That is why I am prepared to grant you permission to travel to London. You must be ready to leave tomorrow morning, and you will take this young girl as your companion.'

Anne Winter sank back into her seat. 'She is so important, then, that you would permit this to me . . . ?' She looked carefully at Manon, some new thought evidently having come into her mind. 'What is your name, child?'

'Manon, your ladyship.'

'Manon,' repeated Lady Anne. 'It is Welsh, is it not? But Manon what?'

Manon opened her mouth and looked to Seeker, who gave a very curt shake of the head. 'Ingolby,' he said, the first name that came into his head. 'Her name is Manon Ingolby, and she will travel with you to London as your companion, and before you register your own arrival in the city at the office of Thomas Dunn, behind the Old Exchange, you will take her to the place named here,' he handed a sealed letter to her, 'and hand her over only to the care of the person named here.'

Lady Anne took the sealed letter and studied the name and address on the front. A puzzled look was gradually replaced by an incipient smile. 'Her father has chosen her friends well, I think.' She pulled a sash and in a few moments Robert had returned.

'Please have the small bed made up in my dressing room, for my young friend here. See that the fire is lit in there, and that everything is in place for her comfort. Then have Lydia go to my bedchamber, and have my trunk taken up there.'

'Tonight, your ladyship?'

'Yes, Robert, tonight. I leave for London in the morning and,' she turned to look directly at Seeker, 'I may be there a good while.'

After Seeker had bid Manon a curt farewell, for which he had prepared her earlier, with the knowledge that they could not properly communicate until she was safely in her new London home, Lady Anne saw him to the door of Fairfax's house.

'I will give you no cause to regret this trust you have placed in me, Seeker. Whatever other differences might lie between us in the past, and in the future – for I make no promises – this child will be safe with me.'

Seeker nodded. 'For all your duplicity, I know that, or I would not have left her with you.'

'And you may also trust,' said Lady Anne, just as he was passing out into the night, 'that no one will ever know her true identity from me.'

He stood very still on the step. 'What?'

'I watched you from the upper window there, as you approached the house. And I saw it as you both came into the light. It's in her eyes, though they are not your colour, and in her face, though how God could use the one set of bones to create one visage so dreadful and another so lovely, I do not know. I would urge you to take greater care, once she is in London. But on all that has ever been dear to me, Captain, no one will ever know of that child's true identity from my lips.'

TWENTY-SIX

A Reckoning

As Seeker walked down the path from the closed and securely bolted double doors of the Treasurer's House and out onto Minster Yard, he felt something clench hard, beneath his chest. One more day, and they would be away, leaving the north and travelling on the road to London, where he could better control things. One more night: and Manon would spend that night in Fairfax's house, the safest house in York. There was no more he could do tonight for the safety of his daughter.

But there was one other task he must perform before he returned to York Castle from where he would set out with his prisoners tomorrow morning. The purse Bess Pullan had sent him away from Faithly with weighed heavy in his bag, alongside the letter he had drafted and sealed to go with it.

He would have to cross the river, by bridge or boat, to reach North Street. The taverns and alehouses were slowly disgorging their drinkers into the ginnels and alleys of the city, and Seeker was in no mood for dealing with drunkards and miscreants tonight – let the men of the night watch deal with them. Seeker chose instead to go by the walls. He climbed the steps at Bootham Bar and headed south-wards. In truth, he wanted, one last time, to look upon the grounds of St Mary's Abbey and the graveyard of St Leonard's. He wanted to assure himself, once and for all, that any apparition he had glimpsed there on the night after the attack on him was but the disordered vision of a man who had taken too much physic.

Tonight, however, the clarity of that night was gone. What there was of the moon was clouded over, and there was little wind to chase the clouds away. Lights flickered through the window panes of King's Manor, as clerks and officers continued to process information coming in for the major-general from all over Yorkshire, Cumberland, Westmorland, Northumberland and Durham. So much information, as if that would bind the country together, when what was needed was more men. How many letters, reports, accounts would it take before Parliament under-stood: without the army, the country cannot hold? He thought of Faithly, where rumours and resentments that had come to the surface and drawn breath in the trier's court had played themselves out or been drawn back again to linger in the shallows and hidden places of village life, until some new storm or tide came to expose them once again. He thought of Matthew Pullan and Abel Sharrock: what use to put power into the hands of local men, be they never so well-affected, if at base those men had known and hated each other all their lives?

The ruins of St Mary's, St Leonard's, the crumbled vestiges of Rome, black lumps against the blackness of the night, told the story of men riven by spite who could not bear that they should not have their way. Seeker stood a long while looking down over the ruin of St Leonard's, but however long he fixed his gaze, he could not see anything there amongst the stones of times gone that might threaten him. Whatever drugs Michael had fed him from the apothecary six nights ago had played with the borders of his mind and called to his vision fears he had not until then known he had. Dismissing the tumbled stones and broken graves from his thoughts, Seeker quickened his pace, and was soon descending at Lendal Tower, calling up the boatman to take him across the river.

An old woman in the first of the straggle of cottages along Tanner Row directed Seeker to the rectory, a fine, timber-framed gable house, the first floor and eaves projecting over the street. The rector had not yet retired for the night, but was busy at his sermon, and not greatly inclined, when he raised his candle to see who his late caller was, to break off for Seeker. Making to close the door, he suggested that the captain might return the next day, at a more convenient hour.

Seeker leaned against the door jamb and put his foot across the threshold. 'It is inconvenient enough that you have lied to me once already,' he said. 'Dress yourself properly and take me to the anchorhold.'

'But the church is all shut up,' the man said.

'I did not ask to be taken to the church, I asked to be taken to the anchorhold. You tried to put me off once before – I won't be put off again.'

It was about ten minutes later that, a torch in his hand, Seeker ascended the rickety steps to the anchorhold by the outer west door of All Saints church. The rector declined to go with him beyond the door of the church. 'She is frightened of men,' he said.

Seeker knocked gently on the door, but the only response was a rustling sound.

'Martha,' he tried. 'Martha.' Still nothing, save the faintest sound of whimpering.

'My name is Captain Seeker, Martha, and I mean you no harm. I am going to come in now.'

The door was secured on the outside. He drew back the bolt and opened the door with caution. Immediately, a miasma of bad air, as from a prison cell or a sick room that has been too long occupied, hit him. There was no light in the wooden chamber other than that he had brought with him, and it was a moment before he saw where she was, crouched, in the far corner, on the rushes of the floor. At first, very briefly, he thought everyone had been wrong – Bess, Seth Whyte, himself – and that it was a child and not a grown woman who was kept in this place. And indeed, it might well have been a poor child that Seeker found himself looking upon when he raised the torch. It was as if someone had taken a young bride and laid over her an old and dusty gauze. Her hair was long and might once have waved as Gwendolen's had done, but it was tangled and knotted, brittle greys merging with what must once have been a flow of deep gold. Grey eyes that might have sparkled years ago, and caught the changing lights of day as Gwendolen's had done, were dull now, red-rimmed and scored with lines at their corners, deeper than they should have been on a woman who was surely not yet thirty-five years of age.

She cowered, pressing herself to the back wall of the small wooden chamber. He closed the door as gently as he could, but went no closer to her. 'I am not here to harm you, Martha. I am here to give you something.'

He looked for a place to plant the burning torch, and found an empty sconce in the wall. He wondered if they let her have light at all, or if only the light of day ever relieved this wood and plaster cabin of a more habitual darkness. There was a degree of warmth in the room yet, although the coals at the bottom of a small stove near the middle of the room had been doused, as he suspected they were every night, for fear of fire. Seeker undid the clasp on his bag, and took out the smaller bag entrusted to him by Bess. Undoing the leather ties, he lifted out a small locket. On their ride from Faithly to York, Manon had told him Bess had said he should find it there. It was silver, engraved with roses and thorns, and had been well kept. The catch gave easily. Inside was no miniature, nor portrait as Seeker had thought there might be, but a lock of burnished red-gold hair, tied in a grey silk ribbon. Seeker very carefully, very slowly, went closer to where Martha still watched him from the corner and held the locket by its chain out towards her.

'This was Gwendolen's.'

At the sound of her daughter's name, hope flashed in the dull eyes and she looked at him as if she would ask him something. She formed the word in a voice clearly unused to speaking. 'Gwendolen.'

Seeker nodded and held the locket out further, so that she might more easily grasp it. After a moment's further hesitation she reached for it and curled her long, dry fingers around it, before bringing it to her lips and kissing it.

'Gwendolen is at peace now, Martha. You understand? No more harm will come to her, and you will be with her again one day.'

He saw the hope collapse in her, the breath go out of her in a huge, uncontrollable sob, and he crossed the last yard of space between them to crouch down and hold her in his arms. For almost an hour he spoke gentle words to soothe her, and only when he was certain she was asleep did he lay her on her bed and cover her with the blankets and rugs that he found there.

The terrified rector was still there, shivering at the bottom of the steps, when Seeker came out of the hermitage. He seemed to shrink into himself as Seeker rapidly descended the steps.

'There is little heat and no light in that room.'

'It's for fear of fire, we—'

Seeker could hardly control his fury. 'Bess Pullan gave you money that she should be properly attended to.'

The rector made an effort at rising to some sort of dignity. 'A woman comes daily to see to her needs – takes up her food, lights the stove, brings clean linens or rushes as they are required, sees to the close-stool.'

'And fresh air? Exercise outside that anchorhold?'

Here the rector was more uncomfortable. 'The shutters are opened an hour or two in the day, though the window barred. As to her being brought outside – it used to be attempted, but there were difficulties, and as time went on it became more difficult to manage. She paces that chamber day and night – she does not want for exercise.'

'And hardly a ray of the sun's light on her face.' Seeker was disgusted. 'Tomorrow, women will come from Heworth Hall. They will be accompanied by a guard from the local militia. You will give the sisters access to this anchorhold, and have the woman Bess Pullan paid you to attend her assist them in getting Martha Sorsby out of that place. You will hand over to them the remains of the money which Mistress Pullan gave you for her care. I will also see to it that the sisters are given this,' he held up the purse, 'which Mistress Pullan has gifted for her care for a good long time to come. You will obey my orders in all points, or you will find yourself in York Castle, answering to the major-general. Am I understood?'

The man nodded vigorously, but Seeker was still too angry. 'Am I understood?' he repeated.

'Yes, Captain,' said the rector, only just audible, 'you are understood.'

Seeker was in such a rage that the soldiers at Micklegate Bar almost sprang out of his way as he climbed the steps by their gatehouse to access the walls once again. It would take another twenty minutes at least of walking out in the night air before he would feel fit for civil speech with anyone again. That a young woman had been left to rot alone in such a place for fourteen years, be her mind ever so sickened and tortured, was beyond his comprehension of any world that God could have intended. Had Bess not found her, she might have rotted there the rest of her life, without again knowing the breath of air on her cheek or any human kindness. But had Bess not found Martha, Gwendolen might still be alive today, and face a better future than the sick old woman had been able to foresee for her.

Seeker looked out into the blackness that led towards London. If he had been glad to leave this place and march southwards all those years ago, he was even more so now. The small doses of bitterness, and the mischances that ruined lives, could be covered and then lost in London, but in the expanse of moss, granite, lime and heath in which the people of Faithly Moor played out their existence, mistakes could not well be covered up nor hatreds forgotten. Whatever game Thomas Faithly played, whether newly loyal to Cromwell or traitorous still, Seeker had learned the rules of that game, Thurloe's rules, understood the odds, and he knew that, in the end, he could beat them. The rules of the life he had been born to, had grown up learning, he also understood. But that was a game he knew could never be won. Eight more hours of darkness. Eight hours until he rode from this place, his daughter with him. Eight hours until they left that game behind.

He was not far past Micklegate when he began to feel a creeping unease. Something, he realised, was wrong with the sounds of the night, and it had been insinuating itself into his mind, his hearing, ever since he had left the anchorhold at All Saints. Only now did he realise what it was. Psalm-singing was coming to him from one of the proliferation of churches down within the walls to his left. Psalms he had marched to, gone into battle to. The relentless rhythm of the words was so ingrained that he felt them vibrate through him. If he had shut his eyes, he could almost have imagined the ghosts of fallen comrades marching by his side, here, on the walls of York, comrades who had never lived to breach them. But it was too late, by some hours at least, for such a service and Seeker didn't shut his eyes. It was matters of the living, not the dead that concerned him. Up ahead, at Bitchdaughter Tower, something wasn't right. Bitchdaughter protruded furthest south of all the towers on York's massive walls; there were two men there, as he would have expected, but neither of them was moving. Each, in fact, appeared to be slumped over slightly, as if trying to see something over the wall.

He quickened his pace, calling out to the two guards, who made him no reply, but simply continued to look down at whatever it was that took their interest over the walls of Bitchdaughter. Seeker began to run. Only then did he realise that neither of the torches set into the wall sconces above the men were lit. A few yards from Bitchdaughter he shouted again; still there was no response. He lunged and clasped a hand to the shoulder of the first guard, but as soon as he did so, the man's head seemed to shift, and then his whole body slumped slowly to the ground. Even as Seeker caught him and lifted his chin that he might look in his face, he knew the soldier was dead. The eyes that looked up at him saw nothing, and the slick black mess at his neck was still warm where his throat had been cut. Seeker let go of him, shouted back towards Micklegate, and spun around to see to the other man. But there was something wrong with this one that had not been wrong with the other. Seeker stopped a foot behind him. The uniform wasn't right, the helmet wasn't right and the man carried no halberd. Seeker's mind was just beginning to make the connections when suddenly the figure he'd thought a corpse spun around and lunged at him, a sliver of gap in the clouds allowing the sudden glimpse of a blade glinting in the moonlight. Seeker dived to the side and kicked out at his attacker's leg. He caught the man in the shin and heard the heavy crunch as the heel of his boot connected with bone. The fellow screamed and rolled over, then from the ground lunged at Seeker's ankle. A hot sharp pain seared through Seeker's leg as the steel found his skin and he stumbled back until he was almost at the edge of the drop. His attacker was scrambling to his feet, and Seeker hurled himself forward to grab him by the bandolier with one hand, using the other hand to knock the blade from his grasp. A muffled curse was soon followed by a helmeted head-butt launched at Seeker's jaw, the top of the helmet catching the still-healing scar from the musket ball that had grazed it by All Saints' church less than a week before, and sending a raging pain reeling up to Seeker's skull. Seeker roared and lunged again, pulling up the face guard of his assailant's helmet, and saw, as he had known he must, the twisted features, the squint, unmended jaw, of Caleb Turner. In a moment Seeker had him slammed up against the south parapet of Bitchdaughter Tower. 'That's three misses, Turner. You'd never have lasted half a minute in the field.'

By way of response, Turner spat in his face. Seeker brought his left arm up, his right occupied in pinning Turner to the wall, and swung his fist to connect with the preacher's jaw. As bloodied teeth flew out of the man's mouth, Seeker heard the sounds of shouting from the Micklegate barbican, and soon soldiers were running down the steps onto the wall. Shouts were coming too from the Skeldersgate end. In the moment of distraction from the sounds, Seeker glimpsed another flash of steel, and then felt a second blade, this time plunged into his left side. He staggered for a moment, letting go his grip. Turner ducked beneath his arm and was a pace from the inner edge of the wall when Seeker caught him again. This time Turner drove a foot hard against Seeker's ankle and tried to push him away, succeeding only in bringing them both to within inches of the edge, and the drop. Seeker leaned backwards, but as he did so, Turner lost his footing and fell, screaming, arms flailing, backwards into the darkness. The strong grip on his arm of one of the Micklegate men who had at last arrived was all that prevented Seeker from following Caleb Turner into a last, silent blackness. Between the screaming and the final silence, over the commotion of the arriving guards and those still approaching from Skeldersgate, Seeker heard the unmistakable crunch of a man landing on his own neck. Before the next soldier to arrive at Bitchdaughter had lifted a flaming torch to light the darkness of the drop, Seeker knew that the man who had cost him more than any other, the man in the world whom he most hated, was at last dead.

EPILOGUE

London, 1st November 1655.
The Black Fox Tavern, Broad Street

At first, Dorcas had not believed what her daughter Liberty was telling her, but the child would hardly be mistaken on the identity of this caller. And even then, it had taken a few minutes more for Dorcas to understand that it was not Liberty the woman had come for.

Dorcas had resolved to meet her openly, Anne Winter, in the public parlour of the tavern, where anything said between them might have been heard and faithfully reported to those who made it their business to know about such things. The woman had had the sense to dress herself in a sober fashion, thank God, but Lady Anne's name still ran through the newsbooks and news-sheets of London like a burning fuse, and Dorcas would not have the Black Fox caught up in the smoke of rumour that surrounded her, not even for Liberty's sake. No one would be able to say that what had passed and been said between the two women had been done in secret.

But Anne Winter, whom Dorcas had never thought to see in London again, made plain to Dorcas that the matter she had come upon was not one for chance eavesdroppers to overhear. Only when she had held out to Dorcas her licence to travel, with the signature of he who had granted it, had Dorcas at last relented, and taken her through the door from the taproom into her business room, the place where her ledgers and her pistols and anything else needful for the smooth running of the Black Fox were kept.

Anne Winter had stated briefly what her business was, and handed Dorcas the letter. 'I think he must think well of you, that he should invest in you such trust.'

'And in you,' Dorcas had said, having read the lines once, then a second time.

It was an hour later, after Anne Winter had gone, after Manon had been welcomed and fed and sent off with Liberty to see the bedchamber she was to share with her in her new life of 'cousin', just travelled down from the north, that Dorcas locked the door of her room of business, again unfolded the letter and read it a third time.

I commit to your care that which is most precious to me on all this earth. She is my child, though neither she nor I can own it to the world. I would ask of you, in all your courage and goodness, to take her in and find shelter and some small employment for her, whatever you think fit, at the Black Fox. You must publish to the world that she is your niece, and, for her safety, tell no one that she is my daughter — deny it

*if ever any should hazard that guess. I will ensure that her
keep and her wages are met, and that you should in no way
be the loser for this act.*

*I know that in doing this, I am committing her to the care
of the one soul I trust more than any other, and that I am
delivering her to a better mother than the one God gave her.
You know where and how I am to be found should ever you
or she need me, and I will make my way to the Black Fox
whenever the business and suspicions of this city allow.*

That was it – no signature, even, although she would
have known the hand for Seeker's even had Anne Winter
not told her it was from him. But read it a fourth or a
hundredth time, Dorcas could not make the words appear
there that she had spent the last six months looking for.
He had told her then that he could offer nothing, and she
had said that she asked nothing, and indeed she would ask
nothing of him.

He had gone directly, Lady Anne had said, with his
prisoner to the Tower. Where he would go after that,
Anne Winter could not tell, although she supposed that he
would make his report to Thurloe. And then from Whitehall, where? Here, to Broad Street? Or to his lodging on
Knight Ryder Street, or Cornhill and Kent's coffee house?
Or would his feet trace their way once more to the house
on Dove Court, where the girl it was rumoured Seeker
had loved, and who it was said had once loved him, lived
in poverty with her troublesome lawyer brother? Dorcas

felt something inside her crumble. She would not think about it. She stood up and unlocked the door. She would ask nothing of him, but when he should ask anything of her, she would be here, as she had promised him. Waiting.

Rest, Barkstead had said, when Seeker had brought his prisoner to the Tower. Rest, Thurloe had said, when he had made his report, his long report, at Whitehall. Rest, Drake had said, as he'd cleaned and re-dressed Seeker's wounds and held out a medicine to him that he knew Seeker would not drink.

And Seeker would rest, soon. The fug of mist and sea coal rising from the Thames enveloped him and he breathed it deep. Here and there, circles of ochre lit his slow and halting way through the darkness and mire of well-remembered alleyways and courtyards. Through high walls and narrow streets the sounds from taverns and coffee shops, stray voices in the night, called him on, as the music of the river lapping against the quays gradually faded to nothing behind him.

Author's Note

'Faithly Moor', where much of this story is set, does not exist – it is a figment of my imagination. However, many of the other locations in this book did and do exist, and can still be visited today. Whilst the York Castle of the seventeenth century is gone, Clifford's Tower survives, and it is possible to walk around the top of it and look out from it over York, as Seeker does at the beginning of this book. It is also possible to walk on the barbican of Walmgate Bar, where I have billeted him, and which is now a very nice tea room. The walls of York, The Merchant Adventurers' Hall, the Treasurer's House and part of King's Manor – now belonging to the University of York – are also open to visitors, as of course are the Old Starre inn on Stonegate, and the museum gardens where the ruins of St Mary's Abbey, St Leonard's Hospital and several Roman graves can be found. The events I portrayed as happening in All Saints Church, North Street, are entirely fictional, but the church itself, with its incredible stained glass windows, has survived the centuries as a living church which is also open to visitors. I would like to thank the custodians, past and present, of all these places for their foresight and tenacity in preserving them over the generations.

The Lion inn, high on Blakey Ridge, is also still there, a welcome sight for weary travellers on the moors. The sheep are still very forward.

Finally, thank you to Jane Wood and Therese Keating at Quercus for all their work on this book, to Judith Murray of Greene and Heaton for her continued support, and to Liane Payne for the map.

February, 2018